KT-232-630

X000 000 025 0379

ABERDEEN CITY LIBRARIES

THE LIEUTENANT'S LOVER

The Lieutenant's Lover

HARRY BINGHAM

ISIS
LARGE PRINT
Oxford

Copyright © Harry Bingham, 2006

First published in Great Britain 2006
by
HarperCollins*Publishers*

Published in Large Print 2007 by ISIS Publishing Ltd.,
7 Centremead, Osney Mead, Oxford OX2 0ES
by arrangement with
HarperCollins*Publishers*

All rights reserved

The moral right of the author has been asserted

British Library Cataloguing in Publication Data
Bingham, Harry, 1967–
    The lieutenant's lover. – Large print ed.
    1. Russia. Armiia – Officers – Fiction
    2. Espionage – Germany – Berlin – Fiction
    3. Cold War – Social aspects – Fiction
    4. Soviet Union – History – Revolution,
    1917–1921 – Fiction
    5. Berlin (Germany) – Politics and government –
    1945–1990 – Fiction
    6. Love stories
    7. Large type books
    I. Title
    823.9'2 [F]

    ISBN 978–0–7531–7712–9 (hb)
    ISBN 978–0–7531–7713–6 (pb)

Printed and bound in Great Britain by
T. J. International Ltd., Padstow, Cornwall

To my beloved N.

"All shall be well
And all shall be well
And all manner of things shall be well."
                    Mother Julian of Norwich

RUSSIA, 1917

CHAPTER
ONE

1

Misha always remembered the moment.

Weeks of war had passed without fighting, just orders to advance, followed almost immediately by orders to retreat. And then one night, on another interminable journey in a troop train, it happened.

It was long past midnight. The train slowed and stopped. The little country platform filled with food vendors selling hot tea, boiled beef, rye pancakes. Misha clambered out to get some clean air and pace the stiffness out of his legs.

As he walked up and down, it began to snow. Small flakes at first, so light they hardly seemed to descend. But within minutes, the flakes had grown into big white feathers. They still seemed to fall so slowly that they were hardly coming down at all, but the ground quickly spread with white. Misha liked the snow, and went on pacing just as before. All around, sounds became softer, rounded, muffled.

Then a new vendor came onto the platform with a bundle of papers. There was a sudden eddy of excitement, men shouting, commotion. And Misha was caught up in it. Acting by some automatic instinct, he'd reached in his pocket for a kopeck or two and snatched a newspaper from the pile. And there, under the lamplight and the falling snow, he had read the headline:

"BOLSHEVIKS SEIZE POWER IN PETROGRAD. WINTER PALACE STORMED."

That was all. There was a full article beneath the headline, one part fact, three parts sensational speculation. But Misha didn't read a word of it. He didn't have to. He was the son of a wealthy industrialist and landowner, at a time when owning industry and land had become suddenly dangerous.

The Tsar was overthrown. The workers had taken over.

Misha knew that his world had changed, utterly and for ever.

2

Tonya too remembered the moment.

The water butt on the landing had been frozen over, but at this time of year the ice wasn't yet thick. A couple of axe-blows was enough to break the surface, and she'd filled the enamel jug, feeling it grow suddenly heavy as the water rushed in. She carried it through to the apartment beyond the landing.

In the living room, a cast-iron stove leaked heat and smoke in equal measure. The room was dim. In the corner by the stove, a man sat and watched Tonya enter and shrug off the thick coat which she wore over her nurse's uniform.

"Not working, Father?"

He grinned, showing a mouth that held just four teeth, and not one of them a beauty. "Why work? It's the revolution." Pleased with his answer, he repeated the word, dragging it out, giving a final kick to the final syllable, *revolutsya, revolutsy-a*.

To begin with, Tonya had ignored him. There was the fire to stoke, water to boil, soup to make, her elderly grandmother, Babba Varvara, to care for. She didn't know what he was talking about, but then again as his excuses for not doing his job as a railwayman were innumerable, she didn't care much either.

But then the old man had nudged the table. There was a newspaper lying there. Tonya remembered picking it up almost angrily, irritated at the interruption. And there it was, in simple words, black on white. The Winter Palace was stormed. The Tsar was captured. The workers were in control.

For a moment, perhaps only a second, Tonya remembered thinking that this must be good news. She was a worker, wasn't she? If their class was victorious, then things would get better wouldn't they? She looked back at her father, who grinned again. His mouth was like a black hole thumbed into the dark grey shadow of his face.

"*Revolutsy-a*," he repeated, nastily. "*Revolutsy-a*."

The word was ominous, and it sounded like death.

CHAPTER
TWO

1

Misha had stood beneath the lamplight, reading and rereading that headline, ignoring the snow that fell continuously on his arms, head and neck. And then, after perhaps twenty minutes of shocked thought, he'd jerked his head up. It had become obvious that his time in the army was over, that it was his duty to desert, to seek out his family, to see that everyone was all right.

Nothing had been easier. He'd simply walked down the platform, away down the track out of the lamplight. He'd sheltered there in the bushes till the train whistled and moved off, taking his commander and fellow soldiers with it. When day had come, he'd wound a dirty bandage around his head and darkened it with blood from a dead pigeon. Going back to the railway station, he'd barged and begged his way onto the first train that came along. It had taken three weeks to cross the country. He'd had to evade the military police, to bribe guards, to walk long distances wherever the train services had completely stopped working. But he'd done it. He'd come home to Petrograd, the city of his birth.

The family home, a big mansion on Kuletsky Prospekt, stood in front of him. At first glance, nothing had changed. The great sweep of steps was still there, the iron railings, the glittering expanse of windows. But something was wrong. The lanterns on either side of the front doors were unlit. A narrow pathway had been trampled through the snow on the steps, but the snow hadn't been cleared, nor had sand been scattered to avoid slips.

Feeling strange, as though in a dream, he approached his own front door and stepped inside. The moment that his foot crossed the threshold, he knew that the world, *his* world, had changed for ever.

The old house, once grand and silent, was aswarm with people. There were families, families of *workers*, in every room. The house was occupied and carved up like any tenement block. In the drawing room, where countesses had once danced, crude wooden partitions chopped the room into three. A stove burned smokily in the fireplace. A washing line hung over the marble mantelpiece. There were beds, and not even beds, mere piles of straw covered over with dirty sheets heaped up around the walls. Misha noticed a woman, dressed in black, grinning at him as she stirred a cooking pot. Around her neck she wore what looked like a gigantic diamond, and he realised that the room's chandelier had disappeared, its crystal pendants stripped and scattered. He stared at her in shock, until she began to cackle. He walked abruptly on.

In every room, it was the same. It wasn't like a tenement block, it was worse. The great house had never been intended for more than a few occupants and its plumbing and drainage were overwhelmed. The stairway had become a urinal. Pails of faeces were slopped from windows or just left slowly freezing for the next person to deal with. The house rang with arguments, songs, whistles, babies howling, children yelling, neighbours bickering.

Misha entered every room in turn. Nobody stopped him or told him to leave. He recognised nobody. Nobody recognised him. No servant from the old days, no groom or footman, certainly not his father, mother or sisters. He felt gathering dread. On the ground floor, nothing. On the first floor, also nothing. The second and third floors were likewise empty of any trace of his family or staff. As he climbed to the fourth and final floor, a floor once reserved for servants, he was convinced of the worst.

At the top of the final flight of stairs, the corridor branched off in two directions. One corridor looked and smelled like everything else in the house: the same ill-dressed, chattering horde. The other corridor was different. Its mouth was blocked off by a makeshift barricade: a door torn from its hinges, behind it a wardrobe, an ebony chest, a silk damask chaise longue, a card table, a bookcase. There was a gap barely big enough for a human to pass through. Misha stared at the ridiculous fortification in astonishment, and sudden joy. He put his hand to the torn-off door, knocked loudly and began to squeeze through.

He was just sucking in his belly to get past an awkwardly placed chair leg, when there was a sudden movement in the half-dark beyond. A hand grabbed him and yanked. He tumbled forwards. There was the click of a pistol being cocked and a shouted warning.

"Easy, easy," said Misha, speaking as calmly as he was able.

Further on down the passage, a door swung open releasing some daylight into the gloom. Turning slowly, Misha looked up. The family's old coachman, Vitaly, recognised his master and pulled his pistol away in a flurry of apology. One of the ladies' maids had been standing behind Vitaly with an antique carbine. She too dropped her weapon.

"Mikhail Ivanovich! Mikhail Ivanovich!"

"Vitaly! Thank God. Mother, is she —?"

But he didn't have to finish. His mother, Emma Ernestovna, a woman of forty-two, but more stately, more queenly than her age, came rushing out. She was dressed as no one these days was dressed: a long gown in violet silk, fur-trimmed at the neckline.

"Misha, my boy!"

She ran to him, her hands out for him to kiss. He kissed her as she wanted, then embraced her properly, kissing her on both cheeks. He didn't let go, but asked the questions that drummed inside him.

"Father? Natasha and Raisa? Yevgeny?"

Yevgeny, Misha's six-year-old brother, answered the last question by emerging from somewhere like a bullet and hugging his legs.

"Hello, Yevgeny. You've grown," Misha said, hoisting him up.

His mother watched distractedly. "Yevgeny, yes, he's here. Natasha and Raisa, bless them, in Switzerland —

we think — it all depends on the trains — I haven't had a telegram — we should have had a telegram — what do you think? — Your sisters, really . . ."

"I'm sure they're fine. No telegrams would have come through anyway. And Father?"

"Your father?" She spoke the words as though struggling to remember someone she'd once known. "He's very well. He's in Zhavalya. On business. Urgent business. He must have been detained. He's in Zhavalya. He must be. He wouldn't leave us here like this."

Misha listened to his mother, hearing her words and not hearing them at the same time. Zhavalya was the family's country estate, about two thousand kilometres east of Moscow. But Misha knew his father wasn't there. He couldn't be. Not now, not in winter, now with revolution surging around the capital city and his family unprotected.

"In Zhavalya?" he said blankly.

But he didn't mean anything by his question. He knew the answer. If his mother were telling herself this lie, then it could only mean that his father was dead. That the dominating industrialist, the man of business, his distant but not unkind father had been murdered. And in that same moment, literally from one moment to the next, Misha realised that his childhood was over. He had become a man, the head of the household.

Everyone now depended on him.

2

Pavel was gone.

Kiryl, Tonya's father, either didn't know where his son was, or more likely wouldn't say. But the boy was just fourteen and delicately built. Two winters ago, he had caught typhus, at the same time as their mother had died of it. He had survived, but only just and Tonya knew she couldn't let him wander the streets, out late and alone. She put on coat, hat, gloves and scarf.

"I'm going to look for Pavel," she said. "We can eat when I get back."

"Comrade citizen Pavel, you mean," said her father.

Tonya ignored him and hurried out. A thin snow was falling, but nothing substantial, just tiny round specks flung around in a piercing wind. Her father's last comment could have meant nothing at all, just another one of the old man's jokes, but it had possibly been intended as a clue. She hurried through the streets, feeling her breath beginning to freeze on the brim of her cap.

After walking for twenty minutes, she came to the intersection of Sadoyava Triumfalnaya and Sadoyava Karetnaya. There was a large building with a broad fanlight over a lighted porch. Outside there was a pile of logs, guarded by a soldier with a rifle.

"Is this where the meeting is?" she asked.

He nodded. "Inside. It's been going two hours already."

"Those logs . . . ?"

". . . are red logs. For the Petrograd Soviet."

The soldier might have meant his answer, or he might just be getting ready to haggle. Tonya thrust her hand in her pocket and brought out a lump of sugar as big as her fist. It was damp, grey and sticky, but good currency all the same.

"I've got sugar."

The soldier shook his head. "The logs belong to Comrade Lenin. You need to ask him."

Tonya stuffed her sugar away, unbothered by the rejection. In this strange new world, money was no longer reliable. In a city where food and fuel were desperately short, Tonya now always carried something with her, in case she came across a good opportunity to trade. Most times she failed, sometimes she got lucky. It was just a question of being always ready to try.

She went on into the building. Down in the basement, there was a meeting of the Borough Housing Commission. At the front of the room, there was a kind of podium, planks stretched across wooden egg crates. The podium was dominated by a speaker, hatless and wearing an unbuttoned leather jerkin. The man caught sight of Tonya as she entered. She knew he'd seen her, because his eyes fixed on her, but there was no change in his voice or posture. His presence commanded the room. He was strikingly good-looking with dark curly hair, worn short, and a lean, handsome, intelligent face. The only bad feature he possessed was a nose that had been badly broken. Though still narrow, it bent sharply where it had been struck.

The man, Rodyon Leonidovich Kornikov, was Tonya's cousin and a rising star in the new Bolshevik administration. He fixed his eyes on her, then directed his glance deliberately across the room, before bringing it back to her. He never stopped speaking for a second. His sentences came out perfectly, without mistake or hesitation. Tonya looked over to where the man had indicated. Pavel was there, his eyes shining unhealthily, his coat unbuttoned like the man on the platform. Tonya pushed her way across to him.

"Pavel! You'll freeze."

The boy, a fourteen-year-old, began buttoning up almost as soon as he saw his sister, and he let her adjust his hat and scarf. But he still kept his eyes on the platform where Rodyon was winding up.

Tonya turned her attention from Pavel to her cousin. Rodyon spoke of the necessity of establishing revolutionary principles "from the first winter on; from the worst slum outwards". The broken nose in his perfect face served to draw attention to his handsomeness, adding something mesmerising to his features. He finished speaking, to a scattering of applause.

Pavel turned to his sister.

"Wasn't he good? When I'm older —"

"When you're older you can go out on your own. Right now, you need to stay warm."

Pavel shrugged. His eyes still shone as though fevered. Rodyon barged through the crowd towards them, stopping in front of Tonya.

"Comrade!"

"Rodya! It's all very well for you to march about like you don't feel the cold. You should think about Pavel. He copies you."

"He will be a good citizen one day. Enthusiastic."

"If he doesn't catch his death first."

Rodyon smiled. He had perfect teeth, white and even.

"Well, comrade," he said to Pavel. "Your sister's right. You should stay warm too."

The boy nodded.

"Are you all right for things? Food and everything?"

"We don't have any wood. We'll have nothing at all to burn by the end of the week."

"You have your allocation of course?"

"If it comes. Last time there was nothing."

"That can't be helped. You can't rebuild a house without knocking down a wall or two."

"They're not walls. They're your precious comrade citizens."

Rodyon smiled. He was an important man, the Housing Commissar of the Petrograd Soviet.

"I can't help you. Everyone's in the same situation."

Tonya shrugged. She hadn't actually asked for help, but didn't say so.

"But if you want . . . Uncle Kiryl is still a thief, I suppose?"

Tonya nodded. Her father, Kiryl, worked on the railway and stole coal. An accomplice threw shovelfuls off the train as it entered the station. Kiryl collected the bits up in a sack and sold it on the black market. "He only gets vodka and tobacco. He wouldn't even think of bringing the coal home."

"But still, you have things to trade."

"Yes."

"Then come with me on my tour of inspection tomorrow. You never know what you'll find in these places once owned by the bourgeois."

"Thank you."

He shook his head. "No thanks and no favours. When we have things running properly, you won't be short of logs."

He held Tonya's eyes one last time. Rodyon was a long-time Bolshevik, with two spells in prison to his credit. His nose had been broken in a brawl with police and he was rising fast under the new regime. He had also, for the last two years, been paying careful court to Tonya. He had been constant and, in his way, generous, but Tonya never quite knew whether he was sincere. She wasn't sure if she was his only girl, or if Rodyon would ever lose his heart to a woman. He seemed too self-possessed for that, too important.

She felt suddenly uncomfortable with him and looked away. But logs were logs, and if Rodyon could help her get some, then she would certainly do as he suggested.

"Till tomorrow then," she said.

3

Misha made changes.

He made them fast, over the tears and protests of his mother and the servants. He began with the barricade at the mouth of the corridor.

"It has to come down. Now. You think the red militias will be stopped by a chaise longue and a couple of armchairs? Nonsense. It has to come down. Vitaly, come here. I want you to dismantle this thing. That horrible old wardrobe is no good for anything. We can use it for firewood. Those other pieces you can share out among the others.

"Next the windows. They're hopeless. They need fixing properly. We don't have any putty, of course. But how do you make putty? It's chalk and oil, isn't it? Linseed oil. I saw chalk in Yevgeny's room. We'll use that. Seraphima, do you know where we can get linseed oil? If we can't get the oil, ordinary flax seeds will do. We can press them for oil. And in the meantime, curtains. Do we have any fabric? No? Then use the hanging in mother's room —"

"The tapestry, Misha! No! It's French, you know. Your grandmother —"

"It's thick and it's heavy. It'll do. Use the carpet too if you have to."

And on it went.

The fireplaces were useless, so Misha stole some empty oil cans and turned them into stoves. He dismissed the servants. He exchanged the ebony chest for a sackful of millet flour, which would see them through winter. He made an inventory of their remaining valuables and concealed them beneath the floorboards.

But problems remained.

Firewood was the worst. They had terribly little, and decent firewood seemed almost impossible to obtain.

And the next thing was his mother. She couldn't adjust to the new conditions. She was always sick with one thing or another. It wasn't just physical illness, it was a sickness that penetrated her soul. Misha was certain that if he couldn't find a way to get her into a place of safety, then she wouldn't survive. Yevgeny too was having his childhood stolen. It seemed clear that the best thing for all of them was to escape Russia, to make their way to Switzerland to join Natasha and Raisa there. But how to do that, with no money, no friends, no help . . .?

It was as he was thinking about that precise problem one evening that inspiration came to him.

He had gone, as he had done often enough already, over to the glass cabinet and taken out a bundle of papers: his father's papers that his mother had managed to salvage. He turned the papers in his hand. Although only a few months old, they seemed as ancient as Egyptian papyrus. Stock certificates. Title deeds. Bank statements. Holdings of land. Everything represented by those papers had been swept away, almost literally overnight. On the top of the pile, there was a coloured picture postcard of General Kutuzov, the victor of the Battle of Borodino a hundred years earlier and a particular hero of Misha's father. It was odd seeing the card. It was almost as though these stock certificates and the struggle against Napoleon both existed in the same far distant past.

But as well as certificates of ownership, the bundle contained letters from lawyers, accountants, brokers. And a persistent theme ran through them. From about

February 1917, his father seemed to have started selling assets. Stocks, bonds, land, anything. There were no huge sales. The country was at war with Germany and Austria, after all. It would have been impossible to sell up completely, even if he had wanted to. But there was a steady stream of sales and yet no evidence from the bank statements that his savings accounts had increased by even a rouble. And yet there were hundreds of thousands of roubles involved. Though Misha had reviewed the papers a dozen times already, he was struck by a sudden thought.

"Mother? These papers. Where did you get them?"

"Oh, your father's study of course. Where else?"

"*Where* in his study? His desk? His cabinet?"

"Oh yes. His desk, the cabinet. Luckily we had the keys. But we had to work fast. One day, we had everything, the next it was a knock at the door and this horrible young man with a leather coat telling us about the new decrees."

"You had the key. Who else?"

"Oh, your father, silly! How else could he have opened them?" Emma Ernestovna laughed out loud.

"His secretary, I suppose?"

"Leon? I suppose."

"And how did you happen to have one? Did he give it to you?"

"Oh no, not me. Why should I have a key to his cabinet? Maria Fedorovna, the housekeeper, had a set of keys. That cabinet! Japanese lacquer. So nice, but the polishing!"

"Maria Fedorovna had a key, did she?"

Misha's mother said something in reply, but he was no longer listening. He felt a sudden shock of excitement. Because it was inconceivable that his father would have left his most important documents in a place where a servant could have access to them. It was almost as if the bundle that his mother rescued had been a decoy to draw attention away from the real ones. Misha jumped up.

"Excuse me."

He ran out, down the corridor and downstairs. His father's study had been on the ground floor, behind the drawing room, a place of high bookshelves, cigar smoke, polished wood and leather. Of course, it wasn't like that now. Two families had been allocated the room, and seemed to fight bitterly over the use of every square inch. A china pisspot tucked behind a curtain constituted the hygiene arrangements. A trail of slops led from there to the nearest window. But that wasn't what caught Misha's notice.

What caught his eye was a grey steel safe, bolted and cemented into the wall behind the panelling. The safe had only been exposed when the room's inhabitants had begun ripping up the panelling for firewood. The plaster around the safe had been smashed off. Misha could see the pale marks where sledgehammers had struck. But the safe had withstood the assault. Steel bars protruding from the side of the safe were deeply set into the masonry. Misha had never known of the safe's existence. Its sudden exposure reminded him of what his family must have been through in those first weeks of revolution, before his arrival home. No wonder his mother was in a state of collapse. Anyone would be.

He looked up, snapping himself out of this unhelpful change of thought. Both families, fourteen or fifteen people in all, were staring at Misha, grinning. They knew who he was, as did all the occupants of the house. An old man, a grandfather spat in the fireplace and cackled, "Come to say goodbye, eh?"

"I'm looking for logs. You don't have any, do you?"

The old man wasn't deterred. He nodded back at the safe. "They're coming to take it away next week. They're going to put a tractor in the yard out there, run chains in through the window, then bang! Out it comes. It's full of gold, they say."

"When are they coming?"

"Tuesday. Wednesday. Who knows?"

That gave Misha three days, maybe four. Except he didn't know the codes and he wasn't a safe-breaker.

4

Tonya went with Rodyon the next day.

The Petrograd Soviet had issued a stream of housing decrees, making bold statements about minimum space requirements, light requirements, heat requirements, water and sewerage requirements. It was Rodyon's job to see those decrees were implemented, or at least not wildly breached. All morning, Tonya watched him stride around his domain, backed by a flurry of lesser officials. And he did stride. He seemed to fly through his duties. Those with surplus space were reprimanded, spare rooms reallocated, disputes settled.

And, Tonya noticed, he was fair. He never victimised the rich. He dealt with them the same way as he dealt with everyone. And he lived by the standards that he set others. Like everyone else, he was thin and hungry, and Tonya could tell from his clothes that he slept in them for warmth.

All morning, they strode around. Tonya didn't find any opportunities for barter. She didn't know why she was here. She felt cross with Rodyon for wasting her day.

"I thought you were going to help me find logs," said Tonya, when they broke for lunch.

"Yes. But first I wanted you to see this."

"See what?"

Rodyon turned to her, his handsome face with its broken nose.

"People grumble because our revolution hasn't delivered the promised land overnight. But how could it? For centuries, the bourgeois have exploited the workers. For centuries, the landowners have stolen from the peasants. It will take many years to put that right. And that's why it's important not to lose a day."

"Why me? Why did you want me to see it?"

"Why you?" Rodyon smiled and his smile turned his face back into an enigma. "Because it's important for everyone to understand. Especially young people. Especially intelligent ones. Especially ones with sparkling eyes and —"

He moved his hand towards her face. Instinctively Tonya drew back and he managed to convert his gesture into a cousinly pat on the shoulder. He smiled as though to laugh away his last sentence, and she smiled as though she accepted his dismissal of it. She felt confused and her confusion made her uncomfortable. She liked Rodyon; liked and admired him. He was a man with power in a world where power mattered. But Tonya still never quite knew where she stood with him. She'd had men — boys really — in love with her before. But then she'd known that love was love. The boys had been goofy with it, soppy with it, angry with it, overcome with it. But it seemed as though nothing would ever overcome Rodyon. He seemed to be a man who could never be mastered.

Rodyon finished his bowl of gruel with a grimace.

"Well then, comrade citizen, let's find you logs." His voice sounded harsh.

The next house was a big mansion on Kuletsky Prospekt. And there it was the same thing. Arrangements were checked, papers filled, orders given, disputes settled. In one room, bone cold even in the middle of the day, a steel safe was cemented into the wall, the marks of sledgehammers and crowbars fresh in the surrounding plaster.

And on the top floor, Rodyon whispered to Tonya. "Your bourgeois await. How you deal with them is up to you."

The family concerned — a mother, a small boy and a young man about Tonya's age — were living in two rooms of a former servants' attic. Rodyon flashed through his interrogation, purposeful and disciplined. Only this time, his usual fairness had been replaced by something harder. Rodyon's questioning had a cruel edge to it, a hint of the police cells. The young man, the son, answered for the mother. Tonya could see that he was taken aback by Rodyon's attitude, but he nevertheless kept his cool. After fifteen minutes, the questioning turned away from the matter of housing.

"There is a safe downstairs."

"Yes."

"You are aware that the contents of that safe belong to the Petrograd Soviet?"

"Yes."

"Do you know what is inside?"

"No."

"Do you know the codes?"

"No."

"You're telling me that your father didn't tell you?"

"I was away in the army. Before that — well, he thought I was too young, I suppose."

"You are aware that theft from the Petrograd Soviet is a serious offence?"

"Of course."

The young man smiled bitterly. And in that smile, for the first time, Tonya saw the revolution from the point of view of the former ruling class. This young man's family had lost all its worldly goods, its enormous house, and now here he was being accused of stealing the things that had once been his. She was struck by his calmness, impressed.

"Do you have any documents that relate to your father's previous concerns?"

"Yes."

Without being asked the young man got them out and handed them over.

"Why weren't these submitted earlier to the proper authorities?"

"I didn't know they were meant to be."

"There were decrees issued and posted. It is the responsibility of every citizen to inform themselves and —"

"I was in the army. I wasn't in Petrograd."

"No matter. You *were* in the army. What about now?"

"No, not any more. I was wounded . . ."

"You have a demobilisation order from an officer in the Red Army?"

"At the time it wasn't the Red Army and —"

"Movement orders?"

The interview lasted another couple of minutes: unrelenting, hard, hostile, tough. The business with the safe was brought up again. The young man insisted he knew nothing of it. Rodyon again reminded him of how seriously "theft from the Petrograd Soviet" would be regarded. He meant either prison cells or the bullet, and the young man smiled grimly in acknowledgement.

And then it finished. Rodyon swept on out of the house, down onto the street, to the next house and the next and the next. But he left Tonya behind him, peering through the half-open door, listening to the silence.

5

Misha was about to bend down to check the stove, when he realised that the door out onto the corridor wasn't closed and that the space outside wasn't empty. He straightened. There was a girl there, dark-haired and serious. There was something very still in her manner, and something remarkable in her stillness. She was still in the way that a white owl is, or a deer grazing in snow. But there was also something watchful about her, untrusting. She didn't come or go. She didn't speak. She didn't even glance away when she saw Misha looking at her.

"*Zdrasvoutye*," he said. "Good day."

"Good day."

She didn't move.

"If you want to come in, then come in. But close the door, it's getting cold."

She nodded, smiled briefly, and came in.

"Well?"

"I was wondering if you had things to trade?"

"That depends. What do you have to sell?"

Her hand went into her pocket and came out with a lump of grey sugar and a pack of tobacco cut in half across the label. She held them out, but even as she did so, she must have seen that neither the tobacco nor the sugar were likely to go far in that house. Her mouth twitched. "Nothing. Just rubbish."

Misha looked at the proffered goods and listened to the girl's description of them with a grave face. Without changing his expression, he said, "Rubbish, hmm. We don't have much call for that here. But perhaps we could find some garbage to exchange."

He kept a straight face and looked directly at the girl. For just a second or so, she reflected his own expression: serious, unsmiling. Then his words got through some barrier, and she burst out laughing. She stuffed her goods away with a blush.

"You want logs too," she said, gesturing at the feeble pile of birch wood next to the stove. "So do I."

"So does everyone, it seems. There are no wooden fences left any more."

"I know where to get logs though," said the girl. "Proper ones. Seasoned and everything. The peasants bring them in from the country, but they don't dare come all the way into town because of the police. Only their prices are high. They don't accept rubbish."

Misha stared at the girl. The Housing Commissioner had only just left, seemingly leaving this strange girl washed up like driftwood on his doorstep. Could she possibly be a police spy? The girl read his thoughts.

"Don't worry about the commissioner. He's gone. And anyway he's my cousin. He brought me here, because he thought you might be able to . . . I mean he thought . . . I don't really know what he thought."

Misha hesitated, then decided to accept what she said. He plunged into the chest which contained those valuables too large to go under a floorboard. He came out with a china figurine, Meissen porcelain touched with gold leaf. It was very fine, very white, graceful.

"Would this do, do you think?"

The girl gasped. Misha realised she had probably never seen anything so fine. He gave it to her to hold and look at. She turned it over reverentially, in silence. Her eyes were greenish, with a slightly eastern slant to her eyelids. Though entirely Russian in the way she looked, her eyes gave her a hint of something more exotic, a dash of the Tartar.

"Well?"

"It's beautiful."

"And would a peasant with a cart full of logs think so?"

She nodded. "Of course. They're not short of food, logs or anything like that. Things like this . . . well! It would fetch a lot."

"Good. And if you had something other than rubbish to trade, you'd be happy to show me where to go?"

She nodded.

Misha grinned a huge and delighted grin. He had numerous problems, of course; all of them important. How to get his mother out of the country. What had happened to his father's money. How to get inside the safe. But of all his concerns, his most pressing was firewood. Typhus was endemic in the city. Bad food and cold weather would turn it into a killer. His mother was certainly at risk. He dived into the chest again, and pulled out a second figurine. He tossed it into the air and caught it.

"One for you, one for me. Is it too late to go there now?"

The girl looked at him and at the china doll in her hand. She was wide-eyed, disbelieving. "For me? Really?"

"If you show me where to go."

She nodded. "It's too late now. We have to go first thing. It'll be a long haul back anyway."

"Do you have a sledge?"

She shook her head.

"Really," Misha tutted, "a pocketful of rubbish and no sledge. I can get one, though. Tomorrow morning then?"

She nodded.

She gazed down at the figurine in her hand and put it down gently on the table beside the stove. "You keep this," she said abruptly. "Until tomorrow. You shouldn't . . ."

"I shouldn't what?"

"You shouldn't give people things like that. Not until you know that they'll give you something in return. You don't know me."

"But I trust you. If you'd taken the figurine, you'd have come back tomorrow anyway, wouldn't you?"

She nodded.

"Well then."

"But that's not the point."

"Isn't it?"

She didn't answer, just turned to go. She had her hand on the door and was about to leave, when Misha stopped her. "Wait! I don't know your name."

"Lensky."

"I can't call you Lensky."

"Antonina Kirylovna Lensky."

"Antonina Kirylovna," said Misha with a very prerevolutionary bow, "I'm Mikhail Ivanovich Malevich."

"Mikhail Ivanovich, comrade."
"Till tomorrow then."
"Till tomorrow."

6

Tonya arrived early the next morning, just as Misha was bringing the sledge around to the front of the house. It was dawn, or just a few minutes after.

They started off quickly. The empty sledge ran so easily on the icy upper layer of the snow that it seemed weightless. At turnings, it bucked and slid sideways like a boisterous colt. Going down hills, even shallow ones, it began to run so fast that on two occasions Misha and Tonya fell backwards into it, steering and braking with a boot heel. Misha laughed out loud for pleasure.

"What's so funny?"

"This is. It's fun, isn't it?"

"It won't be so much fun on the way back, pulling this thing full of logs."

"All the more reason to enjoy it now."

Tonya shrugged and for a few moments they tramped along in silence. Then Misha spotted a side street that dropped in a long curve to a secondary road below. His face twitched. With a quick glance sideways at Tonya, he put out his foot and toppled her backwards into the sledge. In the same swift movement, he pulled the sledge around and directed it to the right, down the hill. The sledge quickly leaped forwards, picking up speed. Misha jumped in next to Tonya, who, apart from a single shout of surprise, had said nothing.

Misha had his foot out, ready to guide the sledge, but where possible he let it find its own direction, banking steeply on the mounds of grey snow.

"This isn't the right way," she said.

"We'll go left at the bottom and pick up our road again."

Tonya kept her face set forwards. "You're going too fast."

"All right then, I'll brake."

Misha jabbed his foot out and deliberately kicked a spray of fine powdery snow high into the air. The sledge swept into the spray, spattering them. At first Tonya didn't smile, but then she too thrust her leg out and kicked up a miniature snowstorm. And then they were both at it, wrestling each other like brother and sister, kicking snow everywhere, letting the sledge plunge recklessly downhill. When they got to the bottom, the sledge struck a big drift lying transversely across their path and the nose plunged in, stopping them abruptly and showering them with yet more snow.

They lay in the bottom of the sledge, laughing, getting their breath and looking up at the piled-up clouds above.

"Antonina Kirylovna?"

"Yes?"

"May I call you Antonina?"

"You may call me comrade Lensky."

Misha looked at her. Her face flickered with a smile, though she was doing her best not to show it. "Very well. Comrade Lensky?"

"Yes, comrade Malevich?"

"May I reprimand you, comrade, for fooling around in the snow when your revolutionary duty is to escort the bourgeois to market."

"You are right, comrade. I believe my political education must be at fault. I will endeavour to correct my thinking."

They got up and brushed themselves clear of snow. Misha had taken his hat off and tossed it behind him into the sledge. Somewhere during their tumultuous descent, his hands had got muck on them, and he briskly washed them in a drift of cleanish snow, as matter of factly as if the drift had been a basin of warm water. Tonya watched him, finding him strangely exotic: this former aristocrat now living in bitter poverty; this tall young man, an outcast from the new Soviet system, laughing and joshing with her, the daughter of a lowly railway worker. Young and fair-skinned as he was, Misha only barely needed to shave daily and Tonya felt herself older than him, much older even, though she guessed their ages must be almost the same.

"Very good, comrade Lensky."

"If you please, comrade Malevich."

They started off again, pulling the sledge, mostly in silence now, though the silence was very different from the way they'd started. After walking for an hour and a half, they got to the railway halt where the peasants brought their produce. There was everything there: food, logs, tobacco, vodka, sugar, meat. Tonya was right. The peasants faced none of the shortages of the city where food and fuel were concerned. Misha wished he'd brought more than just the figurine to trade.

Tonya insisted on handling the haggling process herself. She played her hand perfectly, showing little interest in the stacks of firewood, making little clucks of disappointment when she noted sticks that were too thin or poorly seasoned. At the same time, she allowed the peasant women to handle the two figurines, never for long, but always for long enough for them to admire the extraordinary workmanship that had gone into them. Tonya didn't want Misha with her as she bargained, and she waved him away into another part of the slushy yard. He found a man, a former teacher, with nothing to sell except a stack of books on mathematics and engineering. Misha longed to buy them. The books seemed like a glimpse of a possible future, a future of quiet studies and a reputable profession. But Misha had nothing in his pockets and he had to disappoint the man. Meantime, Tonya had fixed on a particular peasant woman, and soon the bargaining began, swift and sharp. A deal was made, and Tonya came over to Misha, waving her hand at an enormous stack of logs.

"Those," she said.

"Those? All of them?"

Tonya nodded. "It'll take two trips. You'll have to take one load back by yourself while I wait here. I won't let these logs out of my sight, or they'll try to cheat us."

Misha nodded. He thought of pointing out that Tonya must therefore trust him to return later with the sledge. But he said nothing. They stacked the logs on the sledge and tied them down. Tonya had somehow seen Misha's desire for the books.

"You want those?"

"Yes."

"Why?"

"I want to study. I think I'd like engineering."

Tonya shrugged, approached the man, and struck a bargain. Misha thought she'd used her lump of sugar and a half-pack of tobacco, but he wasn't sure. The man leaped away, as though hurrying to preserve his good fortune. Tonya dumped the stack of books on the sledge.

"There."

"Goodness! Thank you! You didn't have to . . . How can I . . ."

Tonya brushed aside his offers of repayment with a cross shake of her head. "Why do you owe me anything? If you don't tie those books down, you'll lose them."

Misha tied the books down next to the logs.

"You'll need to go fast. My place is a mile or two further than yours."

"As quick as I can."

He set off. The way back lay slightly uphill and even though the snow had a good icy crust, the slope and the rutted surface caused innumerable problems. Misha's arms and back were already sore by the time he arrived back in Kuletsky Prospekt. He unloaded the logs, getting Yevgeny and his mother to carry them upstairs. Then he headed back to Tonya, who had been waiting four hours by now, but who looked as immobile and impassive as if she'd been waiting four minutes or four years.

"Comrade Lensky."

"Comrade Malevich."

Without much further talk, they loaded up and began the long journey back. The roads had thawed a little, making the pulling conditions worse. It was heavy, dogged labour, even with Tonya helping. Once a soldier challenged them to produce the right documentation for their load. Tonya didn't even bother to pretend to justify herself. She just swore at the soldier, using deliberately coarse, proletarian expressions. Misha had never heard a girl swear before. And though the soldier swore back, he didn't try to stop them.

"You put him in his place," said Misha.

"Did it shock you?"

"No. Yes, maybe. The way people speak and so much else seems to have changed these days. But I'm pleased we didn't have to stop."

Tonya made a "tsk" noise, as though Misha had said something wrong, and they relapsed into silence as they continued. Tonya's house was further than she had said and it was almost dark by the time they reached her yard. Misha was very tired now, but said nothing about it. They unloaded the sledge. The logs had become wet on the journey and were now starting to freeze.

"Do you want me to carry them up for you?"

"No."

"A good day's work."

"Yes."

"If you want . . ." Misha began, then stopped. If she wanted, then what? Misha knew where the peasants congregated now. He wouldn't need her help again, and without things to trade — things such as he still had and she didn't — the girl wouldn't have much reason to go back there.

"If I want, what?"

"Nothing. Only . . . where do you work?"

"The hospital. The Third Reformed. I'm a nurse."

"I see. And your father works on the railway, I think you said."

"Yes. Why?"

"Nothing, only I need a job."

"Well you can get work anywhere, can't you? I don't think you'd be much use as a nurse."

"No, but the railway appeals."

"Well then. Go to the railway." Tonya picked up an armful of logs. She stacked them in the crook of her arm, piling them until they were tucked high under her chin.

"You're sure I can't help?"

"I've been carrying logs all my life, comrade Malevich. For me, today wasn't an adventure."

"Yes, I see."

Misha picked up the reins of the sledge and began the slow trudge home.

7

He got home, weary but satisfied.

His satisfaction lasted approximately one second from the moment he threw open the door to their rooms.

His gaze fixed first on his mother, silent and white-faced — then Yevgeny, the same — then on two soldiers in the corner by the window, holding their rifles in front of them like walking sticks. A third man in a tie and a dark coat waited on the opposite wall. He had a revolver at his waist. There was total silence.

Misha broke it.

"Good evening," he said.

"Mikhail Ivanovich Malevich?" said the man in the tie.

"Yes."

"Come with us."

"Come? Why? Is this an arrest?"

The man didn't bother to answer. Emma was frozen in her chair by the stove, eyes terrified, too scared even to cry. Misha saw Yevgeny, his "little comrade", clutching his mother as though it was his job to comfort her.

"I'll be fine, Mother. This gentleman only wants to ask some questions. I'll be home soon."

Perhaps or perhaps not. He knew he had no way of telling. With the man in the tie leading the way, the soldiers pushed Misha out of the door, then led him downstairs into a waiting car. There were two more soldiers in the vehicle, also armed. Still no one spoke.

The car, lurching dangerously on the uncleared roads, crept through the city. It was dark now and from his position, seated in between two soldiers, Misha had a hard job working out where they were going. Lamps flashed by in the darkness. The soldiers in front muttered inaudibly between themselves. Once, they hit a patch of ice and slid sideways into a drift. Two of the men had to get out to help push the car out again, while the driver turned in his seat and stared at Misha with unreadable eyes.

After twenty-five minutes they stopped outside a large building somewhere near the centre of town. The building had two large iron lanterns burning outside and a pair of armed guards just inside the doorway. Misha thought he could see a sign reading "Ministry of Economic . . ." but he didn't have time to read the whole sign and wasn't certain of what he'd seen anyway. He was thrust through the doorway and was marched at speed up a broad turning staircase and along wide, ringing corridors. They stopped at a door. One of the soldiers knocked once, got an answer, then shoved Misha through.

The room was around a dozen feet square, with a grey striped rug over a parquet floor. One wall was covered by a dark wooden unit, cupboards on the bottom, glass-fronted shelves above. The shelves were mostly empty, except for a few rows filled by books with titles like *Report of the Commission into the Iron and Steel Industry 1912*. The only other adornments were a map of Russia and a portrait of Karl Marx.

Behind the desk sat a man, formal, neat, wire-rimmed spectacles over a beaky nose. The man wore a carefully trimmed beard and a look of mild busyness. A second man stood on the opposite side of the room by the door, so Misha couldn't look at them both at the same time. Misha was given a low stool and told to sit.

"Malevich? Mikhail Ivanovich Malevich?"

Misha confirmed his identity with a nod. Then it began. Questioning, intense and repetitive, constant and intrusive.

He was asked about everything. Things that mattered, things that didn't. Things to which they must already have known the answers, things that it was impossible for anyone to have known. Misha's time in the army. His purchases on the black market. His father's business dealings. The conversion of Kuletsky Prospekt into workers' accommodation. Their various small breaches of the housing decrees. His acquisition of logs that day. His contacts with other members of the old regime.

Mostly the questions were asked by the man at the desk: a functionary, not a policeman or a soldier, one of a new breed of Bolshevik bureaucrats. Whenever the man at the desk had had enough, he took a sip of water, a sign for the other man to take over for a spell. Nobody offered Misha violence, but they hardly needed to. The disparity in power in the room was so extreme that a kick or a punch would have been almost an anticlimax. The man with the wire-rimmed spectacles never raised his voice or varied the pace of his questions or took notes. But he never relented. He never gave time to pause. If Misha's answer to a question ever varied by even a half-shade of implication, the man burrowed away at the variation until it seemed even to Misha as though he'd been caught in some barefaced lie.

Round and round the topics came.

Misha had been dealing "enthusiastically" on the black market. Could he deny it? Was he not aware that there were official allocations of goods, that black-market speculation was tantamount to stealing from the workers? Misha had acquired logs in this way. He admitted it, did he not? What other items had he bought illegally? The man ticked off a list of items on the tips of his fingers as Misha made his confessions.

But through it all, Misha began to sense the man was play-acting. He couldn't be interested in a few minor black-market dealings. Everyone in Petrograd used the black market. Misha's strongest feeling was an odd one. He felt sure that Tonya must have betrayed him: that the housing commissar had brought her to do a job, that she'd done it, that he'd been its victim. He felt oddly, deeply wounded. He felt taken in and tricked.

The questioning turned off in another direction. Misha answered as best he could. There was something hypnotic in the rhythm of question and answer. To break the spell, Misha looked at the books on the shelves. *Analysis of International Trade from the Baltic Ports 1898 – 1914. Prussia, Austria and Russia: An Enquiry into International Capital Transactions.* The books were as dull as anything Misha could imagine, but they were also used. One or two books lay out on the desk. Others had small paper bookmarks sticking out of them. Misha guessed that he'd seen the sign right as he came in, that he was now in some kind of economics ministry. And in that case, this man, with his private room, his substantial desk, his black telephone, his air of importance, was no minor functionary. Misha guessed he was dealing with a Bolshevik official of some seniority. And in that case, there was only one possible topic of interest to him: namely, Misha's father's business dealings in the months before his arrest and murder.

Misha realised this and felt relief glowing through him. He knew nothing of his father's business. He could answer truthfully and not be caught out. His answers became fuller and franker. Once, in an answer to one question he began talking about the coal mines his father had owned down in Zhavalya. The man listened to him with a thin smile for a few minutes before interrupting.

"Your father didn't own those mines. He sold them in October 1916."

"No, no, I'd have known if he'd done that," said Misha, sincerely.

"He mortgaged them in June with the Petrograd Savings Bank, then sold his remaining interest in October to a consortium of fellow bourgeois. Please confirm the amounts of the relevant transactions."

"No, no, you have that all wrong," said Misha. "Those mines, they were on the estate in Zhavalya, they were his most important . . ."

The man took some papers from a drawer and threw them across the desk. Misha caught them and read them, stunned. The documents were obviously genuine. A brief note written in his father's writing confirmed it absolutely. And the papers confirmed precisely what the man had been saying. Misha was dumbstruck. If his father had done as these documents suggested, then he must have sold virtually everything he'd owned. And the money had gone somewhere. But where? In the middle of a world war, it had hardly been safe to transport valuables out of the country. And as for anything inside the country, the Bolsheviks had confiscated all physical assets and they'd devalued or rendered worthless everything else.

Again and again, Misha's thoughts returned to the safe in his father's old study.

It was obvious that his father kept his most valuable possessions in there. And Misha knew that the Bolsheviks hadn't yet gained access to it. Why hadn't they just put dynamite to the hinges and blown it apart? Presumably because they suspected that what lay inside might be vulnerable to the blast. Not gold then, but papers.

Misha kept his knowledge secret, but he felt the interrogation was becoming increasingly formal, increasingly pointless. Misha didn't have the answers the man needed. The man was becoming increasingly sure of it himself. The man asked again and again if Misha cared to remember any communication from his father he had hitherto chosen not to mention.

"No. For heaven's sake, I've been away in the army for a whole year. He sent letters of course. I've kept them. They're back in the apartment. I can show them . . ." Misha stopped, realising that the apartment was probably being searched as they spoke. "Well," he ended lamely, "you'll see, there's nothing there."

Then suddenly, the phone on the desk rang loudly. The sound was immense: a landslide of noise. The man poked his wire-rimmed glasses higher up his nose and answered it. He spoke a word or two and listened. Then he nodded, said, "Good, very well," and hung up. He looked at Misha.

"You're right. There was nothing there." There was a short pause. No one moved. Then the man waved a hand at the door, tired but almost amused. "Comrade Malevich, you are free to go."

8

Misha was taken home by the same car, the same driver that had brought him. Dawn was just beginning to lighten the eastern sky, but the city was still dark enough that all Misha could really see was the brightly lit channel carved by the car's headlamps. The streets were severely iced and the car had to move slowly to avoid skidding.

They stopped at Kuletsky Prospekt.

"Thanks," said Misha.

The driver shrugged.

Misha entered the house and closed the big door behind him. Something seemed wrong. He felt a draught on his face that he didn't recognise. The hall, never warm, seemed unnaturally cold. From no motive that he could put a name to, Misha, instead of going directly upstairs to his frightened mother, moved across to the room that had been his father's study. He opened the door as quietly as he could, not wanting to wake the families that would be snoring within.

Only he was wrong. There was no one there. The entire back wall had been ripped away. One whole side of the room was open to the night air and the snow. A light snowfall had drifted into the room itself and lay in a fine dust across the carpet and the mantelpiece. In the half-light of early dawn, the room glowed silver.

Misha stepped further on inside, hardly breathing. In the yard behind the house there stood a pair of tractors. A pair of thick iron chains ran from the yard into the room, and lay across the floor like a pair of giant metal snakes. A sentry stood in the shelter of one of the tractors, smoking a cigarette and looking the other way.

So that was it. The Bolsheviks had traced his father's asset sales and hadn't been able to locate the proceeds. And they, like Misha, suspected that this safe held the answers. Having failed to extract any answers from Misha that night, they'd rip the safe out in the morning, then blast their way into it.

Misha had never been close to his father, but he felt his presence in the empty room. His father had been powerful, distant, authoritative, dominant. It was almost impossible to believe that his life could be ended so simply, that his life's work of turning one sum of money into a very much larger one could be ended by a pair of tractors and a few sticks of dynamite. Misha felt his father's ghost, hovering in silence, watching the scene with the grim acceptance of a man who knows he's been bested.

To the right of the safe, and still, ridiculously, in its old position, was an oil painting depicting the 1812 Battle of Borodino, in which Russian troops under General Kutuzov had halted Napoleon before Moscow. The painting was neither especially good nor especially valuable, but, for the dead businessman, it had symbolised everything important about the Russian spirit. The painting had always been referred to just as "the 1812", as though the date said everything that needed saying. Misha remembered the picture postcard that had come with his father's papers, amused at the coincidence.

Outside in the yard, the sentry threw away his cigarette, turned his face to the room, then yawned.

Misha froze. The light was growing now and he could see the sentry as clear as anything. Inside the room it was darker, but still barely inky. Misha pressed himself against a wall, hardly daring to breathe. It was crazy for him to be here, crazy and dangerous. He should go upstairs at once, home to his mother. He should leave this safe and all its contents well alone.

The moment lasted a few long seconds, before the sentry turned away again, back to his post by the tractor. Misha realised that it was the machinery that was being guarded, not the room. The safe was a safe, after all. And he didn't go upstairs. Not yet.

He turned back to the painting. The familiar old picture, lined with the faintest powdering of snow along the horizontals of the frame, seemed to jog a memory. In his father's last letters, he'd kept referring one way or another to the defeat of Napoleon. Perhaps it was his way of reading the disasters that lay ahead and reminding Misha that the Russian spirit would triumph in the end. Treading as quietly as he could, Misha walked up to the picture. A cavalryman on his horse held his sabre high above a cowering Frenchman.

The 1812.

Then Misha got it. In a sudden tumble of insight, he understood it all. Of course his father had been afraid for the future: the asset sales had been proof enough of that. And who could his father trust with his secrets except Misha, his eldest son? But Misha had been away. Letters directed from a Petrograd seething with revolution to a front line crumbling under enemy attack was hardly the most secure form of communication. If Misha's father had wanted to communicate something of the highest importance, he might well have felt the need to use coded language.

And this was the clue: so simple, so utterly simple. The postcard had been another clue. His father's references to the defeat of Napoleon had been yet another.

Misha guessed that this safe would unlock like other safes. He would have to turn its hundred-numbered dial clockwise to a particular number, then anti-clockwise to a second number, then again, and then perhaps again. But there was nothing to say that the numbers couldn't be the same, or repeated.

Misha went to the safe and put his hand to the cold metal of the dial. It moved as soon as he touched it, surprising him. He steadied himself. Outside the sentry was still there, still smoking. In the old picture, the cavalryman still reared, sabre raised over the beaten Frenchman.

Misha turned the dial. Clockwise to eighteen, then back again to twelve. Then again. Then once more. 18, 12, 18, 12, 18, 12. The dial was marked with small

45

black lines on the outside, with numbers marked 0, 5, 10 and so on. In the poor light of the room, Misha had to examine the dial carefully to make sure it was clicking to a halt on the right number. When he reached the last digit, he felt a jab of disappointment. Perhaps he had been foolish to hope, but there was no sound, no sharp click of release. The door didn't gape suddenly wide. Misha half-stepped away. He remembered his mother upstairs and felt guilty at not having gone directly up. But just before leaving, almost as a gesture of farewell, he put his hand to the door and pulled.

It swung open in total silence.

There was a small packet of jewellery and some papers. Misha put his hand inside and took them all.

CHAPTER
THREE

1

The train nosed in, then stopped. Men began to uncouple the long chain of carriages. A short but massive man in a waist-length coat and a flat cap began to bellow instructions in a continual torrent. Half the time, the orders made no sense. The man shouted things like, "Lift it up — up — no up, you wet dishcloth — well, down then if it doesn't go. Down!" He didn't make it clear who he was addressing or what he was talking about. His face was bright with anger, and he had a tic in his upper lip. The man giving the orders was comrade Tupolev and he was Misha's new boss. It was spring.

Tupolev dealt with some other workers, then approached Misha.

"Malevich. Those carriages. They're late. They're required immediately in the port railway. Immediately! Those carriage bodies . . . Well! They're in a rotten state! But, you understand, we have to fix them up. You do. Not that you'd understand. An aristocrat. Anyhow. That's the way it goes. Yes!"

"You would like me to take charge of repairing those carriages for immediate return to the port railway," said Misha, calmly translating his boss's nonsense into logical order. "Yes, comrade."

Misha knew what he was about. In the four months he'd been working in the Rail Repairs Yard, he'd made himself indispensable. He'd learned metalwork from the older craftsmen. He could work a lathe and a welding torch. He could forge, cast, bore and weld. Each night he read the engineering books that Tonya had bought for him, and his understanding grew. The men turned to him sooner than Tupolev. He had become the yard's inventor, organiser and inspiration.

He reviewed the string of carriages.

They were mostly boxcars, wooden boxes on wheels, which would be easy enough to sort out. But along with the boxcars, there were half a dozen grain hoppers too, open steel bins on wheels that looked as though they had been dipped in the sea and left to rust. Their upper halves were in a terrible state. Their wheelbases were so dilapidated, that only about half the wheels still functioned.

"Those hoppers," said Tupolev. "Well, really!"

Misha examined them briefly, about to recommend them for the scrapheap. Then something caught his eye. A flash of white paint, so badly peeled that it was hard to make out. But the script was Latin not Cyrillic. Misha cleared away some grime from the surface and made it out: LAHTI-HELSINKI. These grain hoppers travelled to Finland, a distant world now, all but inaccessible, and one that was out of reach of comrade Lenin's murderous hand. Misha felt a sudden lurch of excitement, a cold wash of adrenalin. His hand shook very slightly as he wiped it clean on his trousers.

"What do you think, comrade?" asked Tupolev, examining him narrowly. "I can see — well, really, the state of them!"

Misha got a grip over his feelings, and replied normally. "These hoppers. They're for the port railway, you said?"

"The port? No. For Vyborg. The Vyborg line. Don't tell me what I said, you exploiter! You want to scrap them, I expect, but —"

"I'll mend them."

Tupolev was taken aback. He might be a fool, but he knew the basic technical side of his job well enough. These hoppers were all but useless and he knew it. "Mend them! Mend . . ."

"After all, they'll be needed for the harvest. Just think how angry the comrades in the Export Bureau will be if they can't —"

Misha never finished his sentence.

From the far end of the rail shed, there was a thundering crash and a loud scream, abruptly terminated. A few moments of total silence followed, succeeded by the shouts of men as they ran to the scene. Misha sprinted over, aware that Tupolev was lumbering on after.

It soon became clear what had happened. A carriage had been raised on the yard's only usable winch. The winch hadn't been properly secured, and the carriage had come plummeting down. A man lay on the tracks underneath. The man wasn't from the repairs yard. He wore an ordinary railwayman's uniform and a bottle of vodka lay smashed to smithereens beside him. The man must have been dead drunk inside one of the carriages. He must have woken up and climbed or fallen from his compartment. Then, when the winch broke, he'd ended up trapped.

Misha pushed through the knot of people. The man was still alive, but his arm and foot were trapped and he was bleeding fast. Unless he was extricated quickly, he could easily die from loss of blood.

"See?" Tupolev was shouting. "Inattention and slovenliness! And there's too much vodka drunk all round, I'd say. Oh yes!"

Misha threw himself down beside the trapped docker and peered in through the steel wheels in order to try to gauge how to release the man. He stared a few moments, then rolled back into a sitting position.

"We need to lift the carriage. That winch is still usable, it's only the loading pin which has sheared off. You, Feodorov, go and find a pin. Volsky, get up the ladder to the drumhead and clear the old pin. Andropov, go for a doctor. Run!"

Tupolev was still shouting too, but people followed Misha's instructions in preference. Tupolev stood clenching and unclenching his fists by the injured man. His whole air was that of a man worried about a delay in his schedule. Misha continued to direct proceedings, feeling the hammer of excitement, the vital importance of speed.

Six minutes later, the winch was ready. The carriage began to sway off the ground. The docker, a man prematurely aged by drink with just four teeth left in his filthy mouth, was unconscious now. Unconscious and dying. And still trapped. Though the carriage was no longer pressing down on him, his arm had become caught between the wheels. The only way to release it would be to climb under the carriage and ease it clear.

Misha checked the winch. Feodorov had found a new loading pin, but it was far too small for the weight of the carriage. At any time, the whole thing might come thundering down, killing anyone who might be underneath. Tupolev brought his huge bulk close to the trapped man.

"Right now, comrade, one big heave and it'll all be over."

He was about to heave, when Misha snapped at him.

"Don't be a bloody fool, you'll tear his arm off. Stand back."

Swallowing once, aware of the carriage's precarious weight looming above him, Misha rolled beneath it.

Under the wheelbase, it was much darker than Misha had expected and for a moment he could see nothing except a knife-blade of pale sunlight between the carriage rear and the ground. Then the carriage's underbelly began to be revealed in a series of gleams and dull reflections. Misha could see the man's arm, badly broken and cut, but not, it seemed, beyond hope. Misha began to tease the warm flesh clear of the metal. There was blood everywhere, splashing on Misha's face and disturbing his view.

There were shouts from outside; something to do with the winch. Misha worked as fast as he could. He thought he'd done it, then found the man's arm still immobile. He was panting with the effort and the

51

danger, when he realised that it was only the man's coat which still held him.

"A knife," he shouted, "get me a knife."

An eternity later, or so it seemed, a knife was slid in to him. He cut the fabric of the man's coat and the man flopped down like a dead fish.

"You can pull him out now. You can —"

Then it all happened too fast to recall.

The injured man was hauled out so quickly he seemed to shoot out of sight. There were screams from up above. The carriage lurched down. Misha rolled sideways to escape. There was another sharp movement, dark on dark. Then something seized hold of Misha and he felt a violent, irresistible tug, dragging him sideways. He struck his head on something dark and cold.

Then that was all: darkness and silence.

2

It was in darkness and silence that Tonya hurried from the hospital.

Her father, that drunken fool, had been badly hurt — numerous bones broken, a lot of blood lost — but he would be fine. He was much luckier than he deserved. The ambulance men said someone had risked his life to rescue him and Tonya felt she needed to go and thank his saviour.

She got to the Rail Repairs Yard — a giant shed which squatted like a massive dark beast over the rail lines that led into it. There were a few lights on inside, but the shed was so huge that the few points of light only emphasised its size and shadows. She splashed up the muddy track that led to it and found a door cut into the wooden sides. Beyond the door, there was an office with a lamp lit, but nobody to direct her. From beyond a thin partition wall, she could hear the noise of a busy industrial site: engine noise, men shouting, the ringing of metal on metal. She explored further. She tried one door, found it locked, tried another. The door opened, she came into a passageway, pressed on a bit further, then found another door which opened right out into the railway yard itself.

The sudden change of scale was momentarily daunting. The shed was wide enough that eight railway tracks could enter it side by side. It was long enough that ten railway carriages could be accommodated end to end. And it was high enough that the roof seemed to disappear off into darkness. Though electric bulbs hung down from the roof girders, they did little to illuminate the enormous space.

A man, short but powerfully built, saw her and approached.

"What, comrade? Looking for your husband, I expect. You'll have to wait. Party work. I'm sorry, but it's really no good."

The man had a bright red face, unhealthily stressed. His plump black moustache quivered.

"No. My name is Lensky. My father was injured here this afternoon. I wanted to thank whoever it was who —"

"Ah, yes! Alcohol, of course. Your father was drunk. Disgracefully drunk. Unsafe, is it? You can't come here and accuse me — oh no! Quite the reverse. The Party gives high priority — very rightly — safety, of course — not that we can let up, mind you —"

The man boomed on as though anybody cared. Other men had obviously seen Tonya's entrance and drew close, from curiosity. News of who she was instantly spread and she began to get snippets of fact.

"— tumbled from the carriage in a stupor —"

"— the whole thing came smashing down —"

"— broken loading pin, you see, it's the only winch we still have working —"

"— the whole carriage — bam! — eight tons unloaded —"

"— at least a bottle, I'd say, I don't think he knew a thing about it —"

"— old Tupolev just wanted to rip him out. He'd have left his arm right there under the carriage —"

"— 'course, the hard part was lifting the carriage again —"

"— I wasn't going in under there. Any fool could see the winch would never hold —"

"— bloody fool Tupolev —"

"— reeking —"

"— so we sent in our very own bourgeois. Ha, ha, ha! The winch is obviously a true Bolshevik —"

"— the loading pin was too small —"

"— almost had his head off —"

"— came crashing down —"

"— eight tons unloaded —"

"— reeking, absolutely reeking —"

"— bloody fool —"

"— bam!"

Tonya felt the men swarm around her. Judging by the smell, her father hadn't been the only one to take a drink that day. The Railway Repairs Yard was an all-male preserve and Tonya felt something charged and predatory in the atmosphere.

"Who is he? Is he here now?"

"No, no, the hospital took him ages ago. You're a nurse, aren't you?" — Tonya's uniform was visible under her coat — "Didn't they tell you?"

"Not my father. The man who pulled him out. He was hurt? Injured?"

"Ha, ha! Thank the bourgeois, is it? He's over there. You won't get much sense from him, though. Not with a crack on the head like he got."

The men were unhelpful, pressing close. With their oily, leering faces and black beards and moustaches, the men didn't just seem like another half of the same species, but like a different species altogether: dirtier, noisier, brutish, dangerous. Unconsciously, Tonya held her coat closed at the front and broke away from the men, heading for the welding bay. Behind her, the fool Tupolev began ordering his men back to work, so she was spared the delight of a fifteen-man escort.

Down in the welding bay, a single man worked with a blowtorch. Showers of flame and sparks were struck into being. The metal glowed red-hot, even white-hot. Nothing of the man himself was visible. He wore a protective suit and had a dark visor to protect his face. Except that he was tall, Tonya could guess almost nothing of his looks. He didn't see her approach. He didn't stop work. He was mending a thick metal tube which must have been heavy, but the man handled it with a rare combination of strength and deftness, turning it with his left hand as he welded with his right. Finally the job was done. He cut his torch and the flame died. He pulled his visor up and off. He stepped back and saw Tonya.

She was the first to react.

"Comrade Malevich!"

"Gracious! Good Lord! Lensky!"

Tonya saw a bright red weal across Misha's forehead and the start of what looked like an almighty swelling. She was disconcerted by seeing Misha, of all people. She didn't know what she felt.

"It's you . . . I had no idea . . . I came because of my father."

"Your father?"

"My father, Kiryl, the drunken oaf whose life you saved this afternoon."

"That was your father, was it? Good Lord."

As a nurse, Tonya was well accustomed to seeing head trauma, shock, and concussion. She could see at once that Misha had a well developed case of all three. He shouldn't be working at all, still less handling dangerous equipment. He rubbed his head again, as though trying to clear his mind.

"You hurt your head. None of the imbeciles over there could tell me what happened."

Misha shrugged. "Your father got himself caught underneath a railway carriage. We had to winch it up and I slid in to get him out. The winch isn't up to much though, and the whole thing came crashing down again. I only got out because Tupolev got hold of my leg and whipped me out. Somewhere along the way, I banged my head. It's fine though. Sore, but fine."

Tonya felt a surge of emotion, a mixture of tenderness, anger, impatience, compassion. She felt angry with her father for being a drunk. She felt suddenly, briefly, angry with all of Soviet Russia for being a place where winches broke, where drunk men tumbled from railway coaches, where injured men were sent back to work, unthanked.

"You're not fine," she snapped. "Come on. I'll take you home."

"No, really, it's —"

"Don't argue. I'm a nurse."

Brusquely, almost rudely, she pushed Misha away from his work and out towards the exit. He let himself be pushed. When Tupolev called out to him to stop and explain his early departure, Misha just said, "Oh don't be such a damned idiot!" and carried on walking. Outside, under the violet night and the first scatter of stars, Tonya felt Misha stiffening and pulling away.

"What's the matter? You need to get home and rest. I'll tell Tupolev, if you like. An official instruction from the hospital."

"Oh, I don't care two kopecks for Tupolev . . . but I'll go home by myself, thanks. I don't need you to walk me."

"You've got a nasty case of concussion. You shouldn't be alone."

Misha, tall, pale, suddenly angry, turned on her.

"Alone? No, I expect not. But then again, I'm not sure if I want to be walked home by you. Our last expedition didn't turn out so well, did it?"

"Our last expedition? The logs? I think I was rude when you left. I'm sorry. I didn't know . . . I didn't mean . . ."

Misha brought his face close to Tonya's. She felt his force, his anger.

"Comrade Lensky, you can be as rude to me as you like. But I had thought we had gone to buy logs together. I didn't know you were on a little mission from the secret police."

"The police? I don't know . . . I didn't . . . I don't know what you're talking about." Tonya felt her voice vibrating with emotion. She didn't really understand why. Only it was desperately important to her that this unusual man did not think badly of her.

"The police. You don't understand, eh?"

"No, really not. Really!"

In a few brief and savage words, Misha explained. His arrival home. His instant arrest. His interrogator's perfect knowledge of their little shopping trip.

Tonya's face was wet with tears. "No. I know nothing of that. I told no one. I wouldn't. It was you who bought me those logs. That figurine! I'd never seen anything so beautiful. I wanted it almost more than the firewood. They must have followed you. Maybe my cousin. Maybe Rodyon. Not me. I wouldn't."

"Really? Really not?" For several seconds, Misha searched Tonya's face for the truth of what she said.

Illuminated and simplified by the moonlight, Tonya's face was a pale oval, surrounded by a halo of dark hair. Her lips and eyes were imploring. They had a softness about them which they seldom or never seemed to have by daylight. A strand of hair had fallen across her face and had stayed there, wet from her tears. At long last, Misha nodded. He put his hand to her face and moved the strand of hair away from it. "All right then. I believe you. I take back what I said. Sorry."

"Sorry."

Tonya breathed the word as if it held no meaning. Misha's apology didn't seem to change things. Her face was still turned up to his. She was still crying, not even she knew why. Then quietly, gently, she raised herself on tiptoe and put her face to his. She kissed him, the first real kiss of either her life or his. The kiss was mouth to mouth, but still quite chaste. It was as though she wanted to break a barrier, but still allow herself room to retreat if she had got the situation wrong. But she hadn't. When she pulled away, slightly frightened at what she had just done, he pulled her back and kissed her again. After a few minutes, they stopped kissing, but stayed arm in arm, suddenly and astonishingly close.

"If this is concussion," said Misha, "then I like it."

She butted his shoulder with her head in mock-rebuke.

"Do you always thank people like this?" he continued. "I should think it makes a good impression mostly, but some people must be a bit surprised."

She shoved against him as if to scold him, but he had his arm so tightly wrapped around her body that the two of them moved together, one creature under the moonlight.

"I wanted to kiss you when we sledged down that hill together and rammed the big snowdrift at the bottom. I wanted to kiss you and kiss you and never stop," he said.

"Me too."

"Well, why didn't you?"

"Why didn't *you*?"

"Because I thought you didn't want me to. You weren't very friendly, you know."

"I know."

"Well then . . . What about you? Why didn't you let yourself kiss me?"

She tossed her head coquettishly, secure now that she was in his arms. "A girl doesn't have to explain," she said.

"But a good citizen always should, comrade Lensky."

"You make a good point, comrade Malevich. But I still won't say."

"In that case, comrade Lensky, I might be obliged to tickle you."

"But first, comrade Malevich, you would be obliged to catch me."

She broke away and ran from him, laughing. He chased her down the muddy street, and caught her. They were both laughing hard and panting hard. He pulled her close and they kissed again, longer and even more passionately than they had the first time.

Tonya did walk Misha home that night, but it took her more than four and a quarter hours to do so. Misha did go to bed that night with his cut head wrapped in bandages and bathed in vinegar, but it took him until dawn to get to sleep. Both Misha in his bed and Tonya in hers knew that their lives would never be the same again.

3

Four weeks passed the same way.

Misha and Tonya were in love: each was the other's "little paw", as the Russian phrase had it. Each day after work, Tonya would meet Misha by the road leading down to the rail yard. Mostly, they spent their time together walking. The spring was a warm one and it was a pleasure to be outside after a long and dreary winter. They strolled through the city parks, or along the banks of the Neva. But they were outside for another reason too. There was nowhere else for them to go. Twice Tonya had come to Misha's rooms on Kuletsky Prospekt. Both times his mother had treated her as she would have treated any member of the servant class. Tonya felt invisible, irrelevant and unwanted. Neither she nor Misha could behave normally in that atmosphere and they burst downstairs and outside as soon as they could.

Things were no better at Tonya's home. Her father had been sent home from hospital, but his arm was healing slowly and it would be months before he was able to return to work. Deprived of his work, the nasty old man was also deprived of his access to tobacco and vodka. When Tonya and Misha were there together, he missed no opportunity to make a cackling joke, a dirty innuendo. He never thanked Misha for saving his life, nor did he ever once refer to the incident. When Tonya had to go next door to look after her grandmother, Misha had to sit and endure the old man's silent, malicious scrutiny until Tonya was done and they could leave.

So, in the time that they weren't at work, or taking care of their respective families, Misha and Tonya walked outside, covering miles and miles, talking, laughing, kissing and walking. They made love too, not once but many times. There was a spot in the park they returned to again and again. It lay inside a thicket of birch trees, screened off by a dense curtain of juniper and broom. They were hardly alone in wanting privacy, of course, and there were times when they found their spot had already been taken ("Give us a sodding minute, will you, mates?" came from inside the thicket), and other times when they sensed a queue forming outside ("Sorry, comrades, take your time").

But, despite the limitations on their relationship, their love expanded. They lived in a daze. When they were with each other, nothing else seemed real. When they were apart, they dragged themselves around as though drugged.

There was one subject, and only one, that had never been broached by them, but, aside from Tonya herself, it was the topic uppermost in Misha's mind. The subject had to come up, and one day it did. It was the middle of May. They were walking through the streets in the deepening shade, listening to the dying burr of traffic and the clop-clop of horses' hooves. Then Tonya squeezed Misha's hand and said, "Your mother. You said she was ill."

"Yes."

"Headaches again?"

"Headaches, yes, and back pain. And if it isn't headaches or back pain, then it's a cough or a fever or something else."

"She's not strong."

"Oh, she's strong enough, or would be if things were easier for her . . . You know they want her to start work as a factory hand?"

"Your mother, a factory hand!"

"At the saw mill down by the Finlyandsky goods depot. Can you imagine? Wearing blue overalls and shouting above the rotary saws all day." Misha laughed, but his face reverted almost instantly to its former serious expression. "I have to get her out of Russia. You know that, of course?"

"To get her out? But . . ."

"Her and Yevgeny. They'll have to join Natasha and Raisa in Switzerland."

Tonya heard his words and something inside her began to freeze. She walked along, silent and tense. Misha was preoccupied and took a moment or two to notice.

"What's up with you?" he said in surprise.

"Switzerland!"

"Yes. Where else? Most of Europe is still at war, you know."

"But if she goes, won't you need to . . . will you . . . who would go with her?"

"Who would go with her?"

Misha stopped and looked full into Tonya's face. He saw the worry gathered between her eyebrows, her green eyes flitting from one place to another on his face. He was still for a moment, then his mouth quivered and broke out in a merry, widening laugh.

"Oh, comrade Lensky, comrade Lensky!"

He took her by the waist and her left hand, and, whistling out a tune to give them rhythm, he led her in a rapid waltz down the empty street. Infected by his mood, she started to laugh, but her anxiety hadn't gone.

"But really . . . wouldn't you need to go?"

"Comrade Lensky, you're missing your steps!"

"No, tell me!"

"One-two-three, one-two-three, one-two-three, one. That's better. Keep going."

Tonya's feet began to move as he instructed her. She was naturally a better dancer than he was, even though he'd been the one with the boyhood dancing tutor. He'd begun to teach her one evening and already she was technically more competent than him, though she still didn't give herself to the dance the way he did.

"Excellent, Lensky! Lensky of the Bolshoi!"

Misha turned from a simple waltz into a complex Viennese one, full of turns inside turns, spinning and circling down the street. Then he fumbled his steps. She pushed him in mock disgust. The dance ended with them leaning against a high stone wall, panting.

"*Charmante, Madame,*" said Misha bowing.

"Tell me."

"My job is to get them out of the country with a little money. Natasha and Raisa are fifteen and sixteen. Mother will be safe enough with them."

"Really?"

"No. I lied. Raisa must be seventeen now."

"Misha!"

He took her in his arms. He wasn't broadly built, but there was something in his tallness and confidence that made him seem bigger. "I won't leave Russia without you. And you have your family to think of — your brother, father, and grandmother."

"Yes. Yes, I do."

"You wouldn't leave them?" It was half statement, half request.

"No . . . No, I don't think I could. Father — well, he needs me, but I don't know if I owe him much. But Pavel's young, you know. Younger than his age. And Babba, my grandmother, depends on me completely."

Misha nodded.

"That's what I thought. You're right."

They walked on.

Tonya wanted to ask Misha if he meant what he had just said about not leaving without her, but she kept her mouth shut, knowing that if she asked him again, he would be certain to bound off again on some teasing diversion. All the same, the thought boomed in her head. Her lover, an aristocrat, a wealthy bourgeois of the old regime, was willing to stay in a country which had, for him, turned into something not unlike a prison camp. *And for her!* She felt light-headed at the thought.

"You say you have to get them out . . . do you know how?"

"Yes. The Rail Repairs Yard. I didn't just end up there by chance, you know."

"The rail yard? You mean . . .?"

Misha told her. He told her about the single-track railway which crept out of Petrograd up to the Gulf of Finland. How it crossed the border between Vyborg and Lahti before turning and heading for Helsinki itself. How six wagons from the Vyborg line had come into the yard. How he had manipulated Tupolev into assigning the repair job to him.

"They do need repair," said Misha. "They're in a terrible state. A couple of them are probably beyond salvage. But that's not all I'm doing."

He told her the rest of it. How he was building a compartment flat against the rear of one of the wagons, built to look like the sloping wagon wall itself. How he would put in a bench, airholes, a sliding entrance panel. How another few weeks' work would see his project completed. How he planned to conceal his mother and Yevgeny in the compartment one summer's evening before the hoppers were loaded for export.

Tonya could well imagine the labour, ingenuity and sheer courage that had gone into Misha's plan.

"Your mother is very lucky," she said.

"Well, we have yet to see if the idea works."

"And money. You said they needed money."

"Yes." Misha hesitated. He trusted Tonya, of course. He could hardly have told her about his escape plans otherwise, but telling her about the money seemed like a still more serious confidence. After all, senior Bolsheviks had been on the trail of the money when Misha had wafted it from in front of their noses. He had even at one stage suspected that Tonya had been involved in the whole affair.

"You don't have to tell me."

"No, no. It's all right."

Misha preferred to trust Tonya than to hold anything back. So he told her. About the safe. The codes. The items inside. "There was jewellery there. Not a huge amount, but — well, plenty." Misha felt embarrassed. It might not have been a huge amount to him, but to Tonya it would have represented vastly more money than her father had earned in his entire life. "And papers," he added. "Father had been buying stocks, bonds, anything he could. But buying it through agents abroad. He was clever about it. He didn't know whether England and France or Germany and Austria would win the war. So he shared the funds about. Some in Berlin. Some in London. Some in Paris. Some in Geneva. Part of that money will be lost of course, but not all. If my mother gets to Switzerland, she will have plenty. She will be a rich woman. Rich enough. If, one day, we go to join them, then we'll have enough to set up in business, to make a good life out there."

Tonya heard his words as though he were talking about taking her to dinner on the moon, or asking her how she would like to furnish her palace. His words seemed ludicrous, but also somehow believable, coming from him. For the first time, Tonya began to believe that things might yet all turn out for the best.

<h1 style="text-align:center">4</h1>

Tonya was home early from the hospital. It was early July, the season of Petrograd's famous white nights, when the nights were so brief that darkness never really set in, a late twilight fading into an early milky dawn.

Normally, she would have gone straight to the rail yard to wait for Misha to emerge. But not tonight. Misha wanted to use the long night to complete the secret compartment in one of his grain hoppers. He planned to stay up all night to do it. He wouldn't see Tonya again until the following evening.

But, though Tonya missed him, she didn't mind too much. She was behind with her housework and the apartment needed cleaning. She spent half an hour with her grandmother, Babba Varvara, then went back into the main room and began working. She hummed to herself as she worked, and sometimes found herself unconsciously repeating the dance steps that Misha had taught her. She was doing just that, twirling as she carried the cooking pot over to the stove, when she sensed the door open behind her. She stopped dancing and put the pot down. It was Rodyon.

He looked tired and thin, worn down. She saw him still from time to time, but not often. She was surprised to see him, and guarded.

"*Zdrasvoutye*," she said.

Rodyon nodded, but said nothing. He sat down.

"Tea?"

"Yes, please, if you have it."

"You can have bread too, if you want."

"I'm fine."

"You're not fine. You look tired and hungry."

Tonya put the kettle on the stove, then jiggled the logs inside to stir up the heat. The apartment was hot even with the windows open wide, and the heat was an unwanted extra. There was also something unsettling about the length of these summer days. When she was with Misha, the long days made sense. But when he was absent, the endless days and shimmering nights seemed mildly insane, as though the world had lost its ability to rest. She cut a slice of bread and spread it with pork dripping and salt.

"Here."

"Thank you."

Rodyon ate it wolfishly, then sighed.

"You know, Marx took a material view of humanity. It was his greatest insight, his greatest accomplishment. But you don't realise how right he was until you've been hungry. All the time I've been sitting here, I've wondered whether you had sugar or jam to go with the tea. I desperately hope that you do, but have been too proud to ask. A spoonful of sugar against a man's soul. Pitiful, isn't it?"

"I have sugar, yes. And lemon."

"Ah, the careful management of the official allocation or the miraculous bounty of the black market. I wonder which."

"You know very well which."

"Yes, and I'm going to enjoy it anyway. You were cooking as I came in. At least, you were dancing with a cooking pot, which I assume is the same thing. Don't let me stop you."

Tonya did as he said. To the pot, she added cabbage, beans, carrot, onion and a thick shin of beef. She put the whole thing on to boil. She worked carefully, guarding her expression. She wasn't exactly nervous of Rodyon, but the two of them hadn't seen each other for a while and Rodyon seldom did things without a purpose. She waited for him to reveal it.

The kettle boiled. She made tea, let it brew, then poured it, adding three spoonfuls of sugar. Rodyon took the cup with thanks. He had barely changed his posture since first sitting down, but she could see his tiredness slipping away, and he wore it now as a mask more than anything.

"We're seeing Pavel more and more at the Bureau of Housing," he said.

"Yes."

It was true. Because of Misha, Tonya had been at home very little. Pavel, never properly rooted since their mother had died, had taken to leaving home more and more. He often ended up at the Bureau of Housing, where his admiration for Rodyon had blossomed into something close to hero-worship.

"He is useful. He runs a lot of errands for us."

"He's a good boy."

"Yes . . . And when did he last wash, do you know?"

"Wash? He washes every day."

"Face and hands, yes. I meant more than that. All over."

Tonya shrugged. "He's fourteen, nearly fifteen. You know what it's like."

"This week? Last week?"

"What do you care? He won't wash in cold water and boiling enough water for a bath in this heat . . . well, he's old enough to boil water for himself if he wants it."

"You didn't always say that."

"He wasn't always fifteen, or as good as."

"But the change came four months ago, didn't it, Antonina Kirylovna?"

Tonya swallowed. Rodyon was creeping around to the real subject and she felt her mouth go strangely dry. Though she wanted to blame it on other things — the endless day outside, the light glittering from the city's roofs and cupolas, the heat of the stove — she knew it was none of those things.

"Maybe," she admitted.

"Mikhail Ivanovich Malevich. Son of Ivan Ilyich Malevich. Ivan Ilyich was one of the country's richest men. Not in the top fifty perhaps, but not so far outside either. Coal mines. Iron works. Land."

"They have none of that now."

"No."

Rodyon stopped as though he'd finished. He finished his tea and pushed his cup away from him.

"More?" said Tonya.

"Please."

"The sugar doesn't come from father's coal-stealing. It comes from Misha. The soup things too. He trades his family's last few possessions. He is generous."

"Bourgeois sugar, eh?"

"That's one way to put it."

"Then I'll have another spoonful."

Tonya poured the tea and pushed it back at Rodyon. Her movement contained an ounce or two of anger and tea slopped over the rim of the cup. He ignored both the anger and the spillage.

"His family's last few possessions. What a piteous-sounding phrase!"

"There's no pity. It's a simple fact."

"Is it? Really? That's another insight of Marx's. Facts aren't necessarily simple, even the simplest ones. His father accumulated possessions by exploiting his workers. Each year, every year, men died underground in his coal mines. Others were cut to pieces in industrial accidents at his iron works. And he reaped the profit."

"He employed them. I don't suppose conditions in his mines were worse than elsewhere."

"He gave them the lowest wage he could possibly pay them, you mean. Yes. And that wage wasn't always enough to give his workers enough food, fuel, medicine or housing. Look at this rat-hole you live in. You have always counted yourself lucky to have it. How does it compare with Kuletsky Prospekt, eh? How does it compare with that? So: you say his family's last few possessions, but if he stole the labour that allowed him to acquire them, then to whom, really, do those things belong?"

Tonya shrugged. "Who cares? In a few months, they'll have nothing."

Rodyon nodded, as though he agreed. He stood up. All at once, the lean tigerishness of his energy seemed to come rushing back. When before he had looked tired, now again, as usual, his face radiated an intense, challenging handsomeness, spoiled and completed by his broken nose. He paced the tiny apartment as though he felt cooped up in it. He leaned out of the open window, traced a line on a cupboard with the tip of his finger as though to check for dust, then came over to the stove and felt it for heat.

"Good soup."

"Yes."

"The smell is almost the best part."

"Maybe."

"A meat bone?"

"Beef."

"You're lucky."

"If it's luck that we've been talking about, then yes."

"Hmm."

Rodyon paced again. Back to the window, behind Kiryl's armchair, which he rocked to and fro on its back legs, then to the table and the carrot ends and onion skins left over from Tonya's cooking. He took some carrot ends and began to munch.

"Babba Varvara's all right, is she?"

"She's fine. No different from ever."

"No. You do well with her. If she weren't your responsibility she would be mine. Thank you."

Tonya shrugged. Then he turned abruptly around, and faced Tonya. She found herself fixed in the sudden glare of his intensity.

"Listen, Antonina, this boy of yours, Mikhail Ivanovich. He is a danger to you. You must stop seeing him."

Tonya opened her mouth to protest. The anxiety that she'd felt since Rodyon's entry had been pointing all along to this one inevitable moment. She felt fiercely, passionately protective of Misha. But Rodyon didn't let her speak. He waved down anything she might have had to say.

"You'll protest of course. But hear me out. At the heart of the Communist Party lies the understanding that the interests of Malevich's class are irreconcilable with the interests of the workers. It isn't any longer a question of living space or property or anything like that. But Malevich knows that the Party is his enemy. The Party knows that Malevich is its enemy. If you align yourself with Malevich, you align yourself against the Party. That's dangerous. It's inconceivably foolish, if I may say so."

Tonya moved her tongue inside her mouth. She found only glue and ash. She couldn't have spoken if she'd wanted to, but Rodyon hadn't finished.

"The second thing is this. The All-Russian Central Executive Committee is about to issue a new set of decrees. Malevich and his kind will be sent into internal exile all over Russia. It's no use having these people

74

crawling over the seats of power in Petrograd and Moscow. They'll be given work to do. They will work of their own accord, or they will be made to work in a labour camp. We find it helps to keep the alternatives fairly simple. The decrees will be published any day now. They will have immediate effect."

Tonya felt the blood rushing in her head. She wanted to find some way to block the sound of Rodyon's words, but couldn't. The words had already smashed aside any possible barrier and were roaring forwards in their destructive progress. Only time could tell what wreckage would be left behind.

"And one last thing. I think I've handled things badly. I should have acted sooner or perhaps later. I kept putting things off. But in the end I realise that the only important thing is that I should act. Antonina — Tonya — I am — I have always been your greatest friend and admirer. I know that this isn't the time — there's Malevich in your thoughts I know. But you will put him aside. You'll have to. And when you do, please know that I'm here. I have loved you for a long time. For ever, so it seems. I would like to be — if you'll let me — I know it'll take time — more than just your friend and your cousin. Don't give me an answer now. The timing is all wrong, I know. Forgive me. But some day. I shan't go away."

Rodyon took a step or two forwards as though intending to grasp Tonya's hands or kiss her. Then, realising any such movement would be profoundly unwelcome, he simply nodded his head, briefly looked around the room, then strode briskly away.

5

Tonya told Misha of Rodyon's visit. She didn't tell him about the first part of what he'd had to say, nor the last part either. But she told him about the decrees, the awful fact of impending banishment.

Misha had listened in silence, then nodded thoughtfully.

"I'd expected something like that," he said, "only I'd hoped it wouldn't come so soon. All the same, there's no reason to change plans. We'll just have to work a little faster."

And work they did. Misha barely slept for working. He finished building a false wall into the back of one of the grain hoppers and got three of the six wagons workable. He couldn't do more.

Nor was Tonya idle.

It was one thing to build a false wall onto the back of a freight car, it was quite another thing to get that freight car onto the right train on the right line at the right time. After consulting intensively together, Misha and Tonya agreed that it was essential to take Kiryl at least partly into their confidence. The old man was utterly untrustworthy in most respects, but there was little he wouldn't do for vodka, and Tonya promised him enough to swim in. Somehow, Kiryl used his railway contacts to attach the wagon to a train bound for Finland. A date was set — then postponed — then set again.

And finally, things were ready. The train would leave at first light, which meant that it would be loaded overnight. Emma, Yevgeny, Tonya and Misha stood in the corner of the freight yard, watching the process.

A locomotive stood at the head of a long line of grain hoppers, moving the wagons forward in short eight-yard bursts, letting each one fill with grain from the loading chute. It was past midnight and the process was accompanied by flares of lamplight, whistles, and the occasional thundering curse. The short season of white nights had passed. The night was dark.

Misha's wagon was near the back of the line, but the line kept moving forwards. It was time.

"Well then," said Emma.

"You've got the blankets?"

"Yes. And the cushions are already inside."

"Good."

Emma had a basket in her hands: food and water enough for three days, plenty of soft wax for earplugs, a candle stub and matches, enough jewellery to bribe any number of border guards. The crucial bank documents, which represented the family's future worth in the new world, were sewn into the lining of Emma's travelling jacket. Yevgeny, absurdly dressed in a neat blue sailor suit, stood wide-eyed with tiredness, looking at each of the three adults in turn.

Up ahead the locomotive jolted forwards. Misha reached out instinctively to pull Yevgeny away from the moving train, then kept his arm around him as they walked the eight yards on to their wagon. The sound of the grain chute was louder now. The farewells could no longer be put off.

Misha climbed into the wagon first, hoisted Yevgeny after him, then watched Emma and Tonya climb in as well. Though from the outside the wagon looked the same as all the rest, and would do even in full daylight, the inside was different. Alone in the repairs yard, working mostly by night, Misha had welded a compartment that lay up against the sloping rear of the wagon. Access into the little space was via a sliding panel which would be completely concealed when the grain was loaded. At the top of the compartment Misha had fixed a grating to provide air, but a plate had been fixed so that nobody could look down through the grating to what lay beneath. The whole thing had been made to look like a permanent feature, inconspicuous. The compartment would be cramped, noisy, sweaty, dirty and uncomfortable. But it would be roomy enough for two people to get from Petrograd to Finland in safety.

Misha slid back the steel panel. It clanked loudly, but the night air was full of clanks and bangs. No one was around, either to notice or care. The compartment yawned darkly open in the lantern's light. The only minuscule concessions to comfort were two low metal benches, little more than sixteen inches wide, and a metal bucket with drainage holes drilled through to the bottom of the wagon. The bucket would be their toilet for the duration of the journey.

"Very well then," said Emma, rubbing her hands together as though needing to keep warm. "Right then."

To Misha's surprise, the prospect of escape had revitalised his mother's long dormant practical streak. It had been she who, without prompting, had opened the lining of her jacket to take the documents that Misha had given her. She had been surprisingly astute and accurate in understanding and assessing the value of the various bonds and stock certificates. She had been brisk and matter of fact about provisioning herself for the coming journey. She had even, to Misha's delight, allowed herself to acknowledge Tonya for what she was — her son's beloved — and had made her feel welcome in their apartment, with a kind of courtly, dilapidated grace.

Misha nodded. "Right then," he smiled.

He embraced his mother. He felt a surge of love for her. He felt himself, every inch, his mother's child. He bent his head down and let her cradle it against her shoulder as she had done years ago. Then they embraced again in the normal way. Her eyes and his were blurry with tears.

"Take care, Mother."

"I will."

"I know."

"Come with us, Misha. You still can."

Misha smiled and shook his head. "I'll be fine." Behind him he felt pressure from Tonya's hand on his back. "Go," she whispered. He could hardly hear her over the noise of the grain chute, closer now than ever. He didn't even bother to shake his head. Picking up Yevgeny, he hugged him once, then eased him through the open panel into the claustrophobic metal compartment.

"Farewell, little man."

The boy nodded, but was too overcome to say or do anything more.

"Mother."

Emma was about to make a movement, when the train jerked forward again, and they all steadied themselves until it stopped. Then Emma simply smiled and kissed Misha on the lips. "You are a good boy." She climbed into the compartment, her basket on her lap, and began to arrange their blankets and cushions for Yevgeny's comfort.

Tonya came close to Misha.

"Go," she said. "I'll follow when I can."

It wasn't a new suggestion. Since Rodyon's visit to her apartment, she'd felt more strongly with each passing day that Misha needed to leave. The country wasn't safe for Misha, and was getting less safe with every month. He ought to go. She felt it in her bones. But though she'd argued with him, pleaded with him, stormed at him, cajoled him, he'd been as stubborn as a rock. "Things'll get better," he said. "Look at the French Revolution. That was bad for a few years, then it blew itself out. It'll be the same here. It's only a question of waiting and being careful."

Tonya knew he was wrong. What did he know of such things? All his life, he'd been rich, privileged, cocooned, lucky. She hadn't. She knew about hardship. She had seen her mother die, and her brother Pavel almost die, from typhus. She knew things didn't always turn out for the best; that for the unlucky ones at the bottom of the pile, they hardly ever did.

"Go," she said again. "Please. I'll follow when I can. Babba won't be around for ever. Pavel is growing up. I can't leave them now, but . . ."

He shook his head. This was a dispute they'd had a dozen times over the last week. Their positions had become locked and irreconcilable. It was the closest they'd yet come to a proper argument. The two of them waited together in unhappy silence while his mother arranged herself in the little metal compartment. Then Emma smiled, took Yevgeny onto her lap, and signalled that she was ready.

"Good luck, Mother."

"Good luck yourself."

Misha reached in, clasped her hand, then stood back and slid the panel closed. The compartment already looked like nothing now: part of the wagon, nothing more. Tonya said something to Emma from outside, but no answer was audible.

The train moved forwards once more. It was about twenty-five or thirty wagons long, and the first dozen or so were already filled. The grain chute itself was lit up and there was a man in the wooden observation kiosk under the chute itself. Misha and Tonya kept back to avoid being seen, but waited long enough to see that their wagon was filled like all the rest. They saw the grain, grey and colourless in the poor light, flood the wagon, then stop. Nobody noticed anything. The train moved on.

Right or wrong, there was no going back.

6

For two days, nothing happened. No good news. No bad news.

Misha didn't dare to hope, didn't have cause to fear. He went to work as usual. He saw Tonya in the evenings as usual. Now, of course, they had a private apartment to themselves, a bed to make use of. Strangely, though, neither of them were able to think about making love while Emma and Yevgeny's fate was so uncertain. Not just that, but the idea of undressing completely and being wholly naked with the other seemed sudden and rather shocking — although they had made love frequently, it had always been outdoors and always at least half-clothed. So for those first two days and nights, they spent time together, cooked and ate together, then sat by the empty stove, holding hands and thinking about the rattle of train wheels in the dark. When they slept they kept their underclothes on, covered only by a thin sheet in the sweltering night.

Then, by the third day, things seemed brighter. The arrangement was that, if the escape was successful, Emma would contact a Helsinki lawyer named Dr Pakkinen, who in turn would write to a Petrograd lawyer named Kamenev, an old friend of the family. The code for "all went well" would be a request to pass on greetings to Misha. It might take weeks for the letter to get through. On the other hand, if the escape had been detected, then Misha's own arrest would follow with swift and bloody certainty. No news was good news of the best possible sort.

So Misha started to hope. But it was Tonya, as ever more careful than him, who urged him to proceed with care. They were upstairs in the apartment, sitting in front of the wide open windows, basking in the warm air and golden light.

"You have to make a declaration to someone," she said. "If you don't do it now, and they find out that you've said nothing, you'll be held responsible."

Misha frowned. "You're right, only not yet. I don't want to risk being too soon."

"And I don't want to risk you being too late," said Tonya, sharply. "It's not only you to think of now."

"No. Perhaps you're right. What do you think? Maybe the house committee?"

"Of course the house committee. I'm not saying you need to go to the Cheka." The Cheka were the new, much-feared, secret police.

They stood up. He was perhaps eight or nine inches taller than she was and the difference in that little room seemed suddenly huge. Tonya, as always, wore her hair tied and pinned at the back. He had never seen it otherwise. Putting his hands gently to the back of her head, he began pulling at the pins. She did nothing to help him except turn her head as he wanted, and she stood silently breathing, feeling the warmth of his hands on her neck. Then he was done. Her hair fell free in a dark curtain, framing her face and softening it. Misha ran his hands through her hair, then dropped them. The two of them stood in silence. It felt like the most intimate thing they'd ever done.

"Well?" said Tonya.

"Well?"

"What do you think?"

"I think you look beautiful."

"Really?"

Misha was about to answer light-heartedly, before seeing that Tonya had been genuinely anxious.

"Really. You should wear it like that all the time."

"I always wanted curly hair. I used to see all these pictures of the ladies at court —"

"I like your hair just as it is. Besides, most of those court ladies wore wigs."

"Really?"

"Most of them were bald underneath. Or hairy like a bear."

"Idiot!"

She pushed him and he pushed her back. But they both knew that they needed to go downstairs to see the old woman of the house committee before she retired for the night. Tonya was about to start putting her hair up again, when Misha stopped her.

"Don't do that. Go as you are."

"I can't go like this. I look like —"

She stopped and blushed. They fought for a moment, then compromised. Tonya tied her hair at the back, but only loosely, so it still fell like a soft halo around her face. They went downstairs and knocked on the basement door, where the comrade chairwoman of the house committee had her room. The old lady was ready for bed, dressed in some voluminous white nightgown which could have served for somebody five times larger. She cackled when she saw the two of them together and

Tonya felt sure that she was staring at her hair and drawing conclusions. Misha explained why they had come. He said that his mother and Yevgeny had gone out to visit friends the previous evening and not come back. He said he was very worried.

"Worried? You should be, comrade. In this city, disappearance is a bad thing. It's not the right thing from a political perspective. If a comrade worker vanished that would be one thing, but for a member of the propertied classes — well! That's a serious business."

The old woman seemed caught between two emotions. The first and strongest one was fear and anger that Misha had brought her this problem. But the other emotion was delight at the scope for gossip and interference. When her chatter turned to the latter subject, her voice became suddenly italicised, full of leering innuendo.

"Oh yes, and you will need to inform the Bureau of Labour. If the disappeared ones don't turn up soon, then you'd do well to send their papers along to the foodstuff distribution committee. You wouldn't want to be found profiting from excess distributions — not someone in your position. Not even if you can think of *other young people* who might enjoy the food. Oh yes, I'm sure you have ideas on *how to use the living space*. Perhaps you already have done. Eh? That would be something, wouldn't it, comrade? Your mother missing, maybe killed for all you know, and *only one thought on your mind.*"

They burst away from the old woman as soon as they could. Going upstairs, they hugged each other tightly. The future seemed suddenly very close, unknown and dangerous. Almost without speaking, by common assent, they stripped silently off and made love, naked and in bed together for the very first time.

7

The decrees were published. Internal exile for the "propertied classes", an old Tsarist tool turned to new uses by the Bolsheviks.

Misha was relocated, but not far. The Petrograd railway authorities didn't want to lose Misha's services, so he was shifted just a hundred miles to Petrozavodsk, on the line north towards Murmansk. Misha was employed as a railway engineer there as part of a small team of four, one of whom was also an ex-bourgeois like himself. The job was pleasant, his fellow workers positively cordial. Meantime, the old lawyer Kamenev had passed on greetings from Doctor Pakkinen in Helsinki.

Misha felt a fierce kind of joy at the news. His mother was safe. His brother was safe. He had done his duty to his father and his family.

Best of all, it wasn't hard for Tonya to come out to see him, often once a week. She'd come sometimes on her own, sometimes with Pavel, and the three of them would go out, looking for mushrooms in the woods, or swimming or boating on Lake Onezhskoye. They got on well. Misha took a liking to Pavel and taught the boy metalwork and how to bait a fishing line. Pavel still hero-worshipped Rodyon, but seemed to have a place in his affections for Misha too.

Then, one late November afternoon, Tonya was in the yard below her apartment. The family's fuel allocation had just arrived and she wanted to get the logs upstairs before they were stolen. She had just taken one load up and had her arms full with another, when she observed, in the growing gloom, somebody bending over the pile and helping themselves to as much as they could carry.

Tonya threw a log at the stooping figure.

"Hey! Get out of there!"

The figure straightened.

"Well, comrade, that's not very friendly."

It was Misha.

Tonya dropped her logs, and ran over to him, apologising and, in the same breath, telling him that he shouldn't have come here to Petrograd, it was too dangerous for him to break the terms of his exile.

"Lensky, Lensky!" he said, kissing her. "I'm here legally, or sort of. I'm here to pick up a new slide valve for one of our engines. The one they send us keeps getting stolen. I'm due back at midnight."

Tonya's emotions turned at once from worry to hospitality.

"Good! Then come up! I didn't know you were coming, or I'd have found some meat for you somehow. I've got a beef stock, though. I could make soup, and —"

Misha brushed away her words as if he were clearing snow from a woodpile.

"I can't stay. I told you. I've got to go and get this valve. But listen. There's a hospital at Petrozavodsk. It's small and not very good, but it needs staff. I've made friends with a doctor there — a real doctor, a proper old bourgeois like myself — and he can get you a position there as a nurse. Just three days a week, mind you. For the winter only. Pavel is old enough to take care of himself for that time."

"There's Babba, too. I couldn't . . ."

"So get Pavel to pull his weight. He's easily old enough and he only does so little because you let him. Or Rodyon. He's always offered to do more."

Other objections rose to Tonya's lips, but they got no further. Tonya knew that she was seeing problems only because she was scared, because she didn't believe in luck when it came, because she distrusted the world most of all when it seemed to promise something. But being with Misha changed things somewhat. His outlook was so different from her own, so boundlessly optimistic, that she couldn't help but doubt her own first instincts.

He saw the struggle in her face and held her gently to him.

"It'll be all right. Just say yes. I'll sort everything else out."

She looked up at him — his earnest face, long and pale in the twilight. She nodded dumbly.

"Yes? Is that a yes? Good for you, comrade Lensky. Good for you." He kissed her. "Listen. I mean it. I do need to go. The hospital will be in touch. It's a Dr Zurabov. He's nice."

And with that he was gone. The yard was empty again and only the pile of logs at Tonya's feet gave any sign that the conversation had happened. She picked up the fallen logs and began to carry them upstairs.

8

Just ten days passed, then Tonya was ordered in to see her hospital supervisor.

"Bad news for you, Antonina Kirylovna," he said, tossing a paper at her. "Some awful hospital out in the sticks needs a nurse. They've requested you. Don't know why. I'd say no if I could, but the request has come through Party channels. I can't say no. It's only three days a week, if that's any —"

Tonya didn't hear any more, but felt a surge of joy at the news. It was almost as though Misha's magic had somehow found a way to penetrate the remorselessly grinding machinery of the state. Tonya made her arrangements and two days later she was in Petrozavodsk. The snow had already come up there, and lay like a clean white mantle over town and countryside alike. When she finished work at the hospital that evening, Misha was there to meet her. But he didn't take her back to his room, a space so tiny there was barely enough space for one. Instead he took her out of town, three miles down a track to a little wooden hut on the edge of the forest.

"It's an old hunting lodge. Run down, but fine. No one uses it."

"Don't we need to . . .? Shouldn't we get authorisation?"

Misha stood up to his knees in the snow, bright-eyed and exultant. "Yes, comrade. You are right. You raise an important point." He opened his arms wide and said in a loud voice, "I claim this house on behalf of the ultra-bourgeois family Malevich." There was a low cliff not too far distant, and his voice bounced off the grey rocks in a series of echoes. He turned back to her with a widening grin. "To hell with comrade Lenin," he shouted. "To hell with the revolution. Long live the bourgeoisie!"

Tonya was shocked to begin with. Shocked, because she'd never heard anyone say anything so daring for months now — let alone shout it at the top of their voice. And shocked too, because she was torn. She knew that the revolution was riven with too many little men: driven by fear, anxiety, power, greed. But there were also the Rodyon Kornikovs: good, hard-working idealistic men, who had pledged their lives to the service of their fellow men. She wasn't as quick as Misha to condemn the changes.

"You say it," he said. "Down with Lenin."

She smiled and shook her head.

"Ah, pardon me, comrade worker, you should be saying 'Up with Lenin! Power to the people!' Go on. Say it."

She laughed, and again shook her head. But this time her denial went only skin-deep. It was a game.

"Comrade Lensky, the revolution will fail if you don't shout."

They looked at each other, grinning, then they both began to shout.

"Up with the revolution!"

"Down with the Bolsheviks!"

"Power to the people!"

"Bring back the Tsar!"

"Up with Lenin!"

"Down with Lenin!"

They shouted as loud as they were able, till the rocks boomed back with the sound of their voices: "Lenin . . . Lenin . . . Lenin . . ." Then, because Misha had the louder voice, Tonya jumped at him and pushed him backwards into the snow. He grabbed her leg and pulled her after him, and they rolled over and over together, as though the snow were the softest of white feather beds. They could hardly breathe for laughter.

They grew a little more serious. They stood up and brushed themselves down. The hunting lodge stood ready for them.

Misha bowed. "*Mademoiselle Lensky, je te presente le chateau Malevich.*"

Until he'd been seven, Misha, like many Russians of his class, had spoken French with his mother, and he spoke it now with a kind of careless elegance, which Tonya secretly found daunting. But she curtsied low and gave Misha her hand so that he could escort her, like a *grande dame*, across the heaped up snow to the lodge itself.

The interior was bleak, dark and cold. It had an intimidating, depressing feel and Tonya's heart sank. But there was a stove and the wooden walls were mostly draught-proof and there were no vermin of any kind. Misha dug a lamp out from somewhere, lit it and got to work straight away on lighting a fire. The red spit and crackle of the kindling immediately lifted Tonya's spirits again. She took the lamp and bustled around the hut, exploring her new domain. There was a bed with an old feather mattress, some store cupboards full of bits of old harness or hunting gear whose use she didn't know. There was a sackful of potatoes that Misha had brought out; also a stack of logs, oil for the lamp, some cooking pots, and, in one cupboard, a small store of tea and sugar which made Tonya gasp for joy. She came back to Misha, whose fire was now beginning to blaze.

"What do you think?" he asked.

"I love it."

Misha stood up, smiling. "Bugger Lenin. And bugger the whole blasted lot of them."

"Apart from Rodya."

"Yes, good old Rodyon, apart from him."

Tonya stepped into Misha's arms and by a shared understanding they began a slow dance around their new room; a waltz again, but not a fast one; slow and deliberately graceful. For almost the first time, Tonya didn't just dance the steps correctly, she gave herself to them and her upturned face seemed shot through with something grave, almost spiritual. Misha didn't try to break into her mood. He just danced in silence, making sure not to disturb her rhythm.

And then, after a while, she changed posture and grinned. Misha suddenly speeded up, and they shot around the room, whirling and stamping, until they spun apart laughing. That night, though they heard wolves howling outside, they slept in bed with each other, feeling absolutely safe, absolutely secure for the first time for years.

9

That winter, Tonya was able to spend half her time or more with Misha. When the weather was bad and the storms came in, they didn't even go to work, knowing that the power would be down and there would be nothing for them to do. Misha had borrowed a shotgun from somewhere, and shot and snared rabbits, pigeon, and other game. They ate well. In the long hours of darkness, they talked, or made love, or danced, or made plans. Misha began to teach Tonya French, then — deciding French was of no practical value — he switched and began teaching her German, which Tonya was quick to pick up. When it was cold, they loaded their stove with fuel until its sides glowed red. They talked about everything on earth, and sometimes just spent long hours in happy silence with each other.

It was, by far, the best period of their entire lives.

But as the thaw came, and snow began dripping and slopping from every roof, branch, rock and slope, their long winter idyll came to an end. Tonya was summoned back to her city hospital full time. Misha received instructions requiring him to relocate to a railway repair depot in Perm, six hundred miles and more east of Petrograd.

Tonya cried at the impeding separation, full of foreboding.

As ever, Misha saw only the positive side of things.

"Perm is ideal. Out there in the provinces, the revolution won't have changed anything too much. I'll be able to get on with things. As soon as you can, you can join me. In a few years' time, you'll see, everything will be different."

He was more right than he knew.

On the fifteenth of April, 1919, he left Petrozavodsk. His route took him first to Petrograd, then east to Perm. He sent a message to Tonya, asking her to meet him at Ladozhsky Station so they could say their goodbyes. There wasn't time for him to wait for a reply so he just went through the tedious business of getting his ticket sorted out, hoping against hope that she'd find a way to see him off. The line moved forward and Misha got to the ticket counter.

"Authorisation?" said the clerk. "Ah, yes, priority. All right for some, isn't it? And I suppose you've got a travel warrant too? Of course, you'll need to get that stamped. Unstamped means nothing at all. That queue over there, by the glass windows. No, they've abolished the special trains. Over there, that window."

The clerk shoved Misha's papers back at him. His wodge of documents had mounted up over the past eight months, until it was now a compact little brick of grey papers, soft and fibrous, like blotting paper. Misha moved over to the window that the clerk had indicated. A crowd of starlings had flown under the arched roof into the station and now couldn't find their way out.

He started again in another queue. The country was well into a civil war by now and there were soldiers everywhere. When he reached the head of the line, his papers were inspected again. There was a minor problem: one of Misha's papers had been stamped but not initialled. Regulations stated that it had to be initialled as well as stamped.

Misha took back the document, and tucked some paper money inside it — *kerenkas* — currency issued by the Provisional government in the months before the revolution. The money was mostly worthless, but not entirely. The clerk took it with a shrug and initialled the offending document himself. Another four minutes and the all-important travel warrant was stamped.

Misha's train had pulled in by now, and there was a surge of passengers towards it. Misha knew he ought to join them if he wanted any chance of a seat, but he still hoped to see Tonya. He went to the main entrance and waited there, hoping to catch sight of her. He saw two nurses, but both of them short and fat. He felt a jab of disappointment. A column of conscripts were being herded into the station at rifle-point. Inside the station, a whistle shrilled.

Misha could delay no longer. He turned back into the station, feeling suddenly lonely and afraid. He made his way towards the train, but his path was blocked by the column of conscripts. A man had just keeled over and there was a knot of other men around him shouting and arguing.

Misha began to negotiate his way through the mêlée, when there was a shout behind him. It was Tonya. She came bursting through the crowds, her face straining with the effort.

"Misha! Dearest!"

They kissed with passion.

"Take care."

"I will. I'll be fine. As soon as I've got myself sorted out, I'll let you know. The sooner you can come, the better. You and Pavel and Babba Varvara and Kiryl, of course."

"Yes, yes. Is that your train? You mustn't miss it. If you want a seat . . ."

"Oh, the seats are long gone. Don't worry. I don't mind standing."

They were interrupted by one of the soldiers who had been herding the conscripts.

"Hey! Comrade nurse, we have a man here who's just conked out. One minute standing, next minute, whack! Over he goes. Anything to get out of fighting, eh?"

Tonya took an impatient look at the fallen man. The man was obviously unfit to fight. He had the pale face and ravaged expression that often preceded typhus, and there was an ooze of blood from where his head had struck the station concourse.

"He can't go," she snapped. "Look at him. He needs to get to a hospital. Take him to the Third Reformed and ask for Dr Griese."

She stood up, seeking Misha's hand with hers. But they were prevented from moving. The officer in charge of the soldiers, an easterner with Khirgiz eyes and a reindeer skin cap instead of his regulation headgear, detained them with a sharp movement of his pistol.

"Well, comrade lovers, it seems you're right. This man isn't fit to serve. But the trouble for you is that we have a quota to deliver. We can't be short."

"That's your business," said Tonya, beginning to pull away.

"Your papers."

The officer ignored Tonya, but a ring of his men stopped Misha from going anywhere. Tonya, already half out of the circle, came back into it, scared and white. Misha handed over his documents, knowing they were in order. The officer began to flip through them, commenting on them in his thick Siberian accent.

"Travel authorisation — yes. Warrant — yes, stamped. Immunisation certificate — you have been thorough, comrade. Authorisation from local party commissariat — no, I don't seem to find that."

"Yes, I have that. Here."

Misha reached out, but the officer anticipated his movement. With a short, sharp jerk of his arm, he hurled the whole meticulously collected stack of documents high up into the station roof. The movement alarmed the starlings who were roosting there, and all of a sudden the air seemed to be alive: the tumbling grey papers and the swooping birds. The papers fell down into the crowd, only a few yards away, but as inaccessible as the coast of Japan.

The officer with the Khirgiz eyes smiled at his new recruit.

"Welcome to the war, comrade fighter."

The soldiers closed around Misha and began to sweep him away.

Tonya watched numbly, but with ever-rising shock. This, she realised was the moment she'd always dreaded. The moment in which the world proved itself to be as hostile as she had always believed it. She had been right to fear, right to be untrusting, right to have told Misha to leave when he could. These thoughts took shape in a sudden awful burst of realisation. For a second or two, she stood woodenly, seeing Misha's form dwindle as it passed down the platform in the knot of khaki-clad soldiers. Then, all of a sudden, she found herself running, sprinting, as fast as she could, her shoes clattering down the platform in a burst of noise that made even the soldiers stop and turn.

She caught up with them, but was prevented from getting close to Misha.

Over the arms and shoulders of the men who held her, she shouted: "Leave! When you can, leave. I'll join you. I'll find a way. Just get out. As soon as you can, get out."

Misha stared back at her. He too was in shock. At any rate, his face was void of all expression, all emotion. He said nothing, just nodded. Then the soldiers pushed him forwards, and Tonya away down the platform.

Tonya didn't know when or if she would ever see him again.

10

It was eight weeks later.

Tonya had heard nothing. She didn't know where Misha was, which unit he belonged to, or where he was fighting. She had received no letter or message of any sort. All the same, he was always on her mind. It was because of him that she had come here — to the Bureau of Housing in Petrograd.

The Bureau was located in one of the old palaces that used to line the banks of the Neva. The large old rooms had been crudely divided with rough block walls to make a row of offices that faced onto the courtyard. Tonya made her way along the corridors until she tracked down the room where Rodyon worked. The door was open and Tonya peeped through it before announcing her presence.

He sat at a desk with his back to the window. Three junior functionaries sat in front of him, taking notes, amending documents, presenting letters. Rodyon dealt with his business with a brisk but even rhythm, as though he were competing in some long-distance race of paperwork, where pace had to be balanced against the importance of conserving energy. Rodyon dealt with one functionary and dismissed him.

Tonya let the official go by, then sidled past him into the room. Rodyon had his head down and didn't look up.

It was summer now, mid June. The courtyard outside was lined with maple trees, their leaves dense, healthy and green. A few moments went by. Then Rodyon glanced up and saw Tonya.

"Ah. Antonina Kirylovna. How long have you been there?"

"The door was open."

Rodyon nodded. He dismissed the two remaining officials with a nod, and invited Tonya to sit with a wave of his hand. Or perhaps invited was the wrong word.

Authority was stamped in everything Rodyon did. It was half invitation, half command.

"You'll have tea."

"You don't need to be formal with me, Rodya."

"No, no . . . but still, tea would be good. I usually have some around this time." He stuck his head around the open door and called down the corridor for refreshments. "The greatest empires have always been tea-drinking. The Chinese. The Mughals. The British, of course. Now it's our turn. The rise of the Russian tea-drinking empire."

Tonya knew that Rodyon's flippancy was carefully managed. It was very unrevolutionary to speak of the Russian empire. A good Bolshevik knew that the revolution in Russia was only a prelude to revolution elsewhere. The only empire that counted was the workers of the world acting in unity. Rodyon spoke as he did to take the ideological sting out of his position of power. He did it as an act of delicacy towards Tonya. She smiled her appreciation.

"You've heard nothing, I suppose?" he said.

"No. I don't suppose I will."

"Well, there's always a chance. Let's hope we hear something soon." In the weeks since Misha had been taken away, Rodyon had done all he could to find out his whereabouts. He had made full use of his official position, bending the rules as far as he was able. He hadn't once mentioned the offer he'd made in her apartment that hot July evening last summer. He had been tactful and generous.

100

The tea was brought in. It came in an ornate samovar with a polished ebony base and an elaborate silver-bound handle. Warming on the top of the samovar was a small teapot containing *zavarka*, strong black tea, to be diluted with hot water from the samovar. A saucer of lingonberry jam, something Tonya hadn't seen for years, came with the tea.

"The reddest of teas in the whitest of pots," commented Rodyon.

"Thank you."

They drank, holding a spoonful of jam in their mouths before swallowing it with the tea. Tonya still hadn't mentioned the reason why she'd come.

"You didn't come here to drink tea with me, Tonya."

"No."

"Well then?"

"Last summer, that day you came to my apartment, you raised a subject . . . you asked a question."

"Yes, I seem to remember it."

"I was wondering . . . I wouldn't blame you if you didn't . . . but if you still wanted to, I'd be able to give a different answer."

She had been sitting with her hands over her stomach. Now she moved them. A gentle swelling was already evident.

Something changed in Rodyon's face as he watched her. Or rather, not a muscle seemed to move. His intense dark eyes, his strong mouth, his focused bent-nosed handsomeness all stayed exactly as they were. But there was some change in his energy. Some quality of attentiveness, even softness came into him.

"You still love Malevich, of course."

"I do like you, Rodya. I wouldn't be here if I didn't."

"No and you wouldn't be here either unless . . . when is it due?"

"I don't know exactly. Maybe five months."

"And even in these revolutionary times, babies need fathers. Ones who are fighting somewhere in the wastes of Siberia hardly count for much, do they?"

"No. I want his baby . . ."

". . . to be protected. Quite right."

Tonya looked down at her hands. They were folded primly on her lap. She felt herself looking like an efficient secretary or a schoolgirl eager for praise. And Tonya was neither. She tried to make herself relax.

"Tonya, you asked if my offer still stands. It does."

"Ah!"

"I know your feelings for Malevich. I think I understand your feelings for me."

"Yes."

"But you do understand that any marriage of ours would be a real marriage? We would share an apartment and a bed."

"Of course."

"If Malevich returns . . . I shan't seek to prevent him. If he comes and you choose him, I shan't stand in your way. The revolution must be total. The heart and the state."

"You are a good man, Rodya."

Rodyon stood up. Tonya did the same.

"Well then," he said.

Tonya swallowed. She knew that a kiss was now expected. Rodyon's physical proximity now seemed sudden and almost overwhelming. She could smell him as though noticing his scent for the first time: a mixture of linen and ice water, ink and tobacco smoke, pierced through with something athletic, the light sweat of exercise.

"Well."

She nodded, and held her arms slightly out as a signal for him to step forwards. Her movements were jerky and abrupt, like a mechanical toy that hadn't been oiled. Rodyon stepped lightly forwards and kissed her gently on the lips before moving back. His touch had been definite, but light; more than familial, less than possessive.

"Thank you," she said stupidly. "Thank you."

She tried to summon up a picture of Misha in her head, but all she could bring up was the soldiers surrounding him on the station platform, his white face looking around at her in shock, the fist in his back pushing him forward, and the train that would take him east to Siberia, out of her life, perhaps for ever.

It was the eleventh of June, 1919 and the future suddenly felt very empty indeed.

GERMANY, 1945

CHAPTER
FOUR

It was the second of May, 1945.

The day was rainy and cold. Dull grey clouds pressed low over the city. Everywhere over the shattered city, smoke continued to rise in dense black pillars, but the flames themselves were already dying back. There was shooting here and there — at the Zoo flak tower, at some U-Bahn stations, in isolated buildings and cellars — but mostly the impression was of silence.

Silence and desolation.

In Prenzlauerberg that evening, a group of Red Army soldiers tumbled out of a ransacked brewery. The soldiers were so drunk, they were barely able to walk. One of the men went to relieve himself in a doorway, then heard shouts from downstairs, where there were men locked in a cellar. The man was too drunk to care much, but as he lurched back out onto the street, still fiddling with his flies, he happened across a SMERSH officer. The man told the officer about the cries, then staggered off. The SMERSH man investigated.

Inside the cellar there were eight men, hungry, their faces black with grime and stubble. The SMERSH man was briefly interested. The Russians were on the lookout for scientists and technicians who would be of value to Soviet weapons programmes. But the prisoners were of no consequence. There were a couple of pastors, some old Social Democrats, a couple of common criminals. The SMERSH officer lost interest. He was only human, after all. This night was the first night of victory, and he too wanted to get drunk.

And that was lucky. Because if the officer had been a bit more inquisitive, he might have noticed that one of the prisoners — a tall, fair-haired man in his mid-forties — looked more Russian than German. For all that his German was fluent, it was almost a little too perfect, as though it had been picked up in the schoolroom not the cradle.

But the officer went on his way without investigating further and the prisoners spilled out onto the smoking street. There was rubble everywhere, rubble and smashed steelwork. The air was harsh and gritty with soot from the fires that still dotted the city.

It was like a scene from the end of the world.

In another area, in Spandau on Berlin's north-eastern corner, a group of Soviet soldiers looked across at the ruins of the city they had fought so long to capture. The soldiers were numb with tiredness. Long exposure to the weather and the filth and smoke of war had given them an almost Asiatic colouring. They sat beside their packs, staring out at the flat, grey landscape beyond them. A few of them smoked. No one spoke.

One of the soldiers was a female driver, somewhere in her forties. She wore the uniform that marked her out as a member of a *shtraf* battalion, a punishment unit linked to the regular Red Army. The *shtraf* battalions had been given the worst jobs in a war full of horrors. The woman had been lucky to survive.

For a while, the woman sat and stared at the demolished city, doing nothing, not moving. Then she stood and climbed up onto the carcass of a burned-out truck. From her vantage point she could see more of the city: the dense black columns of smoke, the jagged edge of the ruins, the smell of scorching. She hung onto the truck and drank the sight in. Her face was too tired to express much emotion, but if there was anything at all in her eyes, it certainly wasn't victory or elation; more a kind of wistfulness, even longing. She had brown hair and greenish eyes, with a slightly eastern slant to her eyelids. She looked like a woman who had seen a lot, suffered a lot. On her right hand, two fingertips were missing, little stumps of dark pink that ended just where the final joint was meant to be.

She got down off the truck, lay down on the chilly road, and fell asleep.

CHAPTER
FIVE

1

Something great had been accomplished.

The war in Europe was won. The Führer's last *Wunderwaffen*, his long-promised "miracle weapons", had turned out to be not miraculous, just laughable: kids on pushbikes, holding anti-tank weapons they weren't trained to use. And as for the other desperate predictions, talk of the *Werwolfs* who would wage ferocious underground war against the invaders, those too had turned out absolutely hollow. The war had been emphatically won. The plague which had ravaged Europe was ended.

But that just raised a whole further set of questions. What now? What next? For Germany, for Europe and the world?

Nobody knew. The Allies, in the urgency of their efforts to beat Hitler, had made almost no provision for what was to follow. About some of the big points, of course, there was agreement. Germany would not be dismembered. There would be one country, Germany, and there would be one capital city: Berlin. The nation would be divided into four zones, each to be administered by one of the four victorious powers, Russia, America, Britain and France. Berlin, too, would be divided and run the same way. But the administrative zones were simply that: lines of bureaucratic convenience. There would be only supreme occupation authority, the Allied Control Council, to be made up of the Military Governors of each zone.

And that was it. All the crucial details had been left undecided. Would political parties be allowed to form in Germany again? Would there be free speech? Democracy? Would Germany's industry be permitted to revive? Or would the country be turned into an agricultural economy, a pastoral nation of no threat to its neighbours? What would the defeated nation use by way of currency? And what would happen to the occupying troops? Would the Americans be home within two years, as President Roosevelt had promised Stalin? And even before the war, Germany had never been able to feed herself. What would happen now? Would Germany be given food, or would she have to buy it? And if she were to buy it, then what would she buy it with, bankrupt and ruined as she was?

To all these questions, there were no answers. Or not too few, but too many. The point was that nobody knew. Everyone simply hoped that the broad framework of what had been agreed would be enough to cope.

One country: Germany.

One capital: Berlin.

One government formed by the four wartime Allies, united.

That, at any rate, was the plan. It was now the eighteenth of July, 1945. Though the war had been over

111

for two and a half months, the Russians had only just permitted the Western Allies into Berlin. The Russians had muttered about the need to restore order and to clear mines, as though the Western Allies weren't more than capable of doing both things themselves, but Western protests were so muted, they were barely audible.

But at least the time of waiting was over. The Americans, British and French had arrived in Berlin. Perhaps now, the old wartime cooperation could begin again. Perhaps relations between the partners would improve.

Perhaps.

2

The major stood at the window and stared out.

The building was one of the few to have remained more or less intact through the battle for Berlin, though there was no glass left in the windows, of course. The sweltering heat bore down hard on the city, lighting the nearby streets with a burning intensity and leaving the rest to waver in the petrol-blue haze.

"The damned thing is," he began, then glanced over his shoulder at a young captain. The captain, blond-haired and untidy, more like a ploughboy than a military officer, was leaning over his desk, correcting a typescript. "You're not listening."

"The damned thing is that I'm not listening?" said the captain, without looking up. "Why should I, if that's all you have to say?" He finished with his typescript, then hurled it into a wire out-tray. "Done. Lucky old Berliners. Everything they ever wanted to know about application procedures for displaced persons interzonal movement orders."

"What? Oh, never mind. The damned thing is that we've been put in charge here with no bloody strategy. Civilian Communications, that's our business. Good idea. Top notch. Medal to the chap who thought it up. But what the bloody hell are we meant to communicate? All we do is transmit these communiqués from MilGov. They don't make much sense to us. They make even less sense to the poor buggers out there. No wonder they've no idea what's going on."

"Don't they?"

"What? Don't they what? Christ, it's hot."

"I think they know exactly what's going on."

"Wish they'd bloody tell us, then." The major picked up a cricket bat that lay beside the window, and began to take dummy swipes at non-existent balls. Block, block, drive. Block, block, sweeping left-angled hook to the boundary.

"The point is," persisted the captain, "the Russians knew exactly what they were doing. They had a system of ration books for the entire city sorted out in less than two weeks. A daily paper in the same time. The Red Army may have behaved like a horde of savages when they arrived, but it's the Russians, not us, who are getting water sorted out. Power, mail, rubble-clearance, the U–Bahn, hospitals — you name it. That's why they have things to communicate, and all we have to talk about is our damned interzonal movement orders. And

113

the Berliners know it. They're scared of the Russians. They hate the Russians. But they know damn well that Comrade Stalin is very, very interested in this city and the country it's supposed to govern."

"Yes, well, I don't suppose there's a lot we can do about it. Friend Ivan has been here two months longer than we have. In any case, what does it matter? Oof!" The exclamation came as the dummy-bowler dropped a wicked ball short at the major's feet, forcing a piece of brilliant defensive bat- and foot-work. "Ivan's only got one voice out of four on the Allied Control Council. That's three against one — at least, it is if you count the French as being on our side."

"Yes, and of course Ivan is a well-known democratic sort, who wouldn't dream of using underhand means to install his loathsome system right here in the heart of Europe."

"God, Hollinger, you are a gloomy sort. That's what too much time in Intelligence does to a chap."

"Yes."

The major practised another couple of strokes and was about to put the bat away, when the captain took a brown roll out of his desk drawer and tossed it in the air, interrogatively.

"Go on then," said the major.

The major moved to a spot on the wall where the outline of a wicket had been drawn in chalk. A line of insulating tape marked the crease. The captain stood at the far end of the room, rolling his shoulders, with a dreamy look in his blue eyes. There was a moment's inaction, when it seemed as though the strongly-built

114

captain had forgotten where he was. Then, rolling into a single-step run-up, he whirled his right arm in a perfect bowling action and released the bread roll.

The roll shot through the air. The major swung at it. The bat nicked the edge of the roll, but couldn't deflect it. The roll broke full-toss against the leg stump, shattering into a thousand glossy crumbs.

"Damn you, Hollinger," said the major placidly, as he bent down to sweep up.

The captain didn't move to help. Instead he stood, still swinging his arm in a scything bowling movement, launching ball after ball at the chalk-drawn stumps.

"You know," he said, "we really ought to do something about it."

"About what?" said the major, knowing better than to expect a reply.

But he was wrong, because Hollinger did reply, albeit crookedly. "D'you know, I think I was wrong to give up my post in Intelligence," he commented. "I thought I'd be more use here."

"You are of use here. Don't go getting it into your head that I'll support you if —"

"You'll support my move back again?" said Hollinger, deliberately mishearing. "Good on you, old chap."

3

Misha picked his way down the street.

The old Berlin quarter of Charlottenberg had changed its name. The sardonic Berliner humour had

115

renamed it "Klammotenberg", heap of rubbish. Similarly, Lichterfelde was now "Trichterfelde", field of craters. Steglitz was now "*steht nichts*", nothing left standing. And that was Berlin now. A heap of rubbish. A field of craters. Nothing left standing.

It was a hot day, the fifth in a row.

Misha had with him a loaf of bread and a thick pat of butter. He wore a cotton shirt and a torn black flannel jacket, items which he'd purchased with the gift of cigarettes given him by an American army unit he'd worked for briefly as an interpreter. And the Americans had been generous. Misha still had six packs of cigarettes left, which made him a rich man in these broken times. Misha opened one pack and began to smoke. The summer sun felt good.

Once upon a time, he thought he'd successfully rebuilt his life. He had spent two years fighting with the Bolshevik partisans in the civil war that had followed the revolution. Every day for those two years he had looked for a chance to escape, but weather, remoteness, famine and the partisan guards themselves had made it impossible. Then, one day in 1921, Misha found an opportunity to slip away from his unit. He'd walked a thousand miles south to Persia, then travelled by sea and train to the coast of Italy, then up to Switzerland. He'd had no money, and had had to work his passage any way he could. It had taken him almost a year to do it, finally rejoining his family in the spring of 1922. For years, he had hoped that Tonya would find a way to follow him there, but it never happened. He wanted to write, but didn't know her address and knew that any letter from him could only get her into trouble. They were separated by a thousand miles and the iron walls of the world's most complete dictatorship. She might as well have been living on the moon.

In 1925 he had moved to Berlin, where he used his share of the family's money to start an engineering business, a pump manufacturer, in partnership with Otto Goldhagen, a Jew. Years went by. Misha had given up hope of ever seeing Tonya again. Goldhagen had a pretty daughter, Lillie, with whom Misha had always got on very well. In time, friendship had turned into something deeper. He and Lillie had married. They'd not been able to have children, but the marriage had been a full and happy one all the same.

At the next street intersection, Misha paused.

Once he had known this district very well indeed. But the devastation was simply extraordinary. What had once been fine rows of grandly built apartment blocks lay smashed to pieces across the cratered roads. Tanks and trucks lay burned-out like the extinct corpses of another age. The places that Misha still recognised no longer seemed to fit together with the rest. The city was like his life. Both Otto and Lillie had been killed in extermination camps. Misha himself, a long-standing Social Democrat, had been arrested and imprisoned both because of his politics and his choice of partners in business and marriage. In Nazi camps for seven years, Misha had survived only because his technical knowledge had been too

117

valuable to waste. He still mourned every day for Lillie, his laughing, dark-haired, olive-skinned wife.

Unable to orientate himself, Misha approached a group of *Trümmerfrauen*, "rubble women". Dressed in skirts, summer blouses and headscarves, the women were systematically clearing the rubble. He asked for directions. One of the women put down her wooden bucket and looked at him strangely.

"You want the old Berlin Pompentechnik? It's there, of course, there."

She pointed. She pointed not to a building, but to a hole, a gap in the skyline, a void.

Misha felt strange, as though big weights were shifting inside him. The tangled geography around him fell into place. Of course he had been disorientated. The place he had been searching for was no longer there. There was hardly even a "there" left.

"*Danke.*"

"*Bitte.*"

Misha offered the woman a cigarette. She took two, but lit neither, just tucked them away in her blouse.

Misha walked towards the void.

Towards and into it.

The place had obviously been bombed out long before the Red Army had arrived. The old factory hall — *his* factory hall, the place which had produced the best marine pumps in Germany — was now a whistling desert. Once, there must have been a tangle of steelwork, but the steel had long been taken away and reused. The old factory walls, once thirty feet high, were nowhere higher than ten feet. In most places the walls no longer existed at all, they were just lines of rubble. Buddleias had colonised the ruins, and their purple flowers released a heavy scent. A few butterflies fluttered yellow and white against the grey stone. The old factory floor caught the heat, and the air hung like a furnace. Except for the butterflies, nothing moved.

Misha stood in the middle of the old factory. He had been prepared to find little enough, but nothing at all? He could feel the burning concrete through the worn-out soles of his shoes. It was the only feeling that made sense to him. The rest of it felt like a dream.

And then he spotted something. A heap of ruins in the corner concealed an opening. One of the offices hadn't been utterly destroyed. Something white hung down over the opening, a sheet or strip of cloth. Misha moved towards it.

And just then, the cloth was torn aside. A figure stepped out, dressed in a Red Army greatcoat worn over shorts and a cotton undershirt. The figure was barefoot. He had a few days' growth of beard on a chin that was only just old enough to need a razor at all. The youth spread his arms wide open, like some dream image of a crazy Jesus.

"*Wilkommen*," he shouted. "*Wilkommen an der Nichtsfabrik-Berlin*." His voice ricocheted off the remaining walls and shot around the empty space in a spreading series of echoes.

"Welcome," he said. "Welcome to the Nothing Factory, Berlin."

4

Tonya stepped out into the glare.

There was something strangely bright about Berlin this summer. For one thing, there were few buildings now high enough to block out the light. On top of that, old stonework had been shattered by explosions, the edges lay sharp and white, glittering with mica, throwing back the sunlight from a million tiny mirrors.

She stood on the steps and waited for her eyes to adjust. She retied her headscarf. There was still so much dust in the air, her hair filled with grit almost instantly unless she wore a scarf. The thought made her think of Misha; of his hands on her hair, that time he'd first unpinned it high up in the old servants' attic in Kuletsky Prospekt. The moment felt like only yesterday. In Russia before the war, Misha had become little more than a memory to her. A much beloved one, of course, but a memory all the same. Here in Berlin, that all changed. It was Misha who seemed real, Rodyon who had become the memory. Had Misha ever succeeded in escaping Russia? Had he made it to Europe? To Germany? Had he married? Did he have children? Had he survived the war? Tonya had no way of knowing the answer to any of her questions, but they drummed insistently in her head all the same.

Her renewed preoccupation with Misha made her feel guilty. Rodyon had only ever been good to her. They'd spent two happy years in Petrograd, but the period was ended by a ferocious and hungry winter which had brought about the deaths, in quick succession, of Babba Varvara, her father Kiryl, and — most poignantly of all — the little baby boy, Vassily, Misha's son.

Tonya had been so overcome with grief that Rodyon, sensitive to her feelings as ever, had sought a new position in Moscow, in one of the economics ministries. Tonya had worked as an administrative assistant in an import-export house. Then, when her talent for languages came to light, she was given further training in German, and appointed translator. Rodyon hoped that the new city and new occupations would help her come to terms with her losses. For a while things had gone all right. They'd had children, two girls, Yuliya and Yana. They'd been happy, or something like it. Tonya loved her daughters with all her heart. Rodyon she liked and respected with such unwavering strength that her feelings there too could easily have been mistaken for true love. But, following Lenin's death, the political climate had continued to change, continued to worsen. Rodyon didn't like the new politics. He had his principles, and refused to let them slip with the times.

And now, almost certainly, he was dead. During the time of the Stalinist terror, he had been arrested twice for "terrorism against the state". The first time, he had been punished by beatings and a year in jail. The second time, he was given fifteen years in the Gulag — a death sentence, almost for sure. Tonya herself had survived his second denunciation by just two years. In 1936, she too had been arrested, charged under Article 58 of the Criminal Code, the most serious article, and had been sentenced to ten years in the Gulag. When, in

1943, she'd been given the chance to fight in a *shtraf* battalion and wash away her "guilt" in blood, she'd jumped at the chance. And despite everything, she'd survived. She hadn't always been sure that she'd wanted to, but she had. Somewhere, perhaps, her two daughters had survived the famines and the purges, the Gulags and the war-making, but Tonya knew that the country was full of *bezprizornaya*, waifs and orphans of the times. She knew she was unlikely ever to meet up with them again. What was even worse, Tonya knew that it was her duty not to seek them out. The children of politically suspect parents were politically suspect themselves. Poor Yuliya and Yana would be better off if they never saw or heard from their mother again. Tonya thought of them all the time — more often even than she thought of Misha — and when she saw girls of about their age in the street, she would often just stop and stare, tears filling her eyes.

With the end of the war, she'd expected to be returned to Russia. But she wasn't. The Soviet occupiers were short of translators and Tonya had become a very good one during her years in Moscow. So she'd been ordered to stay, here in the heart of Berlin. She was delighted. She had nothing to go back for. This Berlin summer felt like a golden interlude separate from ordinary time. She intended to enjoy the warm weather, enjoy her work, avoid trouble, avoid attention.

Smiling to herself, a lunch bundle under her arm, she headed off for the Tiergarten, the park at Berlin's ruined heart.

5

Misha went closer.

"No," he said. "Not welcome to *the* Nothing Factory. Welcome to *my* Nothing Factory."

"Yours?"

Close to, Misha could see how young the kid was, a teenager, nothing more. Young and hungry of course, not that there was anyone with enough food these days.

"Well, it used to be anyway. We didn't always use it to make nothing."

"*Na, ja,*" said the boy, with the true raw Berliner accent, "you missed out then."

"Missed out? How?"

"Look. Look around. The factory's doing a roaring trade these days. Nothing everywhere you look."

Misha held up his loaf of bread and melting paper packet of butter.

"Do you want to eat?"

The mismatched pair headed for the opening from which Willi had appeared. Inside there were two habitable rooms left intact. There was an old bedstead salvaged from somewhere and a pile of bedding. There was no water or lighting, a scatter of unwashed dishes. But it wasn't the primitive living conditions which caught the eye, so much as the décor. There were big poster-sized pen-and-ink drawings of the major world leaders: Hitler, Stalin, Churchill, Roosevelt, Mussolini, Goebbels, Himmler. The drawings were caricatures: savagely accurate and bitingly funny. Mussolini was drawn as a ventriloquist's dummy manipulated by a giant Germany. Churchill's face was attached to the body of a union-flag-wearing bulldog, whose hindquarters were defecating on a map of Africa. Roosevelt was a crippled puppet, dangling from the long strings held by cigar-chomping industrialists. Most shocking of all, there was a drawing of Hitler and Stalin depicted as two middle-aged spinsters in bed with each other, sharing wine from a skull-shaped bottle. There were spare parts of old pumping equipment which had been linked together in a kind of frieze around the room, and a giant communist red flag, with the stars-and-stripes inked over it in black pen.

Misha drew his breath in shock. Willi's caricatures would have drawn certain retribution from any Russian troops or surviving Hitler loyalists. Nor were the British or American forces immune from dishing out a good thumping to anyone whose attitudes they disliked.

"Quite a gallery, Willi."

Willi shrugged. His skinny right arm shot up in front of his portrait of Hitler. "*Heil . . . Ach*, what-was-his-name?" He dropped his arm. "Food?"

Misha got out his treasures. He himself was hungry enough, but the boy was famished. The boy ate like a wolf, tearing huge chunks of the bread and stuffing them into his mouth, with both hands busy. In between mouthfuls, or rather during them, but in between the times when his mouth was too full to do anything but chew, he answered Misha's questions.

His name was Willi Spranger, but these days he called himself Willi Nichts. His father had been killed in France early on in the war. His mother had been killed in an Allied bombing raid just a few months back. In theory, children like Willi had all been called up to save the Reich at its final, most desperate hour. Willi had chosen otherwise. He'd hidden away all through that final battle, and then for the last couple of months had continued sleeping rough and scavenging for food. He finished his story, then said "And you?"

Misha told his story in condensed, almost staccato form. Willi only asked one question, which was, "You said you hid for the last two months. You only came out when the Americans arrived. Why?"

"Because if the Russians had found me and discovered who I was, they'd probably have had me shot. As a deserter, as a political fugitive, as a bourgeois. I didn't fancy finding out."

"No." Willi stopped tearing into his half of the loaf and sat staring at Misha with unblinking eyes. After long contemplation, the boy said, "So, we're related then."

"Related? How is that?"

"I'm Willi Nichts, because I've lost my mother, father and home. You, you're the same. You've lost your father, your family home in Russia —"

"— *Homes*, plural, we were rich then."

"— Your homes —"

"— My wife."

"— Your home here, your business."

"— My business partner and my closest friend."

"— Your money."

"— I lost Tonya, the first girl I ever loved. I lost my country. Imagine that, losing a whole country!"

125

"No, no. Not one, two. You're German now, aren't you? And Germany doesn't belong to we Germans any more. You've lost two whole countries, big ones. That's bad. Careless."

The two of them, man and boy, stared at each other. Misha didn't know whether to laugh or cry. The boy was the same. His mouth flickered with mockery. When he'd told Misha off for being careless, he'd adopted the exact tone of a German schoolmaster issuing a reprimand. But his eyes were different. They were too large for his hungry face. They were full of loss.

Misha put his hand to the boy's back and rubbed him between the shoulder blades. The kid leaned into the movement and was silent. When Misha withdrew his hand again, neither of them spoke and they finished their bread in silence.

Berliners spoke of this time as *die Stunde null*, zero hour. Now for the first time, Misha knew exactly what the phrase meant, exactly what it referred to. This, this moment now, was his zero hour. He'd lived in the world for more than four decades, and now here he was sitting in the very rubble of his life, in the ruins of a city, in the heart of a ruined country. He owned nothing, had no one, was nobody.

It felt like the end of everything.

6

Tonya walked on towards the Tiergarten. Her way took her out of the Soviet zone into the British one. But that didn't matter. The zones weren't meant to be important. There was only one country, after all, and one capital city. Movement in and out of the zones was commonplace, an ordinary thing.

The Tiergarten was a blessed relief. The linden trees cast a welcome shade. The war seemed infinitely distant. Even the bomb craters and shell holes that still pockmarked the park were covered over in green. Song birds sang.

Tonya's path took her around to the lake on the west of the garden. There was an Englishman there feeding the ducks. He was straw-haired and burly, looking more like a ploughboy than an army officer. He had an enormous loaf of stale bread and was breaking chunks off it, as though he were expecting to feed turkeys not ducks. Tonya, wishing she had bread to throw, stood and watched. There were crowds of mallards, tufted ducks, and comical white-fronted Canada geese waddling amongst them all.

The Englishman saw her watching and winked at her. She was about to look away, when he put his huge hands to the loaf and ripped it in two. He dropped one entire half, but, just as she thought it was about to hit the ground and roll away into the pond, he swung his foot and booted it. The half-loaf rose high into the air, then dropped down towards her. The kick was so perfectly judged that Tonya merely had to put out her hands to catch the loaf.

"Well held," said the man in English, before adding in German, "*Für Sie*. One man can't have all the fun, eh?"

"*Danke.*"

127

"*Bitte.*"

Tonya accepted the man's bread, but didn't want to talk to him. The NKVD were everywhere in Berlin, and Tonya didn't want to compromise herself by being caught talking to English army officers — capitalists and imperialists to a man, in NKVD eyes at least. Besides, there was something unusual about the man. He seemed to be staring hard at her right hand, at the darkened stumps of her missing finger joints. As she tucked her hand away out of sight, his gaze travelled up, met her eyes, stuck there for a moment, before being washed away in an affable and foolish grin.

She smiled briefly, then looked away, fed the ducks, and walked quickly back to work, feeling disconcerted by the encounter. She decided she wouldn't go back to the Tiergarten again.

7

Misha found the address he'd been given: a former schoolhouse with American army jeeps drawn up behind. The street was one of the few in the city that had emerged from the fighting mostly unscathed, and the buildings looked tidy and clean.

But the schoolhouse was a school no longer. A sign announced the building's new function: "Interzonal Movement Orders Authorisation Office". Further placards set out complex regulations in English and German for the benefit of applicants.

Misha had come early and was the first to present himself. He was told the office would be open in another fifty minutes. Outside in the sunshine, a little girl, perhaps seven years old, sat on a wooden bench in the sun, eating a plum. She had dark blond hair with golden highlights in two plaits.

"May I?" asked Misha pointing to the place beside her.

"Yes."

"That looks like a nice plum."

"Yes." She nodded. Her eyes were hazel-coloured and grave. "Are you waiting, then?" she asked after a while.

"Yes."

"Me too. What are *you* waiting for?"

"I'm waiting for the office to open. I want a piece of paper that will let me travel to a country called Canada."

"Yes, I know Canada," said the girl, with as much dignity as if she were the daughter of an Inuit and a Mountie. "It's snowy and there are bears."

"Well, I'm Russian — or I was — so I don't mind snow. Or bears."

The girl nodded as though she had been looking for an interesting fact to add to her stock, and she continued to sit, kicking her feet and eating her plum.

Misha had been forced to acknowledge the obvious. There was nothing left for him in Germany now. He had no assets, no income, no wife, no family, just one big Nothing Factory, in whose ruins he now lived with Willi Nichts. Misha had just two realistic options. One was to join his sister Raisa and her husband, Markus, in Switzerland. The other was to leave Europe altogether and head for Canada, where his mother, brother and second sister had emigrated long before the start of the war. He had resisted taking either track, knowing that to do so would mean admitting that everything he'd spent his life on so far had been a failure. But then again, as Willi had so candidly pointed out, everything he'd invested in so far *had* failed. Going to Canada would only mean that he was finally obliged to admit the truth.

He sighed. The girl finished eating.

"Yum!" she said.

Misha gave her an answering smile.

"What are *you* waiting for, then? You didn't say."

"No."

"Well?"

"I'm waiting for . . . something different."

"I see. Have you been waiting long?"

"Oh yes."

"And will you have to wait much longer?"

The girl shrugged. She shrugged by lifting her shoulders so high that they touched her ears. She was famished, of course, you could hardly find any Berliner who wasn't, and her bony shoulders made her look like an elf from a German fairy story.

Misha laughed. "Same here. Always waiting, eh?"

"No, not always. I didn't say always." The girl corrected him, then pulled off her shoe. "It's broken. Can you mend it, please?"

The shoe wasn't in bad condition, but the buckle was broken. Misha went around to the back of the schoolroom, where there were some GIs brewing coffee. Misha borrowed some tools, and a length of wire and repaired the buckle. The girl was a war-orphan, her father killed in Italy, her mother killed just three months back in an Allied air attack. She was theoretically in the care of an UNRRA orphanage, but she didn't seem very concerned about playing truant. Misha finished mending the buckle, then noticed that the shoes were too big, so he padded out the toes with newspaper until they fitted.

"There!"

"Thank you."

"You haven't told me your name."

"You haven't told me yours."

"I'm Misha," he said, wondering at himself. It was years since he'd given his name in the Russian way, let alone the informal nickname that had only ever been used by his nearest friends and family — plus, of course, by Tonya. "Misha Malevich."

"Misha," said the girl, considering it. "Good. That's a good name. I'm Rosa."

"That's a good name too."

"Because I'm like a rose."

"Because you are."

By this time, a queue had begun to form behind Misha and the door of the schoolhouse was abruptly thrown open by a fat-necked Yankee major, smelling of chewing gum and tobacco.

"OK, buddies," he said in English, before adding in German, "let's get moving this morning, one at a time, who's first?"

Misha was. He was shown into an interview room, a former classroom. The fat-necked major sat on the teacher's dais, with a young lieutenant beside him to take notes. Misha had to sit on a narrow wooden chair in the middle of the bare floor.

Things didn't go well. The problems started because Misha didn't have a rations book.

"How come?" said the major. He had learned German at school and spoke it with a solidly American accent, as though it were his patriotic duty to break the spirit of every foreign word that came his way. "The Russkies had got rations books sorted within two weeks."

"I didn't want to collect one from the Russians."

"Why? You say you're a German citizen, but you just gave your name here as Malevich. You a Hiwi?"

A Hiwi, short for *Hilfsfreiwillige* or volunteer helpers, was the name given to Soviet citizens who had volunteered for the German *Wehrmacht* and fought against their countrymen. Most Hiwis had already either fled to the west or killed themselves, but some still lingered. It was certain death for any Hiwi to be returned to the Red Army, but some Allied officers did so anyway.

"No. No, I'm not. As I say, I'm a German citizen. I have been for almost two decades."

"Then you should have got your rations book from Ivan, shouldn't you? If you're not a Hiwi, that is."

"I left Russia twenty-four years ago. Escaped, really. I was the wrong class. It was dangerous for me there."

"Still, if you're a German citizen, why wouldn't you want to collect rations? It don't look as though you've been eating too well to me. Address?"

"Nowhere you could quite call an address, really. I live in the business I used to own; what's left of it, that is."

"What type of business?"

"We manufactured marine pumping equipment."

"Civil or military?"

Misha shrugged. "Either. Both. The pumps were the same."

"Right, sure. That's part of the armaments industry all right. You done a *Fragebogen*?"

"I'm sorry?"

"A *Fragebogen*, questionnaire. Part of the denazification process."

"Denazification? I had a Jewish wife, a Jewish business partner. I spent the war in concentration camps."

The major looked disgusted and muttered something in English to the lieutenant. Misha spoke almost no English and couldn't follow it.

"Why do you want to move interzonally, anyhow? If you're a German citizen, then you have a duty to work as directed by the occupation authorities. It's not just a question of going wherever the hell you feel like."

Misha tried to explain. He had relatives in Canada. The Canadian consulate here in Berlin had been of the view that an emigration application might be favourably received, but he'd have to present himself in person to the appropriate bureau down in Munich. Hence the

133

need for an interzonal movement pass, authorised by the American Military Government.

"Jeez," said the major, looking at the letter from the Canadian consul. "You know, this don't mean a lot to us. If you're a German citizen, then you really belong here. If you're a Russian, then you ought to sort out your problems with your own folk. Still . . . Canada . . . Jeez . . . Listen, we need you to fill out a full *Fragebogen*. Then submit that to the denazification people. Then they'll check it out. If that's all OK, come back to us for a movement pass. Oh yes, and get yourself a rations book. What the hell do you think Ivan's going to do? Eat you?"

That was the interview over.

Misha collected the papers he'd brought with him, and went away with more forms to be filled out, more addresses to traipse to, more bureaucrats to deal with. But it had been neither better nor worse than he'd expected. He walked outside into the sunshine and found the little girl from earlier, still on her wooden bench.

"Still waiting, Rosa?" he said to the girl.

"Um . . . I'm not sure."

"You aren't sure? You still haven't told me what you're waiting for."

"No."

She stared at him with great concentration as though there were some matter it was vital to establish accurately.

"Well? If you tell me, I might be able to help."

"Yes, maybe . . . Can you cook?"

Misha laughed. "Only when I have food, little *Roseknospe*," he said, using the word for rosebud.

"Can you sew?"

"Not very well. Why? What are you waiting for?"

She frowned as though the answer should be obvious. "I'm waiting for my new mummy and daddy, of course."

Misha heard her words and became suddenly grave himself. For the first time in their conversation, he gave her his full attention, kneeling down so his face was on a level with hers.

"Before I went into that office, you said you were waiting. When I came out, you said you weren't sure if you were waiting any more."

"I thought my new mummy and daddy would come both at the same time. But it doesn't have to be like that, does it?"

"No, little *Knospe*."

"Well then."

"Well then, what?"

"Well then, that means I'm not waiting any more."

"Does it now?" said Misha softly.

He stood up and took her tiny hand in his big one. He could stay in Berlin and accept the responsibility that Rosa seemed keen to thrust on him. Or he could emigrate to join his family in Canada. There was no way he could do both. His heart told him to stay. He had no particular desire to go to Canada, it was only that there was nothing left for him in Europe. But his heart hadn't done him much good in his life so far. It

135

was time for his head to rule. He knew what he had to do, and he fully intended to do it.

"I'm sorry, little one, but I'm afraid I can't help."

8

Meanwhile, as Misha and Rosa were talking in the sunlight, inside the building the major and the lieutenant were arguing.

"The guy's Russian," complained the major, shoving another stick of gum into his mouth as he spoke. "He looks Russian. He's got a Russian name. He admits he was raised there. So he's Russian. Why the hell should we be bothering with him? Ivan's guy, Ivan's problem."

The lieutenant protested. "If his story's true, it might be dangerous for him."

"Dangerous? Why the hell would it be dangerous? The guy left twenty-five years back. And if he's a Hiwi . . ."

"The regulations say —"

"The hell with the regulations. How would you feel if you found an American fighting for the Krauts? You'd pretty much want to beat the heck out of him too."

"I guess . . ."

"Yah! His story don't add up. Either he's a German, in which case there's no reason for him not to have a rations book. Or he's a Hiwi, in which case he belongs to the Russkies."

"Yes, sir, only —"

"Only nothing. I bet we never see him again. Did you see his face when I told him we'd need him to disclose

136

all his past Nazi affiliations? I bet he's a Nazi like all the rest of them. Jewish wife, my ass! Send his details around to Ivan. Name, address. Known facts. That sort of thing. Then Ivan can figure out what to do."

"You want me to disclose his identity to the Soviets?" The lieutenant's tone was downright incredulous; insubordinate. The major glared at him and the youngster coloured. "Yes, sir, sure thing. I guess they're part of the team now. Sure."

The lieutenant went to sort things out, while the major went to the window and stared gloomily out.

The queue had lengthened: a collection of raggedy scarecrows with famished faces. "Jeez," commented the major, which was his way of reflecting on the astonishing fact that this same collection of human beings had come so close to defeating the greatest military powers in the world. Then his gaze traversed sideways and he saw something else: the Russian was still there, talking to a little blond girl in plaits. The major rolled his gum into a ball and stuck it in the pouch made by his lower lip against his gum.

"Goddamn Nazis," he muttered.

9

A golden evening was decaying into night. Here in ruined Berlin, darkness always seemed to leak upwards from the burned-out buildings, spreading first to the streets, then upwards to the sky. It was the most dangerous time of day, when the city turned itself over to its darker elements: the black-marketeers and the prostitutes, drunken Red Army men and the speeding cars of the NKVD.

Tonya made her way across town, up the Prenzlauer Allee, walking carefully in the thickening dark. A car passed, too close, with a blare of headlamps and engine roar. Tonya was forced to jump aside and managed to graze herself on a heap of rubble. She thought she heard men laughing as the car screamed away, but she couldn't be sure.

Then she heard something else.

Down a side street, a woman was crying and, in between sobs, calling for help. Tonya hesitated. Of her fellow translators, almost all were either Party members themselves or married to a Party member. Those who, like Tonya, had served time in the Gulag, were rare and the scent of suspicion never quite left them. Few of the other translators would even speak to her socially. Though Tonya didn't mind the isolation, she lived in fear that she would somehow betray herself or be denounced. Anything might trigger it. She knew perfectly well that there didn't have to be any basis in truth for the accusation. So she was careful not to offend, to follow the Party line, to stay inconspicuous. And helping a German woman was not quite inconspicuous.

Then the cry for help came again. It was a young voice, almost girlish. Tonya wanted to walk on, but then the thought of her own two daughters came irresistibly into her head. The oldest of the pair would be just nineteen now. Before Tonya could think further, she found herself running and stumbling over the rubble heaps towards the darkness of the little alley.

The woman heard her coming and stopped crying.

"Thank God. Who are you? I can't walk."

Tonya peered forwards, saw a patch of something gleaming white in the surrounding gloom, and made her way towards it. The patch resolved itself into a young woman, lying propped up against a ruined wall.

"The bastards hurt my ankle," she said.

Tonya looked, but didn't enquire. Almost certainly, the woman had been raped. Almost certainly, she had been raped by a Russian — the Americans and British were generally rich enough in cigarettes or chocolate to get what they wanted without force.

"Let me help you home," said Tonya.

"Thank you."

The woman struggled to her feet and put one arm around Tonya.

"Where to?"

"Just up there. I only came out to get water."

They went a little way, the woman hopping with her good leg, Tonya supporting her other side.

"You're Russian," said the woman, not quite as an accusation, but almost.

Tonya was about to do the sensible thing, to mutter what platitude the Party would want her to say, something about German bandits dressed in Red Army uniforms, but she couldn't bring herself to.

"I'm sorry," she said, "it was bad with us too."

They walked on in silence. The injured woman wasn't as young as Tonya had first thought. She was in

139

her thirties anyway. The building where she lived had had most of its front blown away, but there were some rooms at the back that had been made habitable. They went up some stairs and down a corridor towards the rear of the building. The woman threw open a door and led the way into her flat. There was a large green sofa, some shelving in dark wood, and an elaborate birdcage with no bird. An old Bluthner upright piano gleamed against the wall. Beyond the main room, there was a tiny kitchen, with an oil lamp hanging from the doorway.

And that wasn't all. There was a large leather armchair, made to look small by the big-built figure who sat in it. The figure had straw-coloured hair and an easy smile. He was wearing civilian clothes, but that wasn't how Tonya had first seen him.

"Comrade Duck-feeder," he said. "Thank you for coming."

Tonya reeled back in shock. She might even have gone running from the building, except that the German woman, whose ankle had suddenly recovered, stood behind her and closed the door. Tonya felt trapped and frightened.

"I'm sorry to scare you like this," said the Englishman. "My name's Mark Thompson. I'm a captain in the British Army. And all I want is to talk to you for a few minutes. I'm not here to injure you in any way." Then, speaking to the German woman, he added, "Marta, I think we would all like some tea." The German woman, Marta, nodded silently and disappeared off into the kitchen.

140

Tonya still stood with her back to the door, saying nothing.

"Just so you know," continued the Englishman, "the door to the apartment is not locked. If you go out of it, I won't stop you, nor will anybody else. On the other hand, if you choose to stay, I will make absolutely sure that nobody ever needs to know that you saw me."

"I shouldn't be here."

"No, you shouldn't. But you came because you heard cries for help. You helped Marta into her house. She offered you tea and you accepted. That's all true. That's all you ever need to say to anyone if they ask. Which they won't. I'm fairly sure that no one was watching you on Prenzlauer Allee just now."

"That was you in the car?"

"And some colleagues. Yes."

"You're a spy."

"Yes. Not a word we like very much, actually. *Smert shpionam*, death to spies, as your comrades so pithily put it . . . But yes, call a spade a spade, I'm a spy."

"And your name? Mark . . .?"

"Thompson. No. You've hit the nail on the head, old girl. That's not my real name. But it's safer for everyone that way, you included."

The Englishman, "Thompson", spoke excellent German, but he had the habit of taking phrases straight from English and translating them directly. Sometimes that worked, "*Sie haben den Nagel auf den Kopf getroffen*". More often than not, it didn't — *nenn' ein Spaten einen Spaten* — and the linguistic strangeness

141

made Tonya feel as though she'd stepped into a dream world.

She still stood with her back to the door. Electricity had been restored in most parts of Berlin, and the smoky yellow oil lamp was disconcertingly dim. Everything in Tonya screamed at her to leave, but somehow her legs felt rooted to the spot. She was vaguely aware that somehow she connected this unwelcome Englishman with Misha. They were physically quite unlike, of course. Where the English-man looked like a ploughboy, Misha had looked more like a concert pianist. All the same, they had something in common, their ludicrously unwarranted confidence for a start. And Tonya didn't leave. In fact, she stepped forwards and took a seat, but still dreamily, as though there were a second Tonya in the room standing and watching as the first one sat down.

"What do you want?"

"What do *I* want?" he said. "Easy. Peace in our time. England to win the Ashes. Uncle Joe Stalin to have a nasty accident. Throw in some decent marmalade and I'd be in heaven. But that's irrelevant. It's what you want that matters."

Tonya said nothing. There was a window open at the back of the kitchen, and the oil lamp swung a little in the draught. Light and shadow swam dizzily in the room.

"I don't want anything."

"Really? Nothing?"

Tonya shook her head.

"I'm sorry, but I can't believe you. Listen, do you know that at the Yalta conference, your comrade Stalin promised to create a 'free, mighty and independent Poland'? Perhaps the Poles believed him. Anyhow, they were brave enough and foolish enough to rise up against the Germans in Warsaw, just as the Red Army was on the outskirts of the city. And the Red Army did nothing. Nothing at all. They just waited on the banks of the Vistula and let the *Wehrmacht* troops massacre the Poles. Right now there are, we think, a dozen NKVD regiments throughout the country. A dozen regiments of secret policemen to make sure that Poland is just as free, mighty and independent as Uncle Joe Stalin wishes."

Tonya shook her head. There was a buzzing in her ears, something she knew from the war, a noise that lasted for a few days after any particularly intense battle.

"I'm only an interpreter," she said. "I'm not interested in politics. I don't —"

"No." The Englishman was gentle but persistent. "That's all right to say if you're an English housewife or an American businessman. Politics doesn't have to matter. But for us, for anyone who lives in Germany or anywhere to the east, then politics matters. It has to."

"What do you want?" said Tonya again.

From the kitchen, there was the hissing sound of a boiling kettle, and the sound of Marta making tea.

"I want to save the world."

"*Entschuldigen?* Pardon?"

"Well, you did ask. The point is, I think that your Joe Stalin wants Germany to be every bit as free, mighty and independent as Poland. We think he's working very carefully to make sure of it. And as you know, conditions in Germany are fairly desperate. There's no food. Winter will be abominable. Industry is at a standstill. The countryside has no fertiliser. The harvest will be poor and in any case no one has any money. Meantime, what with anti-fraternisation rules and the black market and prostitution and anti-Nazi witch-hunts, I don't know that our Military Government is winning many friends. In short, if Mr Stalin wants a Communist Germany, then who's to say he won't get it? And if Germany falls, then Italy will follow. And Austria. And would the French hold out? I don't know. But I do know that I'd be jolly upset to have fought this entire war simply in order to pass Europe from Hitler to Stalin."

The buzzing in Tonya's head had become so loud, she could hear no more. She sat forward in her seat, with her hands clamped over her ears. She rocked herself, as she had seen soldiers do in cases of severe combat-trauma. Her eyes were closed against the swaying lamp. Then she found herself not rocking, but being rocked. The big Englishman was holding her head against his chest and soothing her. It felt like being petted by a bear. She pulled free. Marta had reappeared with tea, hot and very sweet. The Englishman was still standing and his big, ramshackle presence made the room appear smaller. He looked upset.

"I'm so sorry. Mostly my work brings me into contact with such worms — not you of course, Marta, you're a brick — that I get clumsy when I meet real people."

"Why me? Why of all the people, why —?"

"Because of your work. Because of the documents that you see."

"How do you . . .? What documents?"

"You work in the *Hauptübersetzungsbüro* of the *Sowjetische Militäradministration in Deutschland* in their Mühlendamm office. I know because I had you followed."

The *Hauptübersetzungsbüro* was the Central Translation Office. The *Sowjetische Militäradministration in Deutschland*, usually called the SMAD for short, was the Soviet Military Administration in Germany.

"You had me followed. Why me?"

The Englishman took her hand and held it up. Her right hand, the one missing the tips of two fingers.

"Because of this."

"My hand?"

"It was frostbite, I suppose?"

Tonya nodded and heard the Englishman's next words as though through fog.

"We guessed that perhaps you suffered your frostbite in the Gulag. We guessed that perhaps you weren't a great admirer of your comrade Stalin. It wasn't hard to guess that you held some administrative post inside the SMAD. Some of those administrative posts give access to important information. It was because of that hope that I had you followed. When I found out that you

145

worked for the translation office on Mühlendamm, I had to find a way to talk to you. That office has access to some of the most important documents anywhere inside the entire Soviet administration. I'm sorry to drop this all on you like this. I'm sorry to remind you of the Gulag and all that you suffered there. If you tell me to go to hell I would quite understand."

But Tonya was a long way from telling him to go to hell.

She felt split between two selves again. The first one was nodding now and crying, copiously weeping. The second Tonya, still standing over by the door, was rocking back on her heels and watching the first one — this crying one — with pursed lips. It was the first time Tonya had cried for more than twenty years. It was the first time she had ever let herself cry about the day when she'd lost her fingertips.

"I was sentenced to ten years," she said, speaking slowly. "Ten years, for nothing. I've no idea who denounced me or why. In those days, no one knew. We were put on a train, me and hundreds of others. We were taken to Siberia. It was spring, but the snows hadn't yet melted. They led us to a snowfield, huge and totally empty. The only thing there was a sign that said 'GULAG 92 Y.N. 90'. We were made to kneel in the snow, in long lines facing outwards. For hour after hour, a roll-call took place. Detachments of prisoners were led off. I stayed. So did others. Then the roll-call finished. The remaining prisoners, some hundred and fifty of us, were allowed to stand. That snowfield was our camp. Everything that was ever built there was built by us. We began right there on that first day, breaking saplings with our bare hands to build a shelter for the night. I only lost my fingertips. I was one of the lucky ones."

The Englishman was moved, but his posture contained as much anger as sympathy.

"And that's why I want to keep Germany free. That's why I contacted you. But if you choose, you can leave now. I promise you we will never bother you again."

Tonya nodded. She still hadn't touched her tea, but drank it now, gulp after gulp, like an upset child. The Englishman watched her in silence.

"I'll go now," she said.

"You do that. Remember. You helped Marta. You drank tea. You can point out this apartment to anyone who asks. I won't try to contact you again, and you won't see me feeding the Tiergarten ducks either. But if you do change your mind, or if you ever want to contact me for any reason, then go to the Tiergarten at midday. Throw bread for the ducks. We will find a way for you to talk to us safely, not then and there, but very soon. Is that clear?"

Tonya nodded. She stood up. She hadn't quite finished her tea and now knocked the little table, upsetting the cup and breaking it.

"Sorry, sorry." The two Tonyas joined up again into one person: a woman clumsily dabbing at the little wreckage of porcelain.

"Don't be sorry," said the Englishman from a huge distance. "It's all quite all right."

Tonya found the door and went running down the hall.

10

Major Grigory Makarevsky of the Soviet 58th Guards Rifle Division yawned. After four years of fighting, in which he'd started out as a humble *frontovik* and risen all the way to his present rank, paper-pushing didn't seem like a proper occupation for a man. But he was a soldier, and choice was a luxury not given to soldiers.

He reached for the next folder in the stack. The folder was thin, containing a couple of dozen typewritten chits sent over by the Americans. Makarevsky looked at the information: a list of "Persons Not in Possession of a Rations Book". Makarevsky looked down the list, not even bothering to stifle the yawn that rose inside him.

Then one of the names caught his eye. His yawn died.

One of the names on the list was a Russian one, "Malevich, Michael Ivanovich — German citizen (?)". There *were* Germans with Russian names, of course. There were those who had left Russia in Tsarist times, whose names now meant nothing at all about their real nationality. But not many of them. Not many, compared with the millions of men who had been swept up by the war and rushed here and there across Europe, across borders, across ideologies. And Makarevsky, like most of his fellows, was a patriot. He

148

loathed the idea of a Russian betraying his country as intensely as anyone could.

He pulled a blank sheet of paper towards him and began to write.

"To Lieutenant-Colonel Klochkov, NKVD administration, Karlshorst . . ."

Makarevsky was a better fighter than he was a bureaucrat. He didn't like the secret policemen of the NKVD. He found words more recalcitrant than the German troops he'd fought for so long. His lips moved as he wrote. His black fountain pen sat in his hand like a gun.

11

The bar was in a cellar, with a low vaulted ceiling and dim lighting. Tables were jammed up close and tobacco smoke hung like river-mist. The Andrews Sisters were on the gramophone singing "Rum and Coca Cola"; not once but again and again. About three-quarters of those in the bar were men. The rest were prostitutes, many of them teenagers. There were American GIs, British squaddies, and a handful of Germans — black-market barons to a man. The sharp eyes and flashiness of the black-market men reminded Misha of that first wave of Russian communists — the swaggering young men in their leather coats, their air of ownership.

Misha stood at the door of the bar, feeling out of place.

He didn't have the money for a place like this. No ordinary German did. But he'd been lucky. He was a member of a work party run by a bunch of British squaddies. The work was menial and stupid, but not unpleasant. Determined to get to Canada as soon as possible, he had taken Rosa firmly back to her orphanage, and set in train everything that was required for his emigration application to proceed. Part of that was learning English, and he had asked his supervisors to help him. Since he was already fluent in German, Russian, and French, the new language came easily to him. The British Tommies were impressed, and started to teach him not just English, but cockney English: *Gor blimey guv; wipe yer dial; would you adam and eve it.* They'd had fun, got on well. That afternoon, the corporal in charge of the work detail had invited Misha to the bar, offering to stand him supper.

Misha located the soldiers and pushed through the crowds towards them. The corporal turned to Misha, his eyes already shining with drink. A few seconds passed, in which the corporal failed to recognise Misha. For an instant Misha felt a surge of anger that he should have been asked to come here and then forgotten about; that he should have to perform tricks for food, like a trained spaniel. But then the corporal remembered, and his expression changed.

"Blimey, it's Mr M, the Russian cockney! Here, mate, have a drink . . ."

A seat was found. A glass of beer was shoved in front of Misha. Words shouted across the cellar in English produced a giant plate of fried potatoes and some thin strips of fat-streaked bacon. Misha began to eat the way he'd eaten that first post-revolutionary winter in

150

Petrograd: slow but fast, fast but slow. Although Misha was careful to chew every morsel, especially the meat, knowing that his stomach would complain angrily if he didn't, his mouth was never empty, his fork never stopped moving. Within a few minutes he had cleared his plate.

"Good on yer, chum."

"Proper chow," said Misha. "I didn't 'alf bleedin' need that."

There was applause, shouts, more beer.

"'Ave a frigging fag, mate," he said. "Oi, come 'ere an' say that. Shove it up yer arse, sergeant-major."

More applause, more food.

Misha drank more than he should, ate until he knew that he'd be awake all night with stomach cramps. His mood changed. He was disgusted with himself for being here. Something in his attitude must have rubbed off on his hosts, because the conversation turned away from him, excluding him.

The gramophone had finally ditched the Andrews Sisters, and was now onto the "GI Jive" by Louis Jordan, and "On the Atchison, Topeka and the Santa Fe" by Johnny Mercer. The prostitutes who had formed a group on their own before had now melted into the crowd. One girl lay across the laps of four GIs, eating chocolate. In the tiny space by the gramophone a huge black NCO was dancing with a German girl who must have been less than half his weight. The NCO's eyes were closed in reverie. The girl's eyes were sharp and alert. Her feet moved nimbly, not dancing so much as dodging her partner's boots.

151

"I'd better bloomin' scarper," said Misha, then, feeling deepening disgust, said the same thing in formal English, then German, Russian, French, and Evenki, a Siberian language he'd picked up during his time fighting for the Bolshevik partisans. He enunciated slowly and clearly, purposely insulting his hosts by displaying his mastery and their ignorance.

He climbed the stairs up from the cellar with a savage intensity. And why shouldn't he feel humiliated, he asked himself. He was German now, wasn't he? In which case, he belonged to a defeated nation, a beaten people. If this was the worst that could be expected from the occupation, what right did he have to complain?

He came out onto the street into a flamingo-pink sunset and the first dim violet of evening. The beer that had seemed so innocent downstairs found its edge outside, and Misha felt drunk and unsteady. The thought of returning home to the Nothing Factory, to Willi's bitter, hungry humour, felt temporarily repulsive. A sudden self-destructive instinct directed Misha's steps west down Alt-Moabit towards the old Reichstag building and the solemn arch of the Brandenburg Gate. Occupation troops stood around at the zone boundaries, not stopping traffic, but not off-duty either. Relations between the western troops and the Russians weren't exactly tense, but they'd become touched by something prickly, a static charge that crackled in the air.

Misha strode on into the Soviet zone. Everything was the same here — the same ruins, the same military vehicles, the same hungry German faces — but it was the same and different too. The Red Army still engendered more fear amongst Berliners than the troops of any other army. The heavy iron heel of occupation was more iron, more heavy when attached to a Russian boot.

Somewhere in between Alt-Moabit and here in the dark destroyed blocks beyond Grellstrasse, the beer had worn off. Turning a corner, Misha almost walked into a group of three NKVD men smoking in an alley. He came close enough to see their blue enamel cap badges, the royal blue piping down the seams of their Khaki breeches. The officer's head jerked up in angry surprise. "Sorry, sorry," said Misha in German, scuttling away to the far side of the street.

He was no longer drunk, just scared. The NKVD had no interest in zonal boundaries. They had no interest in passports or diplomatic niceties. If Misha were picked up here, with his dangerous name splashed all over his identity papers, he'd most likely find himself on a direct train to Novaya Zemlya in the Soviet far north, and the murderous embrace of a labour battalion. There were worse things in life than being patronised by a group of Tommies, after all.

Guarded now, frightened and very sober, Misha began to walk home. He walked at a measured pace, and checked every corner before proceeding on into the street. Crossing back a little south of the Brandenburg Gate, he felt relief break over him in a huge, cool wave. Only now did he realise that the palms of his hands had been sweating, the top of his spine between his

153

shoulder blades was crunched and painful with the tension.

It would be good to get home, good to see Willi.

He reached Charlottenberg, and his old, precious Nothing Factory. The place was torn apart, wrecked, smashed to pieces. Willi lay with his head cracked open, his face blackened and smeared in a drench of his own blood.

12

"It is of extreme importance," wrote Tonya, "that the appearance of domination by the Communist Party be avoided. Efforts must be made to include all classes in the political process. The 'small Nazi' must be also welcomed . . ."

She stopped typing. The typewriter was an old machine from the twenties and each key had to be struck with alarming force in order to penetrate through all three sheets of typing paper, interspersed with some over-used carbons. The missing fingertips on her right hand prevented her from touch typing, but even so the blackened flesh on the ends of her fingers tended to ache after a long day's work.

She looked back at the Russian text: "Social Democrats or members of other authorised anti-fascist parties should be given prominent posts such as that of mayor. But in all cases the chief of the education department should be a reliable Communist, also the chief of police, also the director of communications,

154

also the senior deputy mayor in charge of personnel . . ."

Tonya felt a sudden wave of breathlessness.
Somehow, that first day in the Gulag came back again.
Since meeting the Englishman, she was thinking about
it all the time, dreaming about it at night. And the
Englishman was right. The SMAD was single-mindedly
devoted to the capture of Germany. The whole thing
needed to look democratic — and be anything but. The
Communists planned to infiltrate the country, then
swallow it. Not just their zone, but all of it.

Tonya hated that. But what the Englishman was
asking her to do was inconceivable. She had been
punished once for conspiracy against the Soviet state,
when she had been guilty of no such thing. How much
more violent would her punishment be if she were
genuinely guilty of espionage?

But she needed to breathe.

She jumped up from her desk, thinking that fresh air
would clear her head. She hurried downstairs, past the
bored reception clerk and the NKVD men who
sprawled, smoking, in the lobby. Outside on the street,
nothing quite seemed real. Tiny blue clouds decorated
a hot summer sky. A girl cruised past on a bicycle,
wearing a red-and-white dress, striped like an American
peppermint. Tonya began half-walking, half-running
down Mühlendamm, then kept up the same pace down
Leipzigerstrasse.

She saw the cyclist again. A chain of American
lorries. A Russian jeep. Tonya felt disconnected from
the real world. She came into the Tiergarten and

stopped hurrying. She didn't look at her watch. She didn't know what time it was, didn't want to know. But the sun was high overhead and Tonya's running shadow was puddled down by her feet. She had a bread roll in her pocket that day: rye bread, made in the Russian way, unleavened, dark and heavy.

She reached the lake.

She wanted to run, but the words she had been translating earlier still beat in her head. "*The chief of the education department should be a reliable Communist, also the chief of police, also . . . , also, . . . also . . .*". Her missing fingertips throbbed in pain.

With tears streaming down her face, she stood by the water breaking her roll into pieces and hurling it at the guzzling birds, piece after piece after piece.

13

Misha jumped to check Willi's pulse.

For a second his fingertips could find nothing — not even a ghost of movement. Then he shifted his fingers and closed on the right vein. The blood flow kicked strong and healthy. Misha was almost literally dizzy with relief.

Most of the blood on the floor came from a long gash on the side of Willi's head, and Misha bathed it and dressed it with care. The boy no longer bled. As Misha rolled the lad over to get the bandage in place, Willi came to, blinking but unfocused.

"Christ, Willi, what's happened here?"

"Oh, you know, visitors, the normal thing." The boy's lip was so badly swollen, his words came out soft and misshapen, like spoonfuls of mashed potato.

"Visitors? Who?"

"Friends of yours. Russians. Nice men with khaki uniforms and big boots. I think they wanted to invite you around to their place. We exchanged the normal courtesies. They admired my picture gallery."

Willi attempted a gesture around the room, which was now smashed to pieces. Willi's drawings had been ripped from the wall, torn up, then pissed on. Every item of furniture in the room had been broken — some of it, no doubt, over Willi's body. But the boy didn't manage to complete his gesture. His right arm was certainly broken. Misha guessed that he had one or more cracked ribs as well.

"NKVD?" he asked.

Willi nodded. "Ideological instruction. Most informative."

"And they knew my name? They were looking for me?"

"Mikhail Ivanovich Malevich. That is you I believe."

The kid's voice wasn't nearly as strong or brave as his words. Misha was tempted to comfort him the way a father would comfort a child, then realised that Willi's carefully assumed identity as self-sufficient boy-man was vital to him, more vital than mere comfort. So Misha changed tack.

"Schnapps," he said. "Always vital after ideological instruction. First schnapps, then hospital."

Misha managed to find an unbroken bottle of schnapps in the debris. They'd only ever had one glass between the two of them and that one was now smashed, so they drank from the bottle. The boy sipped a tiny amount, but his cut lip hurt too much to take more.

"They didn't say how they'd got this address?"

"No."

Misha remembered the gum-chewing American major and guessed that he had played a part in this visit. Remarkably though, he had been away and Willi had escaped with nothing more than a bad beating. All the same, Misha felt his anger rise and tighten inside him. It lodged inside him like a black stone, very hard and very dense.

"If they come back . . . ?"

"I don't know, Willi. Not yet."

"When you get to Canada, then —"

"If. If I go there. It's not certain."

Willi stared at him. The boy's eyes were huge, too big for his face. "You're not going, are you?"

Misha looked inside himself and felt only his anger. He traced its outline with his mind, feeling the hard black smoothness, round like a slingshot. He knew that there was nothing for him in Canada. Canada was escape. It was an easy life. But it was also an abandonment, a withdrawal. He'd already been an exile once. He'd been persecuted by regimes of the far right and the far left. He'd been stripped of family, of possessions, of loved ones. And he was sick of it. He'd run no more. Not another inch. He would occupy his own space and damn the consequences.

"No, no, I'm going nowhere at all."

14

Tonya climbed the stairs to the first floor. The corridor that led away from her had a huge gash in the ceiling and front wall, as though some giant bear had slashed at the building leaving ripped stone and torn plaster. Dim blue twilight filtered in through the gash.

Tonya walked down the corridor to the door at the end. She hesitated before knocking, then, feeling somehow more afraid of the emptiness behind her, knocked anyway.

"*Komm!*"

The woman's voice was brusque, Germanic. Tonya hesitated again, then pushed at the door. It was the same room as before: the oil lamp, the big green sofa, the dark wood furniture, the birdcage, the piano. And the German woman, Marta — if that was her name, of course — stepping briskly forwards, her long hair tied behind in a bun, dressed in a long dark skirt and cream blouse. Standing on the seat of the sofa, was an open violin-case, with a violin inside, gleaming in the lamplight.

"Come in, good evening, you may put your scarf down there."

"Here? Thank you."

"*Bitte*. Now your hands, please."

Tonya held her hands out. Marta inspected them, especially the damaged right hand, with little clucks of disapproval and disappointment. She said things like, "Really . . . no . . . it is hardly going to be correct."

Then she asked Tonya to stand. Tonya was in fact already standing, but she tried to stand straighter.

"No, no," Marta said. "Not stiff like a poker."

Tonya relaxed.

"No! Not flopping like a fish!"

Marta pushed and prodded Tonya's body into the right position, then nodded when Tonya had the posture right, or at least not horribly wrong.

"Now relax."

Tonya relaxed.

"Now stand."

Tonya tried to recapture the pose, but somehow got it wrong again and had to be prodded back into shape.

"Now relax . . . now stand . . . *ja*, better."

The next item on the agenda was how to hold the violin and the bow. Not the real violin or the real bow — Marta obviously thought Tonya was a long way from being ready for that — but a pretend-instrument and a pretend-bow. Marta didn't seem to be very pleased with Tonya's undamaged left hand, the one that would actually hold the neck of the violin, but she was especially displeased with Tonya's right hand, which would hold the bow. Tonya meekly did whatever she was told.

It all felt so strange.

With the door closed and the bombed-out, ruined city shut away, this little apartment felt like a glimpse of the old, domestic Germany: quietly, solidly content. For all the ruin outside, for all Tonya's knowledge that the apartment now contained just two rooms, because the other three had been shot away, she felt as though she had travelled back twenty years, to a place and time more prosperous and at ease than anything she had ever known. Tonya remembered her amazement on first entering East Prussia. The farms and cottages, fields and orchards had been so tidy, she had been simply staggered that any country so richly blessed should even have wanted to grab the poor and wild territory to its east.

"You can read music, of course?"

Tonya shook her head.

"You can't read music." Marta spoke as if Tonya had declared herself unable to read at all. "Never mind. The first thing is to stand right. Now then . . ."

For forty minutes the lesson proceeded, as though it were an entirely normal violin lesson. It was half an hour before Tonya was actually allowed to hold the violin itself, and when she did Marta was so appalled by something in the way she held it — too stiff, or too loose, or too rigid, or too something — that the instrument was snatched away and Tonya had to go back to practising her dummy exercises.

And then, just as Tonya was beginning to wonder if this whole thing was based on misunderstanding, there were quick, sharp footsteps in the corridor outside, a triple-tap on the door, then the footsteps passing away again down the hall. Marta turned to Tonya with a

161

smile — the first glimpse of friendliness she'd shown her.

"Good. That means that Mr Thompson's friends have checked the area. There is no one watching you. There is no one who can hear us."

"Thank goodness! You were so strict with me, I thought maybe you really thought I was here for a violin lesson."

"You are here for a lesson. That's very important. Whenever you come, we will play. And you will pay me at the agreed rate, twenty Reichsmarks."

"Yes, yes of course."

"And Mr Thompson promises that there will be somebody to watch. If there is any danger, then we will play the violin, nothing else."

"And the papers? I have a packet with me."

"I will take them."

Tonya handed over a packet of documents. She was both translator and typist. There was no great difficulty in inserting an extra carbon paper and making an extra copy of documents that came her way. The difficulty was in removing that spare copy from the building, which was always alive with NKVD men. The first time Tonya had left the building with a typescript crackling inside the belt of her skirt, she felt as though her guilt were shouting loudly enough to attract a couple of armoured divisions. When she'd managed to walk out, unmolested, unfollowed, she'd been almost dazed with surprise and relief.

"Good," said Marta, as though she were just accepting a pat of butter or slice of ham. "Now before we complete our lesson, there are a few other things to tell you." Without altering her matter-of-fact tone in any way, she began talking about rudimentary codes, secret drops, ways of signalling difficulty to Thompson, ways in which Thompson himself could send warning signals to Tonya. Marta took measurements of Tonya's feet — "We are constructing some boots for you, with a compartment in the heel. You will find the man who will sell you the boots standing in the Friedrichskirche market at two o'clock on Monday. He will wear a grey woollen cap and a green jacket with leather buttons. The price will be eighteen marks . . ."

Instructions followed in a stream.

She nodded as though she had absorbed everything, but felt as though she'd absorbed nothing at all. And then it was back to the violin. Tonya still hadn't played a note. Marta still seemed very worried about Tonya's damaged right hand. But her clucks of disappointment had softened. By the end of an hour and a half, Marta seemed almost content.

"Good. You may finish there. That's a good first lesson. It is hard for you with your hand."

Tonya stood up, realising that she'd come to know this little apartment much, much better before long.

"Please, Marta, could you play something for me, anything? It's just I've never heard violin-playing before, not properly."

"Never? You have never heard a violin?"

"In church sometimes. Sort of. Not really."

"Hmm! Do you like Brahms?"

Marta picked up the violin and half-closed her eyes. Without looking at any music, she began to play. The notes streamed out; pure, liquid perfection. Tonya listened for a while, awestruck by the beauty. Then, without saying goodbye, not wanting to break the flow of the music, she went to the door and crept silently away.

15

The orphanage lay on the outskirts of Grunewald. There was a lodge house set beside the high wrought-iron gates, but the gates were open and Misha walked through unchallenged. The orphanage itself was a neo-classical affair in pale yellow stucco and white pilasters. Misha walked up to the house, then wasn't sure what to do next. He sat down on a bench in the driveway.

He would stay in Berlin. That was one of the few certainties now. Just as the various bureaucracies were beginning to grind out a favourable result for his emigration application, he wrote a series of letters cancelling all the requests he'd made. He'd done so curtly and without explanation, as though purposely hoping to antagonise the relevant officials and so block off any hope of trying again. Meantime, he'd made up his mind that if Rosa should want a father, she should have one. Beyond that, he knew nothing at all.

Every now and then, groups of children would emerge from one door and hurry off in formation to one of the other buildings scattered around the grounds. The front drive saw a stream of UNRRA-stencilled vehicles arriving and departing. Nobody looked long at Misha. Nobody asked him why he was there.

Misha took a yo-yo from his pocket — Willi said that he'd been given it by a GI at the hospital; Misha was fairly sure he'd simply stolen it — and began to play. The yo-yo was an American one, with a looped slip-string, and an amazing ability to hover and glide. Misha played seriously, his engineer's brain trying to understand the play of forces inside the twirling object. He challenged himself to find new tricks to play with it, then was delighted when he began to add more stunts to his repertoire. Time went by.

And then, almost as he'd forgotten that he was there for any purpose, he felt a presence at his right elbow. He looked up. It was Rosa.

"Hello," he said.

"Hello."

"I came back."

She nodded.

"I'm not going to Canada. I changed my mind."

Rosa had eyes too big for her head — most Berliners did, of course, especially young ones, the consequence of too little food. But her long dark-blond plaits, scrawny shoulders and wide eyes made Misha once again think of her as an elf.

"I made a mistake when I brought you back here, but then again, maybe you've thought about it some more and decided that you're happiest here. If you are, you must stay."

She looked at him with her grave hazel eyes and shook her head.

"I don't have much of a house for you," he continued. "Or much food. I'm rubbish at sewing. There won't be a mummy, or at least there certainly isn't one now. You will have a big brother though, a sort of brother anyway. I really can't promise you much. Most little girls would decide they were happiest here."

She shrugged, bony shoulders lifting and falling in careful imitation of the adult movement. The movement said she wasn't most little girls.

"I'll get my things," she said.

CHAPTER
SIX

1

It was the seventeenth of December, 1945.

Snow was falling.

It fell in great white spirals, as though some heavily padded fabric were being unrolled from high above. Then, when the flakes had reached almost to street level, they were caught up in the city's unpredictable winds and eddies and the snow was rushed around, first this way, then that, like a man struggling to pick up papers on a windy day.

It was evening, almost dark. Tonya had stacks more work to do, but a sudden jabbering headache began to crowd the muscles at the back of her neck. She felt wrung out and exhausted. The tone of the documents that spun through her typewriter — accusatory, aggressive, ideological, grasping — felt like a physical pressure on her skull.

Making a sudden decision, she stood up. She'd leave now, get an early night, catch up first thing the next day. She muttered apologies to her fellow translators — Tonya was the only member of her group without an officer's rank; she was also the only woman and the only non-Party member, and she always took care to show the others the deference they required and expected. Then she put on her army greatcoat and cap and walked out onto the street. The night was clear and freezing. In a city still shorn of streetlamps, the stars shone down bright and hard

Her way back to her barracks took her along Prenzlauer Allee, close to Marta's apartment. Tonya was scheduled to have a "violin lesson" that night, but had decided to skip it. But as she passed the little alley, her resolution suddenly wavered. Marta had never been overtly affectionate towards her, but she had always behaved with a perfectly measured courtesy that somehow amounted to almost the same thing. Tonya suddenly realised that she needed human contact more than anything in the world. The muscles knotting in her neck almost tangibly relaxed at the thought of it. Before any conscious change of mind, her steps changed direction and headed for the little bolthole of Marta's apartment.

She reached the familiar door, tapped and entered. Marta answered the door as usual, but almost at once Tonya realised there was something different about the light in the room, the balance of space inside it. She stepped on inside and there, sprawled untidily in the armchair, was the Englishman, Mark Thompson. She felt instant relief at his presence; a feeling of reassurance and warmth.

"Hello, old thing," said Thompson, rising from his seat. As usual he translated his English idioms directly into German, mangling them horribly on the way. "Thought I'd better pop over to see how you were getting on. Damned cold, isn't it? I suppose it isn't by your standards. Probably ice cream and donkey rides on the beach, as far as you're concerned."

As Thompson babbled, Tonya found herself being wafted into a seat, her coat taken, and a steaming drink put into her hands. Marta helped welcome her, then picked the violin out of its green baize case and began to play, imitating Tonya's own level of technique. To anyone listening — and Thompson's presence almost certainly meant that there were British agents posted to give warning in any event — it would have seemed as if it were Tonya, not Marta, drawing her bow over the strings. But after months of lessons, Tonya had become a reasonably competent player, and the music flowed with some grace.

Tonya listened for a while, then brought the drink up to her nose. She had assumed the drink was tea, which she drank often, or coffee, a little-seen luxury, but it was neither of these. She sniffed uncertainly.

"Bournvita," said Thompson. "Malted barley, milk, cocoa and egg. Horlicks with chocolate. What a concoction, eh? I remember when it first came out. Seemed like a miracle, sign of the world becoming a better place. Completely bloody wrong, of course, but it's a damned good drink all the same. What d'you think? Bit too imperialist-capitalist for you?"

Tonya sipped. She knew that Thompson was talking so much so she could compose herself. She held her face over the mug, feeling it steam up. The drink was delicious, the nicest thing she'd ever tasted. It felt like the taste of England; something comforting and parochial, unlikely ever to shine.

169

"I love it," she said, and meant it. She had started spying because of her conviction that Stalin needed to be stopped in his attempted takeover of Germany. She had continued because of her deepening loathing for the Soviet system itself — but also because of this: Marta's minor courtesies, and Thompson's occasional visits, his shambling, genuine warmth.

"I'd give you a tin or two, only that might not be quite the thing. How's your week been? Pretty bloody from the look of you. The comrades bullying you as usual?"

"Oh —" Tonya shook her head. She didn't want to talk about it. "Just the usual. There are more quota shortfalls, though. In Leipzig, agricultural production levels are running at just forty per cent of quota. The published statistics talk about yield increases, but that's all nonsense, of course. I'll be going to Leipzig tomorrow with General Zavenyagin. I'd expect to learn more then —"

Thompson initially looked alert and interested, but then his demeanour abruptly changed. He waved his hands in front of his face, stopping her in her tracks.

"No, for God's sake. Let's not worry about all that for tonight. The comrades are making a pig's ear of things, lying through their teeth, and blaming everyone except themselves, hey? Listen, tell me about yourself. You've been working for us for months now, and you're the best. I mean it. Our best source in Berlin. Our best source in the Soviet zone. And so far, all we've given you is a few music lessons and one cup of Bournvita. We've been a bit stingy, wouldn't you say?"

"Stingy?"

"Stingy. Mean. Tight. Parsimonious. As close as a Scottish money-lender."

"I wasn't doing this to be paid. In any case, I don't think . . ."

". . . that the comrades would be happy to see you swanning around in a mink coat and pearls. No, quite." Unconsciously, Tonya had been fingering the stub ends of her two frost-bitten fingers. Thompson's eye caught the gesture, and Tonya dropped her hands. "There's principle, of course," Thompson continued, "and a jolly good thing that is too. But I thought maybe you might want something else."

Tonya shook her head. She wanted peace. She wanted to do the right thing. She wanted Germany to avoid the fate that Russia had suffered. That was all.

Thompson looked at her hard, then dipped inside his pocket. He pulled out a pouch of pipe tobacco, a pocket knife, a ball of string and a blue booklet with a heavy gold stamp on its cover. Thompson threw the booklet over to Tonya.

"How about one of these?"

She looked at it. It was a British passport, something she'd never seen before. She fingered the grey pages in wonderment. All the time she had been working for Thompson, she had literally never once thought about reward; or if she had, the violin lessons had seemed like reward enough. The passport was Thompson's own. There was no document in the name of Antonina Kirylovna Kornikova, not yet anyway.

"Obviously, if you became a Brit, you'd have to have some money, and a nice little cottage somewhere, a few roses, view of the cricket pitch, that sort of thing. Old HM Government is a bit strapped for cash at the moment, but I expect we could find something suitable. A poky little boarding house in Clapham and a dozen tins of Bournvita at any rate."

Tonya interrupted him. "Yes. If you mean it, then yes. I would be . . . very grateful."

"No, no, you'll have earned it."

Thompson swept his tangle of straw-coloured hair back from his face, and Tonya could see the sharp and solemn intelligence which lay behind his words, his sprawling asinine speech. She read struggle in his expression and realised that she was the subject of that struggle. She didn't know why.

"Listen, I'm serious about the passport. I'm also serious when I tell you that HMG is unlikely to pay you what it ought to, but I'm sure there'll be a job for you as a translator over in London. But we should make sure we have an understanding."

"Yes?"

"How long you go on working for us here before we bring you over into our sector. What seems reasonable to you?"

Tonya shook her head. She had never in her life been asked by anyone in authority what seemed reasonable. "I don't know. For a passport? Perhaps two years? Three?"

"Good God, woman!" Thompson exploded, speaking English, before continuing, "You don't bargain very hard. Listen, I want you here as long as possible, but I'm damned if I want to be the one responsible for letting you injure yourself. Can we say six months? At most. If we get worried about you before that, we'll bring you across without delay. And for Christ's sake, think of yourself. I know that's a damned bourgeois thing to worry about, but just do it anyway, will you?"

He stood up. As usual when standing, he seemed too big for the room. Marta stopped her violin playing and swivelled around on her stool. Tonya realised that the big man was worried about her. That he was facing a conflict between duty, which was urging him to retain her services for as long as he could, and some softer protective instinct. Tonya was now forty-six. Her son Vassily, had he lived, would have been about Mark Thompson's age now.

She nodded. "I will."

"I doubt it. Damned Bolsheviks. Lost any decent sense of selfishness. Listen. I'm interrupting your lesson. I'll skedaddle. Don't worry about your damned agricultural quotas today. Just play."

He was about to go. Tonya had taken the violin from Marta and her fingers were already beginning to find their places on the strings, when she was shaken by a wave of longing so strong, it physically shook her. Thompson stopped and stared at her.

"You asked me if there was something I wanted."

"Yes?"

"A passport . . . I would like that — no, love it. I'd never thought. But in the meantime, there's something else you could do for me. It's probably silly. There's probably no chance. There's somebody you could try to find for me. A man, Mikhail —"

"— Kornikov?"

"No. Malevich." Tonya blushed — what an unfamiliar sensation that was! "I was not married to him. I last saw him in 1919. He was taken off to fight in the Civil War, against the Whites, against his own sort really. He promised to escape if he could. Sort of promised, anyway. He couldn't do much more than nod. But I believe that he would have come to Germany to settle. Here or Switzerland. He was an engineer. Not exactly trained, but a born engineer all the same. Gifted. I have no idea what happened to him. Perhaps it's no use. It was so long ago. But I suppose you have lists of who's who in your sector —"

"Yes. Lists and lists. Rooms full of them. The Americans too, of course. Even the French, if they'd have the grace to cooperate with us about anything ever. Do you know what town or district we should start looking in?"

"No. I have no idea. None. He had family in Switzerland." Tonya gave their names. "But that was so long ago now. Perhaps it's useless."

"Perhaps." There was that grave look in Thompson's eyes again, the look which Tonya guessed was much closer to the true him than all the nonsense about Bournvita and donkey rides. Thompson closed the moment with a long, slow nod. "But perhaps not. We won't know until we start looking, will we?"

Tonya shook her head. "No, no."

Thompson stood up, getting ready to leave the room. He looked down at Tonya and gave her a wink of encouragement and support.

She smiled back, then added, "I loved him very much. I'm sorry to ask you for something so foolish."

He shook his head. "Nothing foolish about it. Enjoy your lesson."

Thompson departed, leaving Tonya and Marta to the violin. But Tonya played this evening like a dunce, as though this was only her second or third time at the instrument. Marta was patient, but also exasperated. And Tonya? She didn't know how she felt. Once before with Thompson there had been this feeling, of a sudden slippage of emotion, like a roof suddenly shedding its burden of snow in the spring thaw. The first time it had been to do with the Gulag, her lost fingers, the pain and awfulness of those first days. And now it was to do with something still closer to her heart: Misha, her first and only true love. Here in Berlin, in Germany, it was he who seemed real, Rodyon who seemed far away and impossible to believe in.

Tonya played the violin for another fifty minutes. When she got into bed that night, she fell asleep instantly and didn't dream about a single thing.

2

The jeweller removed his eyeglass with a sideways twist of his head, but the loose folds of skin over his eye still retained the circular imprint. He tapped the identity documents in front of him.

"A routine matter."

"Good. And how much do you charge for a routine matter?"

"How much? To convert a Malevich into a Müller? We may say four hundred cigarettes."

Misha grimaced. He had three hundred cigarettes in a cardboard carton and the boxful represented his entire stock of savings. "Can we say three hundred? I have it here."

The jeweller rubbed his eyes, blotting out the circular mark. He sighed, as though making a small fortune from forging identity papers was just one of the crosses he had to bear.

"Very well then. Sit."

The jeweller's room lay just near the Schlasisches Tor in the Soviet sector. Since all the watches and most of the jewellery once owned by Berliners now adorned the wrists and necks of the Red Army and their wives back home, the jeweller had turned his hand to the closely related trade of document forgery. Perhaps, Misha wondered, the jeweller had had the same profession in Hitler's time. In any case, the man had a reputation for knowing his business. His little office had a huge glass window overlooking the road, for the light presumably, and the narrow workbenches were crammed with the intricate clutter of his trade. The heavy snow-laden sky outside filled the apartment with clear grey light, toneless and impartial.

Misha found a small fabric-covered bench and sat, always interested in the technical side of any skilled occupation. The man began with Misha's ration book.

He took a scalpel and began to scrape patiently at the offending surname. The scalpel appeared to make no difference, but the jeweller didn't either hurry his movement or apply more pressure. A minute or so passed and Misha could see the black lettering had grown fainter. Another few minutes and it had vanished altogether, leaving the surface of the paper scuffed and abraded. The jeweller inspected his work with the eyeglass, then dipped his finger inside a little pot filled with a thick grey ointment — china clay, Misha guessed, mixed with graphite to darken it. The jeweller compared the paper against the ointment for colour match, grunted his satisfaction, and applied the substance to the paper with a light dabbing motion. He continued to dab and blot, until the ointment was invisible and the paper magically restored. The jeweller inspected the surface of the paper under his eyeglass for almost a minute. Misha had already spotted the rows of neat wooden drawers which would house the man's collection of printing blocks and typefaces. A glass jar contained a couple of dozen tubes of printers' ink. Misha wondered who the jeweller's principal clients were now — Russian Hiwis, Displaced Persons, former Nazis, a whole sea of lost souls.

Misha wanted to leave.

He didn't like being away from the factory too long these days. The factory had become a place of business again. Pump manufacturing was out of the question in present conditions. The entire German economy was at a standstill. There was no currency which meant anything, no money to buy raw materials, no capital to

177

restore damaged production lines. There was no hope that anything would change at all soon. But if running a complex manufacturing operation had become impossible, the extent of the destruction had created new opportunities. Misha had borrowed and begged some timber and built a weaving loom, operated by pedal and hand. He'd got hold of some raw cotton thread, woven headscarves, sold them, bought more cotton, made more headscarves. He had four looms now, all hand-built, and employed women to work them. It was a tiny business — laughable compared with what he'd once had — but it was a start. The business was busy. It now made headscarves, cotton cloth, aprons, anything which sold. It kept Rosa in food and clothes and schoolbooks. It had now, finally, earned enough to "convert a Malevich into a Müller".

And, of course, the factory wasn't the only thing that kept him busy. Misha was not not only a businessman, but also, in effect, a father. Rosa's arrival had turned them into a little family, the Nothing Factory into a sort of home. The girl needed proper food, regular bedtimes, hot baths, family meals. She needed all the things that years of war had stripped from Germany. And Misha supplied it. Willi grumbled at the regularisation of his free-and-easy routines, but Misha realised that the boy needed an ordinary family just as much as Rosa, and his grumbling was just part of the pleasure. The family had settled down. In a modest way, they were happy.

Hours passed. Then the jeweller pushed back his chair.

"Herr Müller," he said, smiling slightly as he handed over the new, carefully constructed papers. "The glue is not yet dry. I would advise you, if you can . . ."

Misha took his papers, feeling the glow of relief like a hot coal inside him. He'd forged some poor-quality documents himself, in case the NKVD came calling again, but he'd feel far safer with these new ones. He walked downstairs and onto the frozen street. Snow particles, blown by the wind, hissed and skittered across the ice.

He pulled his coat tight and set off for home.

3

Anxious to avoid any inspection of his papers before the glue was yet dry, Misha kept to side roads paralleling Skalitzerstrasse and Gitschinerstrasse, thinking that he was less likely to run into trouble in the quieter back roads. But just as he approached the Hallesches Tor, the road network led him back to the main street. A small convoy of Russian vehicles crept eastwards, a Tatra truck, a couple of motorcycles, and a black ZiS limousine, the 101 model which looked like a Russified American Packard. The limousine was the indicator of a high-ranked occupation official. Misha glanced idly at the car.

Glanced, then stared.

Not at the car itself, but at those inside it. And not at the Soviet general who sat flung back in the rear of the car, but at the woman who sat with a bent head on the seat next to him. Misha could hardly see her face. He

179

could see little more than the colour of her hair, the angle of her cheek, the way she held herself. For a moment the world went still. The convoy crept forwards. Misha stood like a man frozen.

Then he moved. "Tonya," he shouted. "Tonya!"

Nobody heard him. The limousine moved on and away. The people inside didn't look around. A couple of soldiers in the back of the truck stared out at him without much interest. Misha ran, slipping and blundering on the new snow back into the Soviet zone. But it was a useless chase. Before more than twenty seconds had passed, the car was seventy yards away and accelerating all the time. Misha's voice pistoled off the nearby buildings into silence. He stopped running and tried to catch his breath, buildings towers of vapour in the freezing air.

Was it Tonya, or not Tonya?

Misha perfectly well knew that he hadn't had a good enough view to tell. The odds were heavily against it. A thousand to one? Ten thousand? But Misha wasn't in a place where he thought about the odds. Over the last awful decade, Misha's reasons for living — his much-loved wife Lillie; his friend, father-in-law and business partner, Otto; his home and business — had evaporated one by one into the maelstrom of history. Then Willi had become a reason to live, then Rosa too. But Tonya was the last, the best reason to live. In a world turned upside down, it was sometimes the things from the far distant past which echoed most strongly in this bombed-out, war-torn present.

180

In an instant, Tonya's image was as real to him as it had ever been. She had been his first and best true love; always had been, always would be. If she were alive, then he would find her.

4

The car was the clue.

The limousine had certainly been a ZiS 101. There were very few such cars in Berlin. There couldn't even have been all that many on the streets of Moscow, since the production of luxury cars had been brought to a total halt by wartime. And Misha had certainly seen a senior Soviet officer inside the car. Probably only a full general could command such a vehicle and such an escort.

But who was the woman? Misha knew that though there had been enough of a resemblance to suggest Tonya, he had been a long way short of making a positive identification. In any case, he knew that he was very prone to seeing Tonya in a thousand and one different women, many of whom barely resembled her at all. In his first few years in Germany, after his escape from Russia, hardly a week had gone by without Misha being sure that he'd seen her, often two or three or four times in the same week.

But still, Misha's "sighting" brought home to him that Tonya might indeed be alive, that she might even be with the Soviet forces in Berlin or the east zone. And though the odds were against it, they weren't ludicrously against it. Germany still swarmed with Red

Army personnel. Tonya had been a good student of German all those years ago, in the little hunting lodge outside Petrozavodsk. She'd enjoyed her lessons. Perhaps she'd continued with her language training thereafter? If so, then her presence in Germany made sense. Perhaps she had even wangled her way to Berlin in the hope of somehow finding Misha . . . His heart beat thunderingly at the thought. He knew already and for certain that he would never rest until he had found Tonya, or learned for sure that she was lost for ever.

But first things first. Misha had to start somewhere, and the car was the clue.

On a cold, bright day, with sunshine glittering over a black, white and grey cityscape, Misha walked into the Soviet sector to the offices of the *Tägliche Rundschau*, the Soviet-backed daily newspaper. The paper was a propaganda tool, of course. Soviet achievements in increasing rations or rebuilding schools were heavily covered and praised. Soviet bullying, deceit and criminality were never mentioned. But alongside the propaganda, the activities of senior occupation officials were usually given a mention, no matter how unreliable the gloss put on them.

Misha, giving his surname as Müller as he always did these days, asked to see the journalist responsible for compiling the relevant column. The journalist a thin man with a dark beard and moustache clipped to be exactly like Lenin's, came down from the offices upstairs. Misha identified himself. The journalist nodded, didn't bother to shake hands, stuck a cigarette in his mouth, lit it and said, "Yes?"

Misha recognised the type. This man, though German, was almost certainly a Moscow-trained communist. If so, his sympathies would be entirely with the country's new occupiers, not at all with their reluctant hosts.

Looking down at the ground, and deliberately stumbling over his sentences, Misha explained that he was a father — he'd been out on the street the day before — he'd seen a convoy — a ZiS limousine — he'd recognised the driver — a good man — a man who'd saved his daughter from a shameful episode. The phrase Misha used was the common euphemism for rape, often gang-rape, perpetrated by Red Army men on the rampage. Misha explained that he was keen to thank the driver properly, to offer a small gift. He wondered if the journalist were able to find out the name of the driver, or even the official who was being driven around.

The journalist surveyed Misha carefully as he spoke. Then, without answering Misha directly, took a telephone from the desk, and made a call. He spoke in rapid, German-accented Russian to the person on the other end. Misha heard that the officer in question was General Zavenyagin; that the journey had been to the Faculty of Agricultural Sciences in Leipzig. He also heard that the journalist had made no enquiry at all about the identity of the driver.

The journalist turned back to Misha.

"What is your name again?"

"Müller."

"All the officials of the *Sowjetische Militäradminstration in Deutschland* were engaged on their regular business," said the journalist.

"Yes, sir, but the driver —"

"All Red Army personnel are instructed to supervise and ensure the safety of all German citizens. If there was an unfortunate incident, it is highly likely that surviving fascistic units in stolen Red Army uniforms were responsible."

"Yes, sir."

"It is not necessary to offer gifts for the ordinary performance of duty."

"No."

The journalist nodded once, then turned away. He had been utterly, deliberately unhelpful, but Misha had already heard enough. General Zavenyagin. Leipzig. The Faculty of Agricultural Sciences. It was a small lead, but it was enough.

5

Harlan Bauer, Hollinger's counterpart in the American military intelligence services, rolled a baseball around his desk with the flat of his hand. The raised seams made a clunking sound as they passed over the polished desktop, and Bauer, frowning hard, concentrated on moving the ball so that the clunking sounds came at exact, regularly spaced intervals.

"Stuttgart," he said, "you been there? Probably not. My grandpa came from there. Grandpa Bauer. A nice place, so he said. And now? We put a mayor in. A decent guy. No Nazi. The *Oberbürgermeister*. A hard worker. I seen a report from him today that says the city has 60,000 pairs of shoes, 220 suits and 71 overcoats. Only 71 coats and it's January and it's freezing hard and the city has a population of 330,000."

"Listen, Bauer, I know all this —"

But Bauer wasn't done. Clunk-clunk-clunk the baseball continued to roll around his table. In the summer, a group of baseball-loving Americans had engaged with a group of cricket-loving Brits and tried to understand the joys of each other's national game. The experiment had failed. The Americans felt that batting in front of stumps was a typically tight-arsed British way of doing it. The Brits felt that the American game lacked technique and that the pitcher's throwing action came suspiciously close to cheating. Bauer and Hollinger were among the few who had enjoyed the experience and maintained easy social relations afterwards. Bauer held up a finger for silence.

"No, no, hear me out. We're getting in our zone alone maybe 5,000 refugees a day from the east. Where do we put 'em? Even as it is, we have maybe one dwelling for every two families. We've set a target ration of 1,550 calories a day — around half of what an active adult needs to eat in these conditions — and we don't even supply that. We need coal for heating. We need it badly. Only — shoot! — we can't feed the miners, so they're too hungry to work, so they don't dig the coal, so Germany doesn't have the industry, so it can't make the goods, so it can't make the money, so it can't buy the food, that it could give to the miners, so that they could dig out the goddamn coal."

On the last word, Bauer brought his hand down hard on the side of the baseball, spinning it, but also preventing it from rolling sideways. The effect was to make the ball jump up off the table into his hand, and he mimed the action of hurling the ball hard at the dead centre of his window. Bauer let a few moments pass in silence, as though to let the imaginary broken glass finish its descent down into the icy street below. Then he said, "I'm doing it, aren't I? That thing Limey grandmothers do."

"Our grandmothers? I think they mostly knit comforters for our gallant boys overseas."

"With eggs. Grandmothers and eggs."

"Ah yes! They suck them. Strictly speaking, it would be powdered egg these days, so I don't suppose they suck exactly. Snort, perhaps."

"You got it. That's what I was doing, right?"

"Right."

"We got all these problems — I say *we* got, but really it's Fritz who's got 'em — and you want us to pour manpower into looking for a guy who might or might not have arrived here twenty-five years back, who might or might not have stayed, who might or might not have been killed, and who means nothing at all to me or to us or to my good buddy, the *Oberbürgermeister* of Stuttgart."

"Yes."

"You've looked already?"

"Started."

"Found nothing?"

"Not a thing."

Bauer grinned, or maybe grimaced. Bauer was a compact, powerful man, with a face that looked as though it had been mechanically pressed from something durable. In Bauer's case, grinning and grimacing were two expressions which sat close together. He stood abruptly and yelled down the hall for someone to bring him two coffees. He pulled his head back in and asked Hollinger if he wanted coffee. Hollinger nodded. Bauer sat back down.

"It's gives and gets, buddy. I'm not saying we won't give, but you gotta trade."

"Can we make this unofficial?"

"How unofficial?"

"Completely. You don't write any of this down. You report this conversation to no one."

"Depends what you got. I might have to talk to my boss. I can't say."

"But you won't if you don't have to."

"I won't unless I have to. Spit 'n' shake." Bauer did a mock-spit on his hand and stretched it out. Hollinger shook without spitting.

"So?"

Hollinger waited till the coffee arrived and the door was closed again. And then he began to speak. About Antonina Kornikova, his source inside the SMAD. He described her position, the documents she had access to. He didn't mention her name or anything that could identify her, not even her sex. Bauer had seemed almost to hold his breath while Hollinger was speaking. Then

187

he blew out, saying, "You got yourself a sweet little source there. Do we get any of the juice, or you just want me to sit and admire your fieldcraft?"

"We've already given you a lot of the juice."

"Right, only you haven't told us where it's come from, so when our intelligence assessment guys sit around, they look at each other and say this stuff's probably come from some Limey faggot who's copied it out of the *Tägliche Rundschau* and made a few copying errors along the way, so we end up throwing the whole thing into the garbage."

"Right, except now I've told you."

"Right, except now I'm not allowed to say."

"You're allowed to say it doesn't come from a Limey faggot and the *Tägliche Rundschau*. In any case, most of our faggots are already on the Soviet side of things. Either there or the Foreign Office. Not MilGov Berlin."

Bauer grinned — this splitting of the thick lips and exposure of the solid, crammed-together teeth bore no other name — and picked up the baseball again.

"Gives and gets, buddy. It's a big give."

"It's a big get. I'll give you — you personally — access to all the source material. You can vouch for its quality to your assessment people."

"OK. It's a deal." Bauer picked up the slip of paper on which Hollinger had written the name. "Mikhail Ivanovich Malevich. We'll take a look."

"Thank you."

Bauer looked at Hollinger, weighted the baseball in his hand, and waited for a small nod from the Englishman. Then Bauer threw the ball — hard —

across the room. Hollinger caught it, one-handed; paused a second, then returned the missile hard in the opposite direction. The ball made a smacking sound as it flew from palm to palm. Then, without breaking off the game, Bauer said, "Normally, if we have a source, we pay hard American dollars. Maybe offer a passport. We don't offer to trace the untraceable."

Thwack — thwack — thwack went the ball.

"Same with us, only obviously we prefer to pay in milk coupons."

Thwack — thwack.

"She a dame? Only a dame would want to trace a guy."

Thwack.

"She is, yes," said Hollinger, stopping abruptly. "A very brave one."

Bauer responded to the change in tone.

"This can be a tough game, huh?" he said quietly.

Hollinger rubbed his face with his free hand, the one without the ball.

"In war, it was easy. Their men were killing ours. Our men were killing theirs. Whatever we were able to do by way of intelligence was all directed towards winning the war. The morality was pretty simple. I never bothered with it much."

"There's still a kind of war going on."

"Yes, you think so and I think so, though not everyone agrees with us. But whatever it is, it's not a shooting war. This girl's already been to the Gulag once. I don't know, but I get the feeling she's already lost a lot of those close to her. I almost can't stand to think about what would happen to her if they found out."

"I understand. You won't find me telling tales out of school."

"No, I know."

"It's her call, buddy. She knows the risks."

"I tell her we'll keep her safe."

"And so you do."

"But we both know I can't."

The two men fell silent. It was the constant moral predicament of their jobs. On the one hand, both men knew that the Soviets were planning for the communist takeover of Germany. Of all of it, east zone and western zones together. From Berlin to the North Sea coast. And the Soviets had to be stopped. Both men knew that their task now was little less vital to the safety of the world, than it had been all through the years of war. But on the other hand, it was harder now to ignore the casualties. The individual agents who, for reasons of money or conviction, threw their lot in with the western intelligence agencies. Bauer and Hollinger protected their agents as well as they could for as long as they could. But there was a limit to what they could do. They had both lost agents in the past. They both knew they would again. Whether their agents succumbed to the bullet or the labour camp was never known. They had simply dropped out of sight, never to return. It was a fate too awful to think about — except that Hollinger never stopped thinking, and of one agent in particular; a woman with remarkable green eyes and two fingertips missing on her right hand.

Bauer understood the mood. He spoke quietly, saying, "If Malevich is in our zone, I'll find him. If I can, I will."

"Thank you."

Hollinger took the ball and tossed it in a gentle rising curve towards the American. Bauer hardly had to move his hand to catch it. Once he'd got it, he made no move to throw it back.

"Howzat?" he said, in a voice so quiet it was almost a whisper.

6

One day, not long after her trip to Leipzig, Tonya found herself accompanying a group of senior officers from the SMAD to a cluster of military security facilities in the scatter of lakes and woodland between Fürstenwalde and Halbe. On arrival there, it turned out that the only Germans present were fluent Russian speakers and Tonya was told that her services were not required. There was no car available to take her back to Berlin; and even if there had been, as a mere corporal, Tonya was never going to be allowed that privilege. But there was a wooden canteen building, where Tonya could wait until her superiors were ready to return.

She entered the building, expecting it to be empty. But it wasn't. As well as the bare tables and the uncurtained windows letting in the wide forest light, there was a woman there, around Tonya's age, sewing.

"*Guten Morgen*," said Tonya, nodding.

"*Morgen.*"

The woman was dark-haired and quiet. Tonya sat down not far from her. There was a cast-iron stove in the room, but the fire in it was small and mostly useless. Both women sat in dark civilian coats and hats. After a while, Tonya spoke.

"You haven't anything to read, have you?"

"No, but you can help with my sewing if you'd like."

The woman was embroidering a white cotton handkerchief, and indicated a basket which held further sewing things. Tonya was about to accept the offer, when she noticed what the woman was sewing: a hut on chicken-leg stilts, the house of Babba Yaga, the witch of countless Russian fairy tales. The handkerchief was obviously intended for a child back home.

"You're Russian?" exclaimed Tonya.

"Of course — you?"

The woman pulled open her coat a little way, to reveal her Red Army uniform underneath. They quickly switched to Russian and began to talk rapidly. The woman's name was Valentina. She had been a driver in the Red Army, then had been ordered to stay on after the victory. Valentina asked if Tonya wanted to take a walk in the woods around about and Tonya leaped at the chance.

They walked and talked, keeping either to the vehicle tracks that curved through the snowy wood, or occasionally branching off onto the trails used by hunters or woodsmen. The woods were mainly pine, and the red trunks, high canopy and filtered sunlight reminded both women irresistibly of Russia. Tonya didn't know what it made Valentina think of, but for her such forests were and always would be about Petrozavodsk, and that magical winter she'd spent with Misha.

For a while they kept to carefully neutral topics. The senior echelons of the SMAD were shot through and through with NKVD men and informers. Anything political was a dangerous topic. Likewise any opinion not endorsed by the Party itself opened the speaker up to possible risk. But at last, and only when they were out of sight of everyone and everything, Valentina raised a topic.

"In the canteen, before you put your gloves on, I noticed your hand . . ."

"Yes. I had frostbite . . ."

"Was it . . .?"

"In the Gulag? Yes. I was there —"

"Oh, me too. When were you sent? What article? How did you get out? You weren't in a *shtraf* battalion too, were you?"

Suddenly a dam was broken, and both women began to speak rapidly of their experiences. Tonya had been sentenced for ten years under the most serious article of the criminal code. Valentina had been denounced by a neighbour who'd been jealous of her apartment. She'd been accused of everything, of course, but only convicted of a minor offence and been sentenced for just three years. Her experiences had been bad, but nothing like as bad as Tonya's. All the same, it was a vast relief to them both to talk woman to woman, political undesirable to political undesirable. They walked for four hours. Before they arrived back at the little cluster of buildings, the two women hugged and vowed to keep in touch as best they could back in Berlin.

Then they arrived back. Valentina's services were wanted — she was reprimanded for being late, in fact — she waved to Tonya and shot away at the wheel of her UAZ jeep. Tonya, on the other hand, was kept waiting another six hours, and was half-frozen before the time came for her too to leave.

But something had happened. She'd half-known it already after her last meeting with Thompson. And that something was dangerous. For twenty-five years, ever since Misha had been forced to flee for his life, out of the country and out of Tonya's life, she had taught herself to suppress hope, to avoid optimism, to keep strict limits on the amount of human interaction she could allow herself.

And that old dam had suddenly broken. Mark Thompson had broken it. A blue and gold passport and the hope of seeing Misha again had broken it. Of course Tonya knew that the odds were heavily against her ever seeing Misha again. Perhaps he had been killed in the Civil War. Perhaps he'd died of gunfire, cold, disease, hunger, wild beasts, or any of a dozen other possible causes. Even if he'd succeeded in escaping, he might never have come to Germany, or even Europe. He might have been killed in the war, or died in a camp, or been bombed sleeping quietly at home. And if he had made it all the way to Germany, then he would surely have married at some point, had children, moved on . . . But none of that was the point.

194

The point was this. For two and a half decades, Tonya had avoided hope, because she knew that too much hope could crush those who held it. Now hope was alive again: spontaneous, eager, combustible, dangerous. After so long, she had begun to trust.

7

"Zavenyagin?" said the doorman, spitting accurately into the wastebin between his boots. "That shit."

"He was that bad?"

"It was all shout and scream for hours on end. We could hear him down here."

The doorman had a tiny wooden kiosk inside the entrance to the Leipzig Faculty of Agricultural Sciences. On a wooden shelf to the side, a simple wick dipped in paraffin made a stove on which a tin of water was beginning to boil.

"Do you want coffee?"

"You have coffee?"

"No, no. Erstaz-coffee, of course. But not so bad. This one has some real barley."

The doorman indicated that Misha should enter the little booth. Misha didn't quite see how he could, but crammed himself in anyway. The doorman nodded approvingly and made the coffee. He began to complain about Zavenyagin — "*der Herr Scheisse-Zavenyagin*" — and about the Soviet occupation in general. Misha agreed with most of the complaints, but he was never really sympathetic to the self-pity of some of his fellow Germans. Did these people really not know what their own countrymen had done in Poland and Russia, the Baltics and the Ukraine? But Misha said all the things the doorman wanted him to say, approving every complaint, affirming every tale of woe.

Gradually, Misha brought the question around to the woman who had been accompanying the general.

"Ach! Some campaign floozy, I expect. A bit of skirt to cheer him up away from home. Our girls are better looking than those Moscow sourpusses."

Misha prodded further, and placed a whole pack of American cigarettes on the wooden shelf by way of encouragement, but the doorman knew nothing more.

"She must be deaf as a nut, though," he commented, "to put up with the way that man shouts. One of the cleaners here, Frau Fassbinder, she said he shouted so loud that —"

The doorman ran on, but Misha was no longer listening.

"Frau Fassbinder?" he asked. "Did you say Fassbinder?"

8

To begin with, Tonya saw little of Valentina. The first time they met up was for an evening meal at the echoing military barracks where Valentina had her sleeping quarters. The canteen was full of male soldiers, male voices, male laughter, and the two women ate quietly and quickly together, enjoying themselves hardly at all. But the connection had been made, and they persisted with their efforts to meet. Sometimes, if

Valentina's duty rosters permitted, they were able to meet for lunch, eating cooked ham and pumpernickel bread, and walking down by the bank of the Spree.

And they *talked*. Not about everything of course. Tonya didn't say anything about Misha. She certainly didn't hint at the activities which brought her into contact with Mark Thompson of British intelligence. They avoided any discussion of politics. They were both careful to keep anything which might be construed as a comment on Party leadership dutiful and respectful. But otherwise they talked freely; about their experiences in the Gulag, about their families, about their times in the *shtraf* battalions, their fears of dying, their relief to have escaped Siberia. It was a particular relief to Tonya to talk about her daughters, Yana and Yuliya. She knew she would almost certainly never see them again — even worse, that she shouldn't even try to get in contact — but they remained in her heart and her thoughts as strongly as Misha did himself. It was nice to be able to tell someone about them. She possessed no photo or picture of the two girls — she had been taken to Siberia with nothing at all beyond her prison uniform — and Tonya felt that talking about them somehow kept her link to them alive.

The two women came to see each other most evenings when their schedules permitted. They spoke Russian together. They embroidered items to send to Valentina's niece back in Minsk. They laughed. They remembered again what ordinary friendship felt like.

Then one day, Tonya was carrying a bundle of documents down to the basement for copying by the typists there, when she remembered something Valentina had said the night before. She chuckled to herself. She was still chuckling, when, at a turn in the stairs, she met an NKVD captain, Arkady Konstantinov. The captain was tall, had glossy chestnut hair that he wore daringly long, and wide observant eyes.

"Something funny, Comrade Kornikova?"

"No, sir, nothing."

Tonya's hands were a bit too full with the documents and a couple of files slipped from the top.

"You are taking these down to be typed?"

"Yes sir."

"Then I'll help."

Konstantinov took the two files that had fallen and left her to carry the rest. He walked half a pace behind her, so she was very aware of his presence, but couldn't see him. The stairs were wide enough that they could easily have walked abreast.

"You laugh at nothing?"

"Only something a friend said yesterday."

"A friend?"

"A Russian, sir. A comrade driver with the 12th Guards Rifle Division."

"Ah." They were downstairs now, in the basement. There must have been damp-proofing once, but if so it had been split or cracked in the shelling, and the basement was heavy with damp. "The name of your friend?"

Tonya told him, along with name, rank and unit. She felt scared now, though for no reason she could think of. Konstantinov nodded slowly. He slipped his two files on top of the stack that she already carried, and left silently, his footsteps inaudible on the soft linoleum.

Tonya felt a wave of fear so strong, she almost retched.

9

Konstantinov climbed the stairs again.

There had been nothing in his conversation with the interpreter, or almost nothing. But Konstantinov was good at his job. He felt the prickle of the *almost*, the way a hunter knows when a stag is hidden in a thicket. At the same time, Konstantinov knew that the interpreter had been thoroughly checked already. She wasn't a Party member, it was true. She had been in the Gulag and in a *shtraf* battalion, but in some ways that kind of past stood as a guarantee of present loyalty . . .

Konstantinov fingered the phone on his desk, toying with the idea of doing nothing. But he was a man who always preferred action to idleness. Knowing that the phone call would almost certainly come to nothing, he made it anyway. He called the unit whose name Kornikova had just given him. He confirmed that there was indeed a corporal driver who served there. The woman's name was as the interpreter had given it. But there was something else too. The driver had also been in the Gulag, had also been in a *shtraf* battalion.

Konstantinov replaced the handset with a tiny smile. The doubt that had been almost but not quite present had widened into something larger — still small, of course, but big enough now to be worth investigating.

It was all very well releasing these men and women from the Gulag, but it was not preferable that they should spend unsupervised time together afterwards. Those with a tendency towards political dissent should be very careful about keeping themselves away from corrupting influences.

Konstantinov pulled a sheet of paper towards him and scribbled an instruction. The issue was a minor one. There was almost certainly no need for any action, beyond perhaps a formal warning from an appropriate Party authority. But the interpreter worked with some highly sensitive documents. No precaution could be too much.

Konstantinov wrote some instructions and signed them, then threw the sheet at his wire out-tray. The whole business was probably a distraction. He had more important things to worry about.

10

The doorman had confirmed Frau Fassbinder's name and managed to locate an address. An hour later Misha had located the house, a place seemingly untouched by war-damage. Behind the painted front door, the yells and shouts of children racketed forth. Misha knocked. A woman answered.

"Frau Fassbinder?"

The woman shook her head, ducked behind the door, called for someone, then disappeared. A second woman came to the door. Misha explained who he was and what he wanted.

"There was a woman with Zavenyagin. It's her I want to find."

"A woman. The interpreter, you mean?"

"Interpreter? Yes, could be."

"Who told you to come here?"

"The doorman, Herr Gärtner —"

"Gärtner, that old fool. It wasn't me who cleaned up in there, it was Frau Wannemaker."

"Frau Wannemaker. Listen, if you have an address —" Misha began to dip into his pocket for another packet of cigarettes.

"Address!" The woman snorted. "That's simple. You'd better come in. On the third floor. If those are cigarettes in your hand, then you're very welcome to hand them over."

Misha let the woman take the cigarettes from his hand; from his pocket almost. He stepped inside. The door closed behind him. The house was narrow, though tall, and it was clear that several families now lived here. The heaps of washing, the low hum of quarrelling, the precisely marked lines that demarcated territory in the communal kitchen were all familiar to Misha from Kuletsky Prospekt in the time following the October revolution. Frau Fassbinder jerked a thumb at the stairs, then turned away, ignoring him.

Misha made his way up. The stairs were steep and narrow. The house smelt of too many unwashed bodies, but also of boiled laundry and starched cotton; an odd mix. He got to the third floor. There were only two doors. Misha knocked on one and swung it open. It felt as though he had opened a door out onto the sky. A bomb or shell must have taken away a slice of roof, and the room lay open beneath the sky. Except for an abandoned dolls' house, there was nothing in the room but rubble and snow. Misha closed the door again and knocked on the other. This time, though he still got no direct response, he could hear the sound of people just the other side of the door. He knocked again, for politeness, and opened the door.

Inside there was a single small room. There were three children, poorly dressed and hungry; also a woman, sitting on the only bed, suckling a tiny baby. The woman didn't move the baby away from her breast when she saw Misha enter. She didn't get up or say anything. She just looked at him through dark and deep-set eyes. There was very little furniture and the room was bare and cold.

"Frau Wannemaker? My name is Michael Müller."

The woman continued to look at him, but didn't say anything. The children, their ages ranging from about four to eight or nine, drew together, but they too remained silent. Doing his best to avoid anything which might look or appear threatening in any way, Misha said, "Frau Fassbinder downstairs suggested I come up. She thought you might be able to help me."

He took another full packet of cigarettes out of his pocket and placed it on the stool in front of him. The oldest of the children, a girl with bare feet, ran over and snatched it up before going back to the others. Misha was conscious of his height in the small room and tried stooping to make himself look shorter. He knew he looked very Russian, and took care to keep any trace of accent out of his German. Since the woman still said nothing, he decided to continue.

"I understand that you were cleaning up in the room where the Russian General Zavenyagin was recently. He was the unpleasant man who shouted a lot. Now what I'm very interested in is the woman who was with him. She was a Russian too. I expect she wore an army uniform, but it's possible that she was in civilian clothes. I wondered if by any chance you happened to learn the woman's name. Or if you were able to describe her appearance in any way."

Misha stopped, leaving plenty of silence for the woman to step into if she chose. She said nothing. The girl who had taken the cigarettes went over to her mother and whispered something into her ear. At least that proved she couldn't have been deaf. Misha guessed that nerve damage from bombs or shells was probably a likelier explanation of the woman's silence. As the girl drew her head back, she caught Misha's eye. It wasn't a nod, exactly, but Misha felt sure there was some gesture of encouragement, but without words he didn't know what to do next.

Then his eye fell on a bundle of paper that the children must have used for schoolwork or writing practice. He took a sheet and drew a pen from his pocket. He carried the sheet into the light of the only window — then hesitated.

His thought had been to draw Tonya, but he found himself seized by sudden doubt. There was the gap of twenty-five years of course, but it wasn't that. He suddenly doubted himself. He doubted that the picture of Tonya that he'd carried for all this time was the true one. Was she real or just a fantasy, a mirage? He put pen to paper, but made no further move. Ink from the nib began to spread out in a tiny spider's web pattern on the coarse war-standard paper. The light coming in through the window seemed empty and unhelpful. Then Misha caught the eye of the girl who had encouraged him. Something in her watchful eyes, her ragged clothes and bare feet prompted him.

He began to draw, hardly even knowing in advance what he was sketching. But there was only one thing he could have chosen. Tonya, in the hunting lodge near Petrozavodsk, dancing. Misha left himself out of the picture, but he knew he was there invisibly, holding her waist, guiding her steps. He drew her with her head tilted back, her hair carrying out behind her. He drew her with bright eyes and an open, excited mouth. As a way of illustrating a person's likeness, it was an absurdity. Misha should have drawn her face, the way a police identity poster might be drawn, showing the head in full detail, ignoring her body altogether. One of Tonya's most distinctive features were her green, slightly slanted eyes, and yet he'd sketched those eyes with a few brief strokes of his pen; capturing the essence, but avoiding all detail. Feeling like a fool, he wrote *Augen* — *grün*. *Haare* — *braun*. Eyes green, hair brown.

He looked at the picture. It was Tonya all right; his version of her perhaps, but a real one all the same. To him, it felt as though Tonya's spirit had been captured on paper. The sight of his own drawing made him catch his breath with emotion. He showed the picture to the woman who still sat silently on the bed. She looked at the picture for about eight or ten seconds. Then she switched her eyes from the picture to Misha's face. She nodded.

He wanted to explode into a thousand questions. Was it her? Could she be sure? Did she appear healthy? What was her voice like? Did she seem happy? But even as the impulse rose in him, it died away in the knowledge that not a single one of the questions would be answered.

And then he noticed that the woman was trying to tell him something. He held the drawing up again and the woman indicated Tonya's right hand, shaking her head. Misha frowned and shook his head. He didn't understand. The woman shifted the baby against her chest and held up her own right hand, with the first two fingers tucked down.

Misha returned the gesture carefully. The woman nodded vigorously. The interpreter — Tonya — had lost some fingers. Had it been war or frostbite? Hitler's army or the Gulag?

Then Misha did something else. He put his fingers to the corners of his eyes and pulled them apart, so that his eyelids would appear slanted, like Tonya's. Again the woman nodded, smiling this time.

Misha breathed out with a long shudder of relief and certainty. In an impulse of generosity, he emptied his pockets of all his money, his cigarettes, everything of value that he kept there. He wanted to give something to the girl who had encouraged him with her nod, but he had nothing suitable. He bowed to the woman and to the girl, then left the room.

Tonya was alive and working as a military interpreter somewhere in Germany, most likely in Berlin itself. She had been injured at some point, and Misha felt with a rush of certainty that the Gulag had been responsible. He wouldn't rest until he found her.

11

It was a treat, albeit a small one.

Valentina had been commended by one of her superiors and had been given her own bedroom as a reward. The room was tiny. The bed filled most of the floor space. There was only about fourteen inches between the side of the bed and the wall, and not much more than twice that at the foot. All the same, it had been literally years since either Tonya or Valentina had had anywhere private to sleep and the privilege felt like a tremendous luxury. The two women took their evening meals there together, when they were able, embroidering handkerchiefs for Valentina's niece and chatting.

In the unfamiliar privacy, both women felt an urge to unburden themselves. At one point, Valentina began a conversation in which she attacked the food shortages that were still desperately prevalent at home in Russia. It was the first time either of them had breached their unwritten rule against talking politics. In a sharp voice, Tonya said something of the sort required — no doubts the rumours were exaggerated; it was a soldier's duty not to believe fascistic propaganda; in any case, if comrade Stalin were aware of the problem, it would surely be rapidly dealt with and those responsible punished. Valentina accepted the implicit rebuke, and hung her head and agreed with everything that Tonya had just said, adding a few more contrite phrases of her own.

It was just as well.

Behind their heads, buried in the light fitting, a concealed microphone picked up their words and relayed them to a tape recorder in a downstairs cupboard. When Konstantinov obtained the tapes, he had one of his men listen to them. There wasn't much there, he reported. Just two gossipy women. One of the two — the comrade driver — was prone to spreading anti-Soviet propaganda. Konstantinov shrugged. He knew, of course, that whenever two Russians came together and spoke without fear, the crime of spreading anti-Soviet propaganda was likely to be committed. But still, it was his task to enforce the rules. Every minor infraction punished now meant a major problem avoided later. Valentina was summoned by her commanding officer, reprimanded for believing false rumours, and punished for spreading them. Her private bedroom was removed. She was given four weeks on guard duty, in addition to her existing work as a driver. She was demoted from corporal to a mere *ryadovoy*, or junior private. Valentina, of course, blamed Tonya for denouncing her. Tonya denied the charge. Valentina didn't believe her and refused to see her again.

In the meantime, there was only one other detail of the report that Konstantinov had seen which bothered him. The interpreter, Kornikova, paid regular visits to a German woman who made a little money giving music lessons. Nothing was known against the German woman. On the other hand, she was not known as a Party supporter either. Konstantinov regarded most Germans with suspicion. Not only had their country-men attacked Mother Russia, but their working class had failed to rise in revolution against its masters. Both were valid reasons for suspicion. What was more, though Konstantinov had nothing against music as such, there was no doubting that playing the violin indicated possible bourgeois tendencies.

His investigation still had some way to run.

12

At the door to the Nothing Factory, Misha paused.

Glass was still hard to obtain, so Misha had sealed the only windows with boards. No chink of light peeped through into the star-bitten night, but there was something else, the chirruping sound of Rosa laughing. Misha opened the door and entered.

Although electricity had long been restored across Charlottenberg, the Nothing Factory had no usable electrical circuits, and the only lighting was paraffin lamps. But Misha didn't mind. He almost preferred the dim, kindly light. And, it was clear, Rosa didn't mind either. Before he had left for Leipzig, Misha had taken some pieces of broken glass and fixed them together with wire to make lampshades. During his two days away, Willi had had the idea of painting on the glass in translucent paint and making wire cradles that would allow the shades to revolve. His latest creation set a chain of comical fairy tale creatures — witches, dragons, tigers, dwarfs, princesses — spinning around the light and appearing in huge coloured shadows on the walls.

Rosa turned to the door, saw Misha, and bounced out of her seat and into his arms.

"Look at what Willi's done!"

Misha let Rosa and Willi display their treasures. They had a fairy-tale shade, a sailing-boat shade, an animal shade, and what Willi called his Berliner shade. The last of these had accurate caricatures of all the senior occupation officials and German party men — Sokolovsky, Clay, Robertson, Schumacher and others. Willi put the shade over the lamp and let it revolve. The walls were suddenly full of red and blue painted figures, following each other in an endless, pompous sequence. Misha watched it turn in silence.

"I don't like that one," said Rosa, and Willi removed it.

Misha didn't quite like it either. The little family group had a precarious subsistence living. Whenever it came to jobs that he didn't like — weaving cotton, repairing looms, selling headscarves, bartering for timber or tools — Willi was a maddening combination of lazy and incompetent. It wasn't simply that he was unwilling, although he was, it was that he did jobs ham-fistedly and badly. Yet when it came to things he loved — painting lampshades and creating little wire cradles — his commitment and dexterity seemed to know no limits.

"Have you had supper yet?" Misha asked. "Rosa, it's after your bedtime. Have you washed your face and hands? Willi, is there enough fire in the stove for a hot drink? You do need to keep it stoked, you know, it's not enough just to paint lampshades."

Misha listened to himself scolding and disliked the sound. All the same, he knew that Rosa especially needed structure in her days and it was his job to provide it. He and Willi, with Rosa helping, quickly ran through their domestic chores, clearing up, heating water, getting Rosa ready for bed and then into it. When she was settled down for the night, Willi and Misha sat over their supper (boiled potatoes drizzled with pork fat) and a glass of schnapps.

"Well?" said Willi.

Misha nodded. "She's here. In Germany definitely, Berlin probably. Working as an interpreter for the SMAD." Misha briefly related his adventures.

"You drew her?"

"Well what could I do? The woman wouldn't talk."

"Can I see?"

Misha produced the sketch. The paper was of the worst quality and the ink had already leached outwards, giving the lines a fuzzy, indistinct look. Willi examined the drawing very closely, holding it to the light to see better.

"It's good, very good work. You should draw more. All this technical stuff . . ." Willi shrugged in distaste.

All he'd ever seen Misha draw were quick technical drawings or construction diagrams. He took the drawing and pinned it to the wall, smoothing it carefully. "You know what Rosa said when I told her where you were?"

"No."

"She just nodded and said, 'Oh, of course. He's gone to find the new mummy'."

"Yes, well I'm not sure we should get her hopes up too far."

"Why? She's in Berlin. Berlin isn't so large. We ask around, put up signs. With all the DPs around, it's not so out of the ordinary." DPs were Displaced Persons. And Willi was right. The war had been like a huge cauldron that had swallowed the people of central Europe, stirred them up, then slopped them out all over the place, with no concern for order or logic. All over the place, mothers were looking for sons, husbands for wives, children for parents, women for lovers. A few more posters would hardly draw attention.

But Misha shook his head. All the way back from Leipzig — and the journey had been a long and slow one — he'd puzzled over the same brute facts.

"Think about it. Tonya was interpreting for a Red Army general. That means she's in a very sensitive position. Perhaps she's already spent time in the Gulag, perhaps not. But, given her position, the security people will be keeping a close eye on her in any event. If we start to ask around, it could be dangerous for her. What excuse could we have for asking? If the NKVD are even

211

a tiny bit suspicious they'll order her away. Out of Berlin. Out of Germany even."

He didn't add, but he hardly needed to, that Tonya's fate could be still worse than that. Willi had once drawn a cartoon of the Soviet far north as a huge genie, sucking whole populations into its belly as forced labourers and political prisoners. The risk was horribly real.

"Perhaps we don't ask, then. If she works with the SMAD, I suppose she must enter or leave their buildings, whether in Karlshorst or elsewhere . . ."

He trailed off. The SMAD had facilities all over the Soviet sector and who was to say where she might be located? But even suppose they were willing to try staking out one establishment after another. Every single SMAD building was protected by Red Army guards and by NKVD men, both uniformed and not. For Misha and Willi to try staking out SMAD facilities in plain view of the cream of the Soviet security services would be simply asking for trouble.

Silence fell. Tonya was here in Berlin, but as distant as the sky. The problem seemed all but insoluble. Willi rolled his schnapps around in his glass. Since Rosa had joined them, Misha had started treating Willi less like a friend and more like a son. He didn't feel himself in a position to withdraw all Willi's old privileges — the boy was seventeen after all — but he did now set limits to them. One small glass of schnapps was Willi's nightly limit. The boy grumbled, but he'd become more secure, more grounded, happier.

"Were you angry about the lampshades?" asked Willi.

"No."

"I didn't pick up that steel wire you wanted. I was going to, but I forgot and then it was too late."

"That's all right. I'll pick it up tomorrow."

Misha frowned into his own drink. It was clear that Willi would be useless as a cotton headscarf entrepreneur. He was more trouble than he was worth even as a simple loom operator. There wasn't a shortage of labour in Berlin of course. The whole city was full of hungry people, who'd do anything in exchange for enough Reichsmarks or cigarettes to buy food and fuel for their families. But sometimes Misha felt burdened by it all, the need to build and mend his looms, find labour, barter for supplies, sell goods, and all the while provide a good home environment for Rosa, cook their meals, attend to their domestic needs. It was a big sackful of troubles to carry by himself. He sighed.

Willi looked savagely into the lamplight. He picked up his glass "Berliner" shade again, settled it back on the lamp and sent it spinning wildly around on its stand. The huge shadows whirled and flashed on the walls.

"I'm not much use to you, though am I? You don't need to deny it."

"You help look after Rosa."

"That's hardly an affliction, is it?"

"And you can maybe help me in one other way."

"*Ja?*" Willi had stopped the lampshade. With a dab of red ink, he adjusted his profile of Sokolovsky, to add more strut, more exaggerated swagger.

"I think it's hopeless for us to look for Tonya. Hopeless for us. Dangerous for her."

"You won't even try?" Willi was incredulous.

"No. She needs to look for us. But first we need to tell her that we're here."

Willi put his brush and ink carefully away. He was more careful of his brushes than of anything else in the happy disorder of his life. He spun the shade again, but slowly this time, solemnly.

"And how do we do that?"

Misha shook his head. "No, Willi. Not we, you."

13

It was three weeks later, dinner-time on a Sunday evening.

Misha always sought to provide meat for them all at least once a week, and Willi, whose stomach was bottomless, was almost never late. But on this occasion he was nowhere to be seen and had left no word as to where he was. Misha kept the stew heating for a while, then decided to eat anyway.

Rosa, reading his thoughts as ever, said, "Don't worry. It's only Willi being late."

"Of course it is," he told her, worrying anyway.

They ate. Rosa was having a phase of not enjoying vegetables, and it took her twenty minutes to finish her red cabbage, which she ate by picking out one long strand at a time and dropping it into her mouth from above. Misha told her that the cabbage would make her grow big and strong. Rosa rolled her eyes at him, in scepticism.

Then, at last, there was the clattering outside which signified that Willi had arrived on his push-bike and had flung it up to rest against the metal dustbins. Rosa clapped her hands, and Misha too felt an immediate lightening of worry.

Willi entered.

"Food! I'm not late, am I? I'm starving. I had to go to Rudi's to get some proper ink. My inks were getting too faint to use."

Beneath his arm, he held a long tube of paper. Misha, knowing what it was, was excited about seeing it, but Willi insisted that the paper was frozen and that it needed to thaw out properly before it could be unrolled. He warmed it through over the stove. Misha cleared a space on the table and moved the lamp back to make room. When Willi was finally happy, he unfurled the paper — a big, poster-sized sheet of it — and laid it out.

Misha caught his breath.

There were six cartoon strips, each four or five frames in length.

Each strip revolved around a single invented character, an ordinary Russian soldier, a Red Army *frontovik*, endearing, tipsy, accident-prone. The character had a pot-belly, an expression of happy and peaceable mystification, and a short wooden rifle that could threaten no one and nothing. The little soldier was an appealing sort — slow-witted perhaps, but charming.

215

The sort of man anyone would take a liking to in an instant, befriend in a moment.

The cartoons were excellent. Funny and touching at the same time. Rosa, who didn't entirely understand the point of them, chuckled at the friendly, dumpy little chap. Misha too was struck by Willi's talent for these things. The cartoon strips told of the little man's adventures in all the situations that so baffled, enraged and exasperated Berliners. No one could read these cartoons and not laugh at the humour, smile at the accuracy.

But their true genius lay elsewhere. Because the good-natured *frontovik* was called Comrade Lensky — the name which gave the cartoon strip its title. Lensky's best friend, who featured in every cartoon, was a brilliant caricature of Misha himself and was called Mikhail Kuletsky. And every single cartoon, every single story contained buried references to a past that only Misha and a certain female Red Army interpreter could understand. There were references to hunting lodges, waltzes, an empty safe, railway repairs, the hot white nights of Petrograd, a woman and boy making an escape under piles of grain . . .

Misha scrutinised the cartoon that lay immediately in front of him. This one, the first, was making a series of well-aimed jokes about the pitiful rations handed out by the Western Allies. The cartoon was pithy, well-drawn, funny and likeable. But there was something missing. Misha sat and pondered without getting anywhere. Willi, with a sudden impatient movement, signified that he was waiting for a reaction.

216

"They're brilliant, Willi. You have a natural genius for these things . . ."

Then he got it — the thing that was missing. The cartoon, of course, had its title in German: *Kamerad Lensky*. That was fine, of course, but Tonya would never have seen her name written that way. Why would she? Misha took the sheet and, beneath the main title of the first strip, he wrote the same thing in Russian: Товарищ Ленски He put pen and paper down. The ink dried from glistening black to a dark grey-purple.

Misha breathed slowly through his mouth.

He felt strange, a feeling of warmth spreading outwards from his chest to reach every part of his body. And though he'd never encountered the feeling before, he understood it instantly. It was a sense of certainty, a recognition of when something was absolutely right. Because this cartoon was exactly that. If Tonya saw the cartoon, she couldn't help but understand its message: the names, the buried references, Misha's own pet name for her written in his own handwriting. And at the bottom of every strip was a name and address: Willi Nichts, the Nothing Factory, Leipzigestrasse, Charlottenberg.

"They're perfect, Willi, perfect."

Misha added the same title, Товарищ Ленски, to the remaining strips, then stepped back, almost shocked at how good his idea was proving to be. Willi hung out with a group of journalists, satirists and artists who produced (very irregularly) a free newspaper called *Die Trümmerzeitung*, "The Rubble Gazette". In return for a few cartons of cigarettes, *Die Trümmerzeitung* would print Willi's cartoons. Misha and Willi would paste them up over Berlin, the Soviet sector especially, using the sides of buildings, trees, burned-out vehicles and anything else by way of hoardings. Such posters were fairly common these days. The Soviet authorities destroyed anything they didn't approve of, but the *Kamerad Lensky* strip was endearing, funny — and consistently mocked only the Western military authorities. The Soviets, hopefully, would leave the cartoons up, till rain and ice destroyed them. Then they'd print more strips, paste them up again, and so on.

And if Tonya saw them she would understand. The cartoons were a love letter, addressed to her. All she needed to do was to walk across town and be in Misha's arms again.

CHAPTER
SEVEN

1

The first winter of occupied rule had been a bad one.

The weather had been cold. In parts of the country, snow had drifted in places up to ten feet high. Old folk, living in cellars, had had their doorways sealed in by snow and only the determined rescue efforts of neighbours and friends had kept casualties down.

In the meantime, the Allies, Western and Soviet, continued to struggle. The loveless peace between occupiers and occupied still held, but things were going downhill. The food rations were set far too low for an active population enduring bitter weather, but even those rations weren't enough. There were shortages of meat, eggs, milk, potatoes, coal, electricity, clothing. The denazification process swelled until more and more ordinary Germans were lapped in its coils. Rumours about the living standards of the occupying forces swirled with increasing bitterness in the freezing air. The French were always drunk like pigs. Black American soldiers could buy a German girl for one bar of chocolate. The English were arrogant and treated Germany like a part of imperial India. The only industries which flourished were prostitution and the black market. There was no money that meant anything, only cigarettes.

And, in the meantime, the Soviets had continued to work towards a Germany that would be united under Communist rule. Their plan — bold in the extreme — was to merge the Communist Party with the pre-war Social Democrats. The intention was to use the new party to win democratic elections — then swallow the country. The whole country that is: not just the east zone, but the west zones too, bringing communist rule to the shores of the North Sea.

But the plan was failing. Badly. Horribly. In the west, the Social Democrats were contemptuously refusing to have anything to do with the proposed merger. In the east, the merger was being forced through, by a combination of lies, bullying, thuggery and bribes. But even in the east, no one trusted the new party. That was good news of a sort — but dangerous too.

How would Stalin react to the setback in the west? What would he do to harden his control over the east? And most of all, what of the original plan? What of the idea that Germany would remain one country, under joint four-power control? Most of all, what would happen to Berlin? The city was completely surrounded by the Soviet zone. If the Russians and the Western Allies finally fell out, what would happen to Berlin? Would Stalin take it, as he had already taken so much else? And if so, then what would happen to its people? Worse still, what would the rest of Europe think of an America and Britain so weak as to let it happen? If

Berlin fell, what else might yet tumble? Austria? Germany? Italy? France?

As so often before, there were a million questions and no answers. The mood was bad. It was late March, 1946.

2

In the schoolyards of Hancock County, Kentucky, a promise sealed "spit 'n' shake" was a promise that could never be broken. And Harlan Bauer kept his word. He'd sent urgent requests to the governor of every district asking them to search their records for a Mikhail, or Michael, Malevich. Negative answers had begun to pour in. But Bauer kept the pressure up. He told those who'd answered too quickly to check again. He told those who answered too slowly to speed up.

And one day he got lucky.

A thick-witted, fat-necked, gum-chewing, German-hating Yankee major from the subterranean reaches of a hopelessly over-tangled military bureaucracy came up trumps. He had met Malevich and interviewed him. A movement authorisation had been applied for, granted, then never claimed. The major was based just a few blocks away here in Berlin, so Bauer went to interview the man. The major blustered, denied, chewed gum and defended — then admitted that as well as processing the movement order, he'd made a point of handing Malevich's details over to the Russians.

Bauer had been furious.

"You say the guy was a German citizen, who'd spent the war in camps? That he'd been persecuted by both the Commies and the Nazis? Then — Jesus — this guy's life hasn't been bad enough, you gotta go see if you can screw it up even worse!"

Bauer was out of line. Both men were majors but the other man was the senior. All the same, Bauer was in the right, the other man was in the wrong, and the sheer force of Bauer's personality made him intimidating.

As soon as Bauer returned to his desk, he called Hollinger and gave him the news. Hollinger sent a man over to the address Bauer gave him, a ruined factory somewhere in Charlottenberg. The man Hollinger sent found a trio of women working some home-made weaving looms. The women told him that no one of the name Malevich lived there now, if ever. The only permanent residents were a man named Müller, a teenage boy who called himself Willi Nichts, and a little girl whom Müller had adopted. Questioned further, the women said that yes, they thought the NKVD had once raided the property. The boy, Willi Nichts, had been beaten and hospitalised. Perhaps there had been an abduction too; but if so they hadn't heard about it.

Hollinger's man checked dates and names with the hospital in question. The facts all seemed to match up.

The conclusion seemed inescapable. Malevich — the man whom Kornikova so badly wanted to find again — had been living right here under her nose in Berlin. A shamefully wrong-headed bureaucratic decision had allowed the NKVD to discover Malevich's identity.

Never ones to allow a supposed crime from twenty-five years back to be forgotten, the NKVD had come crashing in to try and snatch him. Perhaps they'd succeeded or perhaps they'd failed, but if so then Malevich had obviously gone on the run again, maybe changing his name, faking his papers. He could be anywhere now, under any name, impossible to find.

Hollinger's normally sunny face grew cloudy, even brutal.

The agent Kornikova was just about old enough to be Hollinger's mother, but she never seemed that way to him. Quite the reverse. Despite the life she'd led, despite the suffering and loss, there was something youthful about her, something light but also strong and enduring. Hollinger admitted to himself that he was emotionally bound up with Kornikova — not in a romantic way, but not in a mother-son way either. He just cared about her very deeply. It mattered to him, to an excessive and unprofessional degree, that her life should turn out for the best.

The first rule of sound intelligence is to avoid getting personally involved. Hollinger knew that. He believed in the rule. But he broke it anyway. He cared about Kornikova and his attachment blinded him.

3

Tonya had been busy.

She'd been hauled off to interpret on a long tour of industrial sites that took in Frankfurt an der Oder, Guben, Cotbus, the terribly ruined city of Dresden,

Leipzig, Dessau, Brandenburg, Potsdam. She had been interpreting for a party of technical experts from Moscow, and every day had been long and tiring, ending with feasts of vodka and wild boar that ran late into the night. On top of that, the weather had been difficult, a sudden thaw and heavy rain combining to make the roads heavy and often impassable. She ended the ten-day tour with a bad head cold and a mountain of paperwork.

She worked till eleven o'clock that night, then walked back to her sleeping quarters, a former *Wehrmacht* barracks, a place of long concrete corridors, harsh lighting, echoing toilet blocks, and green-painted plywood doors. She reached her dormitory: eight narrow beds under high metal-paned windows. Between each bed, there was a gap of around twenty inches. Tonya was now *starshiy serzhant*, senior sergeant, and her rank had been recognised by the award of a corner bed and a small bedside table. She knew that her past would probably prevent her from rising further, but she liked the little privileges that she now possessed. She didn't allow herself to think of that blue-and-gold passport, or Thompson's rose-covered cottage. As far as possible, she didn't even think of Misha, though that was like asking the bird not to think of the wind.

She made her way to the toilet block to get ready for bed. She washed her face and hands. And she went to the lavatory, one of a row of six doorless cubicles.

There was no lavatory paper, of course, just a pile of newspaper. The most easily available newspaper was the *Krasnaya Zvezda*, the Red Army publication, but most soldiers were scared of being caught wiping their bottoms on one of Stalin's speeches and any alternatives were eagerly seized on. Today, at the top of the pile, there was a strip torn from one of the unauthorised single-sheet newspapers that were to be seen around Berlin. Tonya was just about to make use of the strip, when the drawing on it caught her eye.

The cartoon itself was an excellent example of the genre — well-drawn, characterful, engaging — but it was the title that grabbed her attention. The cartoon strip was entitled *Kamerad Lensky* and beneath the title, in hand-written Russian lettering, the translation: Товарищ Ленски

Tonya stared and stared and stared and stared.

The name itself was not uncommon. It was similar in occurrence to the German "Schneider", or the English "Wilson". But the handwriting! Surely that was Misha's own handwriting, with its characteristic flicked tail to the "Л" and the "Щ"? Tonya desperately wanted to see more — but the cartoon had been torn. She held not even half of it in her hand. The cartoonist's name, or pen-name more like, was given at the bottom: Willi Nichts. Perhaps there was more — more handwriting, some further clues, an address even? — but not in the scrap which was all Tonya possessed. She searched her own stall, then all the others, for further copies. There was nothing. She even went down the hall into the privates' toilet block to search there. Still nothing.

She went back to that first little scrap and interrogated it. The handwriting, which had first

225

seemed so intensely familiar, dissolved into mystery. It wasn't exactly the same as she had remembered it — but twenty-five years had passed since she had known Misha. Of course his handwriting would have changed. Then again, Tonya knew that she so strongly *wanted* the writing to be Misha's that her judgement was hardly likely to be reliable.

Was she crazy to be thinking of him again? What were the odds against such a thing? And yet, and yet . . . great as the odds looked, they shrank away as Tonya thought about it. She had always expected Misha to end up in Germany — he'd always said that Germany was the engineering capital of the world. And if he'd come to Germany, then why not Berlin? And if Berlin, then it was perfectly conceivable that he might have caught sight of her, or heard her name. And if he had seen her, still loved her, still cared about her, then how else could he find her, but by asking in code if she would return to him?

Her heart crashed against her chest.

Back in the sergeants' and petty officers' toilet block, she stood in front of the only mirror, a dingy, fly-spattered affair. She unfastened her hair, combing it behind her with her fingers. She had aged. Her hair — the colour of the forest floor, as Misha had once described it — was flecked with grey now. Lines had crept into her face. Her green eyes were still bright and clear, but she'd never liked her eyes, never quite accepting their slightly eastern look. She had grown thinner too, lost some of her old soft roundness. In the old days, Misha had always been the lean one. Perhaps, as she'd aged, she'd somehow taken on something of him, his energy, his leanness. She hoped so.

Was he here in Berlin? Just miles away? Looking for her?

It seemed impossible and all too likely, both at once. Tonya didn't know what to think. But the art of living without hope that she'd once learned in the Gulag was lost to her now. Hollinger had started her on her new course, Valentina had confirmed it.

She had begun to hope, begun to trust. She washed her face, tied up her hair and went to bed, tremulous with fear and hope, love and anxiety.

4

Marta Kappelhoff, Tonya's piano teacher and "handler", had her day job working in one of the construction crews in Prenzlauer Berg. The phrase "construction crew" was the one favoured by the city authorities, but rubble-clearance not construction was their primary task. Marta herself was too slightly built to be of much use carrying buckets or pushing barrows, so she passed her day using a small hammer to chip mortar off bricks, so that the bricks could be reused. It was slow work. Slow and cold. At the end of the day, Marta either went directly back to her apartment or went shopping for food in one of the street markets that thrived alongside the old Zeiss Planetarium.

But today was Tuesday, and every Tuesday and Thursday she visited her mother who lived on the edge of Berlin, out at Neukölln, not far from Tempelhof airport. Her way took her through one of the most comprehensively damaged parts of Berlin, where the Soviet Eighth Guards Army and the First Guards Tank Army had battered their way through German defences. In that fighting, buildings already wrecked by Allied bombs had been further pounded. Ruins to rubble; rubble to powder.

Marta's shoes crunched on gritty mud. Recent wet weather had made the roads stream with dirty grey. The sun had just set, and the sky was violet streaked with red. One of Marta's shoelaces was loose, and needed retying. She came to a corner, glanced ahead and behind her, saw nothing, then stepped lightly into a ruined doorway and thrust her hand into a pocket-sized gap in the masonry. When Hollinger wanted to get a message to her, he left it here. When she wanted to communicate with him, she did it the same way. But today the gap was empty and the doorway wasn't.

"Marta."

Harry Hollinger moved silently in the gloom, holding his finger up to stifle any involuntary exclamation. The exclamation came, but very quietly.

"Thompson! You shouldn't be here!"

"No, not exactly. But don't worry, we checked the place very carefully before I stopped off."

"What is it? Bad news?"

"No, no, nothing like that. Information for Kornikova, that's all."

"Oh?"

"We've looked for Malevich and we've got news, some good, some bad. The good part is that Malevich is certainly alive or at least he was a few months ago. The Soviets found out about him, tried to grab him, but failed. The bad part is that he's no longer living at his old address. I guess he's tried to run from Berlin into the Allied zones, maybe under an assumed name. That's certainly what I'd do if I were him. You can tell Kornikova all that, and you can promise her that we'll continue to look."

Marta stared furiously at the Englishman.

"You came to tell me that? You could have written it. You didn't need to come here. You shouldn't have come."

Marta lit a cigarette and retied her lace — her excuses for using the doorway. Glaring again at Hollinger, she left, moving briskly and angrily up the street.

Hidden away in the fold of some tumbled masonry, Ekaterina Ershova, junior sergeant in the NKVD, hesitated. Her instructions were to follow this woman, Marta Kappelhoff, but they were also to note and pursue anything out of the ordinary that happened along the way. But what did "out of the ordinary" mean? Kappelhof had stepped into a doorway to light a cigarette and retie a shoelace. Why not? Ershova might have done the same thing.

Only two things bothered her. Kappelhoff didn't smoke much. Only two or three cigarettes a day, according to the report she'd seen. And it was a still night. It would have been easy to light up here on the street, there was no need to find the shelter of a doorway. And why the delay? Ershova couldn't help feeling that Kappelhoff had spent just a few seconds too long out of sight of the street.

Ershova continued to hesitate. If she were going to continue following Kappelhoff, she would need to do so at once, or give up altogether. But the woman was surely on her way to her mother's. Ershova reasoned she could always catch up with her later.

She continued to hesitate, then decided to stay. She remained in position, hidden by the wall in front of her, watching the street turn slowly from grey to black.

5

The night proved as exhausting as the day.

It wasn't that Tonya couldn't sleep. She did. But all night long, the cartoon haunted her. Or rather, in her strange dream-state, it had seemed to her as though she were the cartoon, as though she herself were the little black-ink figure of Comrade Lensky, with his slight paunch, his bulging eyes, his air of slightly baffled mystification. In the guise of this comical little figure, she had spent the whole night wandering Berlin — or rather, the line-drawn, cartoon version of the city — searching for Misha. Every sign, every shop window, every notice was written in Cyrillic; handwritten; with those little flicked tails, once so characteristic of Misha, and now . . .? It hadn't even been clear in the dream whether she was looking for Misha the person, Misha the cartoon, or Misha the artist who had drawn or dreamed the whole thing. The entire intense dream had lasted from the moment she had closed her eyes to the moment that she was physically pummelled awake by her neighbour in the dormitory, long after the reveille bell had sounded.

And now? Well, Tonya knew she had to go directly to her Mühlendamm office. The work there had piled up. She was sure to be reprimanded if she were even a few moments late. But though there were limits on her freedom, she was no prisoner. She was a *starshiy serzhant* in the Red Army. She could come and go as she pleased. In her lunch hour, after work, while out on errands. Surely, surely, she would be able to find half an hour to walk the streets in search of another copy of that precious cartoon. And if all else failed, then it would only be another week before she had her next violin lesson with Marta.

For now, though, waiting that week seemed like being asked to stand still while a century passed. She sped to work. After the night she'd just had, Tonya had expected to find work slow and difficult, but for some reason the opposite happened. She raced through her work like never before. The Russian sentences had formed themselves in her head before her eye had even reached the full stop in the German text. Her fingers flew over the typewriter. The thirty-two typebars of the Cyrillic alphabet danced like a small black cloud of angrily buzzing insects over the page. Time flew by.

Then, at around eleven fifteen, Tonya got up to go to the toilet. There was no chance of finding that cartoon again here: the Mühlendamm office was used by a number of high-ranking officials and all the cubicles were stocked with plain grey toilet roll imported from a

231

factory in the old East Prussia. She began to return to her desk, but in the hall outside her office, she encountered a group of senior occupation officials, including a number of the technical experts she had accompanied over the last ten days. She saluted the Red Army officers, then stood aside, not wanting to barge her way through the crowd to get back to her desk. She didn't listen to the conversation, just waited quietly. A few minutes passed. Then the posture of the group in front of her suddenly changed. Tonya looked up. She saw General Sokolovsky himself stride down the corridor towards them. Tonya, and all the other soldiers present, braced themselves into a stiff, formal salute. Sokolovsky swept up. There was a brief conversation. An important meeting was about to take place in Karlshorst. Some of the technical experts were required to be there. Yes, there would be German-only speakers present also. Interpreters would be required. Sokolovsky jerked his head impatiently, not wanting to be bothered with details. One of the technical experts pointed at Tonya.

"Sergeant Kornikova, there. She can interpret."

Sokolovsky nodded and waved his hand. "Come." It was an order.

6

The thirty-six hours which followed that instruction were among the strangest of Tonya's life.

For one thing, she didn't sleep, not even for a minute. For another, the meeting she was asked to attend — or meetings, rather, because one symposium rolled on into another, in seemingly interminable sequence — turned out to be of the highest possible importance to the future of the Soviet Union in Germany. All the most senior officials were there, Russian and German. The purpose of the meeting was to present Soviet plans for the east zone, and elsewhere in the emerging Soviet bloc. A succession of speakers from Poland, Czechoslovakia, Hungary, Austria, Romania, Bulgaria, and Yugoslavia were there to survey the progress of the Communist Party in their home countries. The meeting rooms echoed with the sound of Russian triumphalism, Russian greed.

And that in turn led to the third strange aspect of the whole experience. A vital document, with the highest security classification available, needed to be translated into German. The document summarised the state of the Communist presence throughout Germany, east and west zones together. The longest single section was on Berlin itself. Tonya was ordered to carry out the translation. It was that task which kept her up the entire night, as all the others were either feasting or sleeping. Page after page swooped through her typewriter. The state of the Communist advance was carefully analysed. Key Communist sympathisers were named, as were the Party's most important opponents. In the latter case, the individuals weren't just named, they were evaluated for their susceptibility to bribery and blackmail. The weaknesses of the Western Allies were listed in precise and remorseless detail. Without question, the document was the most shocking, comprehensive and important information that Tonya had ever come across. She had been asked to type up three copies of the whole thing: three thin white sheets interspersed with flimsy black carbon papers. She typed in a trance, her fingers rubbery with tiredness, her mind spinning with the implications of the text in front of her.

And automatically, almost without consciously choosing to do it, she changed the topmost carbon paper after every page of typing and retained it. By the end of the night, she had thirty-eight sheets of carbon paper. The dimpled black surface wasn't possible to read with the naked eye, but each key stroke had made an impression which would certainly be visible under magnification. As dawn broke over the city, Tonya shuffled her carbons together into a stack and folded them twice. The package was too large to fit into her hollowed-out boot heel. So, silently borrowing some sewing things from the desk of a female worker, she slit her boot lining at the top, placed the papers inside, then sewed up the incision. She was a good seamstress and her work was practically invisible. She continued to work on lesser documents, until the meetings reconvened at around eight o'clock. By this time, she was so tired, so overcome, that she hardly felt the size of the risk she was taking.

But the strangest thing of all was yet to come.

At one point that morning, Sokolovsky was called away to the telephone. It was clear that he was speaking directly to Moscow. A whispered rumour went around the room that the general was speaking to Stalin himself. During the interval, people relaxed and joked.

Cigarettes were lit and the air turned blue with the smoke. Over in one corner of the room, people began laughing and passing some printed poster-sized pages around. The pages circulated around the room. Wherever they passed, people bent over them; read them and chuckled. Then they reached Tonya.

It was the cartoons again. Comrade Lensky, with his little pot-belly and his comical strutting walk.

Tonya's tiredness dropped away from her in an instant. She felt as fresh and clear as if she'd just bathed in ice melt-water. She scanned the cartoons with astonishment. Now that she had them in her hand, an entire page of them, their message was clear beyond doubt. There were references everywhere. To Tonya's maiden name. To Misha's mother and Tonya's father. To Kuletsky Prospekt and the hunting lodge in Petrozavodsk. To waltzes and sleigh-loads of black-market logs and china figurines from Meissen. And the clinching thing was Lensky's best friend, a perfectly drawn caricature of Misha himself. And at the bottom of the page there was a name, Willi Nichts, and an address in Charlottenberg. The entire page was an invitation addressed to Tonya.

All that remained was for her to walk across town, and come home at last.

7

Konstantinov gave a short, sharp nod.

Lieutenant Bezarin, a burly Siberian peasant, built short and square, gave the door a thundering kick about nine inches left of the lock. Nothing happened. Behind Konstantinov and Bezarin there stood a pair of NKVD men armed with axes. One of them made as if to step forwards, but Bezarin shook his head. He stood ox-like in front of the door, his big head slightly swaying on his shoulders. He collected himself, his small eyes narrowly focused on the part of the door that had resisted his kick. There was another second or two of silence, then Bezarin collected himself and crashed into the door again. The wood splintered and broke. The metal lock was torn from the frame. The door smashed open. Bezarin, tumbling forwards, lay happily smiling in the debris.

"*Harasho*," he said. "Good."

The owner of the apartment, the German woman Marta Kappelhoff, was away at work. She would be gone all day. Konstantinov and his men moved slowly into the apartment, savouring the moment.

8

One of the Moscow technical experts was describing the scope for further industrial reparations from the region about Leipzig. His Russian was dense with technical terms, unnecessary jargon, and mangled grammar. His pauses were too short for Tonya to translate effectively. Ignoring her difficulties, the expert ran on, as though deliberately making life hard for her. Tonya, already dazed with tiredness and the events of the previous twenty-four hours, began mumbling and getting her sentences confused. Sokolovsky, who was present at the meeting, banged the table with his fist and glared at her. The room went suddenly silent. Tonya swallowed nervously. Then Sokolovsky's face changed. He had it in him to be genial and humorous, and something lit up in his expression now.

"You were interpreting yesterday also?"

"Yes sir."

"And this morning, since how early?"

Tonya hesitated. How was she to answer that, since she hadn't been to bed?

"Well?"

The general's face was a curious combination of inviting and stormy. On an impulse, Tonya decided to trust him and speak the truth.

"Very early, I suppose, sir. I was translating documents through the night. I haven't slept."

The general's face blackened and he turned to the technical expert. "You haven't slept and now this block-head who can't even speak proper Russian makes your life hell! Idiot!" The technical expert went pale and took a step or two back. The silence in the room continued, as people waited for Sokolovsky's next pronouncement. The great man consulted his watch. It was five to twelve. "Lunch," he roared, adding in a quieter voice to Tonya, "eat well, finish this afternoon's session, then get some rest. Well done."

His attention turned away from her, and towards the meal that would be awaiting them all downstairs: huge bowlfuls of soup, full of beans, cabbage, onion, beetroot, and ham. There would be black bread and the pale yellow butter of the local German creameries.

237

But Tonya didn't want food. In a daze, she began to walk downstairs, heading for the open air. The carbon papers in the lining of her boot formed a stiff band down the outside of her right calf. Although the actual physical pressure was very slight, the crashing significance of those papers suddenly seemed so intense that it was all Tonya could do to avoid walking with a limp. She was suddenly appalled at herself for the risk she was taking. What had she been thinking of?

She knew the answer, of course. Quite simply, when she had taken the carbon papers, she had no real expectation of finding Misha again. Now, just a few hours later, she didn't just know that Misha was alive, she knew where he was living. She had read, that very morning, an invitation conceived by him and addressed to her, an invitation that asked her to find him, to live with him, to marry him . . . In contrast with the crashing importance of those facts, her own feelings on the German situation, on the importance of helping Mark Thompson, suddenly paled into insignificance, a candle flame in sunlight.

She walked into the grandiose Karlshorst lobby, once adorned with Nazi flags, now spread with red banners and Soviet slogans. The blood seemed to pulse with strange forcefulness in her calf, as though her heart had slipped and was beating down there instead. She glanced outside. It was a brilliant day. It had snowed overnight, perhaps the last real snowfall of spring, and the bright March sunshine leaped from drift to drift, splashing brilliant reflections and the hard diamond glitter of ice in every direction. Outside a car stopped.

An NKVD captain, recognisable from the royal blue splashes on his uniform, got out. Tonya recognised him. It was Arkady Konstantinov. There was something alert and bounding in his stride, something that reminded Tonya of a hunting dog at work. The captain, followed by two of his men, strode towards the front entrance.

Tonya recoiled backwards. There was no logic at work that made her do it, just the thumping pressure in her boot. She bumped backwards through a side door, and found herself in a passage from which a number of low-level clerical offices opened. It was the lunch hour and most of the offices were empty. Tonya went into one of them and sat down. Her head was thumping. She missed Misha like a physical pain in her side. A small part of her wondered at the strangeness of seeing him again after so long, but not most of her. Mostly, she knew that after being with Misha for a single minute, it would be exactly the same as if they had never been apart. It was as though a fragile porcelain cup had been carried through the battlefields of the Eastern front, from Stalingrad to Berlin, and ended up exactly the same: unchipped, unbroken, uncracked. It might be a miracle, but if so, it was a miracle Tonya knew she could rely on.

But she didn't want to go to Misha with these lethally dangerous papers in her possession. She unpicked the thread on her boot lining with a pair of scissors. She pulled the thread free and drew out the folded black carbons. Now in her hand, it seemed like a very fragile cargo for a thing of so high a value. She had an impulse simply to throw them away. Who would

239

bother to check some discarded carbon papers lying with other rubbish in a wastebasket? But she held back. Some sense of loyalty to Thompson stopped her. That, and a sense of how important they were, a sense of how much they mattered to the future of Germany, the future of Europe. She hesitated. There was movement in the passage outside, but it was only office workers going to or from the canteen.

She continued to dither.

What had brought Konstantinov here? It could be anything, of course. Karlshorst was the headquarters of the Russian occupation in Germany. Konstantinov could have a hundred reasons for coming, none of them likely to be connected with her. All the same, she remembered the glimpse she'd had of him. His bright face and eager strides. He had reminded her a little of Rodyon, back in the old days, the first days of the Revolution, when he'd stridden around Moscow seeking to put old wrongs right . . .

An envelope lay on the desk in front of her. She shoved the carbon papers into the envelope, then ran the envelope into a typewriter and paused over the keys. She wanted to send the package to Mark Thompson, but she knew that that wasn't his real name, nor did she possess an address for him. What about Marta? But envelopes leaving Karlshorst didn't generally go to German citizens of no importance. Tonya paused another fraction of a second, then began to type. She had decided that the envelope should go to a senior official in the British military government; and the more senior the better, because the envelope was less likely to be tampered with on the way. She typed in the name and address of a major-general in the British sector, whose contact details she happened to know from her other work. She completed the address, then realised she had typed over the carbons inside. Oh well, there was nothing to be done about that. She pulled the envelope free of the typewriter and went to the door of the office.

There were a couple of people in the passage outside, but no one of significance. No Konstantinov. No NKVD men. She went to the door leading into the lobby and peeped through. No Konstantinov. There were a couple of NKVD men, but there always were. No one seemed unusually on the lookout. There was a uniformed driver collecting packages from the central desk. A murmur of conversation carried across the room, amplified by the stone walls and floors. And suddenly, Tonya was walking out across the lobby, striding briskly towards the desk. The driver was only a *yefreytor*, a senior private and a glorified messenger boy. Tonya handed him her envelope.

"And quickly now," she snapped, "this one's urgent."

The driver nodded, acknowledging Tonya's rank. He tucked the envelope in with the rest. Tonya walked towards the door of the lobby, followed by the driver. She stepped outside. The sunlight and the snow stung her eyes, but stung in a good way, stung in a way that marked the end of one thing and the start of another. She heard the driver start up his car and move off.

Karlshorst was on the eastern edge of Berlin. It was here that the Soviet 5th Shock Army had pounded its way into Berlin. It was here that the German armed forces had finally signed the document of surrender. It was a long walk from here to Charlottenberg, to "Willi Nichts" and the "Nothing Factory". But the walk meant nothing. The past no longer meant anything. In two hours, no more, Tonya would be in Misha's arms. She began to walk westwards down the street.

Seven minutes later, Captain Arkady Konstantinov of the NKVD came running into the Karlshorst lobby, followed by his two men. He sprang to the front entrance and gazed up and down the street. There were a few women around, including a couple of Red Army soldiers, but no sign of Tonya. Konstantinov went to the driver of a Tatra truck that was unloading boxes at a side entrance. He asked the driver for information about Tonya's movements. The driver shrugged and pointed.

Konstantinov climbed into his jeep and took the wheel. His two men climbed in after him. Konstantinov raced up through the gears, turning sharply and driving snow upwards in a fine white arc.

The jeep disappeared, heading west.

9

Sixty-five minutes later, at one twenty-two that afternoon, a curious scene took place at the Brandenburg Gate.

A woman, a Red Army sergeant, warmly dressed against the cold, was walking briskly past the gate, crossing from the Soviet sector to the British one. The woman was in her forties and her life had clearly etched its difficulties in the lines of her face. All the same, though, there was something ineffably bright about her, something joyous. Her walk wasn't just brisk, it was also full of life, movement and hope.

Whatever the reason for the woman's optimism, she certainly had a fine day for it. Snow lay around, with the brightness of a new fall. The air was cold and sharp. A brilliant sun marked every shadow with a crisp, clear edge, so the solemn shape of the big limestone arches, all the more solemn for being war-damaged, was repeated in perfect outline on the ground. The air was perfectly still.

The woman had crossed through. That is to say, she had left the Soviet sector and she was clearly inside the British zone. There was a trio of British Tommies just in front of the Reichstag, or whatever was left of it, and those soldiers were absolutely certain of the point. But it made no difference. Why should it? Berlin was one city, Germany was one country. Invisible lines on the ground should make no difference, and they didn't.

The woman, walking fast, was beginning to jink right, as though intending to skirt the Tiergarten to the north. But then, from behind her, a Russian jeep, a UAZ diesel with its engine grindingly loud in the silent air, came hurtling too fast down the snowy roads. The sound caught the woman's attention. She turned. As she did so, she thought to put her hand to her head, pulling down her army cap so that her face was partly covered by its brim. But the movement was an afterthought. It came a second or two later than it should have done if she had wanted to remain concealed. But it made no difference, in any event. There was nothing so uncommon about seeing Red Army troops in the western sectors, but then again there weren't all that many middle-aged female Red Army sergeants to be found in the Tiergarten either.

The jeep driver saw the woman. The driver turned the wheel and the jeep made a long skidding turn that flung it twenty or thirty feet sideways across the snow. But then the wheels got traction again. The woman began to run. But she had nowhere to run to. The jeep caught up with her. Three men tumbled out of it. The woman was still running, her face completely panicked now, all her joy, her zest for life, utterly extinguished by the sight of her pursuers. The woman made a good job of it. She made eighty, maybe even a hundred yards, keeping her footing well on the icy streets.

But it was one against three, a woman against men, fit middle-age against the arrogant good health of youth. The captain caught her. The other men swung around either side of her. Panting breathlessly, the men frog-marched their captive back to the jeep.

The British Tommies saw it all. One of them, a lance-corporal, was unable to control his feelings. He came running over to the Russians.

"You bastards," he shouted. "You fucking bastards lay a hand on her and I'll fucking —"

But his threat evaporated into nothing. What, after all, could he do about it? The men bundled the woman into the jeep. The driver started the car and sped back, around the gate, into the Soviet sector. The British lance-corporal shouted a few more useless insults at the retreating exhaust pipe, then gave it up. He walked back to his buddies, who gave him a round of ironic applause.

"Sodding bloody Ivans," he said and reached for a fag.

CHAPTER
EIGHT

1

"Last one, *Knospe*."

Misha hoisted Rosa up and let her peg the final poster to the washing line, that snaked endlessly beneath a makeshift corrugated-iron roof. Although *Die Trümmerzeitung* allowed them to use their press, Misha had to supply both paper and ink. The only ink he had been able to obtain was an old pre-war batch, that took two or even three days to dry properly in the chilly air. But time didn't matter too much. He and Willi printed three hundred posters each week and, working by night, posted them all across East Berlin, concentrating especially on U-Bahn stations, office doorways, canteens, food markets, anywhere where people congregated. Each day that passed, more and more people would see the cartoons. One day, Tonya would see them too.

He released his grip on Rosa and let her slide to the ground.

Hanging the posters out had made dinner late and would mean Rosa was late getting to bed. But it couldn't be helped. Misha was simply too busy to look after everything. His cooking had become more basic. He had allowed himself to skimp on Rosa's bedtime story, so that now, instead of the long, wild, Russian fairy stories of old, she got little more than a kiss goodnight and a promise to see her in the morning. But Rosa understood. The miraculous little girl didn't like the slight disintegration of the family unit, but she understood that Misha had to work hard to "find the new mummy". She never complained, but helped out where she could instead.

They went indoors.

The stove was hot. A beef and potato stew — lots of potato, a mere tint of beef — stood warming on the top. Rosa ran to wash her hands. Misha told Willi to do the same, then began to serve up. Willi had the lamp up high, and his fairy-tale painted shade threw huge images of dragons, castles and princesses across the walls.

They were just beginning to eat, when Misha raised his hand, motioning for silence. Rosa stopped dead, her spoon hovering between bowl and mouth. There was movement audible outside. It was too late for ordinary vistors. There was no one with business at the factory. Yet there was certainly somebody there, moving around. Rosa's eyes widened. An unreasonable hope began to hammer in Misha's heart.

He had always imagined that Tonya would come by day. But why should she? Perhaps the nights were easier for her to get away. Misha stood up, breathless, excited, his ribs almost cracking with the pressure of so much hope, as his brain vainly tried to persuade him to calm down.

He went outside.

There was somebody moving down the factory wall, under the tin roof where the Comrade Lensky cartoons were drying. The light of a torch poked here and there between the hanging pages.

"Hello?" called Misha, adding softly in Russian, "*Kto tam?* Who's there?"

The movement of the torch changed. There was a rustling of paper sheets. A shape emerged from the gloom. Then a man moved out into the open. He flashed his light onto his face so that Misha could see him. The man was big-built, blond, uniformed but somehow untidy with it, as though the uniform were only a lightly worn disguise. The man had taken one of the posters down and was holding it in front of him. The ink was still wet and heavy, and the paper moved stiffly like a board. Misha felt the iron clang of disappointment, and yet he couldn't quite believe that this unexpected night-time visit was altogether unconnected with his search for Tonya. Misha stood, silently waiting.

"*Guten Abend*," said the man. "Sorry to disturb you and all that. I'm looking for a Herr Malevich."

Misha shook his head, but said nothing. His new name was still a protection to him and he wasn't keen to reveal his true identity for no reason. But the big man wasn't put off.

"Well, now, that's just it. I expect you're going to tell me you're Herr Müller and I'll bet you anything you like that you've got a wallet full of papers to prove it. All the same, it's Malevich, I want to speak to. Either Malevich, or this little fellow, Kuletsky."

The big man held up the poster and waved at the little frozen cartoon men who crawled across it. The man came closer to the light from Misha's front door and he was visible now, a British captain with something cheerful and ruffian-like in his expression. He looked like a man who would get things done. Misha knew without looking around that Rosa was at the front door staring out. He sensed her disappointment almost as intensely as his own.

"Yes, I'm Malevich. Kuletsky too if it comes to that."

The Englishman grinned. "Splendid. My name's Hollinger, Harry Hollinger. I've got some news for you, not mostly good news, I'm afraid."

They went inside.

The furnishing was still very basic. That was hardly a surprise, Berlin had lost perhaps two thirds of its buildings and much of the remaining accommodation had been looted. Misha had salvaged some of the furniture, built some more, compromised on the rest. Misha himself sat on a packing case. He indicated that Hollinger was welcome to do the same. Before sitting, Hollinger fingered the glass shade on the oil lamp and set it spinning. Seeing the images spin and whirl across the walls, he grinned with pleasure. He sat down.

"I've interrupted your meal."

"Not at all."

Russian codes of hospitality, and German ones for that matter, insisted that guests always be offered food and drink. But the etiquette of hospitality always presumed that the hosts had spare food to offer and that the guests might need it. Misha didn't offer.

Hollinger didn't ask. The Englishman glanced around the little family circle. He indicated the sheet of cartoons, which was already softening and unfreezing in the warmth.

"Who's the artist? You?"

Willi nodded.

"It's good stuff. I like it. I'll bet you don't have a license, do you, but the good stuff never does." He pulled a large paper-wrapped packet from his pocket and slid it across to Misha. "Wanted to bring a gift. Didn't know what to bring. Hope this comes in."

The packet was full of cut ham, two pounds at least. Misha took it gratefully. He gave a big slice each to Rosa and Willi, then indicated that they should go next door to their shared bedroom. The pair didn't even try to protest and crept silently away.

"You said you had news."

"Yes." Hollinger frowned. "You're looking for a friend of yours — a lover, for God's sake, let's call a spade a spade, why not?" In Hollinger's German, that translated simply as *lassen uns ein Spaten einen Spaten nennen.* More or less nonsense, of course. His next words were anything but. "You know who I mean. Antonina Kirylovna Kornikova, born Lensky."

Misha nodded. "Kornikova!" The air in the room was very still, very silent.

"You didn't know? That she was married, I mean?"

"No. When I saw her last, she wasn't . . . but I'm pleased. Her cousin, Rodyon Kornikov, was a good man. She did well. I'm pleased." Misha found himself repeating himself, but he thought he probably meant it.

He had never wanted Tonya to stay unmarried all these years. And Rodyon was a good man, would be — have been? — a good husband. All the same, it was odd learning these things. Misha steeled himself for more.

Hollinger smiled, to acknowledge Misha's feelings. "There's more. I'm a captain in British Military Intelligence, bit of a contradiction in terms as you'll see. I recruited Antonina to work for us. She is a translator attached to the SMAD, in a position to see a lot of documents that were of interest to us. She worked for us because she wanted to do the right thing. Because she was scared of what might happen to Germany if her dear friends and colleagues had their way. Perhaps you know . . . ?"

"Know?"

"Well, of course, there's no way you could. She spent time in Siberia. Sentenced to ten years for some perfectly ridiculous reason. Only let out so that she could fight for her country. She lost a couple of fingers with frost-bite. It was what first drew our attention to her. I'm very sorry to be the one bringing you so much difficult news."

"No, no . . ." Misha shook his head. It was true. There was so much news, so much of it difficult. All the same, through all his other feelings, Misha could also feel Hollinger's courage in coming, his courage in spilling all the information, good and bad, in such a candid way. "The Gulag . . . I had always worried about it . . . Things became so dangerous, and principles were the most dangerous thing of all. Perhaps Tonya had too many to be safe. And if she married Rodyon . . . well,

251

he was powerful and principled, the worst combination of all."

"Yes. The dictatorship of the proletariat, eh?" said Hollinger softly. "I've never had a quarrel with the working classes, it's just the dicatorship bit that's hard to swallow. In any case . . . Antonina did first-class work. The best. I have the very highest respect for her. It wasn't easy. She did remarkably well."

Misha noticed that Hollinger had moved from the present tense into the past. The cold air from outside seemed to have entered the room.

"Recently, six days ago, that's all, we hit a problem. Our main point of contact with Antonina was via a liaison agent in the Soviet zone, a German woman whom I trust implicitly. This woman's apartment was raided by the NKVD. Thank God, thank God, nothing was found. This woman had become worried after a security lapse on my part and had taken steps to clear the apartment of anything even vaguely untoward. The NKVD found nothing aside from an old tin of Bournvita. At any rate, it was the drinking chocolate they grilled her about when they arrested her later. Arrested her, then released her. This woman had been giving Antonina violin lessons. That was the cover, but the lessons were perfectly real. As far as I know, the bloody Russians have no firm foundation to accuse Antonina of anything."

Hollinger went silent. But Misha knew he hadn't finished. He sighed before continuing.

"But when did that ever stop them? We've lost contact with her. We have had people watching her place of work and her barracks, and found nothing. She has had instructions, naturally, on fall-back meeting places, emergency drops, all that sort of thing. We've had no indication from her at all. That's all we know. The only bright spot is that the Soviets haven't announced anything. You know the sort of thing. Comrade Whatnotovich found guilty of trading on the black market. Sentenced to three years' hard labour in Novaya Zemlya. There's been nothing like that. Nothing that we've heard anyway, and our ears for that sort of thing are normally quite good.

"And that's it. That's all I know. I don't want to assume the worst, but it's clear that there is a problem. If I had to guess, I'd say she was still in Germany somewhere. Her German was first-class. As good as yours. Better than mine. That's the sort of skill that Brother Ivan doesn't give up so easily. In the absence of any real evidence against her, I'd say they'd be likely to keep her here, maybe shift her somewhere less sensitive. I don't know, but it's a fair guess. I came here because I wanted you to know everything."

"Thank you."

The Englishman wasn't done. He pushed a hand through his thick blond hair, turning it from one shape of mess to another. He still hesitated. He reached for a slice of ham, then remembered that the ham would be very precious to any ordinary German and pulled his hand back again — then thought better of his own politeness reached for it again, took it, and ate it.

Speaking as he munched, he added, "I feel responsible in two ways. One, I recruited Antonina and promised to look after her. Two, I made an error in procedure, a small one, but maybe significant. Our German liaison agent certainly thinks so. In any case, I also want you to know that we will do anything we can to help her. Our first difficulty will be finding her. Our second problem will be getting her out."

Misha didn't know what to think or feel. On the one hand, he had just heard what was possibly the worst news he could possibly have imagined. On the other hand, there was a man, an Englishman, here in the room, who had seen Tonya, spoken to her, known her, perhaps even cared about her a little.

"How did you know to come here?" he asked.

"Ha!" The Englishman grimaced for a half-second, before looking serious again. "That's easy. I asked Antonina what she wanted in exchange for her services. The question surprised her. She wasn't used to being given things. I offered her a British passport, naturally, and she was thrilled at the idea. She hadn't thought to ask for anything at all. Then, that evening, just as I was leaving, she stopped me to ask for one further thing."

"Yes?"

"For you. She asked for you."

Misha opened his mouth, but couldn't find words to fill it. *So Tonya too had been looking for him*. It felt like news of the most wonderful sort. He felt an uprush of love, so strong it caught him by surprise.

Hollinger paused, then continued. "I did what I could to find you, or thought I did anyway. We tracked Malevich here, but only found a Müller. I blame myself. I sent someone when I should have come in person. Then after we lost touch with her, I went back to thinking about the mysterious Herr Müller and I thought it worth a second try. I see from your posters that you've been trying to find her."

"Yes."

"A clever idea. I expect it would have worked." Hollinger shifted in his chair. He was the same height as Misha, but much squarer across the shoulders. He looked like the very prototype of the unsophisticated rural Englishman, but Misha wasn't fooled. Then Hollinger added, "I know almost nothing about you. All I know is that Antonina wanted to find you more than anything else."

Misha nodded. "We were lovers. I was a bourgeois, a class enemy of the revolution. There was not much future for me in the country. We spent about a year together. That was all. I last saw her in 1919. I escaped Russia in 1921. I hoped she'd find a way to join me, but . . ."

Hollinger looked shocked. "Good God. It's been twenty-five years, then. More."

"Twenty-seven years. Almost."

Hollinger nodded, then bent forward. The lamplight caught the shape of his head and projected it onto the wall alongside the comical little cartoons.

"I am very sorry, Herr Malevich. I had wanted to bring the two of you together. I am afraid that, unwittingly, I've pulled the two of you apart."

Misha nodded and at the same time released a long, juddering sigh. He realised that he had been waiting for an apology. The apology enabled Misha both to

255

acknowledge his feelings and to accept Hollinger's offer of help. Something perceptibly relaxed in the room. The door from the bedroom swung open and Rosa stood there in her night-things, with Willi looming behind her. Misha invited them in with a wave. He poured a glass of schnapps for Willi and let Rosa climb onto his lap and snuggle in.

He told them a potted version of what had happened. Something had happened to Tonya. No one was quite sure what, but this English captain was going to help them look. Rosa was upset, and cried a little. Once Misha would have been worried for her and would have tried to pet her out of her tears, but he knew her better than that now. He knew that, with Rosa, grief and other emotions came and went as easily and naturally as changes in the weather. The grief was essential, but it would pass. Not for the first time, Misha found himself learning something from his little *Knospe*.

Once the two children were settled, Misha said, "You said you would help look for her. I don't know what that means. As for me, I don't even like to cross into the Russian zone if I can help it. My papers aren't bad, but they're still fakes."

Misha's papers lay on a low cupboard within reach of Hollinger's long arms. He took them and examined them under the light.

"They're good actually. You used that chap up by the Schlasisches Tor, did you? He's the best."

Misha was astonished. "You know him? You don't mind?"

256

"Ah, well, it helps us really. All these lesser Nazis running for South America. Why not? It cleans this country up on the cheap. And every now and then, when some more important villains come his way, he lets us know and we pick them up, very discreetly of course. The arrangement works well for us both." Hollinger tossed the packet of identity documents up in the air, then tossed it back towards the cupboard. He didn't bother to look where he was throwing, but his aim was perfectly accurate all the same. "We can get you proper documents though, of course. Official ones. Any name you like. Stick with Müller, if you're happy with that."

"Müller's good enough for me. While you're at it, you could do me a favour."

"Yes?"

Misha indicated Rosa, by now fast asleep against his chest. "I've sort of adopted Rosa — or to be quite honest, she adopted me. But I don't have any papers for her. I just took her from her orphanage. I expect UNRRA are still trying to work out if she's missing or if they've just miscounted."

"Rosa Müller. Very good. Why not?"

"And that's not all. I don't have a reason for entering the Soviet zone. It's all very well having the papers, but —"

"But, poppycock! You're an engineer, aren't you? A businessman?"

"Yes. A businessman who owns three hand-made looms, no savings and all in a country with no money."

257

"Brother Ivan is short of everything," said Hollinger. "He's stripped Germany of its industrial assets, but hasn't the faintest idea of what to do with them. They need people like you."

Misha nodded. "Of course they do, but . . ."

"Forget the buts," Hollinger interrupted. "If you had the capital to set up in business — a business which would give you the freedom of the east zone — what business would you choose?"

"That's easy. Castings. Every manufacturer in the world needs castings. It's a business I know well enough from before."

"Castings?"

"Yes, industrial castings. We make a mould, pour in molten metal, and take a cast of anything at all. We can make spare parts, industrial prototypes, components for larger assemblies. As I say, there won't be a factory in Germany, east zone or west, that doesn't need them."

Hollinger smiled, sudden, brilliant, transformative. "Good. Castings it is. And to get started with castings, you'd need . . .?"

"A blast furnace, of course, and then metal handling equipment . . ." Misha began to list the things he'd need, excited at the idea of restarting in industry. Then he checked himself. "It's not cheap. What are you asking in exchange?"

Hollinger pinched another slice of ham. "Mostly, to get Antonina back. She was our best agent. We owe her."

"And?" Misha prompted.

258

"And if you travel the east zone with your eyes and ears open, you will learn things. Economic. Military. Political. Social. Anything. If you choose to tell us, we will always listen with gratitude."

"That's all?"

"It's plenty. As I say, we owe Antonina."

And that was that for the evening, or almost.

As Hollinger left, Misha stood up with him gently setting down the sleeping Rosa without waking her. Outside the front door, the air was still below freezing, but there was a weather front rolling in from the west, a wad of thick cloud that obscured the stars and was lit from beneath by the faint glow of the city. Misha noticed the cloud and his Russian bones felt the coming thaw, the irrepressible upthrust of spring. The two men shook hands, but Hollinger didn't leave. He looked uneasy.

"Listen, I haven't quite been open with you. There's one other thing, perhaps two. The first is this. Just before we lost contact with Antonina, we received a packet from her. Some documents. Carbon papers actually. She didn't know who to send them to, I suppose, but she happened to pick a major-general who happened to possess more than the ordinary military ration of grey matter. He understood that the carbons might be of interest and passed them to us. The documents are — they are simply of the highest possible value — I can't tell you more — but suffice to say that if Antonina wanted to save Germany from her countrymen, then she couldn't possibly have given us more help than she did.

259

"That's the first thing. The second is this. I don't know what to make of it. Maybe nothing. Maybe it's not connected. But I happened to hear of an incident that took place on the same day that the major-general received that envelope. A Red Army sergeant, a woman, was walking past the Brandenburg Gate, when she was stopped and picked up by an NKVD jeep. When she saw it coming, she tried to run. All this was reported by some of our men, who happened to be on the spot."

Misha heard his words against a background of sudden buzzing in his head. He jutted his head forwards, as though trying to poke through the noise. "You say she was walking past the gate . . .?"

"Yes. From the Soviet sector into ours. If it was Antonina — which we don't know — then she was heading in this direction. It may be that she was trying to come to you."

2

Snatched in the shadow of the Brandenburg Gate, Tonya was shoved and frogmarched to the waiting jeep. She saw some British Tommies nearby. One of the men had come running over, shouting angrily. He was armed, of course, but so were her captors. And in any case, what was the man to do? Start shooting? Tonya was thrown into the jeep. Konstantinov drove. In the back, Tonya was obliged to sit in between two NKVD men she didn't recognise. Nobody spoke.

She wanted to cry. Freedom had drifted so close, she'd been able to smell it. Another half-hour and she could have been in Charlottenberg, perhaps even in Misha's arms. Even if she'd just been a few hundred yards deeper into the British sector, perhaps Konstantinov would have thought twice about abducting her. At the same time, she knew tears would be taken as a sign of guilt. She remembered Hollinger's instructions. Never assume they know what you fear they know. Admit nothing. Talk only about the violin lessons. She sat tight-faced and rigid as the jeep tore through the streets, never stopping and hardly even slowing except for corners. The cold wind whipped at her eyes. They stung and watered, but didn't cry.

The jeep headed for Karlshorst. Tonya felt the chilling certainty that her last act of treachery had been uncovered. What a fool she'd been! She could see herself being presented with the evidence of her deeds. She could see the envelope, those lethally incriminating carbons being unfolded in front of her. No crime could be greater than the one she had just committed. Would they kill her instantly? Tonya could bear death, she thought, but never torture, and not the Gulag again. The car whirled on towards Karlshorst and Tonya's worst nightmares.

But the car didn't stop there. It carried on to an NKVD barracks and regimental headquarters a short distance beyond. Konstantinov killed the ignition and the noise of the engine died. With the car motionless at last, the rush of wind had died to nothing. The sun was still shining, but without warmth, an empty promise, a Stalinist smile.

Konstantinov flung open the rear door. The guard on Tonya's right got out. Aside from the three men who'd been in the car, nobody gave her more than a passing glance. Konstantinov indicated an ordinary side door part-way down a brick passage way. This wasn't Karlshorst. It wasn't the NKVD's central headquarters. As Tonya followed her captors, she could hear the clack of typewriters and the sound of crockery being stacked. Whatever her supposed offence, Tonya realised that she was being treated in a very routine, a very ordinary way.

Then why arrest her at all? Why snatch her so abruptly?

Hope and tension flickered and fought. She held tight to Hollinger's advice. Don't assume they know what you fear they know. Admit nothing. Say little.

White-faced and tense, Tonya allowed herself to be led to an interrogation room. Konstantinov and one of the men followed her in. She was given a chair and allowed to sit.

The interrogation began.

3

What did Misha feel?

There was so much to take in, he hardly knew. He was angry with Hollinger, of course. It seemed certain that it had been Tonya's covert activities which had caused the problem. If her last, most daring act of espionage had been uncovered, then Hollinger had been suggesting that Tonya's punishment would have been of the severest sort: Siberia or death. On the other hand, there was something in Misha's anger which was ultimately unconvincing, even to him. Misha knew that Hollinger owed him nothing. On the contrary, he knew that Hollinger was a good man, doing a necessary job. He had been candid about things he hadn't needed to be candid about. And man to man, Misha had liked the Englishman. His anger flared in short and savage fits, but never for long. It was already fading.

Another emotion was admiration. Admiration and love. Tonya had been to the Gulag. She'd been released, most likely into a *shtraf* battalion. Then, all alone in Berlin, a strange Englishman had asked her to run a risk of the very highest kind, and all for an objective — a free Germany — in whose freedom she would never share. She had accepted the risk and excelled at her task. Misha could think of nothing more important, nothing braver.

And the third dominant emotion of the many which surfaced was an odd one; one that he would never have predicted. And the feeling was this: he felt clarified, resolute, certain. He felt an old optimism, amounting almost to certainty, that things would turn out all right. The feeling made no sense. Hollinger had gone as far as to mention the arrest, in front of witnesses, of a Russian Red Army woman of the right age, by a jeep full of NKVD men. How much worse could it be?

Yet Misha wasn't in a mood for logic. Up till now, he hadn't quite believed in Tonya's real existence. It was as though that face he'd half-glimpsed through the window of a speeding car had existed only in some parallel universe, not quite connecting with this one.

263

Now that had changed. Harry Hollinger had seen her, spoken with her, worked with her, become a friend to her. Tonya now felt like a real part of his world — and if that was the case, then he would find her. His belief was as simple and implacable as that. He didn't yet know how he would do it, or where he would find her, but his mood was one of resolution and hope, even expectation.

And thus far, at least, he was right to keep faith.

Just four days after Hollinger's visit, Misha received a letter addressed to "Herr Müller". The letter was from the Displaced Persons Identity Confirmation Office (MilGov, British Sector), asking him to present himself and his "adopted daughter, Fräulein Rosa Müller" at the earliest convenient opportunity so that "replacement papers" could be issued for himself and his family.

And the same day, towards evening, a motorbike pulled up. The driver dismounted and knocked at the factory door, holding two large cardboard boxes. Misha signed a chit acknowledging receipt and tore open the envelope that was taped to the lid of the first box. Inside was a short handwritten note which read, "Unfortunately, my nearest friendly quartermaster didn't happen to have any blast furnaces in stock. He did have these, though. I hope you know what to do next. I wouldn't have a clue. Good luck, old man," — this last bit in English — "Hollinger."

Misha opened the boxes. They each contained ten thousand cigarettes in sealed cartons. It wasn't a blast furnace, but it was a start.

264

4

"You ran."

Konstantinov spoke the words with a light smile, as though he were mentioning the weather or indicating a scenic view. The captain had set his cigarettes and matches on the table. He fiddled with the matchbox, opening and closing it, getting pleasure from the neat movement of the tiny drawer.

Tonya shrugged. "Some fools came chasing after me. I didn't know who. You were driving like a madman."

Somehow the relationship of interrogator and prisoner had supplanted the pre-existing military one. Tonya dropped the "sir" and Konstantinov didn't notice or didn't care.

"Only the guilty run."

"I'm a woman. One hears stories about ... unpleasantness."

"Unpleasantness? Committed by a uniformed officer and men of the NKVD? In broad daylight? Beneath the Brandenburg Gate?"

"You're not a woman. If you were, you would hear stories too."

Konstantinov used his two index fingers to snap the matchbox closed. Tonya realised she had already inadvertently handed him something to feed off. He had asked her if she had felt at risk of sexual assault from men of the NKVD. She had refused to rule out that possibility. That was one small strike against her already.

"Of course, if I had known you were NKVD," she added lamely, "that would have been something else. But one hears so many things. Germans, former criminals, in stolen uniforms, doing such unspeakable things . . ."

Konstantinov ignored her. "General Sokolovsky permitted a break for lunch. Your attendance was required in the afternoon. We picked you up by the Brandenburg Gate one and a half hours after the lunch break was given."

"Yes."

"How long is your break normally?"

"Normally? Perhaps half an hour."

"So you were already an hour late. For General Sokolovsky."

Tonya's face felt numb and taut. Her hands were spread on the table in front of her, but they hardly felt like part of her at all. Although her mind was racing with thoughts, she seemed disconnected from her body. Even Konstantinov's questions and her own answers seemed as though they took place in some different dimension. And she had nothing with which to rebut Konstantinov's point. She shouldn't have been where she was. She couldn't deny being there. Any excuse would look feeble. She hadn't even thought of what to say.

"Yes sir," she said.

"And walking back would have taken another hour or more. So you would have been two and a half hours late. For General Sokolovsky."

"Yes sir. I —"

Tonya began to speak, then tears, coming quite unexpectedly, washed away her words. The thought of Misha, a sudden sense of him, warm and close, an actual living entity not the dream-figure which was all she'd had for so long, came sweeping into her consciousness. Konstantinov and the interrogation suddenly felt like nothing at all: a mere distraction from the only thing about the day that really mattered.

Through her tears, she heard herself saying. "The general . . . I thought he must have a long lunch . . . my boots are old . . . I wanted to get some new ones . . . there was a man selling good boots in the Tiergarten. I didn't know . . . I thought the general would have a proper lunch. I thought . . . I only wanted boots."

It was a good answer.

Of course, no answers, no matter how ingenious, would help her if Konstantinov knew anything about her work as a spy. But just then, from the room next door, Tonya heard the smash of breaking crockery, followed by the angry noise of a Russian shouting at a German kitchen worker. Even Konstantinov allowed a tiny smile to curl at the corners of his mouth.

And amazingly, despite her situation, Tonya began to relax. *They knew nothing.* She suddenly felt sure of it. She felt certain that major criminals would never be interrogated in a room like this. Her tears were still flowing, but they felt like no part of her. They felt like a gift from some other place. A gift that allowed her to come across as an innocent woman, frightened and out of her depth. She realised she was nearly old enough to be Konstantinov's mother. She could make use of that. She could already sense the moves.

"I only wanted boots."

5

It was the middle of April. A fine grey rain pattered down over the surrounding fields, muffling sounds and reducing all colours to the same narrow range of greys, browns and muted greens. Somewhere, a long way away, there was the mournful sound of a steam engine whistling.

Down by the railway's edge, Misha's shoes squelched in the mud. On the track above, six or seven feet up the embankment, a German businessman, Herr Kallenbrecher, stood wrapped in a raincoat, looking down and smoking.

Misha continued to explore. The siding stood on the new German-Polish border, a few hundred yards from the main rail-line that led east to Moscow. The muddy verge was littered with industrial equipment, torn out of German factories by the Soviets and left to rot there. Some of the machines had been so roughly disassembled by the Soviet reparations crews that Misha could see they were ruined. Still others had been in good condition when they'd been removed, but had become badly rusted and filthy after a winter outside. In theory, the equipment was destined for transport to the Soviet Union, but Misha could see that it would either never arrive there or be useless when it did. The engineer in Misha revolted against buying — or in effect stealing — such rubbish. But he was also a realist. And there was some once-good equipment here. He squelched up and down in the mud. He found a usable furnace lining of an excellent size. He found crucibles, tongs, ladles, hoists, a pair of small workshop cranes and other gear for handling molten metals. He found a decent press and a first-class lathe, which wasn't strictly necessary but seemed too good to pass up.

Misha looked up. Kallenbrecher had just finished a cigarette and pinged the butt, still glowing, into the mud below.

"If I wanted to go ahead," said Misha, "how would it work?"

"You bring a truck. One, two, however many. You take what you want. You go."

"And you provide?"

"Peace."

"From the Russians?"

"The Russians, the army, NKVD, everyone."

"And loading up?"

"There'll be men here. And a tractor to pull you out of the mud if you get stuck."

"How about transporting the stuff? What happens if I'm stopped?"

"I can get you clearances for Berlin. Real ones, not faked."

"Berlin? Soviet sector or anywhere?"

"No. Soviet sector only. If you want to take it west, that's your lookout."

Kallenbrecher was charging four hundred dollars the lorryload: far too much. But Misha could bargain. And if push came to shove, he thought Hollinger would give him more cigarettes — the basic currency of the occupation. He gazed again at the siding. It looked like a graveyard, but really, Misha thought, it was the opposite: a place of birth and renewal. It would be good to turn such rubbish, the spoils and wreckage of war, into something valuable again. Misha felt a sting of pride, German pride, in his ability to do it.

"Good," he said. "I've seen enough."

6

Tonya would be found guilty, of course.

She'd known all along that no other verdict was possible. NKVD men didn't swoop to arrest people only to have them found not guilty of all charges. The only issue had ever been of what she would be found guilty.

But the interrogation had never tackled the subjects that had so terrified her to begin with. Konstantinov had tried to hit her hard with the little stuff. He didn't like her previous association with Valentina. He had accused Tonya of not denouncing her friend for spreading anti-Soviet propaganda. He had made a big deal of her being late for Sokolovsky. He had spent a full two hours of the interrogation inquiring into Tonya's relationship with Marta, and ended up establishing exactly nothing except that Tonya had taken violin lessons from an unlicensed music teacher.

And that was it. Nothing about spying for British intelligence. Nothing about a packet of carbon papers which would have killed her if they'd been found.

Following the interrogation, Tonya spent twelve days in an NKVD prison cell in the regimental barracks, while further investigations were made. She was treated perfectly well. For two days, the prison regime — two meals a day, no opportunity for exercise, twice-daily cell inspections — was followed strictly. Then within a further day or two, it lapsed altogether. The guards brought her meals straight from the canteen, and sat with her as she ate them. She offered to do their sewing, and soon sat with a big pile of mending from all over the barracks. Most of the soldiers who came to collect their clothes gave her a little present: two cigarettes, some boiled sweets, a newspaper, a carved wooden keepsake. She soon had a little pile of goodies in the cell with her. The most senior guard, a senior sergeant like herself, worried that her little treasure trove might cause problems for them both and took it away, promising to keep it safe until the "comrade sergeant" was released. When Tonya happened to mention having been cold in the night, the sergeant brought her a stack of four thick woollen blankets, apologising for his thoughtlessness.

On the thirteenth day, Tonya was ordered out of her cell. She was driven, under guard, to a disciplinary tribunal held under NKVD auspices in one of their Karlshorst offices. The tribunal consisted of three people: Tonya's section leader from Mühlendamm, Konstantinov himself, and an NKVD major who had

271

lost one arm in the war and sat with his empty sleeve pinned to the front of his tunic. Tonya was formally charged with various crimes. The first crime mentioned was neglect of her duties as translator. The second crime was indulging in capitalistic black-market activities, a charge relating to her admission that she had intended to purchase a new pair of boots from a Tiergarten vendor. The third charge dealt with her failure to denounce Valentina. The final charge related to her association with anti-Soviet elements — that is to say, that she happened to have taken violin lessons from a German woman not formally licensed to give them. Tonya pleaded guilty to all charges.

She was escorted from the room, while the tribunal conferred. The room she waited in was small. It had a single chair, no table. The walls were chalk-white and bare. Tonya didn't sit down but stood at the window and gazed out, across the roofs and ruins of Berlin. It was spring now. The snow had all gone. Birds seemed to have returned to the city and Tonya looked out at the rooftops, listening to the birds.

CHAPTER
NINE

1

1946. A wet spring crawled slowly into a hot German summer. But though the streets still shimmered with heat, as they did in that first intense summer after the war, the mood in Berlin grew icier with each passing month.

Rumours of arguments in the Allied Control Council spread like wildfire. It was said that the British were reducing their garrison in light of a possible evacuation. It was said that the Americans too were quietly evacuating dependents and retaining only core military personnel.

In one way, the rumours were false. Neither the British nor the Americans — nor even the French, in whom no one had much faith — were depleting their forces in Berlin. But the whispering told a deeper truth all the same. The Russians were becoming increasingly hostile, increasingly assertive. Berlin was surrounded. The Western position untenable.

The summer blazed on. The rumours grew.

2

Misha knocked at the front door.

Behind him, in the neat suburban garden, a shell hole clawed its way into the lawn and fruit trees. Misha waited twenty seconds, then raised his hand to knock again. Before he could do so, the door swung silently open, and a black-coated servant wafted Misha through a ticking marble hall to a flashily luxurious drawing room. The owner, Thomas Brandt, was present, dressed in a dark grey business suit with a loud tie. A leather coat was flung over one of the sofas.

Misha introduced himself: he was a businessman, he said, needing help with supplies. Brandt yawned ostentatiously, and skewed his body around in the sofa to look at Misha better. He shrugged.

"So? Why come here?"

"I came because I read one of the British MilGov bulletins. Specifically, the one in which it was mentioned that you had been fined two hundred thousand Reichsmarks for transporting a hundred and fifty tons of pork from Bremen into the French zone and selling it."

"One hundred and seventy-five tons. One seven five not one fifty."

"All the better."

"Drink."

Brandt spoke the word like a statement not a question. Getting up, he poured whisky into a pair of heavy crystal tumblers, no water, no ice. The whisky was a Scottish brand, expensive and rare.

"Thank you."

"You want to sell or buy?"

"Certainly buy. Perhaps selling too."

"Oh?"

"I'm an engineer. I've assembled a foundry. Not first-class, but not bad. We're ready to start."

"What's a foundry? How did you come by it? I'm not a metal basher."

Misha began to answer, ignoring Brandt's derogatory tone, but he could see the businessman's eyes already beginning to glaze. And in any case, what did it matter? The fact was that Misha had done it. It had taken him months to do it, but he'd done it.

First, he'd got hold of some trucks — four Russian-made UralAZ monsters with huge wheels and formidably low gearing. He'd made a date with Kallenbrecher, gone back to the siding, then loaded his trucks till their rear axles were jammed flat against the suspension. Getting the equipment back to the Soviet sector of Berlin had been simple enough. Moving it through into the British sector had been more worrying, but easy enough in the event. Misha had simply waited until two o'clock in the morning, then covered by a sudden squall of rain, he'd driven straight across the sector boundary.

That had been the easy part. But much of the equipment he owned was in an appalling state of repair, and there were still missing parts to be sourced or fabricated. For fourteen long weeks he and a tiny team had laboured to get his factory set up. He'd drawn on the "Central Bank of Cigarettes", as Hollinger had come to call it. But Misha couldn't afford to flaunt any sudden wealth. There were Soviet informers everywhere in Berlin. The NKVD and other Soviet security forces were becoming ever more brazen in beating or abducting individuals they didn't want around. So Misha kept things inconspicuous. He kept his looms going, and had even built four more. As far as possible, he used his existing income to get the foundry built.

But none of that did Brandt need to know.

"We can make anything," said Misha. "Prototypes. Specialist parts. Replacement parts. Every manufacturer will need castings sometimes. Some manufacturers will need us all the time."

"West zones or east zone?"

"Both. Mostly east. The Soviets ripped out the foundries, but couldn't reassemble them. They're desperately short."

"Maybe. But it's a question of payment. The easy things are the simple ones. Food, steel, coal, paper."

"I didn't come here because I needed help with the easy things. The Soviets are desperate. I have names."

Misha handed over the slip of paper he'd brought with him. A list of businesses that needed castings. Two thirds of the names were located in the Soviet zone.

Brandt stared expressionlessly at the paper, then waved his guest out into the hall. Misha stood there. From another one of the rooms off the hallway, a door opened and a girl stepped out. She was in her early twenties, German but carefully Americanised from her nylon stockings to her bright crimson lipstick. She was pretty and thin, but also brassy, unbelievable, fake.

She said, "Brandt?"

"He's on the phone."

"*Die Scheisse*. He's always on the phone."

She left again by a different door.

After fifteen minutes, Brandt was done with his calls and he called Misha in.

"Castings, yes, everyone wants them. You, what do you need?"

"Coal for the furnace. Metal for the castings."

"OK." He used the American term. "Coal is easy. Metals I can get. You will need to promote your own products. That's not a business I understand. You've got clearance for the Soviet zone? You're willing to travel there?"

"Yes."

"Good. I can give you some contacts too. Take samples, but don't sell anything. Just find out what people have to offer."

"You mean money?"

"Yes, money. Not roubles of course. And Reichsmarks only if we have to. But anything. Food. Timber. Any sort of vehicles. Engines. Barges. Livestock. Scrap metal. Oil or coal, of course. Anything. I'll handle things from there."

"Thank you."

"You speak Russian?"

"No, of course not," said Misha, avoiding any discussion of his past.

"It's better to. It's the Russians who make the decisions these days. But *macht nichts*. I'll handle things."

Brandt nodded. The conversation was over. The girl came into the room again, and hung on the doorpost, rolling around it with her skinny hips like a dancer in one of Berlin's new nightclubs.

Once again, Misha felt a jab of his old, unreasonable certainty. Tonya was alive. She was still in Germany. And he would find her. How could he not?

He felt ridiculously sure.

3

Oderbruch, just west of the river Oder.

A place of low, forested hills separated by broad flood-plains, small farms and scattered villages. Once, the Oderbruch had been well inside the German border. Germany had continued on to the east, reaching as far as Königsberg on the shores of the Baltic. But that had been before the war. After the surrender, Germany had lost everything east of the Oder. Poland had jumped westwards. Königsberg had become Kaliningrad, part of Russia itself. The Oderbruch now marked the furthest eastward limit of Germany. It felt like a place forgotten by time. It felt like the end of the earth.

Tonya saw the landscape unroll behind the truck. She was in the back, along with four ordinary soldiers and a couple of dozen crates and sacks. The other soldiers — all male and twenty years her junior — smoked and talked among themselves. They didn't include her in their conversation. She didn't seek to join in.

More flat fields passed away behind their tailgate. More stone houses and low hills. Then the movement of the truck changed. Instead of the gently curving country roads, the truck made a sudden turn and began accelerating hard down a dead straight track, unmetalled and deeply scored and rutted. The soldiers grabbed the sides of the truck for support as the wooden benches beneath them began to leap and jolt. The conversation died to nothing.

The truck drove for another five minutes, then powered through a pair of wooden gates and drew up in a wide dirt turning circle. Tonya was sitting at the rear of the truck and she was the first to get out. All around, she saw low wooden huts surrounded by a wire-mesh fence topped with barbed wire. There were a couple of watchtowers, the only high points visible anywhere on that flat landscape. A few Russian soldiers marched a work detail of poorly-dressed civilians up a dirt path, towards a building whose purpose Tonya couldn't make out.

The men who had been in the truck with her jumped out. One of them was a junior sergeant. Two of the others were *yefreytor*, senior privates. Tonya herself, having just completed a tedious three-month military detention, had been demoted all the way to *ryadovoy*, junior private, the lowest of the low.

The sergeant ordered them to begin unloading the truck, Tonya included. The loads — flour, salt, potatoes, carrots — were packed in large loads designed by men for men, which Tonya staggered to carry at all. By the time the goods had been unloaded and carried over to the storehouse, Tonya's arms were trembling from the strain.

The sergeant, who hadn't moved or helped, nodded curtly. He called Tonya over with a gesture of his finger.

He pointed to a hut, whose white bargeboards and painted door distinguished it from the others around.

"You need to report to the camp commander. He'll tell you your duties."

Tonya nodded, then remembered herself. "Yes sir," she said, with a smart nod.

She walked over to the hut the man had indicated. A sign on the door in Russian and misspelled German read "Oderbruch Special Camp Number 11", together with a sign in Russian only "NKVD 174th Frontier Regiment". Tonya knocked at the door, heard a shout, and walked on in.

4

The manager fingered the lumps of iron on his desk. Each one was heavy, several pounds apiece, and they made a dull thumping sound as he shifted them around. Overhead light gleamed dully off their rounded surfaces.

"These are iron not steel," said the manager, plaintively.

"Of course. It's easier for us to make samples in softer metals. But we can make almost anything at all."

"Yes, well, we need castings all right. We're meant to make machine tools for the Russians, but we don't have half the parts we ought to have. Not even screws. Would you believe that? If we want screws, we make them ourselves."

"Screws, that's not my business. Parts, I can make. We'd need specifications or a prototype. Then it's only a question of —"

"Payment. You're going to say payment." The manager was broad, but he had a defeated slope to his shoulders. His tone of complaint was firmly settled now, like climate or the local geography.

"I wasn't. I was going to talk about quantities and materials. But, yes, we'll need to arrange payment."

The manager's hands continued to move among the chunks of metal. He was manager of the Eberswalde Maschinenfabrik, a once-thriving machine tool plant, now struggling to remain in business in the new postwar conditions.

"Yes, well, you can say what you like about the old gang" — the manager meant Hitler — "but at least there was a currency that made sense. There wasn't so much silliness in those days. What will you accept for your samples? Roubles?"

"Of course not, no."

"Reichsmarks?"

"Preferably not."

"So, then, diamonds. American dollars. Fairy gold."

"Anything. What do you have? Cement? Sand? Bricks? Trucks? Finished products?"

"You mean anything?"

"Yes."

For once, the manager was shocked out of his despondency. "*Anything?* Really anything? We have a yardful of timber — proper stuff, all hardwood, well seasoned — that we don't want and can't shift."

Misha nodded. "That sounds good. It's a start anyway. Think about what you have or can get hold of. My partner will give you a call."

281

"Brandt?"

"Yes, Brandt."

The manager nodded, still surprised by the possible simplicity of the transaction. The two men began to discuss quantities, materials, specifications, and Misha was surprised by the manager's sudden alertness when it came to technical matters. After their unpromising start, it turned out to be a useful meeting. The manager was talkative and supplied many details about the economic picture, of which Misha took a mental note, for onward transmission to Harry Hollinger in due course. Only when the conversation turned away from technical issues again, did the manager's gloom return.

"This timber."

"Yes?"

"Well, there's a lot of it. You can't just slip it out of here unnoticed."

"No, of course. We'll need proper permits from the Ivans." Misha still found it strange to talk of his own countrymen in that way, but he was Herr Müller now, his Russian past completely wiped out.

"That won't be easy."

"We can handle it. I'll need a translator, though, of course."

"Translator? There's a Polish woman in the factory here who speaks a little . . ."

"No, no, no, no, no. It will need to be a proper translator. A professional. There was a woman named Kornikova who impressed me once."

"Kornikova . . ."

"Yes, Red Army, but very good, very helpful. She'd be able to help with all the permits and so forth.

282

Perhaps if you ask around. I suppose there's a barracks here in town?"

"Yes, of course."

"Try there. But ask discreetly, don't go yelling things out. Otherwise, see what else is available. But I insist on a proper translator, Russian for preference. The Soviets prefer their own. I won't work with amateurs."

The manager's face went glassy behind his spectacles. Up until this point, Misha had been the perfect salesman, flexible and ready to overcome every small obstacle. On this one point alone, Misha had taken a rigid stance. But the manager was a man of the world. If a man requests the services of a particular woman, there could only be one possible reason why.

"I'll ask around," said the manager. "This Korni-kova . . .?"

"She's a friend. But ask quietly. Please don't mention my name."

The manager nodded. He pushed his spectacles higher up his nose. "I'll ask around. If she's here, then it shouldn't be so hard . . ."

Misha left.

Another seed planted. Another two factories still to visit. Misha's certainty about finding her continued, bright, strong, unreasonable.

5

Tonya quickly came to understand the new conditions of her life.

Oderbruch Special Camp was the smallest of the dozen or so camps that still remained active. It had been set up by the Soviets to handle political prisoners: leading Nazis, members of the Waffen SS, other influential Nazis. But, as Tonya soon realised, such prisoners were the exceptions. Most of the prisoners were ordinary criminals, blackmarketeers, landowners who had resisted collectivisation, journalists who had spoken the truth, and many who had been denounced by unknown people for unknown offences. The camp was, Tonya realised, the Soviet zone's own sweet version of the Siberian Gulag. Instead of the snakes and spiders of Soviet propaganda, Tonya saw only suffering wretches, ill-clothed, ill-fed, forgotten. She felt, not for the first time, ashamed to be Russian.

But she herself was fairly well off. Her regular duties were light. Every now and then, prisoners would be summoned for an interrogation at which Tonya was required to interpret. She found these sessions unpleasant, but not awful. The sessions were listless rather than frightful. The NKVD had no real interest in their prisoners, no real interest in forcing confessions or finding out information. Quite the opposite. The principal policy was neglect. There were no beatings and few punishments. Most activities were banned — singing, lectures, language lessons, games — and all news of the outside world was cut off. No charges were brought, no trials held, no sentences given, no release dates mentioned.

And because of the camp's lack of interest in its prisoners, Tonya's duties consisted of simple, unimportant things. She spent her time translating shopping lists for the camp quartermaster, or interpreting for a Russian driver and a German mechanic when there was a vehicle breakdown.

And that was it. Tonya's accommodation was fine. She was one of only three women on the staff (the other two comprised an NKVD sergeant and the quartermaster's wife who also worked as a typist). The three women slept together in a single room. The NKVD sergeant spent the first couple of weeks putting Tonya in her place, but with just three of them together, Tonya knew that things would soon sort themselves out, and they did. The three women were hardly the best of friends, but they got along just fine.

It was known in the camp that Tonya had been demoted and punished for offences committed in Berlin and her security clearance inside the camp didn't permit her to leave it. But she was still in Germany! When she'd heard her new assignment after being released from detention, her heart had leaped for joy. Oderbruch might seem like the underside of nowhere, but she was little more than forty or fifty miles away from Misha. To Tonya, as for any Russian, such distances seemed simply trivial, no more than a step. And yet how to cross them . . .?

She beat her head against that problem, without making progress. She felt the problem must be soluble, yet she saw no way to solve it. She felt stuck — or at least, she was until one gentle summer's night in early July. A nearby farmer had been cutting dead wood out of his orchards and piled together the clippings for burning. The fragrant wood smoke drifted across the camp. She herself felt suddenly homesick. Not homesick for Russia exactly — her memories of her own country were too overlaid with other feelings — but homesick all the same. She too wanted the freedom to roam where she wanted, to lie on her back looking up at the stars, to smell wood smoke, to make and burn fires of her own — in short, to make a life of her own, however simple.

She began to walk up and down the perimeter of the camp fence. She walked slowly, breathed deeply. Strangely enough, the thing she missed most was music. Her violin lessons had made a deep impression. She wondered if Misha owned a musical instrument. Did he still dance?

Her pacing took her to the foot of the main camp gate, the point at which she normally turned and went back the way she'd come. But a figure broke away from the shadows of one of the huts and came moving towards her. The twilight had deepened into almost-night. Deep indigo blue and violet still glowed in the west, but the east showed black beneath a tangle of stars. Tonya watched the person approach.

"Comrade Kornikova," he said, nodding profusely, "good evening. You are well?"

Tonya smiled at the question. Such obsequious politeness told her to expect something interesting. The man — whoever he was — smelt strongly of warm meat juices and alcohol.

"I'm very well, comrade, thank you. I'm afraid I can't . . ."

"Ah! I beg your pardon. All cats are grey in the dark." The man was short, only an inch or two taller than Tonya. There was a squirrelish busyness to his movements. The brim of his army cap hid his eyes. He jerked his hand upwards and snatched his cap from his head. "*Yefreytor* Rokossovsky. But, please, comrade, to you, I am Boris Alexandrovich."

"Boris Alexandrovich, good evening."

"Good evening, good evening. Listen, I feel very bad. The other day when you helped us, I hardly thanked you."

Tonya took a moment or two to understand what he meant. Then she remembered that a week or so back, there had been a problem with the supply of vegetables from the local collectivised farm. She had helped intermediate between the angry Russians and the perplexed locals. The matter had been simple enough and her intervention had lasted little more than ten minutes. Besides, as far as she remembered, Rokossovsky had shown as much gratitude as the situation had warranted.

"That's quite all right. I was only doing my job."

"Yes, but . . . a man should say his thanks. Listen, I brought you this." Rokossovsky put his hand inside his jacket and brought out a roasted onion and half a roast hare, wrapped in a parcel of cloth. The hare was still warm. Though food in the camp was plentiful, for people of Tonya's humble level, any meat provided was little enough and of the worst sort. The hare felt like a real treat. It reminded her, in fact, of those feasts in the hunting lodge in Petrozavodsk when Misha would return clear-faced and exultant from a hunt, simultaneously stamping snow from his boots, tossing a pair of cleanly shot hares onto the table, pulling off his cap, setting down his rifle, and embracing her.

She took the gift.

"Boris Alexandrovich, thank you."

"Ah yes, you are most welcome. I should have thought of something earlier, comrade. I apologise."

"That's all right, thank you."

"Is it good?"

Tonya wanted to eat the hare on her own, but realised that Rokossovsky didn't intend to let her. She began to eat it, picking meat straight from the bone with her teeth. The food was excellent. It was the true taste of Petrozavodsk, and once again the sense of homesickness began to pound at her. Rokossovsky watched her closely, nodding at her every bite, grinning to encourage her. When she bit into the onion, he said, "Onion treats seven ailments, so they say. But you're already well. Very good." Tonya finished the onion and ate part of the hare. Then, hoping to be allowed to eat the rest in peace, told Rokossovsky she'd save the remains for later. He seemed disappointed, but not for long.

"Well done, comrade. Very wise. Best not to waste it, by eating too fast."

Tonya wrapped the hare and folded it inside her tunic. She hoped her companion would leave, but knew he wouldn't.

She yawned loudly. "It's getting late . . ."

"Yes, comrade, but . . . listen, may I speak with you?"

"Of course."

"They say that he who risks nothing, never drinks champagne. And this business is ..." Rokossovsky found himself unable to get further. Somewhere deep in Tonya's subconscious there was a prickle of excitement.

"A fly cannot get into a closed mouth," she said, answering his proverb with another.

"Yes, yes! Exactly! And in this stink of a camp, there are many flies."

"Boris Alexandrovich, is there something I can do to help you?"

He seemed relieved to be asked a direct question. "Yes, my comrades and I ... you liked the hare, comrade? I apologise for ... Listen." He finally mastered his nervousness and began to speak. Once he'd started, he was almost unstoppable. The quartermaster received supplies for the entire camp. But he and others, including Rokossovsky, had contrived to fiddle things so that the camp received supplies sufficient for eleven hundred prisoners, instead of the eight hundred actually present. "He's a shrewd one, that quartermaster. He could cheat a fish of its skin. The winter was a bad one. There wasn't much food. The prisoners seemed to drop like wasps in autumn." Rokossovsky shrugged. The morality of the situation obviously didn't concern him much. "But what isn't written, isn't known. We have food to sell, and when I take the truck into Bad Freienwalde for fuel, then I ..." He broke off, not quite daring actually to name his crime. But it was clear enough. "These

Germans — they're only dogs really — despite everything, they're still rich. Why I saw one man. He owned three handsaws, comrade, can you imagine? Three! And in all my village, there were only two."

Tonya put up a hand to stop the flow. The excitement that she had sensed before had now hardened and condensed into something tangible, almost pebble-like in its density. "I understand. You sell what you have. But you want my help?"

"These Germans. They look ragged and bargain hard. There is gold in their cellars. This I know for a true fact. My friend, Sergei Mikhailovich, has a friend who told him —"

"If you want my help to bargain, Boris Alexandrovich, then you are most welcome. Bargaining is easy if you understand the language."

"Yes, yes, comrade Kornikova!"

"But you know, of course, that I'm not permitted to leave the camp. The terms of my assignment here . . ."

"Ah, yes!" Word of Tonya's punishment and demotion was fairly well known around the camp. Rokossovsky either hadn't known or, more likely, had clean forgotten. But he wasn't downcast. "But still, there are ways . . . I'd have to think . . . we would need it to be safe . . ."

Tonya nodded. Rokossovsky was half-excited, half-nervous.

"You think about it, Boris Alexandrovich. I'd be delighted to help you. You can come and talk to me whenever you wish."

"Yes. But remember, comrade. These things are dangerous. Keep your ears wide and your mouth narrow."

Tonya smiled. "The wolf doesn't eat the wolf," she quoted.

Rokossovsky's eyes lit up. "Exactly, comrade. And we're two wolves together, eh?" He thanked her again, then vanished into the night.

And Tonya's excitement could now burst out like a glorious firework, green and gold against the night sky. Rokossovsky was the opening she'd been waiting for. How it would work, she had as yet no idea, but she knew this squirrelish little man had it in him to open a path to freedom. The apple-branch fire had almost died to nothing now, but its smell still lingered on the air. The night sky was solid black now, dazzled with stars and the first hint of moonrise. Tonya ate the last of her hare, still almost warm. She was happy, gloriously happy.

6

Cotbus.

The town square. A large hall, formerly some kind of agricultural exchange, had been converted into a kind of canteen for Soviet troops and privileged local workers. The place was mostly deserted. Around forty yellow-topped tables and wooden seats stood around under unshaded overhead lights. The service counter was blue with steam and the smell of boiled milk.

291

Misha, holding the ticket that authorised him to enter, looked around uncertainly. A group of cleaning women, certainly local Germans, sat at one table with a clutter of mops and buckets standing behind them. Two Red Army officers sat at another table, playing cards. Otherwise there was almost no one. Misha marked the rank and regiment of the two officers, then walked up to the counter and asked for a glass of ersatz-coffee, which he paid for in worn-out Reichsmark notes.

As Misha moved away from the counter, he heard a noise behind him. Turning, he saw a man hurrying up to him. The man was dressed in a soft brown suit, and had a wispy beard and nervous eyes.

"Herr Müller. *Ja*. I'm sorry. I'm late. Apologies."

"You're Kunz?"

"Kunz. Yes. I should have said. Kunz."

They shook hands. Kunz's handshake was limp and apologetic. The man was of fighting age, but he didn't look as though he'd ever been a soldier. Kunz himself bought a glass of hot milk and a bun so stale that it could have broken teeth. Then they sat down together at a table.

"You need help with translation? Herr Ingenieur Bofinger said that . . ."

"Yes."

Misha sighed, trying not to show his disappointment. He'd been in Cotbus selling his castings. His samples had been greedily accepted, a price agreed, and the plant manager — the forceful and intelligent Herr Bofinger — had arranged this meeting. The man's Russian was halting but not bad, and he'd certainly be able to handle the business that Misha would give him. But no, Kunz had never heard of a female translator used by the Soviets. The name Kornikova meant nothing to him.

After making arrangements for Kunz to handle the various bits of business relating to his transaction with Bofinger, Misha left the canteen. A vague sense of disappointment swirled like milk steam in the air. At first, he assumed that it was simply his continuing lack of success in finding Tonya that accounted for his gloom. But it was more than that.

Thirty-ish, nervous, weak, only moderately skilled, Herr Kunz had been fairly typical of these provincial translators. Tonya simply wasn't like that. She must have been highly skilled to have held her position. And there was nothing nervous or weak in her either. It felt wrong. For the first time, Misha felt as though he were searching for Tonya in places that she couldn't possibly be. A deep instinct, a deep knowledge of the Soviet mind, told him he was on the wrong track. If Tonya had lost favour in Berlin, and if her skills were yet too valuable to waste, then they'd have found some other solution for her. Not this. She wouldn't simply have been sent to fritter away her days working alongside the Herr Kunzes of this world. Misha knew he was failing, but he didn't know how or why.

He drove back home, to Willi and Rosa, past ripening wheat fields springing with wild poppies and blue cornflowers. But he saw none of it. For the first time, he felt his optimism start to crumble.

7

The trip took place just five days after Rokossovsky's approach.

His method of getting Tonya out of camp had been simple and effective. One of his companions in crime, a sergeant, had staged a public rebuke for some trivial offence. Roaring at her, till his face reddened and the ends of his moustache quivered like a northern aspen, he promised that he'd make her "work until she dropped". The first element in her punishment programme was being made to go into town to help with getting fuel. As soon as possible after her rebuke, Rokossovsky had come hurtling around to explain that she wasn't to worry, it was all part of the plan, there would be more roast hare for her that night, and so on. Tonya had just smiled and laughed. If there were risk in the plan, it wasn't hers. She'd simply be obeying orders.

So they'd loaded up the truck and driven straight into the nearby town, Bad Freienwalde. Tonya stared at her surroundings in astonishment. The town was a small miracle. Aside from two or three dozen houses lost to artillery fire in the last months of the war, nothing had been damaged. Prosperous municipal buildings jostled alongside steep-roofed houses complete with clean paint-work and flowering window-boxes. The inhabitants, of course, looked hungry and worn, and the town was home to a Red Army tank regiment, which would no doubt have stripped every house of any remaining valuables. But all the same, the town was the prettiest, cleanest, most well-to-do place she'd ever seen. Tonya drank in the sight.

Rokossovsky gestured at it all.

"These bastards, hey?"

Tonya, not wanting to argue, simply nodded. She didn't see any obvious Hitler Youth. She did see plenty of women, her age, struggling to feed their families.

"Their cellars, I tell you, full of gold. These men from the tank regiments, they're the lucky ones. I bet they've milked the cow dry, eh?"

He imitated the act of squeezing an udder. Tonya had realised by now that her companion didn't always need her to reply. As for herself, she was nervous, though not much. Along with the empty fuel drums in the back of the truck, there was a sack of carrots, two sacks of winter potatoes, long gone soft, and six bags of coal in fifty kilo bags.

"We'll do the fuel first. If the bastards ask about the supplies, we just tell them nothing."

Rokossovsky muttered to himself, as he swept the truck around to the fuel dump set up by the tank regiment. The tankists always looked down on ordinary army units, and their respect for the lowly troopers at Oderbruch Special Camp was somewhere well south of zero. But the fuel made its way from the fuel dump into the drums in the back of the truck. There were a couple of local German men employed on menial duties around the dump and Tonya duly interpreted any orders which were bellowed their way, which weren't many and certainly not ones that needed much translation. Then Rokossovsky signed some receipts for the fuel and climbed back into the truck.

"Bastards."

He swung the truck back out onto the road, then, driving too fast, plunged down a network of side roads to a small brick warehouse built beside a pretty tree-lined canal. The warehouse was built so that its brick sides rose straight out of the water.

"Now then," said Rokossovsky. "Careful. We need to get a good price. These bastards . . . gold . . . but look out, we must keep a good lookout . . ."

Plainly frightened by what he was doing, he went to the back of the truck and opened the tailgate. A German woman, alerted by the noise came out of the warehouse. She was brown-haired, brown-eyed and pretty. Her clothes were in poor repair, but though hungry, she didn't have the famished look that so many Germans now had. Behind her, a group of small children watched with wide eyes. The children, as so often, looked almost properly fed: the result of parents going hungry. Tonya felt an instant sympathy for the woman, who was roughly her own age.

Rokossovsky continued to fuss. She calmed him down, saying, "Ssh! The egg can't teach the chicken." It was logic he instantly accepted, and he went obediently quiet. He tugged the coal, carrots and potatoes from the truck. The German woman inspected them, insisting on burrowing deep into each sackload to be sure that they hadn't been filled out with stones or logs at the bottom. Rokossovsky, speaking Russian, but whispering anyway, began telling Tonya what kind of exchange would be acceptable: watches, clocks, jewellery, gold, china, carpentry tools, saucepans, decent clothes, lace. The list ran on. Tonya shushed him again.

She introduced herself to the German woman, who was called Gisela.

Tonya adopted a very sharp voice, almost a shout, and said, "Gisela, you must make it look as if I'm bargaining very hard. Answer me angrily to begin with."

There was a quick flash of understanding in the woman's sharp-featured face — hunger made every face sharp — then her old suspicious expression returned.

She shouted back, "I will answer you angrily, but what do you want for all this?"

Tonya — using the tone of voice her father had once used, before age and alcohol had rendered him feeble — yelled back, "Anything reasonable. But I can't accept rubbish or this man won't use me again."

Gisela spat furiously on the ground and flung up an arm. "You are very kind," she thundered. "We are all nearly starving here and your *verdammte* cousins in the tank corps have already robbed us of almost everything."

The ludicrous conversation continued. Gisela was little short of a genius at it. Her tone and expression varied between rage, scorn and stubborn refusal to debate.

In the meantime, with her words, she told Tonya that she had four children; that her husband had died in

297

Russia, that Tonya would be very welcome to come to dinner any time, that if only women had been in charge of things the world would be a much happier place.

At times Tonya wondered if they were overdoing the theatrics, but Rokossovsky looked rapt in pleasure and admiration. Slowly Gisela brought out a pile of offerings — a poor-quality carpet, a non-working clock, three old saucepans, some foolish little ornaments made of straw and embroidered cotton, a real oil painting, a few other things besides.

"Do you think my colleague will be happy with that?" Tonya hectored, her voice now beginning to go hoarse. "I don't know what he normally accepts for this sort of thing."

Gisela — who now stood with hanging head, as though cowed and browbeaten into submission — said, "He should be. This is less than normal, but you can tell him that the tankists have been robbing us. That much is true at least."

Tonya nodded. She turned to Rokossovsky and began to apologise for the relatively poor deal she'd struck. He shook his head, eyes wide with awe.

"You were splendid," he cried. "You really had her begging for mercy. That old wet hen! I wish I'd brought you here before. I'm an old fox, but whiskers can't take the place of brains. You sent her clucking from the yard!"

Rokossovsky began to clear his treasures into the back of the truck.

Tonya turned to the woman, who had tears of gratitude standing in her eyes. Tonya wanted desperately to embrace her. How long had it been since she'd felt that kind of touch? She'd experienced something warm with Valentina and something courteous, even gracious, with Marta. But in neither case had she felt the instant rapport she'd built with Gisela.

Crossly, Tonya said, "If I wanted to get a letter to Berlin, could you send it?"

Still humble, still defeated, Gisela answered. "Thank you from the bottom of my heart for your help. Of course I can send a letter for you, but it may be opened on the way. Everything now is spies, soldiers and policemen."

"No, it would have to be secret. There's a man there . . . I want to join him, but I'm not at liberty myself."

Again, there was that quick movement of understanding flashing deep in Gisela's brown eyes. "Let me think. There may be ways. Will you be here next time?"

Tonya nodded.

"Let me think. I'll tell you next time."

"Thank you. It would mean everything."

Again, Tonya wanted to hug her, but Rokossovsky would never have trusted her again if she'd done so. The two women, still in role, nodded farewell. Rokossovsky, exultant at his triumph but becoming nervous, gunned the engine. Tonya climbed in next to him. Rokossovsky put the truck into gear and roared away up the hill.

8

All that summer it was the same thing. More and more, Misha felt he was on the wrong track, but couldn't for the life of him work out what the right track would be. He didn't give up. Apart from anything else, his business was thriving and would have taken him into the east zone continually anyway. But for the first time, he allowed his search for Tonya to slacken in intensity. His bedtime stories to Rosa grew in length again. The family took time off. And — the biggest change of all — they moved house. Rosa, via a schoolmate, happened to learn of a little cottage that backed onto the grounds of Rosa's old UNRRA orphanage. The cottage had been used by a group of British nurses, and as a result, was in good repair and ready to move into. Misha had called on Brandt for some overdue payments, which the blackmarket man had handed over in a mixture of scrip dollars, Reichsmarks, cigarettes and a strange array of other oddments: whole hams, cases of wine, a clock, a forty-litre drum of petrol. The money had been enough to pay for the house, and Rosa, Willi and Misha all moved across one Sunday in September, pushing their belongings in a borrowed handcart. Willi grumbled, of course. In place of his much beloved Nothing Factory, he would now have to put up with the bourgeois cosiness or *Gemütlichkeit* that he, in theory anyway, so detested. Misha bought him a second-hand American camera and a supply of film and the complaints soon evaporated.

As for Rosa, she was, of course, ecstatic. She had charged around the house, feeling the glass in all the windows, opening and closing the curtains for the sheer joy of having them, insisting on laying the table for dinner because that allowed her to spread out the clean linen tablecloth. Misha had watched her joy, wondering if he should accept that Tonya would never be there to share it.

And then, finally, he got a break.

It was one of those back-to-front discoveries that revealed nothing to begin with, but which, when looked at the other way around, promised to reveal absolutely everything.

It had happened in the desolation of a failing optical products factory in Weimar. The plant had been one of the worst he'd seen: an echoing shell, staffed by ghosts. The manager himself had been in wistful, almost elegiac, mood.

"Yes, my choices get narrower by the day. There's no real prospect of rebuilding this business. The local Ivans understand that, but they have their political bosses in Berlin and their bosses' bosses in Moscow. Sooner or later, someone will have to pay. For me, the only real choice is fleeing to the West or a camp in the woods."

The manager had waved out towards the sea of beech trees beyond the town.

"A camp?" asked Misha, surprised by the manager's use of the word. The Soviets imprisoned people freely of course. They deported them to their loathsome labour battalions and the Gulag. But camps?

"No, no, of course." The manager dropped his hand. "I only meant . . ."

He didn't say what he meant. He'd steered hard away from the subject as though regretting bringing it up.

That was it: the breakthrough.

To begin with, Misha had thought nothing of it. He'd begun the long drive back through the woods, heading east towards Berlin. The light was golden, but not as warm as earlier in the summer. The leaves on the trees were just beginning to be tinted with gold, as though too much summer sun had worn away the green. Misha drove fast, wanting to be back in time to put Rosa to bed — something that mattered even more now that Willi had set up as a photographer and his always-uncertain hours had become more erratic than ever. His jeep-style bucket car, or Kübelwagen, jounced and leaped on the rutted roads. Taking a corner too fast, Misha encountered a convoy of Soviet military vehicles heading straight for him, blocking the road. There was no time to brake, so Misha flung his car off the road and came bumping to a halt in a spray of leaf-fall and underbrush. He killed the ignition.

The convoy ground its way past. Misha noted what he could: convoy size, regimental markings, any senior officers' cars. All these details and more he memorised and would relay to Harry Hollinger in due course. He didn't know how much use the

Englishman could make of such reports, but he did know that the Western Allies were worried about Soviet intentions. Every little detail of troop movements could help Hollinger's analysts build up a picture of what was going on. The last truck in the convoy grumbled past in a roar of exhaust smoke, then moved off to leave the road and woods in silence once again. Misha put his hand back to the ignition.

He turned the key.

Or rather, he began to turn the key, until the tumblers inside were engaged. Another one degree of turn would engage the ignition. But instead of completing the movement, he withdrew his hand.

"The only real choice is fleeing to the West or a camp in the woods."

It had been a strange thing for the manager to say, but that wasn't what had suddenly caught Misha's attention. He remembered the man's hand movement. He had originally held his hand so that it was pointing roughly westwards out of the window. Then he'd glanced out at the forest and adjusted his hand so that it had pointed north-west. If there wasn't a camp, then why adjust hand position? If there was a camp, then why deny it?

All of a sudden, those questions seemed suddenly immense, momentous, hanging in the air like artillery smoke over a battlefield.

Moving quickly again, Misha backed the car out of its intimate clinch with the Thüringen forest. Swinging back onto the road, he pointed the car not east to Rosa and Berlin, but back west the way he had come. He drove intently, angrily, first west to Weimar, then north, then west again.

The forest closed and thickened around the car. The sound of his engine was the only human sound audible for miles. The air was full of sunlight and bird noise, the quick scurry of squirrels. When he reached junctions in the road, he hesitated. He examined any road signs and any tracks gouged into the soft roadside grass. He navigated partly by judgement, mostly by intuition. The light began to soften as the big orange sun plunged towards the horizon.

Then Misha found a sign. The sign was in Russian only, not German. It read "Special Camp Number 2" with an arrow pointing up a heavily-rutted road.

Misha felt the sudden clamour and jabber of excitement, a feeling made up of sweating palms, a cold rush of adrenalin, the sudden focused clarity of thought.

Misha took his car off the road and plunged right into the forest, far enough into the undergrowth that the vehicle's flat grey lines wouldn't be visible. Misha kept a pair of binoculars in the car. He didn't ordinarily like using them — the risk of being denounced as a spy was too great — but now was no time to worry. He took the binoculars and darted off into the undergrowth, proceeding uphill, into the fading tree-filtered sunlight.

9

It took Rokossovsky and his accomplices in the quartermaster's office two weeks to accumulate enough produce to be worth selling. The first trip they made, Gisela was away and Tonya had to bargain with a rodent-like man, who seemed to live in another part of the warehouse. Tonya didn't trust him at all. She saw in him the classic black-marketeer, shifty and self-interested. She bargained hard and got a much better deal than the time before. Rokossovsky again was ecstatic.

Two weeks later, things were all set up for the trip, but then one of the NKVD camp staff needed a trip into town and borrowed a ride on the truck. That meant that the whole deal was off again — they couldn't sell camp stores under the NKVD's nose — and they needed to wait again. Four more weeks passed fruitlessly. Either Tonya was unable to leave camp, or when she did she couldn't find Gisela. Then, finally, on the first day of August, she was in the truck again, with Rokossovsky nervous but excited at the wheel, heading for Bad Freienwalde.

Tonya had fallen in love with the German countryside. It wasn't the landscape, so much, that enchanted her. The low hills, little banks of woodland and curving rivers all struck Tonya's Russian eyes as somehow unreal: built on the scale of a doll's house. But more than all that, it was the villages and farms that she loved. They had their doll's house quality too, but in their case it had to do with their neatness, their

305

perfect order. Tonya looked and could never stop looking at the neatly pruned orchards, the tidy fences, the trim cottages, the orderly fields. As Rokossovsky hammered the truck brutally forwards, he talked incessantly, while Tonya said nothing. When they got to town, Rokossovsky sorted out the fuel by himself.

When they got down to the canal-side, Tonya braced herself against the disappointment of not seeing Gisela again, but the roar of the truck engine hadn't even died away, before Gisela emerged in her dark skirt and white blouse, wanting to smile, only not able to because of Rokossovsky.

This time they had no coal to sell, only food: a sack of rice, a sack of flour, five crates of mixed vegetables. Tonya guessed they weren't just taking food from dead prisoners, they were probably stealing from the mouths of the living too. She didn't like it. The poor brutes were desperately hungry and every now and then waves of infection would sweep through the camp and another few corpses would be carried out to be buried in the woods by the prisoners themselves. However, Tonya wasn't in a position to do anything about it, and in the meantime if the food helped Gisela and her family, it wasn't going to waste.

They began "bargaining", keeping their roles from the time before: Tonya angry, bullying. Gisela defiant, then beaten.

"How are you? I didn't see you the last time I came."

"I'm fine. You saw Jurgen. He can be difficult."

"No meat, I'm afraid, or coal. But the vegetables are excellent."

"It makes all the difference. We women have a little collective. We distribute the food so the children never go short. You can see through the doorway there, how healthy they are."

"Despite everything!"

"Yes."

"Last time, I asked you if —"

"I haven't forgotten." This was the first time Gisela's acting slipped, and she gave a bright smile that showed all her teeth, and both women could feel Rokossovsky scowl in displeasure. Gisela stopped smiling instantly and fell straight back into role — "A friend of mine, Herr Kirsten, has a canal-barge. He runs loads of wheat and potatoes straight from here into Berlin."

"To Berlin!"

"The Heiligensee. Near Tegel. The French sector, I think. The barges are searched sometimes. Your countrymen don't like seeing food go west. They interfere with things, make it hard. But if you don't mind lying flat in the bows under some boards, we'll load the produce straight on top. They'd have to empty the whole boat to find you."

Tonya was so happy at the idea, she couldn't keep the jubilation out of her voice, as she thanked Gisela. Gisela responded cleverly, making Tonya's jubilation seem like victory in the bargaining contest. She went — humbly, browbeaten — to the warehouse and dragged out some baskets of knick-knacks, rubbish mostly, which she laid out for Tonya's approving inspection.

As they pretended to haggle over a few remaining items, they began to deal with some of the practicalities.

"When is Herr Kirsten here?"

"It's hard to say. His timetables are very variable. It depends on so much that's out of his control. But every ten days or so."

"It's difficult. I can only come so irregularly myself."

"If you wanted, you could try to hide here, in the warehouse."

Tonya could tell Gisela was unhappy with that idea. And in any event, so was she. "No. That wouldn't be safe for either of us. I don't know how hard they'll try to look for me, but it would be no good if they caught me . . . Listen, I'll try to come here on Mondays. It's not entirely in my control, but I'll try."

"Do you want to say Tuesday? There's a street market on the Hauptstrasse on Tuesdays. That could serve as an excuse, perhaps."

"Excellent. Tuesday. If Herr Kirsten can try to be here then — other things permitting, of course — then we can hope to try something then."

"What about him?" Gisela indicated Rokossovsky, who was crouching down by the pile of bartered goods: scarves, embroidered tablecloths, children's spinning tops, blunt chisels, rush baskets.

"I don't know. He's scared all the time. I'll think of something."

"You will be taking a big risk." Gisela spoke soberly.

"Yes. But less than I risk by not trying. I could do none of it without your help."

308

Gisela shrugged. "We women must help each other. Nobody else will."

Rokossovsky was happy with his haul, pitiful as it was. Tonya made an excuse to go into the warehouse with Gisela, where the two women hugged in privacy. By the time they came out again, Rokossovsky had loaded the truck and was waiting, with engine throbbing, beginning to be nervous. Tonya climbed in, resisting the urge to wave.

10

Misha went straight to Hollinger with his news

They met once a week at what, Misha supposed, he should call a safe house. But the term was too technical, too like the fieldcraft jargon of a paid and trained secret agent. Misha didn't think of himself like that. He toured the east zone. He kept his eyes and ears open. He passed on anything useful to a friend of his in intelligence. What happened to the information after that, he didn't spend much time thinking about. The meeting place itself was nothing special: just the windowless back room of a former tourist information office. The walls were painted in a pale, sickly green, and were hung with pre-war posters advertising the many pleasures of travel in the Third Reich.

"It was an old Nazi camp, Buchenwald," said Misha. "The Soviets just converted it. Same buildings. Same use."

"Well, that would make sense. Birds of a feather and all that." Hollinger translated the phrase direct from the

English, then repeated himself in proper German, "*Gleich und gleich gesellt sich gern*."

"Yes, quite."

"How close could you get?"

"A hundred metres. But I had binoculars."

"Not an easy sight, I imagine. For you especially."

Misha nodded, rubbing his face with both hands.

"It was awful," he said, simply. "I was never in Buchenwald. Perhaps never anywhere that bad. But . . ." He shook his head. For three hours he had lain on his stomach outside the camp, gazing at it through his glasses. It had been little more than a year since he'd been released from captivity himself, and thus far he'd simply tried to wall himself off from his memories. But back there, in the woods outside Buchenwald, staring at row after row of wooden huts and barbed-wire fences surveyed by machine guns, all those memories had come shockingly back to life. Misha had seen the ragged, starving prisoners moving listlessly between the buildings. It had been awful to watch. The old, hopeless depression had seeped into him like February mist, a cold that no summer warmth could ever hide.

"How long were you in camps?" asked Hollinger gently.

"Seven years. It felt like a lifetime. After two years, I was sure I would die there."

"It's unimaginable. Beyond thinking about."

"And it wasn't only me."

"No, no. Your wife . . ."

"Lillie. Yes. I loved her very much. We were happy. And not only her. Otto, her father, died somewhere like that too. I think perhaps one of the reasons why Tonya matters to me so much now is because of what happened to Lillie. To lose one's wife and best friend is awful. Almost the worst thing that could happen to a man. To lose Lillie and Tonya too — as you say, it's beyond thinking about."

Hollinger nodded, allowing Misha as much time and silence as he needed. Misha had always tried to think of Lillie as she had been: laughing, healthy, bright-eyed, vivacious. He had tried never to think about what she must have become before death: one of those walking ghosts that filled the camps. Mostly he had succeeded in keeping her old self alive. The hours spent outside Buchenwald had summoned up his old demons again, and Misha fell silent. Hollinger, with his usual unobtrusive tact, lit a couple of cigarettes and passed one over to Misha. Neither man smoked much, but there were times for everything.

They smoked in silence for a few minutes.

Then, sensing a shift in the mood again, Hollinger drew them back to the main subject. "The prisoners. How many?"

"Thousands. Not less than two thousand. I didn't think more than eight or nine."

"Poor souls."

"Yes."

"Not still an extermination camp, I hope?"

"No. Not that. I'm afraid I know the difference all too well. In any case, that's not the Soviet way. Stalin

311

doesn't mind killing people, but he doesn't do it on a production line like the Nazis. These were prisoners, pure and simple."

"And nationality? I suppose you couldn't tell?"

"Mostly German, I think. Perhaps all German. I couldn't tell."

"And the camp staff?"

"Soviet, of course. But not many of them. The prisoners looked as though they ran things themselves without much interference. The entire camp staff can't have been more than a couple of hundred at the most."

There was a long pause, before Hollinger asked the million-dollar question. "But big enough to need a translator?"

Misha took another cigarette from Hollinger's pack before answering. His hands shook as he lit up. "That's the question. For me, that's the whole question."

Hollinger examined his cigarette with scrupulous care, then finished smoking it with as much careful attention as a philosophy don might devote to constructing an argument in logic. When he was done, he stubbed the butt out and said, "Antonina was never convicted of anything serious. I'd swear to it. Marta, her handler, has been left in peace. And we know — I can't tell you how — that the Soviets are short of translators. I can't believe they'd have sent her back to Russia for anything minor. She's here. In Germany. I'm almost certain."

Misha nodded. "I believe you. I think you're right. I feel it."

"And?"

"The camp must have translators. Must have. It's too big, too complex for it to manage without. You see, I *know* the Soviet way of thinking. In Russia, we've always exiled our people. We did it under the tsars. We do it under Stalin. If the Soviet administration here lost confidence in Tonya, what would they do? In Russia, she'd have been sent off in internal exile. Somewhere a thousand, two thousand kilometres from Moscow. Here in Germany, the country's too small. It's no distance from anywhere to anywhere. But what's the nearest thing you can get to internal exile here? What's the most out of the way, hidden, forgotten place that exists? It's these special camps. Buchenwald is number two. How many others are there? Not hundreds, or you'd already have known about them. Not even dozens."

Hollinger nodded. "I agree."

"And then again, I've been to all the big Soviet-German cities by now. I've asked around for translators. They haven't been hard to find, in fact. Lots of people, eager to help for the money. But that's always been my worry. It feels wrong. The translators I've found are the wrong sort. If Tonya had been convicted of some foolish offence, they'd have made it hard for her to stay in touch with the world outside. Not because they suspect that I'm looking for her or anything like that, but because that's how these people — *my* people — think."

Hollinger finished another cigarette. It was the fourth one he'd smoked since Misha had been with him. He stared at the butt as though suddenly disgusted by the whole idea of tobacco, and threw the pack onto the table behind him.

"So let's take that as an assumption," he said. "Antonina is attached to one of these blasted camps. We need to find the camps, then find her. After that . . ." He blew out. "After that, we'll just have to find a way to get her out."

11

Tonya sat on her bunk: a wooden frame knocked together from rough sawn wood, a mattress of cotton ticking stuffed with straw, an old cotton sheet now grey with age, two army-issue blankets. It was a sunny day outside, but fresh, and the sharpening autumn air brought out the smell of resin and pine oil from the wooden-walled hut.

Tomorrow was a Tuesday. Tonya had persuaded Rokossovsky to make a trip down to the market that day. Her plan was an uncomplicated one. She would give him the slip during the street market and run down to the little warehouse. If Herr Kirsten and his canal-boat were there, she'd hide away on the barge then and there. If not, she'd simply go back into town, relocate Rokossovsky and try again as soon as she could. The plan relied on the fact that Rokossovsky would be too nervous of having lost Tonya to give the alarm. Since he wasn't, strictly speaking, meant to allow Tonya to accompany him into town, she was pretty certain that he'd just scurry back to camp like a frightened rabbit, denying all knowledge of having seen her.

She felt surprisingly calm. On the one hand, the next two or three days might well determine whether she was safe in Misha's arms or bound for a convict-train to Siberia. And yet, though she didn't deceive herself about the risks, she felt calm. If the attempt worked, it would work. If not . . . well, she didn't spend much time thinking about the alternative.

The air outside was still. The ordinary noises of the camp drifted in through an open window. The prisoners themselves created almost no noise. It was one of the saddest things. The Soviets had imprisoned them and then, in effect, forgotten them. There were few interrogations now. There were no charges or trials. No sentences. No letters or visits. As well as physical illness and infection, the prisoners, almost to a man, suffered from depression, lassitude and despair.

Tonya had come into the hut to pack.

The instinct to prepare for a journey was an old one, as old as Russia perhaps. But here and now, there was nothing more ridiculous. It wasn't just that Tonya wasn't sure how much space she'd have in her hidey hole on the barge. It was more that she owned nothing. The Red Army provided her with her uniform: the clothes she wore now and one change of clothes for when those were being washed. She had some basic underwear and some comfortable boots. She had an embroidered handkerchief that Valentina had given her. She had a comb, a tin mug, a bar of soap, a leather hair-tie, a picture torn from an American magazine that showed a pine forest under snow, a pot of petroleum jelly that she used to protect her lips in winter, a pair of jealously guarded sheepskin insoles that made all the difference when walking in heavy snow. And that was it. She had lost everything when she'd been sent to Siberia. She hadn't even been able to take a picture of Rodyon or of her two daughters. She was forty-seven years old. She had no family, no possessions, no home, no status, no prospects. And she had come in here to pack! She laughed quietly at herself. Tomorrow she would put the hair-tie, soap and comb in her pocket, so that she had some chance of making herself look neat when she emerged from the barge and went in search of Misha. And that was it. That was all she had and all she needed.

Would Misha be rich? She was vaguely aware that he might be. Not only had he escaped Russia with his father's money but, more than that, she knew that he was naturally and prolifically gifted. If he had chosen to go into business, she simply couldn't imagine that he might have failed. Of course, though, Germany was a devastated country and there weren't many rich men left anywhere. But then again, rich was a relative matter. Little though Tonya cared about Misha's financial status, she felt fairly sure that he'd have managed to accumulate more than a hair-tie, a comb and a bar of soap.

She laughed again, feeling joyous.

In the yard outside, she heard a car zoom in through the gates and brake sharply. It was a foolish, showy way to drive, but the fashion for such driving had spread through NKVD ranks, as though such arrogance at the wheel reflected well on the splendour of the state that they served. Tonya listened vaguely to the goings on outside. Normally, they sank into a familiar pattern. The cars, voices, boots, doors, all had their own rhythms, their own customary patterns.

But right now, there was something different going on. Alerted, Tonya sat up and listened. There was a new voice. She couldn't make it out, but it had a brisk, snapping quality to it. It was a voice accustomed to giving out orders and reprimands, a far cry from the camp's usual absence of stiff discipline. Tonya stood up and straightened her uniform. Her boots weren't properly polished. Recently that hadn't mattered, but there had been rumours that the camp was to have a new commandant and if a martinet had arrived among them, then grubby boots might become an issue.

Tonya hesitated. She had no polish of her own, but one of her roommates, the quartermaster's wife, had a tin that she sometimes let Tonya use. But curiosity won the day over boots. Tonya checked her uniform one more time, then stepped out into the yard.

The car that had drawn up was a black ZiS limousine, a car that always denoted seniority. The officer who had emerged from it stood with his back to Tonya. She thought she could glimpse the royal blue of the NKVD insignia, but she wasn't quite sure.

She advanced closer.

The man's uniform was perfectly pressed, including even the backs of his trousers. Rodyon had had that ability once: the ability to work like a Trojan all day and

317

still to look crisp and fresh at the end of it — not that this new man was Rodyon, of course. He was too short and too young. The man hadn't advanced more than six or seven yards beyond his car. He had his thumbs hooked into the side of his belt and he stood with his shoulders back and his chest puffed out. His voice had a nasty, carrying tone. The soldiers he was speaking to were plainly being reprimanded, perhaps even being told off for punishment. There were certainly privates included in his audience, but there were officers too, a captain even. Tonya suddenly wished she had taken the time to polish her boots. She realised that her plan for getting down to the canal in Bad Freienwalde tomorrow might have to be called off. There was something frightening, even disastrous in the mild September air.

She came closer.

The officer was a *podpolkovnik*, a lieutenant colonel in the NKVD. Tonya sidled round to join the group of soldiers he was addressing. As he heard her approach, his head changed direction slightly to indicate that he'd noticed her. She sprang to attention. She was no parade-ground soldier — never had been — but she could pull off a smart salute, when called for. She stood stiffly, her chin up, her eyes with that unseeing middle-distance focus beloved of inspecting officers. She saw the man only as a shape, an impression of a head balding from the front, mid-brown hair and that impeccable uniform.

A second or two passed.

The man wasn't instantly acknowledging her salute. She held her pose, waiting. The man had stopped talking. He was coming over towards her. He was smiling, but Tonya knew that smiles didn't always betoken warmth. The man was standing in front of her now, but for some reason she still didn't look at him properly. She kept her eyes blank, her gaze unfocused. He stopped.

"Well, well, well, Antonina Kirylovna Kornikova."

She almost jumped in surprise. Her blank look suddenly concentrated itself on the man's face. She saw the puckered skin, the blue eyes, the loose, full-lipped mouth. It was her brother, Pavel. She hadn't seen him for ten years.

"Pavel!" she exclaimed in shock. Her brother's smile broadened and his eyebrows lifted. She realised he was waiting for her to acknowledge his rank. "Sir!" she corrected herself.

He acknowledged her salute with a brief gesture of his hand and he allowed her to stand at ease. He looked her up and down. His gaze lingered on her boots, but he said nothing. Then he gave a short nod. He turned back to the men he had been addressing. He had been reprimanding them for a slackness in saluting him on arrival. It should have been a short matter, but he went on haranguing the men, privates and officers alike, for a full eight or ten minutes.

Tonya remembered those first revolutionary years. Pavel had been so eager to copy Rodyon. He had so much admired the older man's force, purpose and energy. But he'd understood nothing; nothing that had

319

mattered. Rodyon's drive had always come straight from his sense of injustice, his determination to do things better. Pavel hadn't cared for any of that. He'd liked the power, the power to command and the authority to punish.

And Tonya suddenly realised something else. She'd never known who had denounced her to the authorities that time in 1936. In that paranoiac decade, suspicion had crept in everywhere. Friends denounced friends. Family denounced family. The kind old lady who helped you with your washing turned out to be a paid informant for the NKVD. So Tonya had never spent much time wondering who had denounced her or why . . . and yet now that she saw Pavel again, like this, she remembered that in the weeks before her arrest, he had made a rare trip from Leningrad to Moscow where he had spent a few days staying in Tonya's apartment. On one evening, Pavel had produced a bottle of lemon vodka and the two of them had got a little drunk together. Tonya now remembered that she had grumbled about the kind of communist party that could send a good man like Rodyon to Siberia for imagined crimes. She'd remembered Pavel grinning, nodding, egging her on. But seeing his face now, in its NKVD uniform, with so much delight in its own rank, such willingness to inflict hurt, she realised that she had been drinking vodka that night with her own betrayer. Her brother, the traitor.

Pavel finished his harangue. The camp staff went about their duties, Tonya included. Pavel showed no desire to talk to her. Apart from that first use of her full name, he had shown no indication that he acknowledged a connection with her.

Tonya went back to her hut that night. She knew she wouldn't be going to Bad Freienwalde in the morning. She knew that the world had changed again, changed very much for the worse.

CHAPTER
TEN

1

Weeks passed.

Autumn drew in and with it, the promise of winter. The last winter, the one of 1945–46, had been bad, but people had somehow expected that. It was the first winter of peacetime. The country was occupied. Things were hard. What no one then had expected was that nothing would have changed a year later. Berlin was still a ruin. Yes, rubble was being cleared, but even so it was estimated that, at current rates of progress, it would take thirty years to finish the job. There was virtually no new construction. There were no tools to do it, no machinery, no materials, no cash. People were still hungry, and now they had a whole year's worth of extra hunger to contend with. No one had enough fuel, or enough cash to buy it. For the black-marketeers and the prostitutes, business was still strong. For everyone else, things were shifting from bad to desperate. Patience was running out. Grumbles against the occupiers had become a constant background noise, like the rumble of summer thunder.

And the coming winter would be awful. No one spoke about it, but everyone knew it.

2

Hollinger had been as good as his word to Misha.

In the last year or so of the war, Allied bombers had been able to pass more or less freely over the skies of Germany. Every inch of the country had been photographed from the air. Old pictures and charts had been pulled out and old sites re-examined. It wasn't long before Hollinger's analysts had identified a further six possible Special Camps. Misha had strongly wanted to go and check them out himself, but Hollinger had kept him back.

"You aren't a trained agent. Your memories of Antonina are almost thirty years old. You aren't skilled in this kind of observation."

They were sound arguments, ones that Misha was finally forced to accept. But though Hollinger swore that he had put plenty of manpower into observing the camps, he came up with nothing. "She isn't there. We're sure of it, as sure as we can be. But there are still other camps. There must be. We've found seven camps in all, but one of them is numbered Camp 12. There are at least five others. We just need to find them and check them. We'll do what we can."

Hollinger possibly spoke the truth, but Misha also knew that there were bureaucratic limitations to what he could do. How much time and effort could the British really put in to locating one, now-useless, agent? Misha knew that Hollinger cared about Tonya, but Hollinger was one thing, the system was another. More and more Misha felt that he would have to do the job himself.

But how? To that question, he had no answer. Except eventually one, and that from a most unlikely source: Willi.

Misha's gift of a camera had been inspired. It was as though all Willi's experiments with ink and pen and brush had been simply preparation for this. The boy instantly secured a series of commissions from an American newspaper (thanks to an impressive but wholly fabricated resumé of his previous work) and used the cash to buy himself a fully-equipped darkroom. He continued to work off and on for the Americans, but most of his work now was freelance. He specialised in taking photos of Soviet officers as keepsakes for them to send to their loved ones back home. The officers paid in Reichsmarks or dark Russian cigarettes. Pleased with the results they got, they recommended him to their brother officers all across the east zone. Willi had papers that permitted him to travel freely, and made the most of his privileges. His particular trick was to capture his subjects in arrogant, almost imperial poses — like the Roman conquerors of a barbarian land. The Soviets liked them, because they only saw flattery. Willi was willing to do them, because of the bitter satire that propelled him.

And Willi had made a discovery — or so he claimed. He wouldn't say what it was, just summoned Misha and Rosa into his tiny darkroom. Misha hoisted Rosa up onto the workbench, and leaned back against the wall himself. Willi — carefully showing off, while pretending not to — bustled about, then, when he was ready, pulled the light cord. The room went completely dark, except for a dim red lamp above the sink.

"Now *tovarishch*," he muttered.

Beside Misha, negatives hung in long, seemingly random, celluloid loops on a piece of washing line. Discarded prints sat in the dustbin or in a scatter of rubbish all over the floor. But despite the apparent disorder, Willi seemed to know just what he was doing and he moved with the accuracy and expertise he displayed whenever he was doing something he loved. Rosa sat cross-legged on the end of the workbench, missing nothing.

"Now then. I took this in Bernau," announced Willi, clearly enjoying his audience and simultaneously threading a strip of film into his enlarger.

He flicked a switch and the image displayed itself on the enlarger board in reversed black-and-white. The image was of a Soviet officer leaning up against a truck. He shaded the enlarger light and threw a sheet of photographic paper under the lens. He exposed the image again, counted silently, then cut the light. The paper went straight in the bath of developer, which Willi rocked from side to side to keep the liquid moving. Rosa craned forwards, then suddenly, the image began to spring from the paper. Rosa gasped. Another few seconds, then Willi washed the page, fixed it, and washed it again.

Satisfied, he jerked on the light, and displayed the print.

"NKVD," said Misha.

"A captain, yes. But look. The newspaper."

Willi pointed to a newspaper that was just visible through the truck windscreen. Misha peered. He couldn't make it out.

"It's Polish," said Willi impatiently. "Look. Who else could produce a language like that?"

He handed Misha a magnifying glass so he could see better. The headline came into focus. Something about the city of Szczecin — Stettin in German.

"Willi, I don't understand."

The boy had brought him in here because he'd said he had something vital to show him. Misha didn't know what and he felt exasperated by Willi's insistence on coming at the subject sideways.

"That truck has been in Poland recently. Probably only a day or two back."

"So?"

"This officer wasn't stationed in Poland. He reported to the SMAD. He told me so."

Misha shrugged. "So?"

"So the man is an NKVD captain based in Germany, but stationed close enough to the Polish border to get that newspaper."

"Still, Willi," said Misha, patiently. "There's no shortage of NKVD men in Germany. Just because . . ."

"He was in charge of prisoners."

"He told you that?"

"Yes. Nearly. As good as."

Misha raised his eyebrows. It was hard to know how seriously to take the boy. Willi was still such a mixture of contrasts. He was young in years, but old in experience; prideful, but competent; too quick to draw conclusions, but often exceptionally shrewd where it most counted.

"He had a truck driver with him. The truck was loaded with potatoes. Bad ones. Soft. I laughed at the load, and said that was no food for a conquering hero. The captain told me that the food wasn't for him, it was for pigs."

"Maybe it was."

"You know it wasn't."

Willi was right. The NKVD were an elite. Their commanders reported directly to Beria, bypassing all the normal military routes of command. No NKVD man, still less a captain, would be sent to buy food for farm animals. The pigs in question were human ones for sure.

"You're right. So there's a camp on the border somewhere. Maybe Schwedt an der Oder, somewhere like that."

Willi shook his head, enjoying his moment. "Not Schwedt."

"How do you know?"

"I asked him."

"You *asked* him?" Not for the first time, Misha was shocked by the boy's sheer cheek.

"Sort of. Not exactly. Even I . . . But I thought the same as you. What is there on the border? Nowhere much bigger than Schwedt. So I asked for a ride there."

"*And?*"

"He said no. He wasn't going that far. He dropped me at Eberswalde, before taking the road south."

"Jesus, Willi! You've done well."

Rosa's eyes widened in the lamplight. If Willi ever blasphemed in front of her, Misha was quick to check him. Misha himself had never used strong language in front of her before. But Misha didn't notice or, for the moment, care. The cold thrill of certainty had prickled through him once again. After a barren summer, he felt like a hunting dog, who had just picked up the scent of prey.

3

Pavel, now in charge of Oderbruch Special Camp, had stiffened things up in every respect. There were regular parades for all soldiers, including Tonya. Uniforms were made to sparkle. Any lapses on the part of one individual would mean a compulsory dawn parade for the entire unit. Sleeping quarters were inspected. All decorations, such as Tonya's magazine photograph, had to be removed from the walls. The only pictures permitted anywhere were portraits of Marshal Stalin and other propaganda emblems.

But Pavel didn't limit himself to spit-and-polish type reforms. The prisoners were counted. Their tally fell well short of the number for which stores were being drawn. The quartermaster was demoted to the ranks. (So too was his wife: a source of some pleasure to Tonya, who no longer had to bear her petty bullying.) Rokossovsky crept around for those weeks, eyes popping out of his head, terrified that his own role in proceedings would be found out, but it appeared that nothing further came of the investigation. Interrogations of the more important prisoners were suddenly taken up again with new vigour. Tonya was kept busy interpreting and typing up reports and transcripts. The whole camp had a busier, sharper, feeling to it. But it also became a jumpier place, nervy and tense.

One evening, about a fortnight after Pavel's arrival, Tonya was working alone in her office, typing up a big batch of prisoner interview transcripts. She worked by the light of a single overhead lamp. The evening was chilly and the window was closed, so that the clack of the typewriter was easily the loudest thing in her surroundings. She was already working late and had missed supper, but hoped that she would be able to get finished in time to beg some scraps from the camp kitchen. She kept her head bent over the keys, ignoring the ache in her frostbitten hand, working fast. As a consequence, she didn't hear the door. It was only a sixth sense of a human presence that caused her to look up and when she did, she saw Pavel.

She leaped up from her desk and sprang to attention. He looked at her for a moment with that slightly frightening loose-lipped smile. Then he relaxed into a more human expression. He acknowledged her own salute with a careless hand, and said, "That's all right, Sister."

"Thank you, sir."

"Have you had dinner?"

"No sir."

"Not hungry?"

Tonya wanted to say that she had been working, but somehow felt inhibited. Would he regard that as toadying, as seeking to gain some kind of advantage? She didn't know. She was confused by her recent insight that it had been he who had denounced her. She didn't know what to do with that knowledge, or how to think of him now.

But Pavel correctly interpreted her confusion. "Ah, you've been too busy. Good. Come to my quarters at nine o'clock. We'll have something to eat. We've a lot to catch up on, eh?"

He smiled again. There was something curious in his look. Was it an acknowledgement that he had been the one to do her so much harm a decade back? If so, his expression certainly didn't seem to show any remorse. The look in his eye seemed to suggest that, if anything, he thought the whole episode had been a great joke, rather like the time once in childhood when Tonya had got into bed to find that Pavel had piled ice in thick layers beneath the covers.

Tonya tried hard to concentrate on her work for the remaining fifty minutes. She wasn't able to do it. Her fingers fumbled the keys and she made a mess of sheet after sheet. In the end, she left her desk and paced out the last ten minutes, watching two bluebottles chase each other around the bare light bulb, occasionally hitting it before spinning away in a fury of buzzing wings.

Nine o'clock came.

Tonya walked across camp to Pavel's bungalow, an incongruously ornate affair, with gingerbread-style barge-boards and ornamental shutters. The whole thing would have looked more at home beside a Bavarian lakeside than here, inside the wire and watchtower camp perimeter. Tonya approached. A sentry on the door — one of Pavel's wholly needless innovations — stamped his feet and presented arms. When the sentry saw who it was, he nodded and signalled for her to go straight on in.

Tonya knocked, waited for an answer, then entered. Whatever Pavel had been up to these past years, he had certainly profited from it. His room was decorated in a mixture of what could best be described as occupation kitsch: oil paintings, carpets, a tiger-skin rug, brass vases, a stuffed and mounted antelope's head, a huge gold-leaf and ebony cigar-box, a portrait of Marx and a portrait of Stalin. With the exception of the two communist portraits, the room could have belonged to any Nazi gauleiter, ostentatious, boastful, looted.

Pavel seemed pleased to see her. He waved down her salute and called her sister, though he didn't go quite as far as suggest that she could drop the "sir". As promised, he'd provided dinner: a bottle of red wine and a pair of small birds that Tonya didn't recognise — Pavel told her that they were wood pigeon — served with thick potato-flour dumplings and dark gravy. Tonya was hungry and ate greedily. Pavel appeared to have eaten already, though he took another plateful now, and he toyed with his food, quite happy to devote his attention to the wine.

As she ate, Pavel plied her with questions. He seemed eager — amused — to hear about her time in

Siberia, and wanted a battle-by-battle account of her battalion's progress from Stalingrad to Berlin. "Excellent, excellent," he kept saying. He seemed to take no account of the suffering Tonya must have experienced, only joy in the violence and the victory.

They talked about old times and family. Their father, according to Pavel, had died in 1940, from "too much vodka". Neither Tonya nor Pavel had ever experienced much love or kindness from the old man, but Tonya felt sad that he had gone, all the same. She asked him, of course, about her daughters.

"*Bezprizornaya*," he said. "Waifs and orphans. They will be alive somewhere, but who knows where?"

"They aren't orphans, sir."

"Ah! That's characteristic of you, Sister, if I may say. A typical female, you place biology above politics. Biologically, are they orphans? Maybe not. But politically, of course they are. Kornikov and yourself both convicted under article 58. That's as serious as things can be. Maybe they were the ones who denounced you, eh?"

"No, Pavel, that was you."

He chuckled in merry delight, as though she'd just complimented him. He didn't either deny or admit the charge, but any remaining doubts that Tonya had had vanished on hearing him laugh. Aside from her very first word on seeing Pavel arrive in camp, it was the first and only time that she allowed herself to drop the "sir".

"Saboteurs of the revolution. The country was full of them then. Of course, things are in a more secure position now. A hard purge, Sister, that's the only way to cure a sick cow."

"Rodyon was a good man, sir. He did his best for his country and the workers. He did his best for people like us. You used to love him."

Pavel's mouth, always so mobile, hesitated now between different emotions. Tonya had finished her food. She didn't feel comfortable with her brother. He felt more strange to her than a real stranger would have done. She couldn't bring herself to believe in the closeness of their relationship.

"I did, yes, but did you? I fancy you could never get that other one out of your head. That bourgeois of yours." Tonya said nothing, and Pavel waited a few moments to see if more time would draw a response. It didn't. "I've read your file, you know. You can't hide things from me."

"Hide? What things, sir?"

Pavel threw his head back and gazed up at the ceiling before quoting, perhaps verbatim, from some remembered lines in her file. " 'The accused was intercepted in the vicinity of the Brandenburg Gate, on the point of entering the British sector. The accused attempted to evade arrest. She did not at first submit any reason for her presence there.' Eh, Sister? But the comrades who wrote that didn't know what we know."

"Didn't know what?"

"Malevich. He is in Berlin, or at least he was. His name turned up on a list passed to us by our dear friends in the American administration. You see, Sister, when one gets to a certain rank, one starts to learn

333

things. Interesting things. *I* know why you were crossing into the west. *I* know who you were looking to find."

Tonya felt a sudden horror. If Misha had kept his Russian name, and if the NKVD knew about him, then his position must have been horribly dangerous. Pavel knew it too. He leaned into the silence, extending and enjoying it.

Eventually he said, "We paid him a visit. Not me personally, but . . . He wasn't there. He had moved on. There was a boy there, no one else." He grinned widely as if the whole episode had all been a great joke.

Pavel's willingness to toy with Tonya's emotions on this subject raised a sudden fury in her. She spoke still with a soldierly respectfulness, but with anger shaking in her voice.

"I stayed in Russia for you, sir. When Misha's family left, he would have gone too, except for me. And I only stayed because of you and Babba. *I* stayed for *you*!"

Pavel rocked for a moment or two in silence. Then he skipped back to a topic they'd left some time back, as though the intervening conversation hadn't taken place.

"So, Kornikov," he said. "You say he was a good man?"

"Yes sir."

"He was convicted of terrorism against the state, but you still say he was a good man?"

"Yes sir."

"You're wrong, Sister. And I can prove it."

Tonya didn't respond, but she felt her face go blank and numb. Her plate of food, Pavel, the room itself, seemed to vanish down the wrong end of a telescope. Pavel's voice came at her from a long way away.

"What do you mean you can prove it, sir?" she heard herself saying.

From a long way away, from another planet almost, she heard the answer.

"You said he *was* a good man. And you're wrong. He still is. Oh yes! That's right. Kornikov's not dead, Sister, much as you might wish him to be. Like you, he left his re-education camp in Siberia to join the Red Army. He survived too — a pair of old leather boots you two must be for toughness — and is now serving the state. A beautiful posting it must be too. Imagine the seashore! The lapping waves! The women! I suppose he has a fancy for women of that sort . . ."

"What do you mean? Seashore? Women of what sort . . .?"

"Preobrazheniye," said Pavel, rolling the words. "He is in Preobrazheniye in the region of Primorskiy Kray."

Tonya shook her head. The sounds were Russian, but also strange. She had no idea where Pavel was talking about. The idea that Rodyon was still alive — that she still had a husband! — was astonishing to her. The fact rolled around in her head like summer thunder.

"Your eyes, dear Sister. Always aslant. I'm your own brother. I can tell you these things straight. You look Asiatic. Mongol, one might say. Not that it spoils your looks, now. Not at all! But I'm quite surprised you haven't heard of Preobrazheniye. I'm sure there are more than a few Asiatic women there too. Why, Preobrazheniye is only a couple of hundred kilometres

335

or so from Vladivostok." He held up his finger and thumb, so that they were only separated by a centimetre. "From your precious husband to Japan itself, it's only this far, the merest hop."

4

As soon as he could, Misha drove to Eberswalde. The main road headed north to Schwedt. A smaller one branched south-east to — well, little enough. There was only one town of any note, Bad Freienwalde, and apart from that, scattered villages, sleepy and provincial.

Once again, Misha felt the prickle of certainty, stronger now than ever before. Germany was too small for an internal exile on the Russian scale. But here was its direct equivalent: quiet, backward, unpopulated. If an NKVD man wanted to make use of Tonya's special skills, but wanted to keep her out of the way of trouble, then the Oderbruch would be the ideal place to do it.

Misha took his Kübelwagen into town, then killed the engine. What next? He didn't know, but strongly felt that something would present itself. He strolled down the little Hauptstrasse, under a line of elm trees. With the light shining through the last November-yellow leaves, they looked almost translucent, as though the branches were thronged with butterflies. A once-weekly food market was beginning to clear away. Misha approached one of the stallholders, clearly a farmer, and asked him how far it was to the "Ivan's special camp". The stallholder didn't know or wouldn't say and shrugged the question away. Misha tried another two men, before finding a man who wiped his mouth with the back of his hand and said, "Six, seven kilometres into the Oderbruch. About that."

So Willi was right! Misha's excitement increased further. It wasn't a pleasant sensation, more like the tightening of claws into his skin, than anything else. Of course, this might not be the camp . . . and yet, everything fitted. Misha was still walking, still furiously thinking, when he noticed a Soviet soldier walking towards him. A Soviet tank regiment had its barracks in town, but this man wasn't a tankist, meaning he had to be stationed somewhere outside. The man was easily recognisable as a Russian peasant, most likely from the endless steppe west of the Urals.

Misha put a hand up and stopped him.

"Excuse me, sir," he began, speaking German.

The Russian shook his hands in front of him, meaning both that he didn't speak German and didn't want to.

Misha was undeterred. Speaking in Russian now — but heavily German-accented Russian — stumbling over his words and inflections, Misha said, "Please. Am German businessman. Have difficulty. Need person who also German also Russian speak."

The Russian shook his head. He wanted nothing to do with Misha's request, but Misha persisted.

"Please. Was once here lady, Kornikova, and —"

The Russian jerked backwards in alarm, then thrust his face, stinking of beer and onion — into Misha's. "No, no. Kornikova was never here, understand? It'll be the worse for you — for everyone — if word gets out. If

337

that skinny witch by the canal has been telling tales, I'll come down and cut off her nose." The man grabbed Misha's lapels, but it was a gesture of fear more than threat. "That old hen, you tell her to keep her ears wide and her mouth closed!"

The Russian pulled his hands convulsively away, stared once more at Misha, then pulled away, walking, almost running, back to his truck.

Misha went running down to the canal. It didn't take him long to find the only woman who lived there: a brown-haired, brown-eyed woman, Gisela. Misha introduced himself, and asked if she knew of a Soviet translator attached to the nearby Special Camp, named Kornikova.

"Kornikova, I don't know. I never knew her surname. She was a very nice lady, very helpful. I haven't seen her for a while."

"Her first name?"

"Antonina."

"Antonina!"

"And her eyes?"

"Green. She had lovely green eyes, slightly aslant."

Gisela pulled Misha in through the front door into the kitchen. She pushed the door shut and said, "And I know who you are. You're her friend from Berlin. She was trying to come and find you. I was going to help her hide out on a canal-barge."

Misha felt a surge of emotion so strong that it would have taken him half a day to unpick and explore everything he felt in those few seconds. It felt as though some explosion had detonated inside, but soft, very soft, as though the shockwaves were felt through fifty feet of cotton wool. So Tonya was close! And she had been looking for him! But as well as powerful joy, Misha was overtaken by sudden anxiety.

"You said you hadn't seen her? Why not? Do you know?"

Gisela smiled.

"Don't worry. There's some new man in charge of the camp, apparently. Things have been tightened up, so they say. I don't think Antonina was even meant to come into town. She said once that she was supposed to be confined to the camp. I'm sure she's still there."

Misha breathed out. He was both relieved to have found her and tense because there were still barriers to bringing her away with him. But of the two feelings, the relief was the stronger. He was full of confidence that he'd find a way to get Tonya out. The puzzle wasn't whether it could be done, but only how.

5

Escape had become more urgent than ever. Before, Tonya had been content to bide her time, happy to wait for an opportunity when the risk of escape would be minimal. That had made sense under the looser regime of the previous commandant, but no longer. Ever since their dinner together, Tonya knew, without being able to say exactly why, that Pavel's presence was dangerous to her. It was more vital than ever to get away. If she took more risks than she had first intended — well, that couldn't be helped.

She formed her plans.

The first issue was how to get out of the camp itself. Although Pavel's arrival had caused most aspects of the regime to tighten up, the camp was there to keep the German prisoners locked up, not the Soviet staff. Every day, the camp gates were opened to allow trucks and vehicles in and out. Many of the NKVD officers liked to fraternise with the officers of the tank regiment in town. Even lower down the camp hierarchy, men like Rokossovsky liked to go into town to buy items on the black market, to chase after women, or to get hold of beer, schnapps and vodka. All the same, Tonya was forbidden to leave the camp, and under Pavel's new regime everyone would be too scared to help her evade the rules, Rokossovsky most of all.

And yet she had to get out. She thought about simply walking out of camp one evening. It wouldn't be easy to find a moment when the gates were unattended, but nor would it be impossible either. Beyond the gates, there was a road that led straight to Bad Freienwalde. If the road were too dangerous, then there was a low wooded hill less than a mile distant that would give her plenty of shelter for the night.

But what then? Tonya knew that Pavel would organise a search to catch any of his men who absconded. He would treat her no differently. And Tonya knew herself well enough to know that she had neither the strength nor the skill to evade any determined search.

340

So that left the camp's own motor vehicles. She began to watch with intense interest the movement of every car and lorry that came into the camp.

She watched the procedures for loading and unloading. She observed what crates and boxes were piled in, took a careful note of what was heavy, what was light. One afternoon, a large consignment of timber posts arrived. When the posts were unloaded, the empty truck stood unattended while its drivers went off to complete their paperwork. Tonya could see the back of the truck empty, except for a loose canvas tarpaulin. A persistent rain fell all across the yard. There was nobody about. Tonya froze in indecision. Should she run out into the wet, jump into the truck and hide beneath the tarpaulin? She thought she stood an excellent chance, eighty per cent or better, of getting into the truck unseen. Trucks were never searched on the way out, and there was no indication that the empty truck was going to be loaded up with anything else. But suppose that she made it out of the camp in the back of the truck? What then? She didn't even know where the truck was headed. It might end up in Berlin. Or it might draw up in some Red Army transport depot, swarming with soldiers and NKVD men. She couldn't guess.

For sixteen minutes she froze, then decided against. Her thudding heart quietened to a soft thump. All this time, she had left her work and had been standing at the window looking out and pondering. She sat back down at her desk and the stack of documents to translate. She began typing again. After a few minutes,

341

there was a tap at the door. It was the truck driver, come to ask some question about his fuel requisition documents. Tonya gave him the information he needed, then asked him, "Where are you headed for now?"

"Me? Back to base."

"And the base is . . .?"

"Bialystok. Poland."

The driver nodded, as though vaguely surprised that anyone could have been so ignorant as not to know, then headed out into the rain. Tonya felt the violent chill of the fate she had just avoided. Bialystok lay close to the Polish-Soviet border, hundreds of miles to the east. If she'd jumped into the truck, she'd have taken herself closer to Siberia, not Misha. So though her commitment to escape remained red-hot, her caution increased as well. She thought of a hundred plans for getting away, and rejected every one.

In the meantime, camp life went on. Her working hours had grown longer again, but for the most part, and prisoner interrogations aside, she enjoyed the work. Most of her colleagues liked her. Besides, they knew she was the commandant's sister and took care to treat her well.

Nor had Pavel forgotten her. Indeed, he got into the habit of inviting her around to his bungalow. "Invite" wasn't quite the right word, of course. His invitations were phrased as orders, and he hadn't yet permitted her to call him anything other than "sir". She was usually required to come around at nine or even ten o'clock at night — a late start to the evening, given that reveille was sounded at six every morning. He usually gave her dinner, irrespective of whether she'd already eaten or not. He himself always took a plate of food too, but it was one of his idiosyncrasies that he had always eaten before her, so that he hardly put a spoon or fork to his mouth. Instead, he just drank wine from a large crystal glass — she was never offered any, and never asked for it — and plied her with questions. Sometimes his questions had to do with the present. He asked her about her translations, about the prisoner interrogations, about her observations of her fellow camp staff. At other times, he leaped back into the past, asking her about their very earliest years together, back in the years before the revolution. Or he might ask her about the Gulag: a topic he never seemingly wearied of. He wanted to know everything about it, especially her arrival there, her sensations and impressions. His questions were never orderly, but jumped around. She might have just completed an answer about an interrogation conducted that morning, only to be faced with a question about the way their mother used to bake bread, or asked to relate how cold it became during the Siberian winter.

Gradually, Tonya came to realise certain things.

Firstly, despite Pavel's need to display his authority, she realised that her status as his older sister still carried weight. Once, seeing him bare-headed on a cold day, she chided him that evening.

"You only started doing that during that first winter of the revolution, sir. You were copying Rodya, but you never had his constitution. You shouldn't have done it then, and you shouldn't do it now. It's not just a cold

343

you might catch. Typhus is rampant amongst the prisoners, as you perfectly well know."

The admonishment delighted Pavel. He teased her, called attention to his lieutenant-colonel's rank, pointed out that he could and would go bare-headed as much as he wished — but still the very next day, Tonya saw him wearing hat and scarf, even though the wind was nowhere near as cold as the day before.

Secondly, she realised that Pavel needed her company. Much as he liked to exercise his authority, it left him without close friends. His only real companionship was with his opposite number in the tank regiment down the road in Bad Freienwalde. Several times a week he took a car down there and spent an entire evening eating and drinking.

And lastly, she realised this. Pavel was a drunk. She had seen it first in his eyes: greeny-blue, like hers, but less intensely coloured. But the whites of his eyes were crowded with red-veined blood vessels, and his focus was often loose and slow. Once she'd understood the message of his eyes, all the other evidence fell into place. Most evenings she was there, she watched him consume a full bottle of wine. But often enough, she realised that he opened another one after she had left. He had also often begun drinking, vodka usually, in the time before she arrived.

Though she'd never accompanied him to his friend, the colonel of the tank regiment, she had once seen his car return. She witnessed it quite by chance. She was already in bed, and was only up because she'd needed to go to the loo and had to cross to the toilet block in order to do so. It was after midnight and windy, and a full moon stared out from wildly moving clouds. The car, the ZiS limousine, swirled in through the camp entrance, with a blare of headlamps and a howl of tyres. Instead of parking in the yard, the car drove right across the grass to Pavel's bungalow. Fascinated, Tonya hurried over, keeping to the shadows, watching to see what followed.

The car came to a stop by the bungalow's entrance. Two burly tankists, warrant rank, no more, got out of the front seats. They opened a side-door and pulled Pavel out, taking him by the boots first, then the belt; handling him as roughly as a sack of turnips. In a flash of moonlight, Tonya saw her brother's head loll backwards like a deer she'd once seen shot at a hunt. Then the two men rearranged their load and bundled it up the three little steps and into the house. They were inside just a few minutes, before emerging again. Then they got back into the car and drove away, back to Bad Freienwalde, she presumed.

Tonya went to the loo, went back to her hut, back to bed.

But not to sleep. She'd seen enough. Her alcoholic brother. That loose swaying head. She knew how she was going to make her escape. She knew how she would make it to Berlin.

For five solid hours she lay in bed, staring at the ceiling, unable to sleep, her heart pounding with excitement at the size of her future.

CHAPTER
ELEVEN

1

It was December 1946. It was two in the afternoon. The sky was a whitish blue. Not cloud really, just a thick haze, almost but not quite penetrated by the distant sun. There was no wind, not even a breath. A white duck's feather, which happened to have fallen on the roof of the guard post by the main gate, just stayed there, a little speck of white on the tarred wooden roof. It didn't move, didn't even quiver.

It was very cold.

2

In the fields beyond the camp, Misha lay with his belly against the icy ground, his face pressed up against the long grass that sprouted in wintry hummocks all along the little culvert. He was stiff and cold from lying so long, but didn't want to move now, for fear of being seen. He put his binoculars down, turning them sideways, so that the glass lenses wouldn't catch the light and reflect it on into the camp. He lifted his belly and stretched his spine, shifting his boots back, keeping his shoulders forward, and giving his vertebrae room to unlock from their long afternoon's ache. The stretch helped, but only for a moment. As soon as he dropped back into position, his back settled into the same dull cramp, as though it hadn't shifted for a moment.

He put the glasses back to his eyes and continued to gaze.

3

Tonya left the quartermaster's office with a stack of papers, a confused mass of receipts, usage statements, inventory reports, and requisition slips. Pavel had been haranguing the quartermaster for sloppy management and he in his turn had come to Tonya to beg for help.

Tonya crossed the yard to her office holding the papers against her chest. Because of the cold, she wore a rabbit-skin hat and a woollen scarf. Her hands were ungloved, but she liked the feeling of the cold air on her fingers. She liked the huge white sky and the way that any sounds seemed to carry for ever in the silence. She walked diagonally across the yard, altering her course only so as to avoid the elegant black shape of Pavel's ZiS limousine. As she passed it, she put a hand out to touch the cold metal of its bonnet. She knew, because he had told her so, that Pavel was going down to Bad Freienwalde that night, visiting his friend, the tank regiment colonel. Pavel had implied some major party and Tonya had seen his alcoholic pleasure at the idea of a night spent drinking.

The feel of the bonnet gave her a sudden race of excitement and fear. If all went well, she would escape tonight. If all went well, she would be with Misha in less than twenty-four hours.

4

From his position in the culvert, Misha could see the wooden door open, discharge a single figure, then close again. He put the glasses back to his eye, touched the focus adjustment, and watched the distant image leap to life.

It was Tonya.

Because of the way the binoculars enlarged and concentrated the image, it looked as though she had jumped out at him. She seemed so close that Misha was actually startled into making an exclamation, a low "Oh!" that rolled away across the frozen ground. The way Tonya was headed, she was actually walking towards him, as though she could see him with perfect clarity and there was nothing more normal in the world than strolling over towards him with a bundle of papers against her chest.

This wasn't the first time he'd seen her through binoculars. Over the last three weeks he'd spent as many days as he could lying here, watching the camp, following her movements. He'd identified her office, the canteen, the interrogation block, and her sleeping quarters. He knew the approximate daily pattern of her life and movements. And yet, by odd chance, he'd only ever caught her in partial view. She had always been walking away from him, or had her head turned, or had been wearing a cap whose brim shielded her face. And this was different. Her face was turned directly towards Misha. It was as though she were looking at him.

He'd often wondered what he would feel actually seeing her again. Would he still feel the same way about her now, or had he been in love with a dream all this time? A dream of Tonya as a young woman, clear-skinned and youthful? He needn't have worried. The extraordinary thing was how utterly familiar she was. There was age in her face, of course, but Misha was more struck by how much had remained unchanged. The clarity was still there. The soft roundedness of her face was still the same, the slight slant to the eyes. Misha felt the old love surge in him again, just as it had done back in Petrograd and Petrozavodsk.

He watched her cross the yard. She paused only once to touch the black metal bonnet of the commandant's limousine. It was a curious gesture; something he hadn't expected. Ordinarily, a lowly Red Army private wouldn't think to touch the elevated luxury of a senior NKVD man's car. But perhaps the commandant wasn't entirely a brute. Or perhaps Tonya had seen some speck of dirt and had been cleaning it away. But no sooner had these thoughts formed, than they vanished. Misha didn't have to speculate about Tonya as he would have done about anyone else. Tonya had seen the smoothness of the cold, black metal and she wanted to touch it. That was all.

Her pace picked up a bit as she crossed the rest of the little yard. She was closer to him now and Misha had to adjust the focus of his binoculars one more time to keep her in view. She came to a second building — single-storey, wooden, tin-roofed — opened the door and entered. The door fell shut behind her.

Misha put his glasses down. It was the confirmation that he'd needed. Not just the confirmation of her physical presence there, but confirmation that his own feelings were as unchanged, as strong, as utterly certain as ever. He hadn't known that he'd needed that reassurance, but now that he had it, he was aware of the tiny doubt that had all this time been ringing away in his mind.

For some time — perhaps five minutes, perhaps fifty, he hardly knew — he lay on his belly with his head pillowed on the damp grass and the binoculars dropped on the ground beside him. He held the knowledge of Tonya's presence to his heart, cherishing the feeling like nothing else.

Eventually he looked up.

For no reason in particular, he looked first at the guard post on the main gate. He saw its roof speckled with white. At first, he thought that some small bird had been mauled by a hawk or buzzard, and this scatter of white feathers was the result. But the thought was absurd, as he well knew. They weren't feathers, but snowflakes, and the now was being added to all the time. Nor was it only in the sky over the camp. It had begun snowing over Misha's culvert too; he had simply been too tied up in his thoughts to notice. But now he rolled on his back, to look up at the sky. The snowfall would be a heavy one. The sky was already crowded with flakes. Looking up as he was, the flakes seemed black against the luminescent air. They were so dense, reaching right up as far as Misha could see, that it looked almost as if the sky were turning solid, darkening over with the falling snow. And the snow was settling. Before long, the drab greys and browns of the December landscape would be locked under a covering of solid white.

There were ways in which the snow would complicate his plans, but he was pleased all the same. For one thing, he was Russian. Snow was his element. He could never feel uncomfortable in an icy landscape. And there was one other thing. For some reason — why, he couldn't say — but he was reminded of that snowfall back in 1917, when he'd first read the newspaper headline that had announced the revolution. He remembered being on that station platform reading the article under the lamplight and the falling snow. The world had been turned upside down then. Perhaps it would reverse itself again now.

Misha put the binoculars back to his eyes and rolled back into position. Not for long. The snow falling between him and the camp obscured his vision. But it didn't matter now. She was there and he had come for her. That was all that mattered.

5

Tonya too welcomed the snow.

When she was done with her paperwork, the light had been half-squeezed out of the day. The air seemed thick with the falling snow, as though a mist had come

down and solidified. When she came out into the yard,
lamps were on around all the main buildings in the staff
quarters — the prisoners themselves had no lighting —
but the light they threw out reached no further than a
few yards. Tonya walked back to the quartermaster with
her papers. Pavel's car was still there, slowly
disappearing from view beneath the white. When she
drew level with it, she allowed herself to drop her
topmost folder. She bent to pick it up. As she did so,
she pulled a short kitchen knife from her pocket. She
pressed the blade up against the tyre and pushed. The
thick rubber resisted for a moment, then gave way. The
air escaped in a rush, then died away with a soft sighing
sound. The car settled an inch or two closer to the
ground. Tonya stood up again and looked around.
There was no one there, no one watching. She took her
knife and threw it, as far as she could, over the wire into
the prisoners' compound. She didn't hear it land.

She wiped the snow off her knees, where she'd knelt
to pick up her papers, then walked on towards the
quartermaster's office. She wasn't breathing hard. Her
pulse was normal.

6

Pavel Kirylovich Lensky, lieutenant-colonel in the
NKVD and commandant of the Oderbruch Special
Camp Number 11, dressed with care. His uniform
didn't give him much scope for elaborate dressing, but
he was exacting about details. His calf-length boots
were aglow with polish. His belt buckle and buttons

gleamed. His royal blue cap with its band of red looked as though it had never seen a day's wear in its life. He settled his cap with precision and smiled at his reflection. He had pale gums and eyes, but his lips were blood-red, almost like those of a woman wearing lipstick. When he finished smiling, his mouth didn't quite close. He wanted a drink, but wanted even more to defer that precious first moment of the evening: the first drink clinking with ice, the first sweet bite of vodka.

He walked from his bedroom to his living room. His driver stood with his back to the door, too uncomfortable in those strangely opulent surroundings to come more than a pace or two into the room. The driver saluted. It had become fashionable in parts of the NKVD to salute, Prussian-style, with a sharp click of the heels. Earlier in the war, such copying of the German enemy would have been unthinkable, but now, two and a half years after victory, the conquerors enjoyed any demonstration of their martial supremacy. In any case, Pavel liked the habit and gave it his tacit encouragement. He returned the salute, then indicated that he was ready to go to Bad Freienwalde.

The two men went to the car. It had stopped snowing now — or at least the flakes that still fell were few in number and came down almost hesitantly. The driver opened the rear door for his commander, then took the driver's seat for himself. He started the car and reversed it in a brisk curve, in order to bring its nose pointing towards the front gate. But the manoeuvre failed badly. The collapsed tyre was pudding-soft on the rear wheel and the car simply slid in a long, sideways curve. The slap of the injured tyre on the wheel was easily audible inside the car. The driver swore and jumped out. The damage was obvious and changing the tyre wouldn't be the fastest procedure in the cold and darkness.

Pavel was angry. He didn't like arriving in town in an ordinary Tatra car. On the other hand, he was all set up for that first drink of the evening and he didn't want to delay it any further. His dilemma resolved itself in anger. Getting out of the car, he tore a strip off his driver, ordering him to report in full uniform every two hours through the night to the duty officer until further notice. The driver went still-faced and tense as he bore the rebuke. Then Pavel, still angry, indicated one of the Tatras. They would go to town in that, then the driver would return and fix the wheel. He would need to remain on-call, until Pavel was ready to be collected.

The driver relaxed a little. He couldn't understand why the wheel had gone flat, but these things sometimes happened. His punishment hadn't been too bad. For a moment, he'd thought that his commander was going to strike him.

The two men got in the smaller car and drove out into the night.

7

Misha waited in his car in the woods. The engine and lights were both turned off. It was eight in the evening, cold and becoming colder. He wore a heavy greatcoat, a khaki cap and scarf. The clothes weren't technically identical to those worn by the Red Army, but they were so similar as to make no odds. Certainly, in the dark nobody would be able to tell the difference. On the seat beside him, he had a pair of heavy-duty wire cutters, some string, a short iron bar wrapped in cloth, a loaf of bread and a bottle of water. The iron bar was intended as a weapon of last resort. Misha had wrapped cloth around it to dull its impact in a fight, as he didn't want to injure anyone more than necessary. With luck he wouldn't have to use it at all. The loaf and water weren't strictly necessary under any scenario, but some old instinct of hospitality made Misha feel somehow obliged to have food ready for Tonya when he got her out. Not that she would be likely to make much use of it. For one thing, they'd still have to reach Berlin before they would be safe. For another, both water and bread were well on their way to freezing solid.

The forest was mostly silent. Every now and then, a rook cawed loudly, or some large bird suddenly tore from its perch with a sudden beating of wings. There was very little wind and the normal sighing sound of a pine forest was entirely absent, so that it was almost like standing by a waterfall without hearing the sound of water.

Misha looked again at his watch. The tiny luminous dots which told the time hardly seemed to have moved since he'd last looked. He had determined that he wouldn't make a move till midnight, and he forced himself now to abide by his earlier decision. Four hours to go.

Time crawled.

8

The driver had taken Pavel into town, then come back to camp and changed the wheel on the ZiS limousine, swearing softly to himself as he did so. It was long after dark by now, of course, and he was working in the light thrown by the headlamps of one of the little Tatras. Tonya came up to him with a tin mug of tea.

"Here, comrade," she said in a friendly way.

The driver looked at her with a slight jolt, recognising his commandant's sister. He swallowed the swearword that had been on his lips, and said, "Thanks, comrade. No offence."

She shook her head, indicating that anyone was allowed to swear where her brother was concerned. "He's a difficult one, that."

"Ach! These officers, they're all the same. That tyre though, somebody stuck a knife in it."

"Well, this camp is hardly full of his friends. And I can say that, being his sister."

"Older or younger?"

"Older. He was a handful, even as a youngster."

"Here, hold this a moment." The driver handed her his mug as he repositioned his spanner. Then, before applying pressure to the locking nut, he steadied himself. "Is it true he makes you call him sir?"

"He's a lieutenant-colonel. I'm only *ryadovoy*."

The driver shook his head and spat, then leaned on the spanner. The barrel nut resisted a moment, then gave way. The driver did the same to the remaining nuts, grunting with the effort.

"What time do you have to collect him?"

"Don't know. He phones. This one's a big night, apparently. I probably won't get the call till three or four in the morning." The driver's face contracted as he thought of it.

"He phones you where? At the guard house?"

"No. His bungalow. I have to sit and wait. All those luxuries, comrade Kornikova. They say the poor man pinches kopecks, the rich man steals gold."

Tonya laughed. The driver swigged down his tea with a loud gulping sound. The sweep of light from the Tatra's headlamps made every shadow or fold in the ground appear like a solid object, hard and black. When the driver threw the last few drops of tea away, the steam rose in clouds from the frozen ground. Tonya took the mug.

"Well, then, if you don't need me to help . . ."

"No, the job's half done already. Thanks for the tea."

"It was nothing."

"Oh, and comrade . . . no offence, all right? If I said anything, I didn't mean . . ."

"No, don't worry. I won't say anything. He wouldn't ask me anyway."

Tonya took the mug back to the kitchens, then went to the toilet block to wash. There was no hot water, except for a couple of times a week, and the cold water was like melted ice. All the same, Tonya washed every day, and today she was more careful than ever to wash herself hard. She scrubbed at her face as though trying to remove a layer of skin. Her skin, which was clear enough anyway, tingled with the coarse sponge and the

357

ice-water. She untied her hair, combed it out hard, wished she were able to wash it, but knew that it would be more likely to freeze than to dry. She didn't usually like her eyes — that slight slant tended to attract insults from the European chauvinist Russians — but Misha had always loved them, so she did too. She gazed at herself in the little scrap of mirror. She saw the brightness of her cheeks and the sheer happiness of her smile; a happiness that came from her increasing certainty that in a matter of a mere day or so, she would see Misha again. She knew there were risks to be overcome, but they seemed too trivial to worry about: a little summer brook to be hopped over, nothing more. She turned her head from side to side, enjoying the idea that somebody would soon be looking at her with love, enjoying the sense of being a woman again.

Just then, there was a noise on the snowy path outside. The toilet block was shared by both sexes and there was little privacy at any time. Tonya quickly retied her hair and left the block. She went straight to bed, but not to sleep, just lay awake, listening to the snores of her neighbours. Time passed. Ten in the evening came. Then eleven. Then midnight.

She got up, ready to make her move.

9

The two luminous dots came closer, then closed into one. Misha forced himself to wait another minute or two. The single dot lengthened, then one dot broke away from the other. It was now past midnight, beyond any doubt.

Misha found himself shivering. He was cold, of course, but it wasn't cold but fear that had struck him. He got out of the car, peed in the snow at the edge of the forest track and got back in. He was still shivering, but alongside the anxiety he felt very calm. It was as though the anxiety were just a coat lightly thrown over the top of everything else, indicating nothing about what lay beneath. He turned the key in the ignition and the car came to life, crashingly loud in the silence.

With headlamps on, he drove down the track back to the road, then killed his lights for the slow ride towards the camp. The camp was only about a mile distant, but without lights, he couldn't drive at more than a few miles an hour. He'd intended to stop three hundred yards before the camp entrance, in the mouth of a farmer's gate he'd identified earlier, but he drove too far by accident and had to reverse back to find his spot. His pulse stayed high and he was given to bursts of shaking, but his calmness remained too. He realised that he only shook if he thought of Tonya. If he pretended that he was just going to enter the camp to fetch a package, he felt no nerves at all.

He parked the car by the farm gate, leaving the key in the ignition. The car was tucked well back from the road and its khaki front was camouflaged under a thick pelt of snow. Misha took the wire cutters and his iron bar and walked to the camp. Though the area was mostly flat, there was a corner where the camp dipped down to an area of low-lying ground, marshy in

359

summer, but frozen hard now. The corner was little used by day. At night it was deserted. Misha approached the stretch of fence and listened. He heard only silence. He put the cutters to the wire and began to snip. The frozen metal parted easily and without noise. Within a couple of minutes, Misha had created an opening large enough to admit him. He slipped through the wire, then folded it back in place.

There was little cloud cover now, but there was no moon, just the glitter of starlight over snow, the huge emptiness of sky. Misha now felt nerves for the first time, real nerves; not the fake variety that he'd felt before. He oriented himself carefully. He knew the camp layout well from his time spent watching, but everything felt different now that he was actually there. The buildings loomed larger and more substantial. All the same, he knew where he was and what he was doing.

He located the little women's sleeping hut and walked over to it. He walked carefully, not making any great racket, but also trying to look as though he had every right to be where he was, trying to look, feel and act like one of the camp guards themselves. His boots creaked in the frozen snow. His breath rose in clouds.

10

Midnight.

Tonya stared at her watch until the luminous dots formed a single point at the top of the watch dial. She couldn't quite believe that the moment had arrived and waited until the two dots separated again before she was certain.

She got out of bed, and pulled on her uniform tunic, trousers, boots and coat. The two other women in the hut were heavy sleepers, and in any case, if they heard her getting up, they'd simply assume she was going to the loo. In cold weather such as this, no one went to the toilet block unless fully dressed.

Tonya emerged from the hut, tucking her hair into her cap and arranging her scarf. There was no moonlight, but the sky seemed full of stars. The night always looked brighter when there was snow on the ground and Tonya had no difficulty in seeing her way. She felt nervous, but very clear, like the bright and frosty night air itself.

Walking with firm, decisive steps, she made her way over to her brother's bungalow. There was a light outside, shaded by the fretwork veranda. She walked smartly up the steps, knocked at the door and let herself in.

The driver was there. He'd obviously been sleeping with his head on the desk close by the telephone, waiting for the ring. He straightened up, blinking sleep from his eyes, trying to pretend he'd been awake all along.

"Ah, comrade, it's you. No, your brother hasn't called yet. It's still early for him. That one, he drinks like . . . Sorry. No offence."

Tonya put a hand up to stop him. "No, don't worry. Pavel's been taken ill. He's called the main gate. He wants me to go and fetch him."

"You? Really? But the roads are icy. Are you sure . . .?"

"I drove a truck in the war, comrade driver," said Tonya with a touch of sharpness. "I drove an armoured car across the Neisse in the last offensive."

"All right, all right, sorry. Give it plenty of choke though. I suppose there's not a problem, is there? Your brother . . .?"

"Ill. You can guess what that means. You can go off to bed."

The driver nodded. He looked for his hat, which had fallen off while he slept, found it, and jammed it onto his head. He held up the key to the limousine and laid it on the desk in front of Tonya.

"Thank you, comrade. Listen, I wasn't sleeping, just resting my eyes. You won't say anything, will you?"

"Comrade, if I told him you were making plans to shoot comrade Stalin, he wouldn't be likely to remember it in the morning."

"No."

Both the driver and Tonya found themselves taken aback by the shocking boldness of her remark. A little well of silence formed between them. Then the driver nodded one last time, and clattered out of the door, down the steps and away across the yard.

Tonya picked up the key: the key to a car and the key to her freedom, all in one. She looked around Pavel's little nest. She felt a sudden urge to make a mess of it. To rip up the portraits of Stalin and Marx, to smash the vases, to pour oil on the carpets, to slash the tiger-skin. In all her dealings with Pavel these last weeks, she had never spoken her feelings about his denunciation of her. Indeed, she had hardly even known her own feelings. How could she, when the penalties for expressing them would have been so severe?

But she didn't need to bother with any of that now. She took the key, turned the light off, and walked over to the front gate. There was a guard on it that she recognised.

"Hello there, Yuri Grigorivich."

The guard looked up. "Antonina Kirylovna! You're up late."

"My brother. Taken 'ill'. He wants me to go. I don't know why."

The guard shrugged and nodded. He knew that Tonya was meant to be confined to camp, but an order from the commandant was an order.

"Ill, eh? That's a nice name for it."

"Yes. If I'm not back at once, then don't worry. If he needs to sleep it off there, I'll wait for him and bring him back in the morning."

"Very good. Take care on the roads, though."

Tonya nodded, awed at how simple it all was. The guard, Yuri Grigorivich, left his little wooden kiosk and unlocked the gates. The snow had piled up at the base, and he had to yank hard to break the crust. The big gates swung open.

Tonya was in the car by now, the engine had started after only a little coaxing. She kept the choke out, as the driver had suggested. She released the handbrake and put the car into gear. She drove forwards slowly, not wanting to start off by letting the big car skid. She

363

had no problem. The car passed through the gates. She raised a hand of thanks. Yuri Grigorivich nodded back. And that was that. Tonya turned out onto the road. The big car had powerful headlamps that illuminated the road well into the distance. The gates closed shut behind her. She only had to drive now, not too quickly, not too slowly.

She'd be in Berlin by morning.

11

Misha saw movement and stopped dead.

There was a figure moving around, caught against the low lamplight coming from a couple of the buildings there. Misha held himself down low, but wasn't too worried about being seen. The night was dark, and he was a long way from the nearest lamplight.

The figure entered a bungalow on the edge of the camp and was inside for a few minutes. Then someone left the bungalow, followed a few moments later by the first figure, who walked over to the gate house, then back to the car. The gates opened. The car left. Misha flattened himself against the snow to avoid the headlamps. The guard who had opened the gates closed them again. Silence returned.

Misha let five minutes go by. There was no further movement, no noise. The camp was so fast asleep, it almost snored.

Misha got up and dusted himself down. He was about to reach the most delicate part of the entire operation. The idea was a brazen one, but rack his

364

brains though he had, Misha hadn't been able to think of anything better. Walking upright, and looking boldly ahead of him, Misha walked over to the women's sleeping quarters. A black electric wire ran into the hut to give it power. Misha cut the wire, then quickly used string to tie it back in place, so that the cut cord wouldn't flop down across the yard and draw attention to the damage. Then he stepped around to the wooden door and opened it. He could see sleepy heads rising from pillows and staring at him.

"Kornikova," he said, gruffly, disguising his normal voice in case the shock of hearing it caused Tonya to cry out. "You're wanted outside. Now." He flicked the light switch on, but nothing happened. "The light's gone," he added.

Misha had expected to hear the sound of Tonya sliding out of bed, grabbing clothes, maybe muttering grumpily at being disturbed. But he heard no such thing. In that first second, the first tiny seed of trouble appeared, and bloomed quickly.

"Kornikova!" he repeated.

One of the other women that he'd woken pointed in the near-darkness to the right bed. "There's no need to shout. She's in that one there. Either that or she's on the toilet. Thanks for waking us all, comrade."

Misha, feeling the presentiment of disaster grow more and more strongly with every passing moment, checked the bed — found it empty — then ran with soft steps outside to the toilet block. He snapped the light on and ran in. There was one soldier, a man, squatting on one of the loos. The stalls had no doors and it was obvious that Tonya wasn't in there. There was a smell of diarrhoea. The solider stared at Misha, said nothing, then spat on the ground and frowned as he returned to business. Misha ran out of the block and gazed around the wide snowy yard.

Where could she be? The extraordinary truth crowded in on him. That second figure to have left the bungalow — the one who drove the car — surely there had been something terribly familiar about that step, that posture. And Misha remembered something else. The car door had been frozen. The person who'd opened it had needed both hands to yank it open. Surely, surely, only a woman would have needed both hands . . .

All of a sudden, Misha knew without doubt that Tonya had stolen the car and was driving to Berlin to be with him. God, what a woman! Scared now, not for himself but for her, scared that his intervention might have disturbed her plans, he went bolting for the corner where he'd come in. He found the broken stretch of wire, wriggled through, then closed the gap. He didn't bother to make a good job of it. The cuts would be obvious enough in the morning. By that time, the game would have been completely won — or entirely lost.

He ran to his car. He searched his pockets for the key, couldn't find it, felt a cold wave of fright, then remembered he'd left the key in the ignition. He started the car, and swerved out onto the road. He drove for half a mile without headlights, then, when the camp had disappeared well behind him in the distance, he switched to full beam. The road up to Bad Freienwalde was potholed and icy, and would need caution. After that, he'd be on better roads all the way.

He'd be in Berlin by morning.

12

The party was a good one.

Colonel Mikulitsin and his brother officers were in fine form. Toast succeeded toast. The vodka was cold and good. Dinner was a huge haunch of roast boar, and the remains of the joint had been left on one side, so the merry-making officers could continue to cut meat for themselves. Mikulitsin produced his cavalry sword and insisted that they carve with that. One of the officers, a Cossack, took the sword and slashed into the joint with a savage skill that had them all roaring with laughter and applause.

Then the phone outside rang. It was answered and a moment later an orderly came in.

"Lieutenant-Colonel Lensky, it's for you."

Pavel lurched to his feet. "What is it? Is it the camp?"

"No sir. Karlshorst, Berlin."

"Karlshorst!"

Pavel wiped his mouth with his hand, a useless gesture. He couldn't think why Karlshorst should be seeking him at this time. He wiped his mouth again, nervously, wishing he weren't drunk.

He went into the stone-paved passage outside, closed the door, and took the phone. Compared with the brightly-lit room he'd just come from, the passageway was cool and dark.

"Lieutenant-Colonel Lensky here."

The voice on the other end of the phone, impersonal and distant, informed him that Lieutenant-General Lukyanchenko was waiting to speak to him. There was a short pause, when only the buzzing on the line told Pavel that the line was still open, then a second voice came in.

"This is Lukyanchenko . . ."

Pavel knew who the man was, of course: he was General Sokolovsky's chief of staff, and one of the most important men in the administration. Pavel had once been at a reception when Lukyanchenko was there, but the two men had never met. His nervousness increased.

But then Lukyanchenko began to explain why he was making the call. Concerns had been growing in the SMAD about disaffection among "reactionary elements" of the German population. Such disaffection was expected to swell during the winter months. Lukyanchenko was ordering a sweep against all prominent "counter-revolutionary propagandists, black-market profiteers, and criminals". The sweep was in progress now. Lieutenant-Colonel Lensky should prepare his camp to receive up to one thousand additional prisoners.

Pavel heard the news in something of a haze. In part that was the drink, but it was more than that. This firm, authoritative voice, the unexpectedness of the call, the weighty nature of the news, even the solemn darkness of the stone passageway, all contributed to his slightly unreal feeling. He acknowledged the information, confirmed his understanding of it, and replaced the receiver. His drunken state bothered him and he leaned his head against the wall, for support and coolness.

He picked up the phone again and dialled through to his bungalow. The phone rang and rang, but got no response. Puzzled and angry, he rang the gate house instead. The guard on the gate was surprised at the call.

"But, sir, you already called for your sister to come and fetch you. She left just twenty minutes ago. She should be with you any moment, unless there was some problem on the road."

"My sister? *Ryadovoy* Kornikova, you mean. I never rang for her . . ." Alcohol, surprise, and the honour of being spoken to by Lieutenant-General Lukyanchenko himself all swam around in his head. Pavel was hardly subtle in his political analysis, but he was a patriot through and through. The firm hand of authority acting against dissident sections of the German population warmed and delighted him. He believed in his country's leadership. The idea of a thousand new prisoners — responsibility — the powerless confusion of the western Allies and the next great step forward for Mother Russia all swirled in Pavel's head. What was this nonsense about his sister? He was inclined to dismiss the whole thing. His own driver had probably just fallen asleep. The rest of it was all some cock-and-bull story to deflect the blame. But why should Antonina have left the camp? She wasn't allowed to. And in his car too! He'd haul her over the coals when she got here.

He rested his forehead against the wall again. He still had the receiver in his hand, but held it down by his side, where the guard's voice sounded tinny and faint. *Why his sister?*

Then, as though suddenly drenched by something freezing, he jerked upright. His sister had stolen the car and left the camp without authorisation. That was not only forbidden. Given her past, any such move could only be because she was hoping to flee to the arms of her bourgeois in the western half of Berlin. Or had Malevich himself come to get her out? The Soviet part of the camp wasn't so strongly guarded that the thing would be impossible. Pavel literally shook with terror. What would Lieutenant-General Lukyanchenko say if he heard of this? He would blame Pavel's negligence, for sure. But what if Pavel himself was thought to have helped her? Conspired with her? Indeed — he accused himself — he *had* conspired. He knew that Tonya had been trying to escape to the west when she'd been picked up under the Brandenburg Gate, yet he'd told no one. He'd protected her. He was guilty of conspiracy against the state. Either the Gulag or Novaya Zemlya awaited him. Pavel felt a wave of fear so strong, he almost fainted.

Somewhere, though, he knew what to do. He lifted the receiver and, still with his head against the wall, he heard himself giving instructions to the guard.

"Summon five men to help you. Take torches and search the camp perimeter. Not the section for the prisoners, but the section for staff. Look for any damage to the fence. Do it now. Don't hang up the phone. I'll wait while you do it."

Down the line, Pavel could hear a bit of shouting, the crashing of boots, the loud report of a door closing, then silence. For a minute or two, nothing happened. Pavel's certainty drained away from him as he waited. Perhaps there was a reasonable explanation for all this. Perhaps Tonya would indeed be arriving to collect him in just a few moments. The guards would find nothing wrong with the fence, then laugh behind his back the next day. He felt anger tightening in his throat. Unreasonably, he held his sister accountable. If she had anything to do with all this, he'd make her pay.

Another minute drifted by. Then, somewhere on the other end of the line, a door smashed open and the guard's voice, highly excited, returned.

"You're right, sir. There's been a break-in. Kornikova's nowhere, sir. Whoever it was must have come in by the hole in the fence, then left with her in your car. We've sent out an alert . . ."

Pavel heard his voice without quite consciously guiding it. Like most drunks, he had a way of operating on automatic that served him well enough most of the time. It served him remarkably now.

"Phone the NKVD barracks at Eberswalde, Finow, Tiefensee, Bernau . . . Have them close the roads to everything coming from this direction. Inspect every vehicle. They're not just looking for the limousine, but everything that moves. Detain everyone, even those with proper papers . . . Do it now."

The guard at the other end repeated the instructions with something like awe in his voice. Pavel noted the tone of voice and loved hearing it. He held his own superiors in the same awed respect. He admired and loved the men who held the east zone in their grip. Today the east. Next year Berlin. Thereafter, the rest of Germany and as much of Europe as they could swallow. In the meantime, he, Pavel, would prove his loyalty by foiling his sister's escape, by catching the bourgeois who had provoked it. He felt a savage joy in his task.

He hung the phone back on the hook, picked up his hat and settled it squarely on his head. A roar of laughter from the room he'd just come from tempted him briefly, but not for long. For him that night, one sort of party was over. A second one was just beginning.

13

Misha reached Bad Freienwalde without a problem. He navigated the back streets, and headed out on the main road to Eberswalde. The route through Tiefensee was more direct, but the road surface would be worse and, in any case, his Kübelwagen would be less likely to attract attention on the major roads.

He passed through Falkenberg, Hohenfinow, and Tornow. The starlight was beginning to vanish under a thick grey pelt of cloud, but the weather made no difference to anything. Misha's car ate up the miles. At this rate, he'd reach Berlin well before dawn.

Villages and farmhouses passed by in the darkness. There were no lights visible anywhere except the towns, but he occasionally saw a flash of light where his head-lamps caught a window pane. He could see the humped black shape of forests, the occasional silver gleam of water. He was neither calm, nor anxious. Rather, he was in some middle state between the two, where he simply wanted to get through the minutes more quickly than they were prepared to come. If he could, he would simply have wound forward the hours to his arrival in Berlin, wound forward to the time when Tonya would be in the western sector, presenting herself to the authorities, searching for him. Until then, he was in a limbo, doing nothing but eating up the minutes.

Then Eberswalde.

Eberswalde and catastrophe.

There were cars, trucks, lights. Sandbags thrown across the road. The trucks were military, showing one red star against the khaki. The line of sandbags was only two or three high, and couldn't have been more than an hour or two old. Misha slowed abruptly. He looked in his mirror. There was another army truck and a jeep pulled up off the road seventy yards back. He was trapped.

He brought his car to a halt.

The bright lights, a combination of car headlamps and floodlights raised on poles, drenched the area. Misha could see a limousine parked there, a black one, its roof still frosted with snow. Was that the same car he'd seen leaving Oderbruch just two hours ago? If so, then he knew who'd been driving it. A sudden agony of despair gripped him so hard, he could barely breathe.

A soldier, NKVD not regular army, approached, requesting papers. Behind the NKVD man, a pair of sentries held rifles at the ready. Misha wound down his window and presented his papers. The man took them, but looked at them without interest. Whatever was about to happen had already been decreed. Misha was told to get out. He and the car were quickly and efficiently searched. There was nothing there for them to find. The only questionable items had been the wire cutters and the iron bar, and Misha had jettisoned both a long way back.

The soldier who had first approached him took the car keys and drove the car around the sandbag barricade to a siding where three other cars, including the limousine, were already parked. Those arrested were led off towards a pair of trucks, men in one, women in another. From the back of the women's truck, he saw a pale face peering out.

It was Tonya. He had seen her and she had seen him. Her face was full of love, and full of tears.

14

Through the night, the clouds thickened. When morning broke, the clouds lay piled up as thick and impenetrable as a pile of wolf furs. When eventually it managed to filter through, the first light of day appeared greenish, like ladlefuls of pea soup. It was still cold.

Pavel hardly bothered to look out of the window, but when he did, the livid skyscape only suited his mood.

He could still feel the vodka inside him, but he'd been drinking coffee and water for four hours now and his head was starting to clear. He knew that Tonya had been arrested, and felt sure of having snared Malevich too. He now felt both the hunter's glee and the hunter's slight depression. When he tried to focus on his next steps — what to do with his sister and her one-time lover? — his mind turned away in rebellion.

And he had other things to think about. Bigger things. For every five minutes he spent thinking about Tonya, he spent fifteen thinking about his conversation with Lukyanchenko. The camp would take a thousand extra prisoners. He'd need more land, more huts, more bedding, more supplies . . . Only then again, such materials were scarce and needed elsewhere. It wouldn't do to be soft on reactionaries and criminals. Pavel began to ponder the logistics of his new arrivals. How little could he get away with? And not only that, but the deeper implications of Lukyanchenko's words sank in. Once again, it was being proved that only Russia was strong. Only Russia had the necessary determination to do what needed to be done. Sooner or later, Russian strength would force the Western Allies to leave Berlin. Italy would waver. Austria would crumble. The western half of Germany would totter and fall. To Pavel, these seemed like the big facts of the night. The little subplot involving a Red Army translator and a German — Russian bourgeois seemed irrelevant by comparison.

Or so he wanted to think. But he noticed in himself a restlessness that he couldn't explain away. He had himself driven back to the camp, but couldn't rest, or even sit at ease. Instead he issued a stream of instructions about things ranging from minor to the utterly inconsequential. With subordinates, he was irritable and snappish. Before long, the whole camp knew their commander's mood. People were summoned from their beds, given orders to be fulfilled immediately, reprimanded for some trivial offence committed a day or two before. Those who were not involved, sat on their beds wearing greatcoats pulled over their undershorts, scratching their heads and wondering what was up.

The greenish dawn was still wrestling with the solid mass of cloud, seeking admittance, when the first truck pulled into the camp yard. Pavel heard the crash of a tailgate, the bark of orders, the heavy steps of soldiers moving in excitement and triumph. Pavel tweaked aside the curtains and saw that the first truck had brought the male prisoners. He waited impatiently, pacing up and down until he heard the expected knock at his door. He shouted admittance.

An NKVD man he didn't recognise, from Eberswalde presumably, opened the door and reported that the prisoners had been brought. Pavel asked for Malevich to be brought in, only to be told there was no Malevich.

Impatiently, Pavel asked for the list of prisoners. The NKVD man produced a list. Whoever had drawn it up was obviously uncomfortable with Roman lettering, because the German names had been written out, letter by letter, in a childish, careful hand. Pavel scanned the list. There weren't many names. There was only one with the first name Michael. The man's surname, Müller, was obviously a cover for Malevich. Pavel asked for that man to be brought to him immediately. The escaping private, Kornikova, was to be brought in as soon as the truck of females arrived. The rest of the prisoners could be released, unless their papers betrayed any irregularity, in which case they could be sentenced as appropriate.

The man left. Pavel jumped to the window again to see what was going on, but the light was still poor and he couldn't tell much about the commotion in the yard. He put his hand to his belt, found that he'd loosened it at the Party the night before, and now re-tightened it a notch or two. He snatched up his uniform cap, put it on, tore it off again, then changed his mind and jammed it back on. His palms were moist.

There was a second knock. Gaining control of himself, Pavel walked carefully to the door and opened it. There was a man in handcuffs, flanked by two soldiers with more behind. The prisoner was clearly Malevich. In the poor light of early dawn, with the lamplight from within blocked by Pavel himself, Malevich looked hardly changed at all from a quarter-century before. It was as though some impatient artist had taken an earlier drawing, sketched in a couple of lines, thrown a dash of grey into the hair, then pushed away the revised sketch as though it were finished. In a rough voice, Pavel told the soldiers to remove the prisoner's handcuffs and to remain outside while he conducted the interrogation. The men did as he asked. Pavel turned his back on the prisoner and brusquely directed him to a sofa with a jerk of his hand. Malevich sat down as instructed, clearly bewildered, perplexed at what kind of interrogation would take place in surroundings like these.

Pavel kept out of the lamplight, taking the opportunity to study Malevich before he himself was recognised. In the brighter light of the room, Pavel could see that his first impression wasn't precisely right. Malevich had aged. Those weren't simply ordinary lines on his face, they were the lines of a man who had experienced a lot, suffered a lot. Pavel digested the information slowly, taking his time. Then he said, "So, Mikhail Ivanovich, aren't you going to say hello?"

Misha looked up, startled, almost as though he'd been struck. Then his face changed. He smiled what seemed like a smile of genuine pleasure. He sprang to his feet.

"Pavel Kirylovich! Pasha — may I still call you that? — Good Lord! What a surprise!"

Pavel's expression changed three times in as many seconds. He showed pleasure, annoyance, superiority, coolness.

"You may call me Lieutenant-Colonel Lensky." Pavel found himself swinging his shoulder around so that Misha could read the message of the stars on his epaulette. "May I remind you that you are under arrest for the abduction, if I may put it like that, the attempted abduction, of a member of the Red Army? Right here from this camp. A most serious offence, if I may say, not to mention any crimes that may have been committed back in the first days of the Soviet time."

"Yes, yes."

Misha sat down again, defeated in his first impulse of warmth, but also baffled. What an extraordinary coincidence that it should be Tonya's own brother to foil their escape and capture him! But the whole thing was strange. If Pavel really wanted to be a stickler for rules, then why conduct the interrogation here, in Pavel's own bungalow, just the two of them alone? Misha looked around at the furnishings, the fat black-and-gold cigar-box, the looming portrait of Karl Marx. He thought about Pavel as a boy — Pavel on their fishing trips at Petrozavodsk — about what Pavel must have done to rise as far as he had, and in the NKVD, of all detestable institutions. But he couldn't think straight. His head was too full of images from the night: the camp under snow and starlight, the car ride, the road block, Tonya's face gazing at him from the back of a prison-truck. He thought of Tonya, of course, but also of Rosa. He hated himself for putting her through what could easily prove to be a second orphanhood.

His thoughts, and those of his captor, were disturbed by the arrival of a second truck in the yard. Misha jerked his head up, but Pavel was already at the window.

"It's her all right," he commented. "My sister and your — I don't know what to call her. Her husband is still alive, you know. Rodyon Leonidovich. He's over in

379

the east now. Near Vladivostok. I can't understand why that plays no part in your plans, the two of you."

Misha said nothing, but something inside him turned a somersault, like a small beast turning in its burrow. Rodyon was still alive! Did Tonya know? And if so, what did she feel about it? Misha didn't know how to take the news, couldn't work out his feelings amidst the turmoil.

There was some business outside, supervised by Pavel. Then Pavel came in with Tonya. He told her to sit, indicating an armchair away from Misha. But she sat down next to Misha and took his hand. The pair of them exchanged an endless glance that left Pavel out of things altogether. He had to cough and stamp for them to turn slowly and face him. They kept their hands locked together, as though able to transmit their innermost thoughts that way. They didn't speak. They sat in front of Pavel, waiting for him to determine their fates.

CHAPTER
TWELVE

1

It was January 1947. A Tuesday evening.

A thin cold wind blew down from the Baltic and sent a chill through everything. The snow which had been present ever since the night of the abortive escape had stayed hard and crisp for just two days. Then a temporary thaw had set in. The snow had subsided into heavy piles, thick and wet. Then the thick grey heaps dissolved into slush and trickles of dirty water that seemed to run everywhere through the camp. By now, even the slush had disappeared, and all that was left was endless mud, grey clouds, wet grass, and the present chill wind.

Misha was a prisoner. Of all the places in the world to be held, he was being held in camp Oderbruch itself, on the other side of the fence from the area that had been Tonya's home for the past eight months.

Had been, because Misha no longer knew where Tonya was. For the first seven days of his imprisonment, he'd stayed close to the barbed wire on the edge of the prisoners' enclosure, trying to catch a glimpse of her. He never succeeded. He was fairly sure that she no longer slept in the women's sleeping hut. He guessed that she was either being kept captive herself or she had been transferred somewhere else altogether — perhaps back to the Soviet Union, perhaps to Siberia.

He was still close to the barbed wire now, still looking for a sign of Tonya, but without any real hope. His feet had got wet earlier that day and they were still wet because he had no way of drying them. Over in the canteen hut, there was the banging of a metal spoon against an empty fuel tin — the sign that the evening meal was ready. Misha was too cast down to have an appetite, but made himself go over to get food anyway. He knew that if his imprisonment were to be long-term, then death from malnourishment-induced disease would become a real danger.

He entered the hut, collected his food and sat down at a table with three others. There was almost no conversation. Misha had still not made the effort to make friends. He knew the names of almost no one there. The prisoners ate their slop — a watery stew made with potatoes and turnip. Misha had eaten no meat since his arrival. He had already lost about nine pounds in weight. Rumours spread that dozens, maybe hundreds, of new prisoners would be arriving before long.

A gust of wind threw a sudden flurry of rain against the window. The window fitted poorly, and the rain seeped through, making a dark mould stain on the inside. The man opposite Misha looked sourly at the pane.

"*Verdammte Wetter*," he remarked. He lifted his spoon and poured the watery gravy in a long spout back into his tin. "*Verdammte Iwans.*"

Then, as well as the wind, there were noises from outside: a truck engine, the clash of gates, the sound of tyres carving through water, a skirl of brakes. Then other sounds: men, energetic and well-fed, stamping through the muddy ground. The door of the canteen hut burst open. Six Soviet soldiers stood there, armed and resplendent in their immaculate uniforms. The low hum in the canteen fell to an absolute hush. Visits such as these were rare — Misha hadn't seen one in the ten days he'd been present — and they betokened either something very good or very bad. The senior officer, a captain, holding his chin so high in the air that he must have been seeing more of the ceiling than of the room itself, snapped out a short command.

It took Misha a second to realise what he'd said, then heard the officer repeat, "Prisoner Malevich, present yourself."

Misha pushed away his food and stood up. Every eye in the room followed him. There was no further instruction from the Soviet captain, but Misha walked over to the doorway. The Soviets didn't move until he had reached them, then he was brusquely ordered to follow and was led outside.

The grey light was far brighter than the dim canteen and a gleam of sunshine was reflected off the wet ground and numerous puddles. Misha contracted his eyes against the glare. The Soviets led him to the back of the truck and shoved him inside. They made no attempt to handcuff him but they did tie his ankles with a short piece of dirty string, as a crude way of preventing him from seeking to escape. All the soldiers carried rifles, but the safety catches were on and the soldiers handled them negligently. Nobody spoke. The captain climbed into the front of the truck and the engine started up. The truck ground its way out of the camp and the heavy double gates were slammed shut behind them.

The truck headed out on the open road. One of the soldiers pulled at the cord that held up the back panel of the canvas canopy. The cord was wet and wouldn't loosen, so the soldier took out a knife and slashed at the knot, until the wet canvas shot down, splattering them all with raindrops. Misha couldn't see where they were going. When the soldiers spoke, they did so quietly and in subdued tones.

The truck moved on. Night fell. The truck slowed down, no doubt because the roads were poor and unlit. Misha tried to guess whether the roads were getting worse — in which case Poland was the likeliest destination — but he found it almost impossible to tell. At one point, one of the soldiers lit a cigarette. Misha, thinking to demonstrate that he was one of their countrymen, asked in Russian if they had a spare cigarette. The soldiers looked at each other and shook their heads, even though Misha could count at least two large pouches of tobacco among the men. Any conversation that there had been ended abruptly.

Then, after about two hours, the conditions outside the truck changed. The road surface was clearly better.

384

The truck's motion began the twists, turns, stops and starts that indicated they were in a city. Based on the size of the city and the time they'd taken to get to it, Misha guessed they must be in either Berlin or one of the larger Polish cities. Every now and then he heard snatches of conversation from passers-by outside the truck, but over the noise of the engine, he couldn't tell whether the speakers were German or Polish.

Then the truck stopped.

There was light outside and the sound of traffic. Footsteps came down the side of the truck from the front. The canvas canopy was pulled back. Outside, there were lights and a huge dark shape; some masonry structure, with its clean lines now war-damaged and ragged. Misha was told to get out. He did so, needing assistance because of the string around his legs. He was half-helped, half-pulled from the truck. The soldier tugging him didn't bother to let him find his balance on reaching the ground and Misha promptly fell over. The men got back into the truck and the truck roared away, sending a blast of exhaust into Misha's face. He fumbled at the cord around his legs, trying at the same time to see where he was. He couldn't make out the large building or monument in front of him. Cars and headlamps were moving fast only a short distance away.

Then he heard footsteps coming towards him; footsteps and the beam of a powerful torch. The torch caught him in the face.

"What's up, mate?" said a voice in English, then, in German or a version of it, "*Sind Sie all OK?*"

Misha got the string off his legs. The English voice and the big masonry arch fell into place. This was the Brandenburg Gate. Misha had been dropped back in the British sector. The torchlight moved away from his face and a rough, friendly arm heaved him to his feet.

He began to laugh in shock and relief.

2

He ran home quickly, of course. Rosa had come running to the door in her nightdress, tears streaming down her face. The poor girl had been convinced, quite reasonably, that her precious "new daddy" had gone the way of the old one. She had to climb right into Misha's arms before she could quite believe the reality of this unexpected return. And Willi was not so different. He stood embracing them both, his skinny face illuminated by wide dinner-plate eyes. Misha came on inside, hugging Rosa tightly against his chest. Willi, after accepting one long hug, jumped away again and busied himself at the drinks cupboard, pouring two large whiskies — the bottle itself a present from Hollinger — and fetching cigarettes. But Misha noticed that the boy's hands had been shaking and that every two or three seconds he was snatching a glance across at Misha.

Misha took the whisky and promised both children, not once but repeatedly, that he wouldn't enter the east zone again. Rosa had snuggled herself inside Misha's coat, curled up like a rabbit in a burrow. Without moving from her lair, she asked, "Did you see her?"

"Yes, *Knospe*, I saw her."

"And?"

"And they wouldn't let her come with me, I'm afraid. I'm sorry. I did my best."

Rosa nodded. She was disappointed — somehow she'd always had a faith in the "new mummy" that had gone beyond anything Misha had ever told her — but it was clear that she couldn't bear the idea of losing Misha again. And Misha too had given up. He had been imprisoned and then released. Why? There could only be one reason. Pavel had wanted Misha to be out of the way while he dealt with his sister. But dealt with her how? Misha couldn't believe that even Pavel could have had his sister shot. Indeed, since Pavel could have had Tonya shot on the spot if he'd wished it, then the length of Misha's imprisonment could only be a good sign. But Pavel would certainly not have allowed Tonya to remain in Germany. She must have been sent back to the Soviet Union. To where? To Moscow or Leningrad? To Siberia or one of the labour battalions in the north? Or internal exile? Or to join Rodyon in the Russian Far East, a full half a world distant? It was too much. The possibilities seemed too endless, the Soviet empire too large, too dangerous and inaccessible. Deep inside himself, Misha grieved for the woman he loved and would never see again. Rosa too, in her childish way, understood all this, and she grieved along with him, hiding her tears inside the folds of his coat.

3

Three months later, April 1947, and the thaw had come to Russia too, almost in a single day it seemed.

Tonya first knew of it one night, when her dreams were full of images of water. She dreamed of water in every conceivable form: tiny springs gurgling from the wet earth, heaps of snow trickling and melting, huge lakes stretching as far as the horizon, river rapids hurtling over rocks. And her dreams didn't just take in the sights of nature. She dreamed of water in every human manifestation too. She dreamed of water in glasses, in decorated enamel jugs, in wooden water scoops and butts, in tin baths, in sinks and drains. Any image at all seemed to count as long as there was water flowing, splashing, glittering and streaming through it.

And when she woke, she woke to a world transformed.

She was on a train to the Far East. Pavel had had her sent as translator to an NKVD camp in Poland while he arranged for her move to join Rodyon. The move had been approved and she was on her way, travelling the vast distances of Soviet central Asia.

The train was in the middle of one of its interminable halts, but it must have made good progress in the night, perhaps taking a southward dip on its way. Because when Tonya stood up from her cramped wooden bunk and looked out of the open window, the whole world seemed to have turned to water.

As far as she could see, in both directions, the fields and roads were lying under a sheet of water, gleaming pale blue and silver in the first light of day. The flooding was obviously an annual affair, because all the farms and villages around were built on low mounds and earth banks that rose muddily out of the shining water. But everything else — trees, hedges, telegraph poles, even cows and horses — were one, two, even four feet underwater. The railway line itself was raised up on a low embankment with the floods surrounding it on both sides, so it seemed almost as though the twin steel lines had been laid across the water itself. The whole world smelled of water and damp earth.

Tonya went to the door and climbed out onto the thin strip of land between the train and where the embankment dropped away into the water. The air was unbelievably fresh and new-smelling. She felt utterly sad, but also somehow reconciled. She had lost Misha, lost freedom, lost the chance to escape from the cold grey hand of the Soviet state. But already, deep in the heart of Russia as she now was, those things had sped away into the distance like dreams of something utterly impossible.

And Pavel had, in his way, been kind to her. Not kind enough to let her go with Misha. But kind enough to spare her the bullet or the camp. It had somehow mattered to him that she was still married to Rodyon. Perhaps in his own unfathomable way, he thought he was doing right by bringing the two of them together again. She could hardly imagine seeing Rodyon again. More than a decade had passed since he'd been torn from her — and the intervening years had been so full of imprisonment, loss, battle, and then the whole adventure of Berlin and Germany. How would she feel? She asked herself the question almost incessantly, but in truth she already knew the answer. She would feel about him as she always had. As a friend. As an ally. As a man she deeply respected. But not as a lover. Not as a husband. But still. It would be good to see him. She hoped he was well.

CHAPTER
THIRTEEN

1

Tonya arrived in Preobrazheniye one spring evening. She didn't know where she was meant to go. There was no one on the platform to meet her. She put down her bag — her life's possessions packed into a bag small enough to swing easily from her shoulder — and waited. In the lee of the station canopy, the shadows grew thicker. A quince tree hung its blossoms over a fence. The air was curious to Tonya: it felt heavy, thick and moist, almost like the air in a communal bath house. She supposed it was the unseen presence of this eastern sea, so unlike the cold northern sea she remembered from Petrograd. Some way away, a bird sang, in a voice Tonya couldn't recognise.

An hour passed. It became darker. Tonya wondered what to do — realised that there was nothing she could do, not this late in the evening — and determined to wait. Another forty minutes ran past. The smell of the quince blossom grew more intense as the evening breeze dropped away.

And then, she heard boot steps running across the dirt yard in front of the station. She stood up. The steps approached. A wooden door was thrust aside with a hollow boom. A man emerged onto the platform and stood in the thin iron lamplight above the doorway, looking around. Tonya realised that she was standing in the shadow, effectively invisible. The man couldn't see her.

But she could see him.

The man was thinner than he had once been. The old flash and fire in his eyes had gone, his former tigerish energy sunk away almost to nothing. But it was Rodyon, all right. She walked towards him, hands outstretched.

2

It was the evening of June the 18th, the end of a fine, warm day. The linden tree in Misha's back garden was just budding into early flower. A honeysuckle had clambered up into the lower branches then collapsed downwards as though fagged out. The scents of both hung seemingly for ever on the still air.

It was eight-thirty in the evening. Rosa was usually required to be in bed by that time but, uncharacteristically for her, she had hung around downstairs, making excuses and dragging her feet. Misha, after a couple of attempts to shoo her up, had given up. He'd mixed her a drink of lemon juice, water and sugar and the two of them had gone outside to sit in the garden and enjoy the last of the sun. They didn't speak much. Willi was out somewhere with his camera and his journalist friends. Misha had erected a hammock under the linden tree in the garden and Rosa swung on it, while Misha sat on the grass beneath. She sipped her drink.

There was almost no sound except the bedtime songs of birds and the squeak where the hammock rubbed against its fixing.

Suddenly Rosa spoke.

"Harry's coming now," she announced.

"Harry? Hollinger?"

Rosa nodded.

"I don't think so, little *Knospe*."

The truth was that Misha hardly ever saw Hollinger now. There was a real friendship between the two men, but their professional relationship had come to an end. It was no longer possible to reach Tonya, and Misha could no longer safely travel in the east zone, and consequently no longer had nuggets of information to feed the Englishman. Hollinger still came around from time to time, but he was too busy to come often.

Rosa didn't argue against Misha's verdict — she hardly ever did — but she just nodded again to demonstrate that she didn't agree. In any case, her occasional bursts of intuition had nothing to do with logic. She went on rocking. Misha saw a spider lower itself onto her head from the branches above and he stood up to brush it away. And just as he did so, there was the sound of a car engine outside. The car slowed and stopped. Rosa raised her eyebrows in a silent told-you-so. Surprised, Misha stood up and walked around the side of the cottage — its stone walls still warm from the day's heat — to the front. There, sure enough, was Hollinger struggling with a large cardboard box.

"*Guten Abend*, old bean," said Hollinger. "Here, take an end."

The two men carried the box around the house into the garden. Rosa had jumped down out of her hammock and came skipping to greet the Englishman with a big hug around the neck.

"Hello there, Rosie. Still up, eh? Here, do you want to see what's in this box?"

Using his car key, he ripped the tape on the box and opened the lid. The box inside was crammed with tinned goods from England and other things that had seldom been seen in Berlin for almost as long as Rosa had been alive. There were tinned peaches, condensed milk, golden syrup, tea, Oxford marmalade, bars of soap, and much else. Hollinger let Rosa dig around in the box emitting shrieks of excitement and delight, then he himself reached down into a corner and pulled out a bottle of whisky. Misha went into the kitchen and came out with two glasses for himself and Hollinger, and a bowl, spoon and tin opener so that Rosa could enjoy her first ever taste of tinned peach. He poured the whisky and decanted the peaches. Rosa bent over her bowl breathless with excitement.

Hollinger's face had been beaming while Rosa was being sorted out, but as soon as Misha stood up again and faced him, the Englishman's face looked sombre.

"What is it?" Misha spoke in French, a language that Hollinger knew well enough and that Rosa didn't.

"Nothing, nothing . . . well, I hope nothing."

"And if it weren't nothing?"

394

Hollinger sighed, swilling whisky around his glass, staring hard at the glittering liquid.

"More and more, I'm getting a bad sense of things."

"The Soviets?"

"Yes, in a way. In the western zones, things have become very bad. In some of the bigger cities, the daily calorie count was down to just 900. That's awful, but at least it's had the effect of waking people up. The Americans, more. Our chaps were awake, but too poor to do much. Anyhow, as you know, this fellow General Marshall has offered real help. Money. Increases in permitted industrial production, even steel. There'll be reform of the currency as well. There'll have to be. You can't get a country to function on cigarettes and banknotes that everyone knows are worthless."

"And comrade Stalin won't like that."

"No. He'll never permit a western currency reform to take place in his sector, which means that the country will be effectively split in two."

"And Berlin?"

"I don't know. The Russians have it surrounded. If they want to cut it off, they can do so easily. We'll never start a shooting war to stop them. Even if we did, we don't have the troops to do it. If Stalin wants Berlin, he'll take it."

Rosa had almost finished her peaches now, but she was making the last peach half last by chasing it around the painted china bowl with her spoon, watching it squirm and squeal away from her. The box full of goodies had taken on a darker meaning now. It was Hollinger's way of protecting them against what was about to come; the starvation and the hopelessness. But a cardboard box, no matter how large and wonderful, would not go far against a Soviet attempt to starve the city.

"It won't be soon," said Hollinger, reading his thoughts. "That box isn't meant to be . . . well, it's just a gift. But if you want to get out of the city now, I'd help clear the paperwork."

Misha breathed out, watching his girl playing on the grass. A brown caterpillar with purple spots had crawled over the lip of the bowl and Rosa was intent on seeing whether the caterpillar liked peach.

"I ought to do it, I know," he said. "For Rosa's sake, if not mine. But I can't. Somewhere, back in the early days with Willi, I realised I could never run again. I still can't."

Hollinger nodded, then changed the subject.

"How is Willi?"

"Well. Very well. His photography is getting better all the time. He is getting commissions from the best American papers now. He's still doing cartoons for *Die Trümmerzeitung*. He's always busy."

"He's got a talent, that boy."

"Yes."

Hollinger opened his mouth to say something, then closed it, then decided to say it anyway. "You know, your little family here?"

"Yes?"

"It's Germany, isn't it? Germany as she was always meant to be and now is."

"I don't understand."

"You, the engineer, the bourgeois, the businessman. The man who'll fix anything, make something of nothing. And Willi. The democratic spirit, the freethinker, the journalist. The sort of person to put an end to any number of Hitlers."

"Yes, and Rosa, the future, the one who gives hope to all the rest of us."

Rosa had finished her peaches and rolled over on hearing her name. Misha smiled at her and pulled her over onto his lap. The three of them played and chatted until the sun went down, and Rosa couldn't keep from yawning.

Hollinger stood up, ready to go. He spoke in French one last time.

"Your Antonina, she was very special. She did a lot for us. I didn't know her well, but what I did, I liked very much. I'm sorry we couldn't get her out. God knows, if anyone had deserved it, she did."

Misha nodded, and found himself repeating Hollinger's last sentence.

"Yes. If anyone deserved it, then she did."

They used the past tense. Both men knew they were never likely to see or hear from her again.

3

Half a world away, Tonya's life began again.

Rodyon had taken her back to his apartment, a single room really, with a communal toilet at the bottom of the stairs, and a small cooking stove crammed into the

397

corner of the room. There was no chair, but a bed big enough for them both to sit.

He didn't apologise for the accommodation — how could he, when the apartment had never been of his choosing? — but Tonya didn't mind it anyway. Of all the futures that Pavel could have arranged for her, this one was the least bad by a long distance.

That first night they sat together and talked until dawn. Rodyon told his story: prison camp in Siberia; the harshest of conditions only barely survived; then war in a *shtraf* battalion; his pleasure at the idea that he might at least die in the fight against fascism, rather than waste away in prison. After the war had ended, his remaining prison sentence had been cancelled. He had been posted here, to Preobrazheniye, and given a job as a warehouseman down at the docks. He liked the sea, he said. He found it peaceful.

Then Tonya spoke about herself. Her imprisonment. Her wartime experiences. At times, it appeared the two of them had been located on the same part of the front, just a dozen miles or so away from each other. But it could have been a million miles for all the difference that it had made or could have made. She skipped over her time as interpreter in Berlin and then Oderbruch quickly enough. She didn't mention Misha or her attempted escape.

They spoke about their daughters of course, Yuliya and Yana. Neither of them had heard what had happened to the girls. Even if they were alive, they would be best advised to make no attempt to contact their parents, political outcasts as they were. Tonya realised that the girls had somehow come to mean more to Rodyon than she did. She accepted his feelings. She had never fully given herself to her husband. It was only right that he had now managed to pull away from his long-standing obsession with her. He told her that she was to be given a job in a fish-packing factory close to the waterfront. "It's not the nicest work, but it's not the worst. Maybe in time they'll let you move to an office job somewhere."

She shrugged. "Maybe. In time."

Only late on that night, when a huge pink sun had reared itself from a pale blue sea so smooth you couldn't tell where water ended and sky began, did Rodyon mention Misha.

"You saw him," he said.

Tonya wasn't sure if it were a statement or a question. She didn't know how much, if anything, he knew. But she wasn't going to lie. She was too old for that now, and too much had happened.

"Yes."

"In Berlin?"

"Yes."

"Of course you must have wanted to go and . . ."

"I tried, yes."

"But you were caught, I suppose. So that's why they sent you here."

"Not they. Pavel."

"Pavel?" Rodyon was genuinely astonished. He'd had no idea. "Really? You know that brother of yours . . . There was always something not quite right about his

399

political convictions. I used to think in those early days, that he might . . . well, perhaps . . ."

Tonya nodded. She knew what he was saying. "He denounced us. First you. Then me. Why, I don't know. I think I never understood him at all."

Rodyon nodded. He got up from the bed to make a fire in the stove and put on a pot of water to boil. He had some coffee beans from somewhere, which he ground by putting them into a cloth bag and thumping them with the end of a stick. Tonya realised he must have gone to extraordinary lengths to find coffee for her. As the stove grew hot it leaked gritty smoke and coal fumes into the room because the chimney joints fitted poorly. It was the sort of problem Misha would have sorted out on his first day, with his long fingers and incessant, deft creativity. Tonya missed that beloved man more than ever now, useless though that feeling was.

Rodyon went downstairs to shave, politely leaving the room for her to change in if she wanted. She didn't bother to change, just untied her hair, combed it out, then tied it again. The water boiled and Tonya made coffee.

All through the night, sitting side by side together on the bed, they had held hands. Once, Rodyon had brought her hand to his lips and kissed it. She had let him. And that had been it. He had made no attempt to take her to bed and, she realised, he never would. Though they would sleep side by side of course — the room had only one bed in it and no room to fit a second — they would never make love again. Tonya felt

400

a little sorry for him: Rodyon, who had only ever been good to her.

At seven o'clock that morning, she went down to the fish-packing factory and reported for duty. The air smelled of fish guts and warm tin.

4

Months passed and, little by little, Hollinger's prediction began to prove itself right.

The Western Allies had finally chosen to rebuild Germany from the rubble. The decisions were timid at first. The vast bulk of American aid under General Marshall's scheme was to go not to Germany, but to her former enemies or conquests. The money had to be spent on American goods, shipped in American vessels. But a change had been made, and the change proved unstoppable.

And the Soviets knew it.

In March 1948, American trains were prevented from entering Berlin. Twenty-four barges were prevented from moving because of some nonsense about permits. The Allies protested, and the Russians softened their stance.

But nobody was fooled. If the Russians had tried something successfully once, they'd try it again in full force before too long. And so it began: a war of pinpricks, none of them too bothersome in themselves, but cumulatively painful and threatening for the future.

In April, fifty barges were held up. The Allies made their protests. The barges moved again. In May, there was another spat over the arrival of parcels into Berlin. And this time, there was no instant loosening. On the roads, traffic restrictions were put in place and then administered by nit-picking Soviet officials, immune to reason. Goods piled up in warehouses and factories, unable to reach their buyers. Berlin began to wither, like a flower left too long on the stalk.

In the meantime, in the western half of Germany, progress towards something like an independent state was growing all the time. A currency reform was being talked about. Any such move would be interpreted by the Soviets as a breach of their wartime agreements, and an immediate response was certain.

Rumours spread.

It was said that the Americans were making plans to evacuate all their women and children from the city. It was said that the British were about to halve their garrison. The Americans were lazy, the British feeble, the French cowardly.

It was 17th June 1948.

5

Tonya walked to the refrigeration area and heaved another crate of fish from the waiting stacks. The chilled area was closed off with heavy rubber doors and large signs in red paint. But the refrigeration plant itself was defective and worked only sporadically. Today wasn't one of the good days and the stacks of fish smelled high.

402

Tonya took the crate to her work station on the packing line. A large red sign above her head said, "FISH PACKERS! YOUR WORK IS FOR PEACE AND TO FEED THE RUSSIAN HOMELAND!" In smaller letters, the sign added thoughtfully, "*The Soviet trade is our immediate concern.*" Maybe so, but the factory manager's immediate concern was meeting quota, and everyone in the factory knew that four months into the plan, they were already four weeks behind it. Tonya's job was, in theory, to gut and descale the fish, then remove head, tails and fins before sending them down the line for boiling and packing. But, because of the pressure to fill the quota, the factory foremen (all men) were constantly patrolling the line shouting at any of the packers (all women) who spent longer than about ten or fifteen seconds on a fish. Time after time, Tonya was being forced to send fish down the line that still had their heads hanging half-on, half-off; fish with a thin spill of guts trailing from their open bellies, even fish that were obviously diseased, with grey eyes and dull, lustreless skins. This crate wasn't too bad, but even so, Tonya cut corners to keep up. She wasn't thinking about fish, however. There had been a storm the day before. Fishermen's boats had been feared lost. Rodyon, a reserve lifeboatman, had been called out when the seas were at their highest and the winds at their angriest. He should have been back within two hours, but hadn't been back after twelve. Tonya wanted to wait for him down at the docks, but had been obliged to come into work as normal. She had heard nothing and was acutely worried.

403

It was the end of the day now. The storm had passed and evening light leaned up against the grimy windows. The smell of fish had thickened and thickened until it came to feel like some solidly physical artefact. The voices of the foremen buzzed like wasps.

A whistle blew for the workers to stop. But no one was released until the last crates of fish were tipped straight from the refrigeration unit onto the line, heads, tails, guts and all. There was a rush of women towards the washrooms. Tonya followed, found a basin, and scrubbed at her skin until it was pink and raw. But she didn't spend as long at the tap as usual. She hurried out of the factory, taking the crooked road down the hill towards the docks. The air was rosy and warm, quite unlike the sea air she'd known in her youth.

She turned a corner and saw the dock lying spread out in front of her. She tried to find the white and blue lifeboat with her eyes, but the port was crowded with fishing and she could see nothing. But she was looking in the wrong place. Rodyon's lean figure, tired but smiling, dressed in his old black suit and dark tie, was there climbing the hill towards her.

"Hello, dreamer," he said.

Tonya jumped at the nearness of his voice, then ran towards him. "Rodya! I was so worried! They said you only had fuel to be out a few hours, and then you were gone so long . . ."

He kissed her cheek and took her hand — the most physical intimacy they shared these days. "We were low on fuel. Just as we were turning to come back, we saw one of the boats in distress. We thought we could go to it, take off the men and drain some of the fuel for our tanks . . . well, we got the men but getting the fuel was another thing altogether. With what we had left, we decided to head on out to sea, rather than risk getting caught up against the shore in the storm. Our radio had packed up somewhere along the way, which didn't help."

"You went out to sea?"

"To Japan almost. Can you imagine? We were picked up by a Japanese trawler fishing for sea bream and horse mackerel. They were nice. They didn't have spare fuel, but they radioed for some."

They began walking home, but then Rodyon was struck by an urge to do something different. "Let's not go back just yet. Let's go to Smirnov's."

Smirnov's was a restaurant famous for its cream cakes and fruit jellies. It was patronised mostly by party officials and those whose jobs gave them a second income through bribery. Rodyon and Tonya certainly couldn't afford it. She objected, saying she didn't feel hungry, but Rodyon insisted and took her there anyway.

They got a table quickly, even though the waiter looked daggers at Tonya's working clothes and her faint but persistent smell of fish. Feeling uncomfortable, she stole a lemon from a fruit stand and went off to the toilets to rub her hands and arms with the juice. By the time she came back, Rodyon, looking like a man utterly used to these exclusive surroundings, had ordered tea for them both and a tray of cakes. Tonya protested mildly, but her protests were waved away. In his present mood, she glimpsed again the charismatic young commissar of Petrograd some thirty years before. He was commanding and charming; smiling but purposeful.

They talked inconsequentially for a while. Then Rodyon changed the subject.

"On the boat, they had a newspaper. A Japanese one."

"Oh?"

"One of the men on the boat spoke a little Russian. Enough to translate for me."

"The newspaper?"

"It talked about Berlin. The Western powers have brought in a new currency. Stalin — well, he must have been furious. So he's ordered Berlin to be cut off. There's no traffic permitted by either land or water. He wants to starve the Western half into submission."

Tonya stared at him in shock, wordlessly.

"The Americans and British have started to fly in supplies by air, but I doubt if they'll even be able to feed their own garrisons like that. The city's airports were never intended for heavy use."

"But if they — if the city — if Berlin —" Tonya began three times and stopped herself each time. It wasn't only Berlin she cared about, it was Misha. If the city fell, then the Soviets would be able to settle scores with everyone inside it, Misha included. Tonya wanted to talk about it all, but held herself back. First, because she generally steered clear of politics with Rodyon. Despite all that had happened, she knew he still thought of himself as a good communist; a true follower of Marx and Lenin. And it wasn't just that. This Soviet assault on Berlin felt like a direct attack on Misha, a last throw of the dice against him. If Berlin fell, would he be able to escape? Would he even try to? And if he didn't escape, would there be any hope that he'd be left to live his life out in peace? Tonya didn't think it likely. She wanted to cry, but felt inhibited by Rodyon's presence and the restaurant's cream and gold formality. She was sure she still smelled of fish, and stared straight ahead of her, her face and eyes stiff and unmoving. Rodyon examined her for a moment, a cream cake halfway to his mouth.

He put the cake down.

"If Berlin falls, then the Americans will lose face all across Europe. That's a big incentive for them to do what they can."

"But food for a million people? And fuel? How will they bring in enough coal when winter comes?"

"It's thought they'll need to bring in ten thousand tons a day when winter comes. But perhaps they'll do it, all the same." There was a long pause. His voice was very gentle. "I sincerely hope they do."

"You do?"

Rodyon had the cake in his hand again, on its way towards his mouth. He stared at it as though baffled as to how it came to be there, then put it down on the little white plate and pushed it away.

"When I read Karl Marx, I find myself agreeing with every word. When I read about Lenin's life, I find myself cheering every action. But when I look out of the window in the morning, I can't recognise a single thing . . . Yes, I hope Berlin holds out. If it does, it won't be because the Americans have flown in so many tons of food, or the British have carried so many tons of coal. It'll be because the Berliners have seen the Soviet system — *our* system — up close and have decided they'd rather starve than submit to it. The system will never recover from that. It has always been based on the belief that given a fair choice, the people would choose it over the alternative. They haven't done. If they don't in Berlin, even under bullying of this kind, then they won't anywhere else. In some ways, this is the end."

Tonya put out her hand and took his. She couldn't say she was sorry, because she wasn't. But she felt for him and his sense of failure. They held hands in silence for a while. At a table a few yards away, a group of Party men looked over towards them, someone spoke in a low voice and there was a burst of laughter. Tonya felt sure they were laughing at her.

Then Rodyon said, "It's not just about Berlin for you, is it?"

"No. There's Mikhail." With Rodyon, Tonya never used Misha's diminutive, only his full Christian name.

"Do you . . . Did you ever love me?"

"Yes. I love you now. I think I always have loved you. Only not like that. Not in that way. I can't explain myself."

Rodyon's eyes glittered. There was some surge of energy in him, but he kept it suppressed. He didn't say what it was about.

"If you could, you would go to him, I suppose?"

"That's a foolish question, Rodya."

"But if you could?"

"Japan you mean? Escape in a boat? No. I've tried to run away twice already. I shan't try again."

"But if it weren't a question of escape. If you could just snap your fingers and be with him?"

"Then I would. I'm sorry."

"No, you mustn't be sorry." Rodyon held her gaze for a few moments longer. The surge of energy was still there, still suppressed. Then something changed again, abruptly. Rodyon dropped his eyes and called for more tea, more cakes. His manner changed. He became once again a man of authority, the vigorous commissar of old. The tea came, but it wasn't hot enough. Rodyon sent it back imperiously, had more fetched, picked out the best cakes for Tonya and insisted that she eat.

"We can't afford this."

"No. And why not? Three decades of socialism and a man still can't afford cakes! I shall have to copy my fellow dockers and steal from the ships. Eh? That's the way to do it! You know what capitalism is? It's when the rich steal from the poor. And you know why communism is better? It's because it's fairer. We all steal from each other."

For the rest of the meal, Rodyon stayed in that mood: witty, brilliant, delightful. Tonya laughed and laughed. They ate more than they could manage and far more than they could afford. When they finally walked home, Tonya kissed her companion lightly on the lips.

409

It was true. She had always loved him. Not like Misha, but in some other way altogether. She didn't bemoan her fate. In some ways, she was happy.

CHAPTER
FOURTEEN

1

June 1950.

The Russian attempt to strangle Berlin had failed. The little airfields of the western sector had been improved and rebuilt. The Allies had poured aircraft into the region. In Britain, the RAF had provided its entire available stock of transporters, then increased capacity yet further by hiring in commercial transports too. The Americans had all along owned enough aircraft capacity, they had just hesitated to commit it to Berlin. But perhaps the British example stiffened them. Or perhaps the example of the Berliners themselves. In any case, they did it. In October 1948, President Truman had authorised the dispatch of a further sixty-six C-54s to Germany. The airlanes had become a steel pathway, constantly roaring, leading from the western zones over a hundred miles and more of Soviet territory into Berlin itself.

Even so, things had been desperately close. Food stocks were never more than a few weeks away from exhaustion. Fuel supplies were bitterly low and the entire city was left colder than it had been even in the darkest days of the war or its immediate aftermath. A hard winter would have finished things.

But the snow never came. The winter was the warmest in memory. Even through the darkest months, the aircraft continued to fly. Coal came in. Also food. And it was enough. As spring came, the Allied flights made the most of the reviving weather. The tonnage of food and supplies crept up month by month, even week by week. For the first time in Russian history, winter hadn't come to the rescue. The weather gods had turned against the Soviets. The Allies had won.

But in truth, the battle hadn't been won by the aircrews of the RAF and the USAF, but by the people of Berlin themselves. For years, they had been bullied, bribed and blackmailed by the Soviets. For an entire year, they had lain under siege. Adults had gone hungry to feed their children. A whole city had survived on dried potato and powdered egg. Families had shared cellars to eke out the tiny quantity of coal available. After more than fifteen years of rule by dictatorship and foreign occupation, the democratic passion of the German people had blazed out so strongly that the entire Soviet empire had been unable to quench it. The Berliners had won. Germany had won. Europe and the world were the beneficiaries.

But, although it was a victory, it was a sad one. Germany, that great country at the heart of Europe, was split in two. The Soviet zone became the German Democratic Republic — an utterly undemocratic police state, riven by spies, party officials, and informers. The Allied zones joined together to become the German Federal Republic, a country that stood set to become the most powerful force for peace and prosperity in that war-torn continent. The Soviet empire might have been checked in its westward expansion, but that still left a vast population imprisoned behind an ideology in which no one now believed. And Berlin remained a city of two halves. The dividing line between the two parts was still open, but it couldn't stay open for ever. Refugees from the east zone drained over to the west; the clearest possible example of what its people thought of the government that ruled in their names. People muttered that one day a wall would be built to divide the city in two. It seemed impossible to imagine it; but some days it seemed impossible not to.

2

Some of this Tonya knew, and she guessed more than she knew.

It was a Saturday evening in June. The sea was as smooth as rippled silk, stretching out to the horizon in pale blue, deep green, and gold. The line where sea joined sky was so faint as to be almost not there at all, as though some artist had thought better of the division and rubbed the original mark out with his thumb. The sun, of course, was dipping towards the land horizon to the west, not the ocean to the east. Tonya, who remembered her Petrograd childhood and the great sun dipping below the Gulf of Finland, still found it a strange inversion of the natural order that the sea should give birth to the sun and the land should swallow it. It was just one more way in which this far eastern existence felt like the exile that it was.

413

Tonya sat on a wooden jetty with some fisherman's nets spread over her lap, like a Siberian peasant's apron. Rodyon had moved from the docks to work on an ocean-going fishing vessel now. It was a move he'd long cherished. When the chance had come up, he'd jumped at it.

In some ways, the move was a good one for Tonya. They always had plenty of food now, fresh fish brought home from the catch. But the hours were long and irregular. Tonya often spent evenings and nights alone; and she felt lonely without him. All the same, she knew that he found peace and fulfilment out at sea. Since she hadn't been able to offer him the marriage he had always wanted, she couldn't begrudge him his fishing trips.

Each man on the boat was responsible for his own nets, and Tonya had learned how to take care of Rodyon's. It was work she enjoyed. She plucked the net over her lap, fold after fold. She found the places where the net was torn, and bound up the gaps with more twine, quickly and expertly knotted into place. Her fingers knew the work so well, she spent half her time gazing out to sea, watching the colours slowly change.

The evening was very quiet.

3

A man walked down the beach towards the jetty.

He saw the figure of the fisherwoman mending her nets, but couldn't see much more than a back, and a face turned out to sea. He came closer, his boots

414

making a soft crunching noise on the sand and seashells.

As he got closer, the woman heard him coming. She didn't turn. Rodyon was down at the harbour attending to some mechanical problem on the boat. He wouldn't be home this evening until late. Whoever the man was, it didn't concern her. She went on working.

The man stopped at the base of the jetty. He didn't speak. Tonya felt a crawling sensation at the back of her neck, like a slow prickle of anticipation that ran up her spine and into her scalp. Her breathing became shallow and watchful. But still she didn't turn. The man behind her still didn't speak. The golden ocean maintained its rhythm.

Then the man moved. He stepped onto the jetty. She could hear the creak of the wooden boards, the ever so slight adjustment of the structure to its new load. Tonya wanted to turn, but couldn't. Her breathing stuck in her throat like a fishbone.

There was another long moment of silence. Then the man spoke.

"Comrade Lensky? Is it you?"

Tonya jumped. Every muscle in her body leaped and tightened. Though she stayed sitting, she was completely braced now, wired tight. She still didn't turn, but her hands let the net drop back in her lap.

"Maybe. Who's asking?"

"It is the comrade engineer Malevich, who's asking."

"Then the comrade engineer is very late. He was wanted a long time back."

The man stepped a few feet further onto the jetty. He was now only ten or twelve yards from Tonya. She dropped her nets and stood up. She still couldn't quite bear to look up, as though scared that she might find herself trapped in some terrible deceitful dream.

"Comrade Malevich sends apologies for his unrevolutionary lateness. He attributes it to his fascistic bourgeois tendencies and class imperialism."

Tonya shook the nets away from her feet and walked down the jetty towards her love. She looked at his feet, his legs, his waist, but somehow she couldn't yet bring herself to look on his face itself. She was crying, but her tears fell soundlessly and without meaning..

"Does the comrade engineer still dance?"

Misha took her in his arms — she felt the same as ever, as though they'd been parted only a minute — and he led her in a dance she didn't recognise down the jetty towards the sea. The dance was very slow, more of a rhythmic sway than anything else, but Misha as usual knew what he was doing. The dance was perfect for the moment and the whole enormous ocean kept time for them. They kissed, long and passionately; lips and tongues remembering the love of thirty years, and not a thing forgotten.

They reached the end of the jetty. Misha gently pulled back from Tonya and the pair of them looked at each other properly for the first time in three decades. They had aged. Both of them had grey in their hair, new lines on their faces. But neither of them noticed the marks of age. She saw the true Misha: constant, imaginative, ceaselessly creative. And he saw the true

Tonya: patient, courageous, ever-loving, strong. She had stopped crying now, and he brushed the marks of her tears away with the back of his hand.

"How can it be true?" she said.

"He didn't tell you?"

"No."

"Your husband, Rodyon. He was caught out in a storm a year or two back. He was rescued by a Japanese trawler. Before he left them, he wrote a letter to me and asked the fishermen to see that it got to the British Embassy in Tokyo. Of course, he didn't have an address. He knew from you that I had been in Berlin. That was all. Anyway, the letter took a little time to find its way to me, but it did. He said where you were. He asked me to come and find you."

"Oh, Rodya!"

"He has always loved you very well."

"Yes." Tonya gathered up her nets. She didn't know where they were going now, but years of thrift wouldn't let her leave valuable nets lying around to be stolen. "Have you come to stay or . . .?"

"No. I don't think I'd be very welcome here. I've come to take you home."

"Home?"

"Yes, I've a little cottage in Berlin, a little girl called Rosa and a boy — a young man now, really — called Willi. You'll like them both. And if we want more children of our own, younger ones I mean — well, it may be a little late for us, but we live next door to an orphanage. If we wanted to adopt some children, there are only too many to choose from."

"Oh!"

Tonya was speechless. She had accustomed herself for so long to making do with very little, the sudden profusion of gifts was overwhelming. Her happiness had grown so large, it was like an almost painful physical pressure against her heart. In the midst of everything, she felt sudden fear, even terror.

"How are we going to escape? Oh, Misha, we've come close so many times. I don't think I could bear another disaster."

He kissed her again and they sat down on the sand.

"We haven't been very good at escaping, you and me. So I've called in the Royal Navy to do it for us. They've got a submarine waiting out there. They'll send in a boat this evening."

"The Royal Navy? The British navy?"

"It's a little present from Harry Hollinger. You know him as Mark Thompson, I think. He's a major now, still in Berlin, doing a very good job I expect. He sends love."

"Captain Thompson! Hollinger? A submarine!" Tonya was still so shocked, she could do little more than repeat these stunning facts. The happiness inside her was still expanding, but it was becoming lighter and brighter as it did so. The pressure on her heart was easing with every second.

She shifted position, so she was nestled right up against Misha, and every part of her body could feel his presence, his reassuring warmth. She had nothing to worry about any more. She let herself give way to the happiness within.

EPILOGUE

9 NOVEMBER, 1989

1

It was typical late November in Berlin. The sun shone, but without much warmth. The trees were mostly bare, but a few pale yellow leaves hung on like the last shreds of summer. The air was still.

But, though the air might have been calm, the city was anything but. West Berlin, the old Allied sectors, teemed with people. And not just any old people, but *Ossies*, easterners, the long-suffering citizens from the Soviet-controlled East Germany.

It had all happened so fast. That summer, thousands of East Germans holidaying in Hungary entered the West German Embassy and refused to return home. That autumn, crowds began to gather outside the Nikolaikirche in Leipzig, in peaceful protest against the regime. Each week, the protests had grown. On November 9th, seventy thousand people marched through the streets of Leipzig calling for peace and an end to travel restrictions. The East German leader, Erich Honecker, ordered the armed forces to crush the demonstration. The army refused. Honecker stepped down. A new leader was chosen. In an emergency broadcast, it was announced that travel restrictions would be lifted "as from tomorrow".

But those listening to the broadcast ignored the phrase. In their tens of thousands, East Berliners turned up at the Brandenburg Gate. The border guards, long instructed to shoot anyone who tried to cross over the wall, had received no instructions. For decades now, East Germany had been a prison state. Now it was different, and no one knew what to do. Then, somebody, somewhere decided to open the border — and all of a sudden East Germans began to pour west. An impromptu party began — the wildest, happiest, most joyful party in German history. Something else happened that night too. Something astonishing. Young men brought hammers and chisels and began to smash away at the concrete wall.

And nobody stopped them.

The Berlin Wall was tumbling down.

2

Today was just nine days later, the 18th of November. In those nine days, the celebrations had settled down as though intending to be permanent. The government of West Germany offered a hundred Deutschmarks *Begrüssungsgeld*, or welcome money, to every citizen of the east who wanted to visit. It seemed as though every single Easterner wanted to do just that.

The city had been busy before, but this was the first Saturday when everyone had recovered their wits. West Berlin shops threw open their doors and let the Easterners come to witness what had been denied them for so long. On the Kurfürstendamm, the gleaming car showrooms of BMW, Porsche and Mercedes had given up any attempt to sell things, and simply allowed the Ossies to come and look at machines of a beauty and sophistication they had never seen in their lives before. Kids clambered over car seats. Dads stared in at open bonnets, open-mouthed in awe. The mothers looked out of the windows and saw a city cleaner, richer and more cared for than any place they'd ever lived, or seen, or dreamed of.

But the traffic wasn't all one way.

In particular, one elderly couple walked hand in hand in the opposite direction, from the Brandenburg Gate through into the east zone. The gate had been completely restored now. There was no sign of the bomb damage that had once scarred it. Its shadow fell crisp and sharp across the pale autumn sunlight. At the border, the man and the woman were asked to show their passports. They did so. They had no visas or permits to cross, but with the world turned upside down, what use were permits? The border guard looked at the passports and stamped them.

The old man said, "*Danke sehr.*"

The border guard responded, "*Bitte,*" but with a strong Russian accent, indicating that he was on secondment from some Soviet unit.

The man smiled.

"*Spassibo,*" he said, with a faultless accent.

The guard stared at him with pale eyes and said nothing.

The couple walked on into East Berlin. On the wall behind them, young men and women were still struggling up onto the wall from the western side. As they watched, they saw a young man, fair-haired, haul himself up onto the rounded concrete top, followed soon after by a larger figure, also fair. They were joined by others. Then still others again. The top of the wall had become a party ground, a picnic place.

The couple walked on. They were very close, very physically affectionate for an old couple. They walked hand in hand or, when their hands got cold, so close that their arms and shoulders were touching. It was a way of moving that neither one of the two appeared to think about. It was an instinctive thing by now, automatic.

They walked through East Berlin. So many of its citizens were on the other side of the wall now, that the place felt like a ghost town, depopulated and eerie. They walked mostly in silence, but every now and then the woman would point things out, saying, "That's the Mühlendamm. My offices used to be there, that building. Top floor." Once she said, "Marta's house. You remember. Harry's agent. She died twenty years back. She was nice." She would have pointed out other things too: her barracks, the SMAD headquarters in Karlshorst, the prison where she had once been locked up. But the two of them were ninety years old now and not as energetic as they once were.

Besides, like them, the city had changed. Brutalist concrete constructions had replaced the war-torn city they'd once known. They ended up at a café near Alexanderplatz. The place was deserted: a large yellow-painted room lit by fluorescent tubes, with sixty or seventy Formica tables and cheap wooden chairs. A single waiter took five minutes to come to them, then another fifteen to bring coffee and cakes.

"Willi's in his element," said Tonya.

"Yes. He's lived for this in a way."

Willi had led a happy-go-lucky sort of life. He'd worked variously as a cartoonist, an artist, a photographer, a journalist (probably the journalist with the worst spelling and the least concern for deadlines anywhere in the Federal Republic), and lately as a documentary film-maker. Everything he did was touched with his own unique style. Right now, he was as busy as an ant, working twenty hours a day with his film-crew catching all the exhausting glory of the moment.

Rosa was happy too. Married now, with three children, and a good job as an administrator with the Free University of Berlin. She lived not far from Tonya and Misha, and saw them most days. But that wasn't all. On settling in Berlin in that long ago summer of 1950, Tonya's only possible regret for the wasted years was that she hadn't been able to have children with Misha. But as Misha had pointed out, why have kids when the orphanages were still so full? So they'd formally adopted another four children, two boys, two girls, and had the largest, happiest, youngest family they could have wished for. They had kept their cottage by the orphanage — twice extending it as their family had grown — and most of the orphanage children had treated the cottage as a second home.

Misha had started up his foundry again. With a proper currency and free movement in and out of the city, there was no stopping him. His factory grew to employ two hundred people. His products were among the best in a Germany that now brimmed with excellence.

Harry Hollinger had been a close friend all the time he'd been in Berlin. But with the partition of the city and the withdrawal of the bulk of the occupying forces, Hollinger had been transferred back to London. He was still a family friend though, and visited often.

As for the others they had known, old age had carried most of them away. Rodyon had had the opportunity to leave Russia too — another case of rescue by a Japanese trawler — but he'd preferred to live out his days in the motherland he'd done his best to serve. He had died eighteen years back of a lung problem, caused by the kind of damp and inadequate housing he had once sought to eradicate.

Pavel too was dead. He had risen one more step in the NKVD, from lieutenant-colonel to colonel, but he hadn't been able to hold onto his position. In the turmoil following Stalin's death and the arrest and shooting of Beria, Pavel had been caught out in a game of politics. He'd been briefly sent to the Gulag, before his sentence was commuted to internal exile. His drinking problem had returned with a vengeance, and liver disease had carried him off in 1969.

The two old folk drank their coffee and tasted the cakes. The cakes were very bad — old, stale, made from cheap and bad ingredients. Well, it wouldn't be for long. The unrest on the streets of Leipzig had begun with the slogan "*Wir sind das Volk*", we are the people. But the slogan had already changed to "*Wir sind ein Volk*", we are one people, one Germany. The divided country would unify once more; and its reunification would seal the new order in Europe. In a reunited Germany, Berlin's cakes would soon improve.

Misha dropped a lot of money on the table, a hundred Deutschmarks or more, everything he had in his pocket. Tonya watched him, smiling. They walked back out into the sunshine, heading back to the Brandenburg Gate.

"Well," said Misha, "I was right."

"Right? You're never right. Right about what?"

"I said it would all be over soon."

"What would all be over soon?"

"The revolution, comrade Lensky. We had a discussion about it in 1918, if I remember right. I said that the French revolution hadn't lasted long, that our own Russian revolution would have to change."

"Idiot."

"Well, it has changed, hasn't it? Not just here, and Poland, and Czechoslovakia, and Hungary. But everywhere. Russia can't go on as it is. It'll change too. It'll have to."

He smiled at her. Her hair was now completely grey, but her eyes, always a little slanted, were still the same clear green of old. He used to think they were the most beautiful eyes in the world. He still did.

"Well?" he persisted.

"Well what?"

"I was right. You haven't admitted it yet."

"I've admitted that you're an idiot."

"Comrade Lensky, you have to admit it or I will make you dance, right here, right now."

She laughed at him. He pushed her gently. She pushed him back. The pair of them, old as they were, walked like young lovers back under the shadow of the Brandenburg Gate.

Also available in ISIS Large Print:

Voyage of Innocence

Elizabeth Edmondson

In 1932, three young women go up to Oxford: Verity, a clergyman's daughter, her aristocratic cousin, Lady Claudia, and Lally, a senator's daughter from Chicago.

Verity falls under the influence of the intense Etonian communist, Alfred Gore, whilst Claudia is drawn to the urbane, pro-German economist, John Petrus. Lally simply watches on, keeping her own council and earning respect and affection from the whole circle.

Verity's convictions lead to agonizing decisions, which affect her own future and also that of her family and friends. In the fearful days of 1938, almost destroyed by her choices and disillusioned with her beliefs, she embarks on a journey to India — a stormy voyage, overshadowed by danger and the fear of war: a voyage that changes her life.

ISBN 978-0-7531-7638-2 (hb)
ISBN 978-0-7531-7639-9 (pb)

The Rules of Perspective

Adam Thorpe

It is April 1945, and the small provincial town of Lohenfelde is about to be overrun by the Allied Third Army. Huddled in the vaults of the Kaiser-Wilhelm Museum are Heinrich Hoffer and his three colleagues. Their petty rivalries and resentments surface quickly in this claustrophobic confinement, and the vaults become a stage for an intense psychological drama of secret histories and shared terror.

Above the ground, picking through the rubble, is Corporal Neal Parry, who wishes he was studying art and not dodging snipers. When he finds an exquisite painting in what remains of the museum vaults, he is immediately reconnected with a lost world of beauty and order: the world of art. It is this small 18th-century oil that is the poignant link between the young American soldier and the four charred corpses he finds at the same time.

ISBN 978-0-7531-7525-5 (hb)
ISBN 978-0-7531-7526-2 (pb)

Making It Up

Penelope Lively

In this fascinating piece of new fiction, Penelope Lively takes moments from her own life and asks "what if some outcomes had been otherwise?" What if her family's flight from Egypt in 1942 had taken a different route? What would her life have been like if she had become pregnant when she was eighteen? If she had married someone else? If she had become an archaeologist? If she had lived her life in America?

In this highly original piece of work, Penelope Lively examines alternative destinies, choices and roads not taken.

ISBN 978-0-7531-7495-1 (hb)
ISBN 978-0-7531-7496-8 (pb)

His Coldest Winter

Derek Beaven

On Boxing Day 1962 it began to snow. Over the next two months England froze. It was the coldest winter since 1740. The sea iced over. Cars could be driven across the Thames.

Riding home from London in that first snowfall, on the powerful motorbike he was given for Christmas, 17-year-old Alan Rae has a brush with death. Immediately he meets a girl, Cynthia, who will change his life. But someone else is equally preoccupied with her: Geoffrey, a young scientist who works with Alan's father in the race with the Americans and the Russians to develop the microchip. Alan, Geoffrey and Cynthia become linked by a web of secrets which, while the country remains in icy suspension, threatens everything they ever trusted.

ISBN 978-0-7531-7461-6 (hb)
ISBN 978-0-7531-7462-3 (pb)

The Sons of Adam

Harry Bingham

An epic tale of love, war and fortune

On 23 August 1893, two boys are born. Alan is the son of Sir Adam Montague, Tom is the son of his under-gardener. They are raised together and it seems that nothing can come between their friendship.

A tragic misunderstanding in the trenches of WWI turns them to the bitterest of rivals, struggling in the most cut-throat business of them all — oil. Only one thing remains more important than making their fortune . . . revenge.

Across three continents and two world wars, their conflict continues. Until, on the eve of the D-day landings, with world history hanging in the balance, the two men meet again . . .

ISBN 978-0-7531-7253-7 (hb)
ISBN 978-0-7531-7254-4 (pb)

ISIS publish a wide range of books in large print, from fiction to biography. Any suggestions for books you would like to see in large print or audio are always welcome. Please send to the Editorial Department at:

ISIS Publishing Limited
7 Centremead
Osney Mead
Oxford OX2 0ES

A full list of titles is available free of charge from:

Ulverscroft Large Print Books Limited

(UK)
The Green
Bradgate Road, Anstey
Leicester LE7 7FU
Tel: (0116) 236 4325

(Australia)
P.O. Box 314
St Leonards
NSW 1590
Tel: (02) 9436 2622

(USA)
P.O. Box 1230
West Seneca
N.Y. 14224-1230
Tel: (716) 674 4270

(Canada)
P.O. Box 80038
Burlington
Ontario L7L 6B1
Tel: (905) 637 8734

(New Zealand)
P.O. Box 456
Feilding
Tel: (06) 323 6828

Details of **ISIS** complete and unabridged audio books are also available from these offices. Alternatively, contact your local library for details of their collection of **ISIS** large print and unabridged audio books.